A
FATAL
TIDE

A FATAL TIDE

STEVE SAILAH

BANTAM
SYDNEY AUCKLAND TORONTO NEW YORK LONDON

A Bantam book
Published by Random House Australia Pty Ltd
Level 3, 100 Pacific Highway, North Sydney NSW 2060
www.randomhouse.com.au

First published by Bantam in 2014

Lyrics from the Kalkadoon song of war were published in *Taming the North* by Sir Hudson Fysh (Angus and Robertson, 1933) and are reproduced with the permission of his son, John Hudson Fysh.

Quotes from the diary of Chaplain George Green (1881–1957) can be found amongst the 2nd Light Horse Association Records in the State Library of Queensland.

An excerpt from *The Man Who Was Greenmantle: a Biography of Aubrey Herbert*, by Margaret FitzHerbert (John Murray Limited, 1983), is reproduced with the permission of Giles FitzHerbert.

Addresses for companies within the Random House Group can be found at
www.randomhouse.com.au/offices

National Library of Australia
Cataloguing-in-Publication Entry

Sailah, Steve, author.
A fatal tide/Steve Sailah.

ISBN 978 0 85798 450 0 (paperback)

Historical fiction.
Gallipoli Peninsula (Turkey) – Fiction.

A823.4

Cover illustration (soldier) © CollaborationJS
Cover design by www.blacksheep-uk.com
Internal map by Alicia Freile, Tango Media Pty Ltd
Typeset in Goudy Old Style and internal design by Midland Typesetters, Australia
Printed in Australia by Griffin Press, an accredited ISO AS/NZS 14001:2004
Environmental Management System printer

Random House Australia uses papers that are natural, renewable and recyclable products and made from wood grown in sustainable forests. The logging and manufacturing processes are expected to conform to the environmental regulations of the country of origin.

To four special women

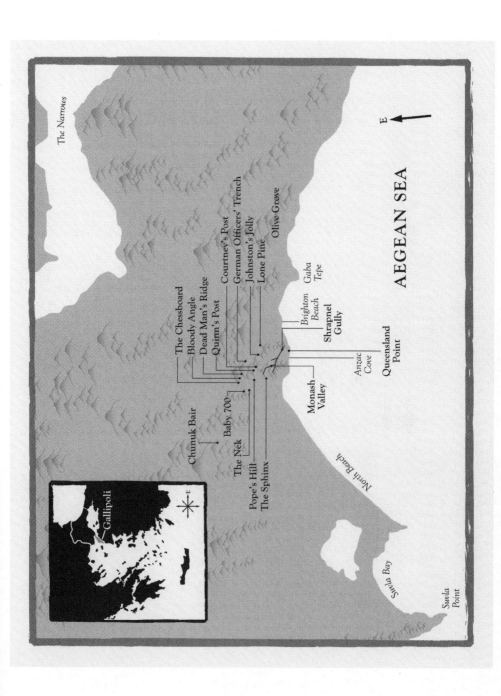

The Narrows

The Chessboard
Bloody Angle
Dead Man's Ridge
Quinn's Post

Courtney's Post
German Officers' Trench
Johnston's Jolly
Lone Pine
Olive Grove

Gaba
Tepe

Brighton
Beach

Shrapnel
Gully

AEGEAN SEA

Anzac
Cove

Queensland
Point

Monash
Valley

Chunuk Bair

Baby 700

The Nek

Pope's Hill
The Sphinx

North Beach

Suvla Bay

Suvla
Point

Gallipoli

E

Achilles glared at him and answered, 'Fool, prate not to me about covenants. There can be no covenants between men and lions, wolves and lambs can never be of one mind, but hate each other out and out and through. Therefore there can be no understanding between you and me, nor may there be any covenants between us, till one or other shall fall and glut grim Mars with his life's blood. Put forth all your strength; you have need now to prove yourself indeed a bold soldier and man of war . . .'

– Achilles addressing Hector before slaying him, *The Iliad*, Homer, circa 8th century BC, (translated by Samuel Butler, 1898)

May 1915

THE NOISE BATTERING THEIR EARS came from all sides as they filed into Quinn's. It echoed off the surrounding hills and gullies, so that every shot seemed doubled or tripled. The parapet shook with the impact of bullets and dirt poured from holes in sandbags, filling the trench with dust.

One of the officers – Thomas couldn't see who in the dull air – stepped up to fire his pistol over the bags and immediately fell back with a bloodied arm.

When a trooper further along with more courage than sense jumped up to fire his rifle, he was dragged down by a tall, middle-aged man, who shouted, 'Don't be a fool. This is a ruse.'

Thomas recognised him as Captain Guy Luther, the 15th Battalion's doctor. 'Mark my words, they know you're new,' Luther shouted above the noise as he passed down the line, stopping several times to repeat the warning. When Captain Luther reached Thomas's section, he barked, 'Don't fire, lie doggo.'

They sank to the bottom as bullets whistled overhead or thudded into the sandbags. And if their officers objected to a non-combatant from a different unit, and a medico at that, giving them orders, they said nothing.

'Wouldn't raise my noggin for all the tea in China,' declared Kingy, saying what was in everyone's mind.

There was a break in the firing, a sudden blessed silence, during which a voice in a heavy accent rang loud and clear across no-man's-land. 'Come on, 2nd Light Horse, you bastards.'

'You first,' an Australian sang out, to nervous laughter among his mates.

Thomas felt a stab of fear in his guts. How could the enemy know them? Was a Turk already looking at him down the barrel of a Mauser? What madness to place novices in a position overlooked by an enemy on both sides and immediately opposite! What sort of awful mess had he got himself into?

For some reason, he was reminded of cricket. At school his favourite place on the field was silly mid-on, so close to the batsman that evasive action was all but impossible. He had been hit several times, but still found the position thrilling. *Ridiculous comparison*, Thomas smiled to himself. *A ball won't kill you.*

At least he was safe at the bottom of the trench.

'Welcome to Turkey,' Kingy grinned with gallows humour.

'Empire of our Ottoman enemy, the unspeakable Turk,' Teach added, 'cradle of mighty Troy and beautiful Helen, a piece of history lost in the mists of time.'

'I got time for a piece of Helen,' Kingy suggested.

A few men tittered and Sergeant Lucky Les hissed, 'Shut your effin' mouth, Trooper King. From 'ere the Turk can hear ya fart.'

'Ah, "we happy few, we band of brothers",' whispered Teach, after the sergeant had moved along.

'"For he today that sheds his blood with me shall be my brother",' Kingy said.

'Well, I never!' Teach slapped Kingy on the back with affection. 'You know your Shakespeare. The Battle of Agincourt, 1415, half a millennium past, by George.'

'Ya ain't the only sod what can read,' Kingy said dryly.

'Kennel-up, confound it!' the sergeant spat through gritted teeth. 'Shut ya fookin' cakehole, or I'll shoot ya m'self.'

Too late. A black ball fell with a plop at Thomas's feet. A cricket ball. It sat there, fizzing on the yellow clay, its fuse blinking red. Thomas froze. He stared at it for a full second until another iron ball tumbled in an arc of smoke over the parapet.

'Look out, there's a bomb,' someone called.

'Thomas!' cried Snow.

'Don't *look* at 'em,' yelled the sergeant. 'Chuck 'em back, fer Chrissakes.'

Thomas and Snow grabbed a bomb each and turfed them over the parapet towards the Turkish lines. They stared wide-eyed with relief at each other, until explosions further along the trench blasted them with blue smoke and yellow dust. Cries of wounded men filled the air as more balls with smoky tails sailed across the strip of sky.

'Steady, lads, play the game, throw cleanly, jolly them up a little,' said Lieutenant Chisholm, his words clear and purposefully slow and full of anxiety.

Along the line, the Light Horsemen put down their rifles to catch the bombs. They grunted and strained as they heaved them back with a manic intensity. They were throwing blind, unable to see where the balls landed, and Thomas wondered whether the Turk was doing the same.

The sound of a blast on or close to the enemy was like the distant thud of a penny bunger on cracker night, compared to the ear-splitting bang of a bomb exploding nearby.

Dust and smoke raced in a cloud along the trench. Through it, Thomas saw two men dive suddenly into the narrow space beside him, followed immediately by an eruption of dull red flame.

One man landed on his stomach at Thomas's feet. It was Wag Scully, a farmer's son from Murgon, who'd earnt his nickname as a scallywag upsetting the fruit carts of Cairo's street vendors.

'Warm work, Tom,' Scully said as he picked himself up.

'You all right, Wag?'

'Tip-top, cobber.'

Without a word, Wag and his comrade returned to the bay they'd abandoned just as another fizzing black ball rolled over the parapet and slipped down unnoticed.

Thomas felt the rush of air before he heard the explosion. The blast blew the larger of the two men into him, slamming him into the wall. Thomas pushed back as if he had the plague and watched in surprise as the big man fell in a heap. There was a wind in Thomas's ears that seemed to shut out every other sound.

Instinctively, he moved his hands across his face, ears, arms, all over, and looked at his legs. Then he checked his hands. No blood, thank Christ.

Wag sat on the trench floor with his arms hanging loosely, staring at the remains of his foot. The boot had disappeared, leaving a mess of toe-less flesh. His face was hideous with pain and his mouth wide with silent screaming.

As Thomas stared, frozen at the sight, he wondered why he couldn't hear the screams, and why he felt a hand twisting his guts into knots. *Help him.* 'Buck up, Wag, it's just your toes,' he shouted.

Only minutes earlier, or perhaps it was hours, Wag had pushed Thomas playfully in the back to hurry him up the steep climb to Quinn's, so keen was he to be in it. Thomas reached into Wag's pocket and retrieved his field dressing and began to bind up the foot. 'It's a Blighty, lucky devil, you can go home.'

Wag seemed not to hear, but clenched his jaw and Thomas wondered at the effort it took him not to scream again.

Where's Snow? A quick glance showed him to be with the other trooper laid out on his back. The big man was unconscious as Snow worked on him, applying dressings to numerous gashes on his legs.

When Thomas's hearing returned, he could hear random detonations all along the line, many of them on either side of the trench, where they did no harm. But the Turk knew his distance and others fell inside with a loud bang, punctuated by screams and smaller agonies.

'I've been hit, chum.'

'Jesus . . . Mother.'

The sergeant arrived quietly and saw Thomas and Snow's bloodied hands and the smashed men. 'Pass the word – stretcher-bearers,' he said. 'Do it quick before you get another bomb in ya bollocks.'

Thomas looked along the trench to find Teach and Kingy preoccupied, one with throwing back a bomb, the other on alert for the next one. He stepped around them to pass on the sergeant's order. When he returned, Wag was already disappearing on a canvas stretcher between two bearers.

'Chap in the 15th Battalion tells me Major Quinn reckons it's amusing to dodge bombs,' Teach said.

'Strike me handsome, which war is he in?' Kingy said, with a look on his face close to madness. 'Fish in a bloody barrel, that's us.'

'Fish got a better chance,' said Snow.

'A bloke's not safe,' Thomas said.

They chuckled, a fearful version of laughter, and didn't meet each other's eyes.

MEN

Queensland, August 1914

'Is it suicide, or is it murder –
that's our first question, gentlemen, is it not?'

– 'The Valley of Fear',
Arthur Conan Doyle, 1914

Chapter 1

THE BOY WITH THE RIFLE squinted down the sights and began to imagine the final act in the wallaby's short life. He would foresee the moment and he would send the bullet there, where he wished it to go, just behind the eye. The creature would hop with the shot, topple on its back, feet up, long tail curled around, and be dead before it landed. That was the way it went, for as long as the boy could remember, from the very first time his father put a rifle in his hands.

He would not miss. Whether for a dingo half-hid in the trees or a fox slinking away or a roo on the fly.

A *gift*, so his father said.

As rare as praise.

Even in the fading winter with the chill in his bones and the breath smoking in his face, the bush was where the boy was happiest and the hunt when he felt most alive.

He squeezed the trigger.

They emerged from the scrub with a swagger, for game was scarce in a time of drought and they'd had a good hunt. Each

wore a line of skinned rabbits on rope around his waist and a
red-necked wallaby curled about his shoulders.

They hopped over a fence and stepped onto the main road to
town. Lamb Street was long and broad, built – like so many in
such Queensland bush towns – to accommodate a big herd or a
bullock train bound for the railway yards without troubling the
shopkeepers on either side.

Thomas carried the pea rifle easily. Snow had already hidden
his weapons in the usual place. It wouldn't do to take a spear
and boomerang to town.

From a distance, they appeared to be men. They'd shot up
over the past year to become six-footers like their fathers –
Thomas lanky, his ginger hair cut short, while Snow was more
muscular with a thick black crop of wavy curls.

They strolled through the twilight in no particular rush,
stepping around the leavings of horse and ox. As they entered
the town, they quickened their pace and kept to the shadows.
To be seen together would set tongues wagging, and they had
no desire to disturb the townsfolk at rest from the struggle to
prosper, tame the land and control the blacks.

Best not invite trouble.

A rare treat drew them back onto the road – an elegant
new Delaunay-Belleville tourer recently arrived from Brisbane.
Neither boy had so much as sat in a motor before.

'What a beauty!' Thomas said, sliding his fingers over the
gleaming metal. 'I'm gunna have one some day.'

'You will,' Snow agreed, 'and you can drive me . . .' he paused
and added, 'to the opera.'

The boys laughed, softly so as not to draw attention to themselves, then hurried on under the bullnose shop fronts, past
the Queensland National Bank, beside the picket fences and
cottages still pleasant with the smell of the saw. Lamps burned

dimly behind curtains. Thomas imagined a mother sewing, a father reading to a child in his lap, together around the hearth.

Once, he'd had something like that, when his ma was alive. Thomas shivered. 'It's bloody freezing.'

'Only for city slickers.'

The same old tease. Back when they'd met for the first time, Snow had been skinny and barefoot. He had danced and weaved around Thomas in a fair imitation of the 'black hurricane', Jerry Jerome, middleweight hero to all the Barambah boys. Snow had punched the air and offered to beat the white boy sense-less, while their fathers watched on, amused. But Thomas had declined, swearing that out of respect for his left-handed ma he never hit a southpaw or a girl. And Snow had laughed, their fathers had laughed.

Their fathers' relationship dated back to the war against the Boers, after which they worked and hunted together, often with the boys in tow. In the bush, the boys became fast friends, a bond that was rare for the times. Later, Thomas went on to college in the city and Snow became a jackeroo for a local farmer, under an arrangement imposed by the mission as soon as he turned fourteen. It was hard yakka, Snow confessed, but better than being stuck in a classroom doing sums. *Can't argue with that*, Thomas thought.

As the moon rose orange in the cooling sky, the boys arrived at a cottage marked with a sign POLICE. Thomas groaned. His father's filly was hitched to the rail, instead of warm in the stable.

'Rosie Girl not yet abed. Not a light showing, by Jove,' Thomas said, assuming the role in their usual game. 'What do you make of it, Watson?'

Early on in their friendship, Snow had found him reading. Thomas, to cover up a certain embarrassment, had boasted of his father's personal connection to the author Arthur Conan

Doyle, a brag that was only partly false. Snow had surprised Thomas by asking to have the stories read aloud to him, then and whenever bad weather forced them indoors or the fish in the creek weren't biting. While Snow had admitted that he wasn't too good at reading, having had only a few years at school, Thomas had been delighted to discover that his mate remembered slabs of dialogue word for word, and had an ear for accents and a lively talent for impersonation.

'I'd warrant our Lestrade is absent,' Snow said brightly, 'though it's hardly surprising under the circumstances, Holmes.'

'Good old Watson!' Thomas laughed, then dropped the character. 'He'll be at Tiernan's again and full as a boot. Be hell to pay in the morning.'

'Nah, you'll be right, you brung enough tucker,' said Snow, patting the rabbits around his middle. 'I better get back to my mob.'

The mission lay several miles away, down the road that skirted the creek. It would be dark by the time Snow arrived. As a dormitory boy, he wasn't allowed out late, but the guard would turn a blind eye if he handed over a fat bunny. 'Go again tomorrow?'

'Yep,' Thomas nodded, as he untied the filly and led her past the outhouse to the stable. It took only a few minutes to settle her in and close the stable door.

When he turned, he found Snow still there and staring hard.

The moon, pale and huge, had picked out the silvery bones of the big ghost gum. Thomas smiled at the sight, until his eyes caught something odd. A sliver of rope hung from a bough and the moon framed the loop at the rope's end in an unearthly halo.

It would be an age before Thomas would get the image out of his head. Though far worse sights were to come, the moonlit noose stuck and seemed to define everything that happened later.

Intrigued, Thomas strode purposefully down the yard towards the tree, only to trip over a small boulder and fall on top of a large khaki sack from which two legs and boots protruded.

The light caught on the familiar buttons, and Thomas – frantic at the implications – grabbed the sack and with a sudden surge of a grown man's strength pulled the uniform towards him before realising that it was a corpse and that the corpse was headless.

Constable First Class John Robert Clare.

Jack to his friends.

Beneath the rope, Thomas hugged the body. He buried his face in the policeman's chest, screaming into the jacket because, terrible though that was, he did not want to look at the neck. He hardly heard Snow pleading for him to come away and dimly felt his friend grasp him by the shoulders in an attempt to separate him from his father.

Snow stood bewildered and appalled, watching the body rock back and forth in Thomas's arms. He yearned to be at home with his own father and mother, away from this bad place. No birds sang, no dogs barked, or horses whinnied. Only the soft hoot of a predatory owl disturbed the windless night. Nothing out of the ordinary, apart from Thomas's whimpering.

A short distance away, Snow saw the moonlight glint white on the bloodless, bald head that Thomas had tripped over. The least thing he could do for his friend was to put the head back with the torso. With an effort, Snow forced himself to grasp it around the ears. He lifted it gingerly, his hands suddenly sticky, surprised at its weight, heavy as a saddle. Snow kept his eyes on the ground, away from the shattered neck and the face in particular. He imagined its terrible expression, did not want to see it. The last thing he wanted was to be holding the head when its angry spirit came looking for it.

Thomas saw what Snow was carrying and moaned. He watched as the head was placed at his feet. Thomas let his father's torso slide through his arms to the ground. He lay back on his elbows and stared into his father's lifeless face and loud racking sobs cracked the night.

The chill seeped into his bones as he sat in the dirt, shivering and alone, staring at blind eyes that once held humour and anger and knew Thomas.

In the haze of horror that had blanked his mind to anything else, he hadn't noticed Snow's absence until he returned with a thumping of hooves, mounted two-up behind a woman astride a large black horse.

'I brung the doc, mate.'

Doctor Ellen Woods slipped from the saddle and strode purposefully to the body on the ground.

'Oh, holy Jesus,' she said and slapped a clenched fist to her mouth.

A slender, handsome woman in her mid-thirties, she was shaking as she squatted down beside Thomas. She looked quickly at the head and put her hand on the torso, on the uniform, over the heart, and clenched her teeth in a struggle to choke back tears. After a minute, she stood and hitched up her long skirt so the hem would not disturb the fluids staining the dirt. She walked slowly around the body, taking in all the details, the position, the head, the noose.

The last thing Thomas remembered about that night was the dancing lights as men with storm lamps came to load his father onto a cart and take him away.

Chapter 2

WHEN HE AWOKE, HIS BACK ACHED. He was lying on a blanket, with another covering him, below an iron roof. For a moment he wondered why he wasn't in his own bed. Then he jerked upright, eyes wild.

He's dead.

Opposite, Snow sat cross-legged. They stared at each other, both lost for words, until Snow said, 'There's breakfast. You hungry?'

Thomas shook his head, got a whiff of smoke and roasting meat outside, and felt sick to the stomach.

A burst of light blasted the room as Tubbie Terrier threw aside the sugarbag door. His face was black as night, framed by a grey beard and wavy hair, and scars decorated his chest and shoulders. He bent his long body to enter and sat down heavily beside Thomas on the rough timber floor.

'Your old man at hospital, Tom. Dunno what for, can't fix him up there, can't fix him nowheres.'

He was Snow's father. He and Jack Clare had met during the Boer War, where Tubbie was a tracker in the army and Jack was a mounted trooper. Thomas had once asked Snow why a man so tall and lean could be called Tubbie Terrier. Snow said it was how his Kalkadoon name sounded to whitefellas.

'I wasn't there,' Tubbie said miserably, with eyes red from weeping. 'I wasn't there.'

The words came to Thomas through a fog. *My father is dead.*

Snow said, 'Nothing you could have done, Dad.'

'We was good mates,' Tubbie said again, his head shaking in his hands. 'I shoulda known . . . don't understand . . .'

Seeing the old man's tears, Thomas felt his own returning and wiped his eyes quickly with his hand.

Tubbie Terrier was the best tracker in the state of Queensland, as Constable Clare told anyone who would listen. They went bush for days at a time, chasing cattle duffers or runaway Aborigines or people lost in the vastness. Together they hunted, drank, didn't give two hoots what respectable folk thought.

Eventually, Tubbie stood up. 'Breakfast ready. Your old man never knocked back good tucker.'

The old man. Would have been forty in November, Thomas recalled.

With each step the frosted ground crackled as Thomas and Snow went over to the fire. Tubbie handed them each a hot saddle of rabbit. Thomas took a bite, forced himself to chew, more grateful for the fire warming his back than the food.

Tendrils of smoke rose here and there among the trees. Hundreds of people huddled around small fires, while others carted tins of water up from the creek, or emerged shivering from their simple bark and branch gunyas and miamias.

Barambah was growing so fast they called it Murgon's black twin, a government reserve for Aborigines removed from land and kin. Tubbie once told him they'd been taken from all over – the Kullilli from out west, the Sundowners from the stone country near Birdsville, the local Wakka Wakka, and plenty more tribes besides. Tubbie had stuck with the Cooktown mob, he'd said, because they were from the far north, up his way.

'Oh, you poor darling,' came the familiar voice of Snow's mum, and Thomas was enveloped in large breasts and a soft belly. 'A good man, a fair man, a friend to us, he was. You remember that, Tom,' said Iris.

Held tight, it was hard to breathe, but Thomas let himself sink into her warmth and the smell of smoke and wild honey. She was large and brown-haired, with a skin of burnt coffee, same as Snow and his sister Winnie. Thomas knew Iris better than his own mother, whose memory grew dimmer with every day.

When his mother died, it was Iris who dried the boy's tears, fed and washed him, and sang him to sleep in her language. It was Iris who'd put him in a clean school uniform with a shilling in his pocket for the train taking his father and him and the coffin to Brisbane. After Rose was buried and his father went bush, it wasn't long before Thomas felt trapped by tie and blazer, study and rules. Hemmed in by crowd and concrete and constrained by the sobriety of his aunt's table, it was Tubbie and Iris, Snow and Winnie, whom he longed for.

She relaxed her hug and grasped him by the shoulders, pushed him back and looked him in the eye. 'He loved you more'n everything, though he weren't the sort to show it. Was always telling us how proud he was, about your schooling in the city, about that shooting and sports stuff you was doing. You don't think of nothing else but that. You listening to me, boy?'

Thomas nodded. *If he loved me so much, why did he hang himself?*

'Oh, Constable Jack was a hard man,' Iris continued. 'That war did things to him, Tubbie will tell you, and when Rose died, well, he always blamed his self.'

'Enough, woman!' Tubbie snapped.

'Don't hush me, mister. It all gunna come out, and this boy need to hear it true.'

Before he could ask her what she meant, they were interrupted by a wallop of hooves. A large man rode into view on a horse that matched him for size and stature. He wore a khaki uniform with stripes on his arm and an air that tolerated no dissent. Those in his path melted away until he reined in before Thomas. He looked around the camp with disdain, and drew a deep, disappointed breath, before his gaze settled on the only other white face. 'Thomas Clare?'

'Yes.'

'My condolences,' said the policeman. 'Your father was a good man.'

A *good man*. The description struck Thomas as faintly ridiculous. His father had hanged himself and botched it so badly that he had left himself in two parts. *Not much good in that.*

'I'm Sergeant Griffin from Wondai. Been riding all night. You're to come with me.'

'What for?' Thomas said with a sudden anger.

'As next of kin, you are required to formally identify Constable Clare.'

'Already seen him. It's my dad all right.'

'Still and all, you are required to do so before witnesses in the presence of the body.'

Thomas gritted his teeth.

'And I have some questions concerning the circumstances of his suic– err, his passing.'

There it was, the copper's unfinished word, and for the first time Thomas began to feel the shame of it.

There was no one else on the road to town as they rode double. Sergeant Griffin was a big man and Thomas felt sorry for the horse. Bareback, he gripped the rear arch of the saddle and kept his hands clear of the copper's backside and his leg away from the rifle lodged in its bucket. Thomas's face was close enough to the man's heavy back that he could smell the sour sweat in the uniform. He concentrated on watching the yellow fences and the gums pass on either side and not thinking about the head and the torso in the moonlight.

After they'd ridden a mile or so in silence, the sergeant began his questions easily enough. 'Your father and I were mates,' he said. 'Did you know that?'

'I saw you both in Tiernan's couple of times.'

'He liked to talk . . . when he'd had a few.'

'Not to me.'

'I understand. I've a boy 'bout your age.'

Thomas grunted.

'Men talk to men but not father to son, eh?'

'Yeah,' Thomas said.

'Was he drinking by himself a lot?'

'Didn't notice.'

'What were you doing with the blacks?'

'Nothing.'

'Will you go back to school?'

'Suppose so,' said Thomas, the obedient son. *He would have wanted it.*

Thomas didn't see much point in the questions and he didn't care for the burly copper. He wished Griffin would hurry the horse on a bit, so they could get to wherever they were going, though he dreaded what he might find there.

'Why would a man like your father do himself in?'

The question cut Thomas like a knife. *How the hell should I know?*

But the sergeant saved him from trying to answer it. 'Poor bugger. Must have been Rose's death and the drink.'

That cut deeper. What did a son know of his father? That he was drunk, yes, often enough, though never loud and coarse like some, and never violent. No, he never beat him. Thomas couldn't remember his dad laughing much, except when they went hunting. Thomas loved him then, trusted and admired him, wanted to be like him – a capable man of few words.

Once, when Thomas had spoken of his fondness for Winnie, his father had replied, 'Don't get serious about her, son.' Nothing further was said. What did that mean, *serious*? Thomas had no idea. He had been so full of his own concerns, in such a hurry to fill up his life with achievement and adventure that he'd not thought to ask.

He swallowed hard. Now he'd never know. Now, whenever he wondered about his father, he would remember the torso and its head in a pool of cold moonlight.

'Jack and me,' the sergeant said suddenly, 'we were in South Africa together.'

Thomas jerked back to the present. 'Ma told me he was in the Queensland Mounted Infantry during the war. Then he served with some famous bloke called the Breaker. Was that you?'

'God, no.' The sergeant laughed. 'That was Harry Morant. We'd met him before the Boer bloody War, when Jack and me was just starting out as coppers. A horse could buck all day and not throw the Breaker. An artist in the saddle, he was, and a fair bush poet. Ladies' man, broke a host of hearts, so I heard. But a pig's pile o' woe when the drink got a hold. We arrested him once for being legless and picking fights, did Jack tell you that?'

'He arrested a lot. Chained them to a log.'

'Bush lockup,' the sergeant chuckled. 'Had one meself till they built me a proper cell. Nothing beats a good log, rain or shine. Gaol's too good for some.'

'That's what he used to say.'

The policeman stiffened in the saddle. 'Did Jack ever talk about a court-martial or executions?'

'No.'

'Or missing papers?'

'No.'

'Did he ever give anything to the colonel?'

'You mean Uncle Harry? I dunno.'

'Jack had no brothers, so Harry Chauvel's not really your uncle, is he?'

'I call him uncle, that's all. He's a mate of my father from the war. They used to meet sometimes, talk about Africa, but Dad never said much about it.'

They went quiet for a time, until the sergeant said, 'You don't remember me, do you?'

'No,' Thomas admitted.

'Neither should you, I s'pose. You were a kid and it was a bad time. I was the cop who investigated the circumstances surrounding your mother's death.'

'Oh,' said the boy.

The telegram had gone to St Joseph's. The headmaster sat Thomas down in his office and handed him the opened envelope with a mournful expression and words that scraped like a fingernail on the blackboard. 'Dreadful news, I'm afraid.'

Four years later, her face had grown hazy, though one clear image remained. He saw it every day thereafter on the wall at his aunt's house – a family stiff in sepia, the farewell photograph from the old country. Rose shone in front, a pretty girl from the Levant, the youngest of seven gathered about the parents, emigrants all for the steamer to take away. The ship had loaded more passengers in Bombay, including Jack Clare – who followed her to Brisbane and contrary to the family's wishes married her.

'He stole my heart. The thief who became a copper,' she'd said in that thick accent of hers.

On Sergeant Griffin's horse, Thomas smiled to himself.

That day in Brisbane, she'd worn the latest clothes ordered from the catalogue specially – a daring blue tie on a frilly white blouse above a fitted skirt, and a broad sunhat – and she'd skipped like a girl beside him as if the city was where she truly belonged, as if time spent with her son was the happiest of her life.

Just the two of them, he remembered, hanging out the window of the Dreadnought as it rattled the tram tracks up Albert Street towards the new school. Then back over Victoria Bridge in one of the Toast Racks, whose open sides allowed them to stand full by the crossbar so the summer wind cooled their grins.

They'd left the tram to amble past crowded pubs, banks and drapery shops near her sister's place in Stanley Street when Rose had stopped suddenly.

'Your father decided . . . we decided,' she'd said in a voice hoarse with sadness. 'I'm sorry I can't be with you. But it's for the best.'

Thomas hardly needed convincing. He'd jumped at the chance to go to a big school with proper cricket and football and new friends to make.

'And you'll have my family, cousins to play with.'

'But you'll be lonely, Ma.'

'I'll be all right, Tommy.'

Tommy. To his dad he was always Thomas.

'Why didn't I have a brother, Ma?'

'God did not will it and your father did not wish it. Better you should ask him.'

Easier said than done. 'It would have been such fun,' he'd said. 'Even a sister would have been better than nothing.'

She'd laughed and the sadness went. She hugged him then, kissed him on both cheeks and on his forehead.

Sergeant Griffin reined in his mount, startling his passenger. 'It was Jack found her while you were at school. You know she drank cleaning liquid, Lysol.'

'Yes, by mistake,' Thomas said miserably.

The policeman turned in the saddle to look sideways at him. 'There's more to tell. Now that your father's gone too, you should hear it. Or maybe you're too young.'

'No, I'm not.'

'What happened wasn't pretty. You sure?'

'Yes,' Thomas said clearly, though with a sinking feeling in his stomach.

The sergeant turned back and clicked his tongue. The horse resumed its easy walk. 'Jack was out bush. When he returned, he found your mother in the stable, stone cold. She'd taken so much that the place was filled with the gas from the poison in her. Her horse was dying from the fumes. He tried to revive her, stayed too long, and collapsed. Luckily he'd left the stable door open, and a neighbour saw him, pulled him out.'

'I never knew.' *I should have been there . . . would have saved her.*

'There's more, son, and it bears upon your father's death.'

'He was pretty knocked by that, my dad was.'

'You also, I expect.'

'We didn't talk about it.'

'Your mother's death was not an accident.'

'What?' Thomas said, stunned.

'I know that's not what you were told,' the sergeant said, then added bluntly, 'Rose took her own life.'

Thomas felt light-headed. He grasped the saddle to prevent himself from falling.

'You were a child at the time and it was up to your father to tell you,' the sergeant continued. 'There was no note. Some people said Jack filled her bottle with poison . . . murdered her to be with another woman.'

'That's a lie!'

'Of course it was a lie. Gossip from some evil bastard with a grudge against an honest cop. You meet plenty of 'em in this line of work, I can tell you. During my investigation, with a few drinks under his belt, Jack told me things.'

That he wouldn't tell me, Thomas finished the sentence in his mind. He wanted the sergeant to stop, was afraid of what he might hear next. Miserable but curious, he said nothing.

'She tried to smother you once.'

'No,' Thomas cried.

'You were just born. She had a pillow over you. I heard it from Jack himself. He put a stop to it, but things weren't the same between them afterwards.'

'I don't believe you,' Thomas said, bewildered. This wasn't the mother who'd loved him. *She'd never do that.*

'She was sick in the head, son.'

'She never . . .'

'She never had another baby, did she? Look, son, I'm telling you this because it's what he told me and it explains a lot. Rose was a country copper's wife, moving from one bush station to the next, shunned by folks who didn't take to her Arab ways, her funny accent, and maybe some of them heard what she'd done to you once. Anyways, she pleaded with Jack to shift back to the city where you could grow up with your cousins. But your father's word was iron. He liked the life and took a promotion to move to Murgon. They agreed that you would go to school in Brisbane and board with her sister. After that, things broke down between them and, with Jack in the bush for weeks on end and without you for company, she got to drinking.'

Sergeant Griffin took a deep breath. 'Jack was a mate – we'd been through a lot together in that war, ya know – so between us we cooked up a story for the official report, said she mistook Lysol for alcohol, marked it accidental death due to intoxication. Your father wanted to spare you and Rose's family from the shame of it.'

Oh Christ, Thomas thought, *two parents, two suicides.*

'It knocked Jack for six,' the sergeant continued. 'He blamed himself. Did he ever talk about . . .?'

'Ki– killing himself?' Thomas hesitated. 'No.' *Never. He was a rock. Solid, stone.*

In the years since his mother's death he and his father had hardly talked. Thomas had been in Brisbane most of the time, struggling to fit in at his Aunt Mercia's and intent on sport and study.

'Never said much. Once I saw him crying. I used to put him to bed when he was . . .'

'Sozzled,' the sergeant suggested.

'Yeah, but I never imagined he'd do . . . *that.*'

They rode on without speaking. The horse's hooves beat a rhythmic clip-clop on the stony surface. A breeze was shifting the gum trees and every so often a wallaby would thump away into the undergrowth.

'I hear you can shoot,' the sergeant said.

'He taught me.' Then, a sudden thought, 'Why didn't he shoot himself?'

'Hanging's neater, son, less mess.'

'Well, he sure buggered that up,' Thomas said bitterly.

'Show some respect,' the sergeant snapped.

The boy stopped talking. He'd had enough. There was a pain in his guts and a nasty taste in his mouth as if he might vomit. And he couldn't stomach Sergeant Griffin for the way he seemed to know more about his father than Thomas did, for the way the copper called him *son*, for calling his mother *Rose*, for all the man's certainty about every awful thing.

His father's head nagged dreadfully. Why had it come off? *That wasn't supposed to happen.* Why did his father lie to him about how his mother died? He'd been twelve then, old enough for the truth.

Both of them left me. Thomas began to tremble. *She never said goodbye.*

For the rest of the ride to the hospital, Thomas didn't care what the sergeant thought, he wept.

Chapter 3

DUDLEY PRIVATE HOSPITAL SAT FLAT and wide on a low hill on Murgon's outskirts. It had a commanding view of the rail line, the lifeline from the coast through the forested hills of the South Burnett, along which prosperity, dried American apples, city newspapers and new settlers came to town.

Waiting on the front steps was a large woman in a white pinafore who introduced herself as Matron Davies. As Sergeant Griffin tethered the horse, she touched Thomas on the shoulder.

'My girls and I patched up Constable Clare after many an outback pursuit,' she said. 'Your father fought his own demons and the drink, and lost the battle in the end. Now, young Tom, you just remember this – he had his faults like all of us, but he was a good man for all that.'

Thomas nodded dull thanks and Matron Davies led them away from the main building to an adjoining grassed area where numerous tents stood.

'These are for the open-air treatment of patients. Pure air is nature's tonic and most efficacious in cases of tuberculosis. We have saved many a patient.' Matron Davies patted Thomas's shoulder again and pointed to a particular tent. 'Sadly, not in every case.'

'Wait here,' said the sergeant as he pushed the tent flap aside. A few moments later he reappeared and called Thomas in.

Inside the tent were the doctor and a man with a thick mous-tache whom he recognised as Mr Armstrong, the captain of the town's rifle club. They were standing beside a wheeled trolley bearing a figure beneath a white sheet.

Thomas looked away and concentrated his gaze on the gurney's bicycle wheels and polished wooden handles.

'It's a rum duty all right, boy,' said Sergeant Griffin.

Thomas glanced at the body. A deep fold in the sheet marked where the two parts had been placed together. He stood uncer-tainly, arms by his side, clenching and unclenching his fists, and wondered what he was supposed to do next.

Doctor Woods stepped up and took his arm. 'Come with me,' she said gently and led him to the fold in the sheet. Deli-cately, she peeled back the sheet, stopping at his father's chin.

'Thomas, is that your father?' the policeman asked.

He looked at the face, prominent nose, wide ears, tufts of red hair separated by the bald crown, eyes locked closed in a serene, grey face.

'Yes,' he said quietly.

Thomas felt an urge to touch his father's face, but feared it might roll away again. He swallowed hard and looked up at Doctor Woods with a plea in his eyes.

'The boy needs some time,' she demanded. 'Alone.'

'We'll leave you, then,' the sergeant said. 'Come by the station later, we need to sort out some of your father's –'

'I'll bring Thomas when he's good and ready, sergeant,' Ellen Woods said sharply, prompting the men to leave.

Thomas looked to the doctor. 'Is it all right, I mean, can I . . .?'

'Of course,' she said.

He bent down and pressed his lips against the cold forehead.

Some time later, it might have been hours for all he knew, Thomas found himself sitting on the bare earth beneath a tree with his eyes fixed on the tent with the corpse. It was impossible, but he let himself imagine for a moment that a terrible mistake had been made, that the flap would open and his father would walk out with a grin on his face.

Doctor Woods sat beside him, all buttoned up in a long skirt, coat and black bonnet, cutting a figure that might otherwise have passed for a grieving widow.

It had surprised the young town when Murgon's first physician turned out to be a handsome woman, and an unmarried, unaccompanied one at that. Women doctors were rare, rarer still in the outback, and Ellen Woods was a frequent topic of conversation. Many judged it most unladylike to see her ride from patient to patient, on the rough tracks between farms and cottages, in all weathers, in her jodhpurs and long black boots, while declining the side-saddle favoured by ladies, and always perfectly in command of her stallion. Despite his present circumstances, Thomas was in awe of her.

'Can I be blunt?' she said. Without waiting for an answer, 'I'm required to certify the death of your father and the likely cause. I want to say some things that you may find difficult. You don't need to say much of anything, but please stop me if you think I'm wrong. All right?'

Thomas nodded.

'We all know your father was a fine policeman. Sergeant Griffin tells me his report will say "zealous and capable", but he will also report that on more than one occasion he was seen to be drunk and brawling. I know that your father was still grieving over your mother's passing.'

Thomas said bluntly, 'Ma drank poison while he was out bush. I always believed it was an accident, but the sergeant says it was suicide. Like my dad.'

'Oh dear,' Doctor Woods cried.

'Sergeant Griffin said Ma tried to kill me when I was born, but Dad stopped her.'

'I find that hard to believe,' said the doctor. 'Though, I have read of rare cases where a mother is not in her right mind for a time after childbirth. Hysteria, they call it.'

'Dad used to say he never treated her well enough.'

'He was a soldier once and wounded, wasn't he? Some doctors I know have treated men back from war who were never the same again.'

'He never said much about that.'

'Well, I imagine it was difficult after your mother's death. Loneliness, a hard life in the bush, and the drinking – that's a great deal for even a strong man like your father to cope with.'

Thomas wondered how she knew so much.

Doctor Woods continued, 'Sergeant Griffin found no evidence of foul play, neither signs of a struggle nor witnesses to your father's last moments. He believes it's an open and shut case. Suicide while temporarily insane.'

Thomas buried his head in his hands.

She got to her feet, brushed the back of her skirt, and stretched her legs. Slowly, she paced back and forth with her hands clasped behind her and her head down, while the hem of her skirt slid gracefully around the heels of her boots. Finally she exhaled a long breath, and resumed her place on the dirt beside him, as if she'd made up her mind about something.

'I gather you enjoy Sherlock Holmes?' she said.

He looked up. 'Yes, how did you know?'

'Your father mentioned it.'

'When I was little, he used to read to me before bed.'

She raised an eyebrow. 'Crime at bedtime?'

'He did the voices really well, especially the accents of the English constables and the rascals,' laughed Thomas. 'Ma hated it. She said there was too much murder and violence in them and that I should read the Good Book instead.'

'The Bible has its fair share of murder and violence.'

'Whenever I did something smart, he would say, "Capital, Sherlock!"' Thomas smiled at the memory. 'He used to say there was no more useful tale than Sherlock Holmes.'

'And he's brave and clever.'

'That's why I like him.'

'But solitary, a little sad, and a trifle odd, wouldn't you say?'

Thomas looked sideways at her. *What did that matter?* Sherlock's brilliant adventures had helped to fill the hole left by an absent mother and father, a shield held against sorrow. 'He has Watson.'

'Of course he does,' Ellen Woods answered quickly. 'Though he's hardly your average country copper.'

'My dad reckoned we'd leave the bush one day for the big smoke. He'd be a private detective and nick the clever city crooks.'

Doctor Woods sighed. 'For all his hard ways, Jack had a bit of the boy in him. He liked to joke that I should come to Brisbane too – and be his Doctor Watson.'

What? Thomas looked sharply at her.

She met his glance. 'Murgon's a long way from anywhere, Thomas, and Jack was a widower. He and I were . . . well, we were both lonely.'

Thomas was seeing Ellen Woods in a new light. Clearly, a great deal had happened while he was away at school.

She noticed his surprise and chuckled. '"The copper and the quack", that's what they called us, though not to our faces, of course. We didn't care. We'd ride to the river or the lake, beautiful places he'd come across while on duty.'

Thomas didn't know what to say.

'Your father met the author Arthur Conan Doyle, you know,' she continued.

'Yes, in Africa.'

'Conan Doyle was a doctor in a tent hospital in Bloemfontein,' she said, with a brief glance back at the tent. 'Jack had a bullet wound and enteric fever and was one of his patients. Did he ever tell you the story of how Conan Doyle was examining him one day when Kitchener and Churchill turned up beside his bed?'

Thomas shook his head. 'Who?'

'One a general, the other a newspaper correspondent, come down on the train from Pretoria to inspect the sick and wounded.'

'And my dad met them?'

'The way he told it, Conan Doyle introduced Jack as an example of how splendidly the colonials were fighting the Boers. Jack said those two bigwigs wished him a speedy recovery, but they were far more interested in the doctor.'

'Because of Sherlock Holmes?' Thomas guessed.

'Exactly. So, there's Kitchener and Churchill pretending they'd never read the stories, claiming they were low art or some such drivel, but nevertheless appealing to Conan Doyle to *resurrect* him.'

'What! Sherlock dead?'

'Oops!' she said. 'You haven't read "The Final Problem"?'

'Not yet,' he grumbled.

'Oh dear me, I've spoiled it for you. Well, Conan Doyle killed off Holmes in a struggle with Moriarty.'

Thomas groaned.

'No, no, don't worry! Let me tell you the rest of the story. So, there's Jack in his hospital bed listening to Churchill going on and on about the British bulldog being full of pluck, daring and higher intelligence, and Kitchener saying, "Dammit, man, it's a time for heroes, for Britain, for Empire, for Victoria, God bless her."'

'And what happened?'

'Conan Doyle insisted his role as a doctor was more important than as an author, and that the fever was killing more men than Boer bullets. But, the way Jack described it, the general and Churchill scarcely listened. They wanted Sherlock back. "Raise him!" Kitchener demanded. "That's a direct order, though you didn't hear it from me."'

'Can a general tell a doctor what to do?'

'I certainly wouldn't stand for it,' Ellen Woods said firmly. 'Jack said that Conan Doyle was furious, grumbling that Holmes must once again save the day.'

'Which he does.'

'Always,' she agreed.

'But how could he, when he was already dead?'

'That's where your father came in,' Ellen Woods giggled. 'To hear him tell it, Conan Doyle paced up and down the hospital corridors for days, wondering how to revive Sherlock. It annoyed Jack so much that he told Conan Doyle a tale of his own - how a wild dog saved his life.'

'I know that story,' Thomas cried. 'He said a snake crossed his path and his horse panicked and threw him and he got knocked out cold. When he woke up, the horse was gone and the snake, a big brown fella - "longer than anyone could remember", he used to say - was hissing in his face and a dingo was slinking around the scrub.'

'That's the one, all right,' said Doctor Woods, and they were laughing together.

'And he reached into his pocket and got out his lunch, a bit of beef jerky, and flicked it at the snake. The dingo went for the meat quick as a flash and the snake went for the dog. He just dragged himself up against a gum tree and watched. Every time the dingo got close to the meat, the snake went for him. Except, after a while the snake got tired and took off into the bush and the dingo grabbed the jerky. Dad reckoned it was the "best bloody lunch I never ate".'

In between their gasps of laughter, Ellen Woods took up the story. 'It's the same yarn Jack told the doctor – "How a dog saved my arse". Pardon me, but those were your father's exact words.'

Thomas laughed again. *No wonder he liked her.*

'And Conan Doyle says nothing for a bit, just chews his teeth, then says, "The canine would have to be British, of course. A rather large, diabolical hound might suit Holmes." And – lo and behold! – a year later, up pops good old Sherlock in "The Hound of the Baskervilles", saving the day.'

'So Holmes is not dead after all?'

'He's very much alive.'

'Thanks to my dad.'

They lapsed into a warm silence, sitting opposite the tent, each with their own thoughts yet not alone.

Thomas Clare didn't tell her, not then anyway, that he wasn't entirely certain of the case of the snake and the dingo. By the time Thomas had entered his teenage years his father had swapped the snake for a wild pig, and later the pig became a croc. In each retelling, usually around a campfire, the lunch was also different – once a piece of apple pie, then a handful of tobacco; although always it was the dingo that saved the day.

Jack Clare was no liar, but he could spin a good yarn. There might be a blue between them, some row over something or other when they might be unflinchingly silent, but when the storytelling urge came upon Jack Clare, rare as it was, the son made sure to listen.

Chapter 4

WHEN THOMAS RETURNED TO THE police station, Sergeant Griffin was loading a packhorse with his father's revolver and carbine and a bag full of documents.

'Got anywhere to stay when the new man arrives?' the sergeant asked.

Thomas shook his head, surprised. Until then, he had not realised he would have to leave.

'Tom be all right with us,' Tubbie said from the steps where he sat with Snow.

'I mean somewhere decent,' the sergeant said, with a distasteful glance at the tracker.

'I'll be looking after him too,' Doctor Woods put in.

Sergeant Griffin grunted. 'There's something else. I was going through his papers.' The policeman held out a piece of notepaper. 'Is this your father's hand?'

Thomas glanced at it. The script was familiar – careless, uneven, and heavy-handed, like his father. 'Yes.'

'It's for you.' Sergeant Griffin gave him the note and Thomas felt his stomach sink.

My son,

I can no longer live with myself. I am most grievously sorry to leave you. I hope you will understand. I regret having been a poor father, a failure and a drunkard. The fault is all mine. Above all do not blame yourself. Thomas, you are now at an age to choose your path in life, which will be better for my absence.

Your loving father

John Robert Clare

In a daze, Thomas stared at the words and struggled to make sense of them. They swirled around his head. *Grievously sorry . . . the fault is all mine . . . a failure and a drunkard.* Words on a slip of paper. That wasn't his father. He never confessed to such things, never admitted any wrongs, never took a step back. Thomas passed the note to Doctor Woods, happy to be rid of it.

Ellen Woods had tears in her eyes as she handed the note to Tubbie, but Sergeant Griffin intervened, 'I'll take that.' The policeman tucked it away inside his jacket. 'I almost forgot,' he said, pulling out a wristwatch from the same pocket and handing it to Thomas. 'This was with the note.'

His father's watch, with the luminous numbers that glowed in the dark. Automatically, Thomas put it to his ear. *Still ticking.*

The sergeant mounted his horse and saluted the doctor. 'Right then, I'll be away. Got an official report to write . . . Be back for the funeral. You'll receive your father's back pay and benefits in due course, lad. Good luck to you.'

Doctor Woods sat with Thomas beside Tubbie and Snow on the police steps. They watched Griffin ride away over the hill until only his broad-brimmed bush hat was visible, before it too disappeared.

No one said a word until finally, Tubbie spoke: 'Tracked ten year with Jack Clare. He never do that.'

'Jack left a note, Mister Terrier,' the doctor reminded him.

'Maybe forced to write.'

'Sergeant Griffin found an empty whisky bottle under the tree and Jack's body smelt strongly of spirits,' the doctor said. 'You and I both may not think it in his nature to take his own life but, as much as it may pain us to admit, we know that when he was drinking he was not in his right mind.'

'Jack seen plenty execution,' Tubbie said.

'As a policeman, of course,' Doctor Woods said.

'What are you suggesting, Uncle?' Thomas interrupted.

'He not gunna bugger it up.' Tubbie gestured for them to follow him.

They walked around the side of the house to the ghost gum from which the noose still hung.

The black tracker stopped beside two half-moon gouges in the dirt. 'Heels. Jack's boots hit ground first.'

The gashes were next to a smooth patch and a deep brown stain. A foul bitterness rose in Thomas's throat as he looked again at the place where the torso had fallen and the head had followed.

'Mister Terrier,' Doctor Woods said, exasperated, 'this is hard enough for Thomas to deal with.'

'There's not much worse than suicide,' Thomas snapped. 'Uncle?'

'Jack not gunna leave his head so son gunna fall on it.'

Thomas winced and turned to Doctor Woods. 'Why did his head come off?'

'Oh, please don't concern yourself with that,' she said, with a pained expression on her face. 'You've been through enough already.'

He looked her in the eye. 'Tell me.'

Doctor Woods took a deep breath. 'All right. I consulted the texts, Thomas. As I told the sergeant, most people who hang themselves die slowly from strangulation. In Jack's case, with decapitation, death would have been sudden and relatively painless. In an execution, the hangman measures a man's height and weight and calculates the length of fall from the scaffold so that his neck breaks. However, if the drop is too long . . .' She paused, leaving the sentence unfinished.

'Dad's a big bloke and that's a high branch,' Thomas said, glancing up, 'and it . . .'

'Yes,' Ellen said reluctantly.

They were all looking at the high bough, a good twenty feet up, when Snow asked, 'Why would he climb up there?'

'He never,' Tubbie said. 'Was pushed.'

'Oh, for pity's sake, Mister Terrier!' Ellen cried.

'Why, Uncle?' said Thomas.

As an answer, Tubbie squatted and, with the backs of his fingers, lightly swept the dirt. 'See them marks. Too even, all in line, covering up deeper marks, some deep, some not deep. Them's horseshoes, swept over with gum tree branch.'

The old tracker moved back beneath the noose and pointed to a smaller horseshoe mark. 'Heel plate. This boot not belong Jack.'

'Oh,' Thomas sighed.

Again, Tubbie squatted and traced a finger beside a line of tiny pits in the dirt. To Thomas they appeared to be the faintest of dimples.

'Hobnails?' suggested Ellen.

Tubbie shook his head. 'Not hobnails. Them's tacks and smooth sole, not get stuck on stirrup.' He got to his feet, brushing dirt from his hands. 'Trooper boot.'

'Trooper – you mean *cavalry*?' suggested Thomas.

'Not cavalry,' said Tubbie. 'Army horsefella boot. I seen same heel, same sole before. In Africa.'

Was Tubbie in the Boer War too? But before Thomas could ask, the old Aborigine had turned to the tree trunk with a wave to his son. 'Snow, give ya old man a shin-up.'

His son cupped his hands and Tubbie put in his bare foot and was propelled up the trunk of the eucalypt, grabbing hold of the lowest branch. Like a man half his age, he hoisted himself up and walked sure as a cat along the heavy bough to the hangman's rope high above them. He slid the rope aside and pointed to the bark beneath it.

'Here. Marks cut deep,' Tubbie called down. 'Rope was pulled this way, that way, like wood saw.' The old tracker slipped back down the trunk and dropped nimbly to the ground, careful to avoid the tracks.

Thomas shook his head. 'You'd expect rope marks, wouldn't you? It means he jerked about in the noose.'

But Doctor Woods groaned, 'Oh sweet Jesus, the bruises!'

'What sort of bruises?' Thomas said.

'I saw them at the hospital . . . couldn't explain them.'

'What sort?' Thomas repeated.

'Fingers, quite clear. Around Jack's ankles.'

'Oh hell,' said Thomas, shaking his head miserably. He sat down heavily in the dirt.

'And his face . . .' added Ellen Woods. 'At first, I thought his head had simply hit the ground hard, but now . . .?'

'What?' said Snow.

'One cheek was caked with dirt. The other was bruised badly and cut.' She paused. 'As if he'd been branded.'

Tubbie pointed to the pits in the dirt. 'Boot?'

Doctor Woods nodded. 'I think so.'

'What's it mean?' said Snow.

'A policeman makes enemies, doesn't he, Thomas?' said Ellen Woods. 'He arrests people for stealing stock, for petty theft or highway robbery, for being a public nuisance. Sometimes they're only trying to feed their families. Sometimes they're locked up for a long time for offences you and I might think trivial.'

'Blood oath,' Tubbie agreed, ''specially blackfellas.'

She looked hard at Thomas. 'Did anyone have a grudge against Jack?'

Thomas shook his head vaguely. 'The sergeant asked me that. I said no.'

'Did he seem more worried than usual?'

'No. Oh, I dunno.'

Doctor Woods blinked often, as if holding back tears. 'You know what it means?'

'It means my father didn't commit suicide,' Thomas said bluntly as a cold fury came over him. 'The tracks tell us that men were here on horses. They threw a rope over that branch. They pulled him up by the rope and dragged him down by the ankles, up and down many times, tortured him.'

'Like the rack,' sniffed Ellen Woods.

'Then they threw him down.'

'So hard his head got torn off,' Snow said suddenly. Then, seeing the look on his friend's face, he added quickly, 'Sorry, Tom.'

Thomas nodded grimly, silent now that his questions had been answered.

'They stamped on his face and murdered him,' Ellen Woods said as she took the boy's hand and held it to her cheek and began to sob. 'Why, in heaven's name . . .?'

Thomas stood stiffly beside her, gripped by a flurry of emotions. Horror, bewilderment, and a relief that his father had not taken his own life. But most of all he felt himself grow hot with rage.

After a minute Doctor Woods let his hand go and wiped her eyes with a handkerchief. With an effort, she recovered her composure. 'Mister Terrier, I assume you will inform Sergeant Griffin?'

'That cop not worth possum piss.' Tubbie spat in the dirt. 'Tell him nothing. Might say I was making trouble. Lock me up.'

'Nevertheless, we must inform the police. Sergeant Griffin won't have ridden far. Best that I advise him immediately.' She mounted her horse and looked down at Thomas. 'It is a mercy that Jack did not take his own life, yet what we have before us fills me with dread.'

'Too right, missus,' said Tubbie.

'Will you be all right, Thomas?' she asked him.

Clenching his teeth, Thomas nodded, and Doctor Woods rode away.

Snow said, 'What are you going to do, Tom?'

Thomas barely heard. He was staring hard at the noose. No one had taken it down. That would be his job, he decided, that and whatever else needed to be done.

Chapter 5

JACK CLARE DIED ON THE night of Tuesday, August the fourth. At any other time, the death of Murgon's first policeman would have galvanised the town like an approaching bushfire. But the death, while noted and remarked upon, was soon dwarfed by events far away.

Every day on the train from Brisbane the newspapers arrived with grand statements and gushing rhetoric, for Australia had quickly joined Britain and her allies to pledge war against Germany and her allies.

The excitement became the town's heartbeat. Visions of gallantry and glory pulsed through the streets. Every young man on horseback dreamt of a cavalry charge or imagined how it would be to abandon the humdrum of farm, yard and shearing shed to answer the call of the Mother Country, and quickly too, in case the war ended before they could get to it.

'I know bit 'bout soldiers,' said Tubbie Terrier, rolling a smoke while they sat on the police station steps. 'Met your dad in one of them whitefella wars.'

Many a time they had sat around a fire to listen to Tubbie the elder tell a story. Thomas suspected he'd heard this one, but

Snow was watching his father closely and nodded at Thomas to do the same. And so, despite the sense of outrage that made Thomas want to let fly at his father's killers, anything to keep him moving, to stop him from screaming, he took a deep breath and with a supreme effort of will sat still.

'You know that big chief fella, the one visit your dad in hospital?' Tubbie began.

'Kitchener.'

'That old general ask us blackfellas come track Boers, and this old fool Tubbie says yes, sir, you beaut, sir, and off I go. And while I was out catching them Boer commandos, you whitefellas was getting rid of your colonies, changing all your bloody rules.'

'Federation,' Thomas said. He'd studied it in class. 'We voted to abolish the colonies, to become one nation – Australia.'

'One nation! Ha, no one asked me,' Tubbie laughed. 'There I was, old muggins, stuck in South Africa coz this place, my country, wouldn't let no blackfellas come home, reckoned we was not dinkum, tough shit Abos.'

Snow shook his head and chuckled.

Thomas gave him a disapproving glance. 'What's so funny?'

Snow shot back, 'Not funny . . . a farce. While Dad's off being a good citizen, the new parliament made a law to stop blacks coming in.'

'My ancestors been here thousands of years before the white man,' Tubbie said.

'Was bad for us too,' Snow said. 'Mum was by herself looking after me and my sister in Brisbane when some other whitefellas decided that we got to move to the mission because Tubbie's deserted us.'

'And me stuck in Africa like every other black bastard,' added Tubbie. 'Anyways, Tom, by this time your dad was trooper with them Bushveldt Carbineers. Old Jack was mad as a cut snake when them British shoot his officers, Breaker and Handcock, so he quit that mob. Then he sees me and got more mad as hell coz they was not gunna sell me a ticket to go home. Good fella, your dad! He snuck me onto that ship and smuggle me back in. We was mates ever since.'

Tubbie laughed, now a little sadly.

Thomas knew the rest. When Jack Clare became Murgon's first cop he employed Tubbie as his number one tracker. With a regular wage coming in, Tubbie had built a small timber and iron-roofed house on stilts at the mission and had enough to keep the family in good food and clothes.

Barambah Creek skirted the Aboriginal settlement named after it and meandered through rich grazing land south of Murgon and beyond. In winter, if the grey gum and silver wattle were sparse overhead and the sky was blue, you could sit on the bank with the sun on your face and savour the water bubbling about your feet.

Winnie sat beside him with her feet dipped in the current. The most beautiful feet, Thomas thought. Bare and brown, they were, with soles tough as leather, and when she ran or swam he could see the shape of her legs. She was tall and coffee-skinned like her brother and with Iris's delicate nose. Her eyes under strong brows were large and brown, and – depending on her mood – danced or burned. Once, she'd told him her grand-father was a white man, though she didn't know his name.

While every other girl Thomas knew was covered impec-cably from neck to toe, Winnie wore her dress loosely as if it was a size too big, or as if she might chuck it off any moment for a good enough reason. He was sure the buttoned-up girls in Brisbane would regard her as common and vulgar, but he didn't give two hoots.

The first time Thomas met her she was bald, the punishment for a dormitory girl with head lice. As they became
friends, she took pride in revealing her latest wounds from
the sub-matron's cat-o'-nine-tails for making mischief or giving
cheek once too often. Sometimes Winnie and another girl
would escape their chores to join the boys for a swim in goona
gully or the bogey hole. At other times, while Thomas set
about with his rifle and Snow with his spear, the girls would
collect mussels from the creek bank, or berries and wild honey,
and when they were in season the native peach *quandong* and
the orange *bumbril*. Then, sure of a feast, they'd prepare a fire
and await the triumph of the hunters. Once Snow impaled an
emu and Thomas finished it off with a bullet, and they cooked
it up, enjoying the dark steaks, the juice running down their
faces, reliving their prowess in hunting and cooking late into
the night.

It was an uncommon friendship for the times, frowned upon
by white and black, town and camp-folk alike. When she was
alive, Thomas's mother had barely tolerated Jack Clare's easy
relationship with Tubbie's family and had complained if he
took the boy to see them, which he did on Saturdays, when the
superintendent granted Snow and Winnie leave to visit Tubbie
in the camp.

After Rose Clare's death and his father's decline, they had
come to mean everything to Thomas, and it was a hard parting
when the school holidays ended and Thomas left for a new term
in the city and the sober care of Aunt Mercia.

Lately, he and Winnie had started up a correspondence,
he to Miss Winifred Daisy Terrier, domestic, care of Supt
Lipscombe, Barambah Aboriginal Mission, via Murgon, and
she to Thomas James Clare Esq., St. Joseph's College, Gregory
Terrace, Brisbane.

Each time he returned, Iris would embrace him as a second son and he would notice how much Winnie had grown in ways that delighted and disturbed him.

'Why'd she do it, Win?' Thomas blurted out, as he watched the water stream around her ankles. 'Why'd she leave us like that?'

'I dunno, Tom,' Winnie said, 'but she musta loved you.'

'Strange way of showing it.'

'She was sick. Wasn't her fault.'

'Was it his?'

'Dunno,' Winnie sighed. 'The drink changes people.'

Thomas looked at Winnie, saw the truth buried in those brown eyes and wished he could disappear into them.

Chapter 6

THE MORNING OF THE FUNERAL came bright and chilling. A westerly swept the little cemetery at the bottom of Lamb Street and the small group of mourners shivered with bowed heads.

Thomas knew them. Shopkeepers, farmers and their wives, victims of petty criminals that his father had put away. They squirmed and fidgeted round the empty trench, uncomfortable on unconsecrated ground that was newly hacked from the surrounding bush and set apart from the hallowed graveyard. No wonder they were anxious, Thomas thought grimly. It would be the last rite for a man declared guilty of self-murder, an offence against God. There was no cleric to conduct the service and, so far, no body.

'What's keeping the beggars?' Sergeant Griffin said, tapping his hand against his thigh. Beside him, a shire councillor shook his head irritably and consulted his fob watch and prayed for the clatter of hooves and hearse.

The cart might have broken down on the way from the hospital, Thomas supposed, and wondered what would happen if it never arrived.

He was in his father's only suit, surprised that it fitted tolerably well. He knew his father wouldn't mind, would be pleased to be laid out in his constable's uniform.

In the city, at the burial of Thomas's mother, Rose's family had mourned with loud weeping and wailing. On that terrible day, Jack Clare had remained ramrod straight. Yet, Thomas remembered, when he had looked up into the rock of that face, had seen him blink over and over, he had understood something of his father. *A copper's face, a soldier's bearing.*

Thomas straightened his back.

Finally, the cart-hearse arrived accompanied by Doctor Woods on her stallion. Now Thomas understood the delay. He had asked her to make his father complete and it must have been a long and difficult suture. *Whole in the hole,* he thought, and then rebuked himself for such disrespect.

Doctor Woods dismounted and without a word joined him at the graveside, dressed all in black except for the white handkerchief pressed to her face, hiding silent tears.

Tubbie and his family stood behind him. The tracker wore his best police jacket and had cap in hand, jodhpurs tucked inside knee-length polished boots; Iris, half her husband's age, and Winnie and Snow were in their Sunday best. From time to time, Thomas felt their eyes on him and was grateful.

'Never been to a whitefella funeral before,' Snow whispered in his sister's ear.

Thomas heard and didn't mind, but Iris shushed the boy with a sharp elbow. 'We sending a spirit on his way today.'

Without further delay, the coffin was offloaded and Jack Clare made a brisk descent to his resting place. The gravediggers recovered their ropes, and one of them flicked a cigarette into the trench before he strolled away.

It was an uncomfortable silence that followed and drew

attention to the absence of a clergyman and the mourners' reluc-
tance to speak. Until William West, once Thomas's teacher at
Murgon's little school, stepped forward and nervously cleared
his throat. Tall and thin, with heavy eyebrows and stick-out ears,
he was dressed in a black three-piece suit and in his big hands he
clutched a grey homburg hat close to his heart.

'We may not judge a man by his last moments,' Mr West
began. 'Only God knows the pain that tortures the mind, what
despair, oppressive and excruciating, what misery, lies there.
Constable Clare is deserving of our compassion.'

The teacher glanced at Thomas with a strained smile before
continuing, 'We shall remember him as an honest servant of
the people and the law, a brave soldier of the realm and a fine
father. Let us pray for the soul of Jack Clare. *Requiescat in pace*,'
he concluded in his beloved Latin.

'Amen,' the mourners mumbled. One after another, they
threw a handful of dirt into the hole, replaced hats on heads,
or opened parasols, and took their leave quickly with a parting
nod to Thomas.

William West approached Thomas and shook his hand. 'My
condolences for your loss.'

Thomas was now as tall as his former teacher. Face to face,
he noticed how the man's lower lip trembled. 'Your father and
I shared a drink from time to time, Thomas. He was a good
man, who despised hypocrisy. Had more townsfolk attended,
Jack might have raised himself up, arrested them and charged
them with fraud.'

'Sir?' said Thomas, puzzled.

'Why, for attending his funeral in the guise of friends, of course.'
Mr West chuckled and Thomas smiled weakly.

'Consider, Thomas, the calamities of Job,' Mr West went
on quickly, his voice breaking and his eyes shining. 'The Lord

tested him and took everything from him. Yet He restored Job and gave him . . . "twice as much as he had before".'

Thomas doubted that God would provide him with two more fathers but he thanked Mr West for his kind words and watched him depart with affection.

Beside their shovels, the diggers sat swigging a bottle, awaiting the signal to fill in the grave. Sergeant Griffin went over to them.

Tubbie and his family threw a handful of gum leaves onto the coffin. The old tracker brought out a plain hardwood cross he'd carved. 'Black *gidyea*, special wood of my people,' he said simply.

While Tubbie hammered in the cross, Thomas stood at the edge of the trench and studied the coffin at the bottom. He wondered whether his father might have wished to lie beside Rose in her family plot in Brisbane. The idea hadn't occurred to him until now. He shook his head to make it disappear. *Too late.* Anyway, Rose's family would never have agreed. They had been generous to Thomas but not to Jack Clare, had never forgiven him. None of them had bothered to turn up today. If only he had spoken up more for his father, made them understand how happy it was before his mother . . .

Most of his memories were of the hard cop and the ruin of the man Thomas hadn't the courage to confront or the wit to change. He'd failed his father. *The craven son,* he thought, who rolled the drunk into bed and pulled off his boots, only to pretend the next day that it hadn't happened.

But there had been that one morning when Jack Clare had said, 'It's been hard on me . . . your mother's death.'

'Yes, sir.'

'You also, I expect.'

'Yes.'

'You're a good lad.'

'Yes, sir.'

Nothing more was said. Thomas's heart had swelled with it. It had been enough, then.

'Goodbye, Dad,' he muttered and threw in a handful of dirt.

'What will you do now?' Snow asked.

'Dunno. Got no family left, except in Brisbane. Don't want to live there.'

'You got us,' said Winnie. She put her hand in his and he grasped it gratefully.

Sergeant Griffin returned with the gravediggers and set them to work. 'Shame there's no grog-up,' he said. 'No wake with a suicide.'

'That's enough, sergeant,' said Doctor Woods sharply.

'Yes, it was uncalled for,' Sergeant Griffin conceded. 'He was my friend too. Have no concerns, lad, about the cost of the burial and headstone. All taken care of, courtesy of the Commissioner.'

'Thank you,' Thomas said. 'But I reckon my father would be more than happy with the cross Mister Terrier made for him.'

'As you wish.' The policeman cleared his throat. 'Duty calls, so forgive me for raising this now, but I must speak to you about this half-baked theory concerning the causes of Jack's death. I have reviewed the evidence and revisited the scene. I've looked at the supposed tracks below the tree and the markings on the bough and I considered the theory put forward by Doctor Woods. I can only say that none of it constitutes compelling new evidence. Certainly nothing that would suggest murder.'

'But what about . . .?' interrupted Thomas.

The sergeant held up his hand. 'Hear me out, son. My black-tracker did not confirm Tubbie Terrier's suspicion of recent activity under the tree. My tracker believes the marks in the bark were the result of your father's struggle in the noose during his . . . ahem, his last moments.'

'Your tracker not worth shit,' Tubbie said.

Sergeant Griffin pretended not to hear and addressed himself to Doctor Woods. 'There is no motive for murder, let alone torture. It simply does not make sense. I'm sorry to say this, because Jack Clare was a mate, but his history of drinking, the note he left behind, and the obvious distress at his wife's passing are generally known and lead me to conclude there are no suspicious circumstances. None. I have closed the file to that effect.'

'But, sergeant . . .' began Doctor Woods.

'The case is closed, madam.' Sergeant Griffin mounted his horse and straightened his khaki hat.

'Whitefella justice,' Tubbie muttered.

Sergeant Griffin ignored him, and reached into his satchel to retrieve a small envelope, which he passed down to Thomas. 'Telegram arrived for you today. Once again, my condolences.'

As the sergeant rode away, Thomas felt only sadness.

'C'mon, what's in it?' said Snow. 'Never seen a telegram before.'

'Me neither.' Thomas gave a weak laugh and opened the yellow envelope. Inside were two cables. He read the first aloud:

DEEPEST SYMPATHIES STOP REGRET UNABLE BE THERE STOP SHARE GRIEF STOP JACK GALLANT COMRADE DEAR FRIEND STOP JACK CONFIDED GREAT LOVE AND PRIDE IN YOU STOP WELCOME OPPORTUNITY ASSIST YOU STOP MUCH AFFECTION UNCLE HARRY STOP WAR OFFICE LONDON STOP

'Jack never mentioned a brother,' said Ellen Woods.

'He used to visit us sometimes. They'd drink whisky and smoke cigars and talk and talk. Dad saved his life in the war!'

Doctor Woods nodded. 'A brother in arms.'

Thomas read out the second telegram – Uncle Harry recommending him to any employer or school that would have him.

'Two cables in one day,' Ellen Woods observed.

Tubbie spat. 'That's the bloody army for ya.'

The second telegram had given Thomas an idea. He wouldn't be going back to school. Not for him the sober masters and the dreary routine. Not on the eve of war. Not with a killer to catch. A killer he would most likely find in the army.

It was only when Thomas returned to an empty house to feed his father's filly that he remembered that it was August the seventh, his birthday.

Chapter 7

WINTER HELD THE PENULTIMATE SABBATH in its dying embrace as August drew to a close. In and around Murgon and in churches across the nation, preachers and priests rallied their flocks to duty and the young men flocked.

The boys caught the train to Brisbane, their carriage filled with youths and men from Kingaroy to Kilkivan. Some faces still shone with parting tears, but all were bright with the promise of adventure and the good fight to come. Thomas waved gaily at old school chums, like Edward the butcher's son and Freddie the baker's boy, and one or two others recently laid off at the butter factory.

Soon enough they joined the queue of lively youths and men in suits and boaters that stretched down Albert Street to the recruitment depot, flanked by a parade of motors that clattered past with their horns blaring in loyal salute.

It seemed as if they had chanced upon a festival or jubilee, for the Union Jack flew here and there from the heights, outnumbered all around by the flags of the new nation, star-crossed with the Mother Country's icon safely tucked into the corner. And when a band of gleaming brass struck up, the long line burst forth with the hymn they had sung all their lives:

God save our gracious King,
Long live our noble King,
God save the King!
Send him victorious,
Happy and glorious,
Long to reign over us;
God save the King!

Ahead in the queue, they saw the teacher William West singing lustily and in the same suit he'd worn to the funeral.

'I'm surprised he's here,' Thomas said to Snow. 'He has a wife and babe to support.'

'That makes him brave, patriotic, and mad as a dingbat . . . just like us,' Snow laughed, as the band began another verse.

O Lord our God arise,
Scatter His enemies,
And make them fall:
Confound their politics,
Frustrate their knavish tricks,
On Thee our hopes we fix,
God save us all.

For their efforts they were rewarded with three hip-hip-hurrahs from the passers-by and the admiring glances of young women in their smart city clothes. As the column of city boys and country lads inched forward, the band launched into 'Rule Britannia', and when it took a break, someone struck up a familiar chorus and everyone sang:

Kaiser Bill went up the hill, to have a shot at France,
Kaiser Bill came down the hill, with bullets in his pants.

'We'll show 'em what Australians can do,' declared a young voice, sending a ripple of excitement through the line and prompting others to cry out.

'Queensland heeds the call.'

'Rally to the Mother Country.'

'Loyalty to King and service to Empire.'

'To the last man and the last shilling,' someone said, repeating the Prime Minister's words from all the newspapers.

'And six bob a day for us,' said another, to general laughter.

A well-dressed businessman said earnestly, 'My store will close, but I shall bear its loss and gladly too.'

'If England's defeated, it'll be our turn next,' a voice called out.

'Isn't this exciting?' a wide-eyed youth told Thomas. 'It's the chance of a life. I really don't give a fig if I never see a Hun, but what an adventure it's gunna be.'

'Better hurry, lads, it'll be over by Christmas,' said another, who turned to Snow. 'And what about you, darkie, running from your missus or from the coppers?'

Snow answered evenly, 'Same reason as you, for home and country,' for which he was congratulated with a slap on the back and a 'Good on you, cobber!'.

'Never been called cobber by a whitefella before,' Snow said quietly to Thomas.

The boys climbed steps and passed through double doors beneath a large sign, ENLISTING DEPOT. They entered a hall merry with bonhomie, and were soon at the head of the queue.

Behind a table piled with papers sat a sergeant in the khaki jacket of the Light Horse. 'Next.'

A feeling of dread rose in his stomach as Thomas handed over the paper with his aunt's address in Brisbane and her signature forged by Snow.

'Parents?'

'Both dead, sir.'

'Don't call me sir,' the sergeant said severely, tapping the stripes on his arm. 'You're a bit young.'

'Born young, sergeant, and just turned nineteen,' Thomas said, grateful that a birth certificate was not required. He guessed the man was fed up with cocky youngsters, so he quickly handed him the telegram from Uncle Harry. 'Will this help? My father fought with Chauvel's Mounted against the Boers.'

'Was in that one meself,' said the sergeant and read the cable.

THOMAS CLARE SON OF JOHN CLARE OIC MURGON POLICE SERVED DISTINCTION QUEENSLAND MOUNTED STOP YOUNG THOMAS BRIGHT HONEST DILIGENT STOP RECOMMENDED STOP HARRY CHAUVEL COMMANDING 1ST LIGHT HORSE BRIGADE WAR OFFICE LONDON STOP

The sergeant whistled. 'If you're good enough for Colonel Chauvel, that'll do me. As long as you can ride, or even he won't want you.'

'Weaned in the saddle, I was,' Thomas said.

'Save your cheek for the riding test. Move on to the doctor. Next!'

Thomas lingered as Snow stepped up smartly and snapped to attention as if he were on parade, his eyes fixed firmly at the wall above the sergeant's head. He was wearing new clothes and Thomas's best shoes and Thomas was by his side.

'Twins, is it?' said the NCO with a raised eyebrow. 'Born in the saddle too, I expect.'

'Indeed, sergeant, a most astute observation,' Snow said in his best Doctor Watson imitation. 'I'm a drover, sergeant, and can ride any horse you'd care to choose.'

'I know some feisty ones,' said the sergeant, looking him up and down. 'A touch dark for the Light Horse, aren't you, young fella?'

It was an old joke and raised a snigger in the queue behind them.

'Suntan, sergeant,' Snow replied evenly, 'from riding all day long and night too.'

The sergeant's mouth twitched. 'Rules say no darkies allowed.'

'Dad's a Maori warrior, Mum's as British as they come. That's her, there,' Snow said, pointing to Iris's signature.

'So if you're Maori,' the sergeant said doubtfully, 'where's your tatts?'

'Oh they're all over, on my back, belly, arms, bum.' Snow turned his backside to the sergeant and made to unbuckle his belt. 'Here, I'll show you my favourite.'

The sergeant chuckled, 'Won't be necessary, lad.'

Thomas stepped forward. 'Him and me are mates, we hunt together, he never misses a shot, and Uncle Harry . . . Colonel Chauvel vouches for him.'

The sergeant looked from one to the other, then back to Snow. 'I suppose you've a letter from the colonel too?'

'Yes, I do as it so happens.' Snow reached into his pocket.

The sergeant smiled. 'Won't be necessary. We're all khaki in this army. Pass on to the doctor. If you're fit, you're in. If you're not, you're out. Next!' he called and signed Snow's papers.

Thomas congratulated Snow with a slap on the back. 'I didn't know your dad was a Maori.'

'Me neither,' whispered Snow. 'But whitefellas like them better than Abos.'

'Never seen a tattoo on you, neither.'

'Oh, I intend to get some.'

'A princely deception, Watson.'

'We lied like the devil, Holmes.'

Thomas tapped the side of his nose. 'And Uncle Harry doesn't need to know, eh?'

'How many boots are there in the army?'

'Thousands . . . millions,' Thomas snorted, then paused. 'It's a long shot, but it's our only clue. Gotta start somewhere, eh?'

'What the hell, we're in!' cried Snow, and they laughed together as if it was the best day of their lives.

When they arrived back from the big smoke, the boys found Tubbie Terrier furious. 'I fought for my people, not for them that killed them.'

'That war was long ago, Dad. The whitefellas won,' said Snow. 'This is my country and I'll fight for it . . . like you did.'

'Don't see no war here. Maybe some faraway place, not here.'

'It's exactly like your story, Dad. The Huns attack one tribe, then another mob, and it'll be us next,' said Snow. 'You did it, you went to South Africa.'

'And still be there, 'cept for Old Jack getting me back, no thanks to no Empire.'

'Uncle, I'm an orphan,' Thomas broke in. 'What's left for me here?'

'You reckon this place my home?' said Tubbie, indicating the camp with a dismissive motion. He looked at Snow. 'My home gone, no one left there. Us blackfellas not citizens in our own country. You gunna fight for that?'

'There's no black and white in the army, only khaki,' said Snow.

'And red, son, blood red, plenty red.'

'I can look after myself.'

'Not like fists in a ring, boy. In war, you knocked down, you don't get up.'

'I'll be looking after him,' Thomas said, 'and he'll look after me.'

'Won't make no difference. Them buggers bury both your sorry arses and won't mark your graves neither.'

'Now, Tubbie, you stop that,' Iris said. 'This blackfella's gunna make us proud.'

'Not a bloody picnic, Iris, blast you,' Tubbie grumbled, still furious that she had signed Snow's papers.

'It's done, mister.'

Tubbie sighed with a low growl and said to Thomas, 'You whitefellas lucky fellas, got good job, get outa this place, live good in big smoke. This gunna waste your life.'

'I'll do my part for King and country, and I'll see the world.'

'On a ship! I never seen the sea!' Snow added with enthusiasm. 'And France, I wanna see that place.'

'And in the army Uncle Harry is the boss,' Thomas persisted. 'That'll count for something.'

'Won't stop no bullet.'

'And you said *boots*, Uncle, army riding boots. That's what they wear in the Light Horse.'

'Bloody army!' Tubbie spat. 'You gunna lick officer boots and they gunna piss on yours.'

'Tubbie!' complained Iris.

But there was no stopping him. 'And you reckon you gunna find them what killed Jack?'

Thomas and Snow looked at each other sheepishly.

Tubbie snorted. 'Only boots you gunna find are them stamping on your head, kicking your guts, and thems they bury you in.'

'Oh, don't say that, Daddy,' said Winnie. 'You'll come back, won't you?'

'We will,' Snow declared. 'And the money's bonza. Six bob a day, ten times what I get now.'

'Plenty,' Tubbie agreed, 'for a fancy funeral.'

'You stop that kinda talk, mister!' Iris insisted. 'It gunna be over soon. Probably they never even gunna get to France, whatever that place is.'

'Women, boys . . . know nothing 'bout war.' Tubbie sighed heavily and sat down on a log, defeated. After a moment he forced a sad smile onto his face and looked up at the boys.

Winnie saw it and gushed, 'I'll write to you, brother . . . and to you, Tom.'

He beamed. Already he was a hero.

Chapter 8

IT WAS TUBBIE WHO INSISTED Thomas join them on the last day. Somehow, Iris had convinced the superintendent to sign permits allowing Winnie and Snow a day off work to visit a dying relative. Snow reckoned that if the superintendent knew he'd enlisted, the native police would be after him in a flash. And the grazier who employed him as cheap mission labour would report his absence soon after Snow failed to show up. He estimated he had a few days' grace before the coppers started searching for him. In Brisbane, he'd joined up using Iris's family name to put them off the track and in the hope that once in uniform the Australian Imperial Force wouldn't hand him back.

Tubbie promised to send any police he encountered off in the wrong direction. Even so, Snow couldn't tell whether his father had surrendered to the inevitable or was still furious.

The old man led them along the banks of the creek. Thomas hung back, knowing that Tubbie and Snow wanted time together. While Iris and Winnie made camp, he walked away by himself.

After Thomas had bagged a wallaby, he sat down on a log beside the creek, listening to the tinkling brown water and alert to sounds in the undergrowth. When he heard a movement behind him, he and his little rifle spun around.

Winnie stood there wearing a radiant half-moon smile and her hip cocked. 'Gunna shoot and hang me on your belt?' she said.

Thomas frowned nervously. The thought of Winnie anywhere near his belt was intoxicating. 'How'd you find me?'

'Ha!' Winnie laughed and shook her head at him as if he was thick. 'A shiny white boy in the bush – not difficult, Sherlock.'

'Don't call me that.'

'You like it.'

'I do, but . . .'

'Well?'

'It's what Dad called me.'

'Oh dear,' she said with mock sympathy. 'So now no one else can?'

Thomas gritted his teeth. She could be infuriating sometimes. 'Aren't you supposed to be helping Auntie?'

'You want me to go?'

'No.'

'Ha!' she cried and sat beside him on the log, with her arm in his and her head resting on his shoulder, so close so quickly that Thomas almost jumped out of his skin.

Winnie laughed. 'You ever have a girlfriend?'

'Once, after school in Brissy sometimes.'

'Did you like her?'

'Of course I did.'

'Did you kiss her?'

Thomas frowned. No city girl was ever as straightforward and as disarming as Winnie.

'Well, did you?'

'Why should I tell you?'

'Because I don't want no first-time kisser kissing me.'

Thomas looked Winnie squarely in the face. He took in her bright eyes, curly black hair and teasing smile. 'She wasn't a patch on you,' he said. 'You're so beautiful it makes me want to shout.'

'Shout what?'

'That you're my girl.'

'Ha!' Winnie grunted in triumph and kissed him sharply on the cheek.

Thomas flinched. 'And you're my best friend's sister,' he said reluctantly.

'Oh, it's all right, I don't want to *marry* you. I've been engaged since I was six.'

'What?' Thomas said, open-mouthed.

'Of course, silly.'

'Well, that's a damn shame,' Thomas said, crestfallen. But, since he was leaving tomorrow and some things needed to be said, he took a deep breath and blurted out, 'Because when I'm with you I feel happy, Winnie. All the bad stuff goes away.'

Thomas saw Winnie's face take on a deeper glow. 'Better kiss me, then,' she said.

And who could argue with that?

They lay down on the grass, all nervousness forgotten, and Thomas couldn't believe his luck.

His hand moved to the inside of her thighs and found her wet. Amazed, he was, that he was actually stroking a girl's secret parts, even as his mouth was on hers, her lips soft and yielding and her breath hot, while another part of his mind kept exploring the marvellous reaches between her legs.

Winnie shuddered. Her thighs tightened around his hand, and her mouth burst in a warm moan into his. She gently reached down and took his hand away. Instead her fingers reached into his breeches and he was lost in a rush of pleasure so unexpected that his mouth froze on hers. He moved to pull away from her but Winnie hugged him closer, both of them speechless and a little frightened by what had happened.

At the end of the day, the three hunters returned to find Iris and Winnie attending a fire between two fallen logs.

Winnie greeted Thomas with a dreamy look so obvious to her mother that Iris took her by the arm and marched her into the trees. 'Women's business,' she told Tubbie, but once out of their hearing, she demanded, 'What's going on, girl?'

'Nothing, Ma,' Winnie said with a glance back at Thomas.

'You been doing *niggi-niggi*?'

Winnie looked outraged. 'No, Ma.'

'Make sure you keep it that way,' Iris said, and then clipped Winnie across the ear.

'Ow,' Winnie yelled. 'What's that for?'

'For fibbing to your ma.'

'I weren't,' Winnie said, but her mother had stopped listening.

They cooked up an echidna and a goanna, and as the sun went down the animals filled the night with delicious smells. Thomas wouldn't eat the echidna, reckoned it was like eating leather, though they laughed at him.

Tubbie passed around a small keg of beer. 'Whitefellas say booze bad for blackfellas, but it never stop them drinkin' it. Don't take no shit from whitefellas, son,' said Tubbie, putting his arm around Snow. 'Remember your people. You Kalkadoon warrior.'

'Yes, Dad,' said Snow.

Tubbie took a deep swig from the keg and cleared his throat. Thomas knew the signs. It meant the old Aborigine was going to tell a story. Snow listened closely too, and it soon became clear that the story was for them both.

'My people from way up north, eh, Snow?'

'Yes, Dad.'

'Never told you this, Tom,' began Tubbie. 'Twenty year ago my father was chief of Kalkadoons.'

'Oh,' said Thomas, surprised.

Tubbie saw his son's pride, yet shook his head. 'Never told you much 'bout that place what whitefellas call Battle Mountain.'

Iris interrupted him. 'You sure you want to tell this story, when these boys just going off to war?'

'Best time, missus.' Tubbie took another swig and continued, 'My people was Kalkadoons, warrior tribe, fight whitefellas ten years. Started when I was your age, boys.'

Tubbie paused to catch his breath. He looked far into the fire and then began to sing with a deep, gravelly voice, and though the words were incomprehensible to him, Thomas felt their power. Haunted and proud, the old man punched out the song in time with his foot and his eyes burned with each word, cruel and brutal as a blow.

When he'd finished, Tubbie smiled at Thomas.

'What was that?' Thomas asked.

'Tribal war song.' Snow looked at his father, who nodded his approval.

'Kalkadoon,' Snow began to translate,

'have our glory and strength gone?

'Our hunting grounds destroyed, our water stolen by cattle.

'Kill and eat beef forever! Kill the white man, kill the white man!'

Thomas shuddered.

'Do our women mock us?' Snow continued. 'We are many and can conquer the white man's magic.'

The fierce light was still in Tubbie's eyes and it scared Thomas. A song to kill, a song to kill Europeans. He'd never heard the like. He looked anew at Tubbie – tall and broad-shouldered, scarred and wrinkled, all beard and unkempt hair – and for the first time he saw the old man as his enemies might once have seen and feared him.

Thomas had read *Boys' Own* stories about the way American 'redskins' had danced and chanted before they wiped out Colonel Custer and his cavalry to a man. Tubbie's was that kind of song, he thought, but surely it had never happened in Australia. Everyone had heard stories of blacks murdering and raping just a generation ago, and he'd heard some of the old hands, when they'd had a few, recalling how they had tracked the blacks and 'dispersed' them; 'frontier justice', they'd called it.

Yet Thomas was so surprised that this gentle man could sing such a bloodthirsty song that he was lost for words. Best not to say anything, he decided.

He must have looked discomforted, because Tubbie was grinning at him. 'Kalkadoons was fierce warrior tribe up north there. Till one day plenty big fight. You heard of Battle Mountain, Tom?'

'No, Uncle.'

'Big battle there long time ago, thirty years. We was gunna finish them whitefellas that took our land, poisoned waterholes, stole our tucker. We was gunna have no more hit and run, was gunna be whole mob in one place. Well, we was waiting for them, every Kalkadoon, brother, cousin. Them whitefellas and native police got guns, Snider carbine repeaters, dumdum bullets, but we got plenty spears, nulla nullas, shields, fighting poles, the lot, and plenty warriors, hundreds. We was ready for them, hiding behind rocks in that real hard place full of gullies and gorges, good fighting place. They got to attack uphill, was tough for them, you understand?'

'Yes,' the boys said together, wide-eyed.

'That whitefella boss, Urquhart the copper, he yell, "Stand in the Queen's name." Ha, we just laugh, throw rocks down on them. Them native police start riding up, silly buggers, too steep for horses, and one bigfella Kalkadoon he throw a piece of ant-hill, hit Urquhart in the face, laid out he was.'

Tubbie chuckled at the memory, then quietly told the rest of the story, how Urquhart recovered to command a flanking manoeuvre. Confused at the change of tactics, Tubbie's father ordered an attack. The Kalkadoon warriors left the cover of crags and boulders and charged Urquhart's posse of white settlers and native police.

'We was running down, spears out,' Tubbie continued. 'We was singing "Kill the white man, kill the white man", straight at them.'

'Like the Charge of the Light Brigade,' Thomas said enthusiastically, drawn along by the tale, all nervousness forgotten.

'Showing whitefellas that blackfellas can fight true,' Snow agreed, his eyes bright.

'Brave . . . so gallant,' murmured Winnie. She winked at Thomas with such warmth and anticipation that he felt his heart might burst.

'Spears against guns, running into bullets . . . stupid!' Tubbie snapped. 'Was slaughter. Plenty warriors killed, my dad too. One of them Snider slugs cracked me head, knocked me out cold, while them native police chase women, old men, kiddies, finish them.'

'Why weren't you captured, Uncle?' Thomas asked.

'Native police, pah!' Tubbie spat in the dirt. 'Blackfellas from other tribes, they chased us, they shot us.'

'But you fought them face to face like soldiers,' said Snow.

'We was dogs to them.'

Thomas said, 'You should have been taken prisoner.'

Tubbie looked from one to the other and shook his head. 'Dogs,' he repeated and took another swig.

'Me last warrior, maybe some others, maybe not. Dunno,' he continued. 'Anyways, this bloody good whitefella Macdonald on the Leichhardt River gimme job, looking after his kiddies, teachin' them bush skills, huntin' wild bees, gettin' bush tucker. That Macdonald was callin' me Tubbie Terrier, never could say my Kalkadunga name. Snow and Winnie was born there, then the missus and me we move to Brisbane, to that Musgrave Park place.'

Thomas had listened with astonishment. In the past Tubbie had talked about bushcraft and stories from the Dreamtime, but never about that part of his life. It wasn't only Thomas who was affected. No one spoke for some time.

'All dead, 'cept me, few others,' Tubbie said finally. 'Listen to old warrior, boys. Brave is good, clever is better. Don't jump in front of no bullets.'

The old man looked back into the flames so Snow wouldn't see his tears.

Eventually, Tubbie rose to his feet and beckoned Thomas and Snow to follow him to a gum tree at the edge of the clearing. There, the tracker looked and listened, alert to any movement, and when he was sure no one else was watching he poked a stick inside a hollow in the trunk.

'Go-way snake, this my place,' he said with a grin. Next he put his arm in to the elbow, and pulled out a small oilskin bag.

'Your dad say look after this,' Tubbie said simply, handing it to Thomas.

They returned to the campsite, where Thomas opened the bag in the light of the fire. Inside was a single sheet of faded

paper. Official-looking, he saw, a document curling ͞
It was signed: *ROBERTS, Headquarters of the Army in*
Pretoria, 14 August 1900.

Beside the typewritten lines, *Field Marshal Lord Roberts will vigorously suppress guerrilla warfare by every means, which the customs of war prescribe,* Thomas noticed a handwritten note in the margin:

Bulala

TNP

K

In the dancing glow of the flames, the writing made no sense. 'What *is* this?' Thomas said.

'From Boer War,' Tubbie replied.

'Why hide it here?' Snow said. 'Why didn't he keep it at the police station?'

'Jack not trust no one 'cept me,' said Tubbie. 'Worried get him killed one day.'

Those last words hit like a sudden blow. In the raw silence, Thomas's eyes filled with tears and remained fixed on the document. When at last he looked up, Winnie was slicing pieces off a steaming wallaby. She handed him a portion, sat beside him and hooked her arm in his.

Tubbie and Iris caught each other's eye but said nothing.

Thomas took a bite, and declared in his best Tubbie voice, 'Good tucker, missus. Blackfellas sure can cook bloody good.'

Iris chuckled, Tubbie smiled.

From the other side, Snow put his arm around Thomas's shoulders.

As he ate, Thomas's thoughts were about the document. So important that even under torture his father would not reveal its location. Why had his father hidden it? Why had he not spoken of it? Was it worth dying for? *Those bastards!* Why did they want it?

The questions raced through Thomas's head. First the boots at the scene of the crime, now his father's concealment of a document from an old war. Pieces of a puzzle, with the army at the centre.

He would be sad to leave them, especially Winnie, when things were just getting started. He would miss the creek, the bush and the hunt, and there was nothing for him in Brisbane except the formality of his mother's family. At school they would whisper behind his back, *the son of suicides*. One or two boys might sympathise, but more would jeer and mock. Of course, he could suffer it or beat them bloody, but why bother?

There was no family, no home, not any more.

Even here around the fire, among good friends, he was an outsider on the fringes of his society.

What remained was the hunt. A new kind. That was what really mattered.

Yes, it was the right decision, he thought. A path dark with danger and uncertainty but bright too with adventure and glory and the company of his best mate.

Tomorrow they would take the morning train. Thomas would say goodbye to his friends and the bush country, to school and to civvie street, farewell to everything he knew.

The Light Horse.

If he were to find who killed his father, it would be the place to start.

LIONS

Quinn's Post, May 1915

'There's an east wind coming, Watson.'
'I think not, Holmes. It is very warm.'
'Good old Watson! You are the one fixed point in a changing
age. There's an east wind coming all the same, such a wind as
never blew on England yet. It will be cold and bitter, Watson,
and a good many of us may wither before its blast. But it's
God's own wind none the less, and a cleaner, better, stronger
land will lie in the sunshine when the storm has cleared. Start
her up, Watson, for it's time that we were on our way.'

– 'His Last Bow: an Epilogue of Sherlock Holmes',
Arthur Conan Doyle

Chapter 9

HOW FITTING, THOMAS THOUGHT, THAT his first encounter with the enemy should be a boot. It stuck out from the roof of the arch he'd squeezed through at the entrance to the post. Beside the boot were the grey fingers of a man's hand and Thomas wondered whether the boot and the hand belonged together.

Other boots poked over the parapet. Decomposing feet in bullet-holed leather, and impossible to tell whether they were Turk or Anzac.

Dead men's boots at the door to hell, still there because no one dared to drag them in.

From his crouch in the fire trench, Thomas could not see over the sandbags into no-man's-land, but the smell told him all he needed to know. It told him what he would see if ever he were foolish enough to stand.

Army boots were why he'd enlisted, he recalled, and he might have laughed had the joke not been on him.

It was the day after he and his comrades came ashore on Gallipoli. They were occupying Quinn's Post, a rabbit warren of narrow trenches, saps and tunnels. Quinn's was not a mile from the beachhead, but as deep in Turkey as any Anzac and closer than anyone to the enemy a mere cricket pitch away.

The Turk lay out of sight over a gentle crest of dirt and prickly scrub shredded by shell and shot. Thomas had never seen a live Turk, but he knew with a certainty that they might charge at any moment, ferocious and mad-eyed, to bayonet and mutilate him and push them all back into the sea. He had heard talk of attacks so fierce that rifles jammed and bayonets became twisted in the heat of firing.

Worse, he realised, crouching deeper in the trench, Quinn's was so exposed to the enemy high up on the flanks that he could be shot from both sides too. Thomas gulped and cursed himself for being afraid and hoped his mates hadn't noticed.

For a fleeting moment he glanced sideways. Snow was beside him, pressed against the bank, then Teach, Kingy and the other Queenslanders on the left, while C Squadron's blokes from New South Wales stretched out of sight on the right, in trenches that ran about the ridgeline up to Lone Pine less than a mile away.

Thomas's greatest fear was that he would be a coward. Or worse, that he would be the only one. He crouched lower and prayed not to let his mates down.

Think of lovely Winnie, or his father, his mother too, he thought, struggling to distract himself. But he could not hold them for long. He wondered if Uncle Harry hadn't made a terrible mistake in ordering them to the forward trenches the day after they'd arrived. After all, like most of his comrades, he was a novice, straight from training, hardly a Light Horseman at all without Rosie Girl. Yet here he was holding the most vital part of the line and never having fired a shot at anybody.

The slow faraway rattle of an engine grew in intensity as an aircraft drifted between clouds towards them. Despite orders not to fire and with little chance of hitting it, Thomas raised his rifle and saw the others do the same. As a dozen rifles silently traced the aviator's progress, Thomas imagined his bullet skewering the pilot and the aircraft tumbling onto an enemy trench, or better still falling upon Turkish officers sitting down to tea or whatever foul heathen mixture it was that they drank.

Thomas closed his eyes and there was Cairo spread out before him. He and Snow were there, at the very top of the pyramid, playing the six-bob-a-day tourist for all they were worth. They'd been eagles then.

He knew the enemy pilot and his observer would see the lot. They would peer into the tangle of ravines and gullies and down into Bloody Angle, Chessboard, German Officers' Trench, The Nek and Dead Man's Ridge. They would look over The Narrows and the Sea of Marmara, perhaps as far as Constantinople. They would spy the men carting water and rations up Monash Valley and those carrying the wounded down to the beach. At a glance they would take in all of the destroyers, transports and battleships streaking the shiny blue Aegean and even the dark slash of a U-boat. Not for them the dismal hole in the ground or the crumbling hillside that left you gasping or the gorse and holly that tore clothing and skin. And soon enough, having taken their fill of photos, they'd putter home to a green field bursting with May wildflowers, somewhere cushy and safe.

Lucky bludgers, he thought and, like the others, lowered his rifle.

Thomas longed to raise his head to look down the Valley to the sea.

He might . . . if he were foolish enough, if he wanted a machine gun bullet in the head or a sniper's slug between the eyes.

Thomas prayed the sandbags gave him enough cover, for the enemy in the heights was a very good shot and otherwise, he'd be gone.

Before their war began, they had been aboard the SS *Devanha* on that clear spring evening. Big country fellows, browned by months of training under Egypt's desert sun, all good shots and riders, packed the rails.

'Hear that?' said Snow, the sharpest ears of all.

Thomas could hear nothing above the rumble of the ship's engines and the hubbub of excited men. But he knew from a hundred hunts that whatever Snow could hear across the placid sea, it was there all right.

A minute later off the starboard side came a distant booming.

A cheer went up from the Light Horsemen. Their brass buckles gleamed, their leather boots shone and their eyes burned with anticipation. They were keen, ready and thankful for it: the Royal Navy giving the Turk a pasting.

As they approached Gallipoli, Thomas cast a last admiring glance at the setting sun, then back to where the flat, fading rays had turned the hills into sharp yellow teeth.

On either side of the troopship, the squat beasts of battleships shivered in black billows as their broadsides punched Turkey with little flames of hell.

Someone along the khaki rail said, 'Struth, this is better than the pictures.'

Like everyone else, Thomas laughed. They were the best of men, from all walks of life, sworn to obey the King's commands and fight his enemies. Plenty, like his father, had fought the Boer. Some officers had enlisted as privates just to have a go.

Thomas's heart swelled with pride in the company of Snow, Kingy and Teach. What pals they were, their friendship cemented in the tortures of training and the carouses of Cairo. They were his family now.

Teach was the cleverest trooper in B Squadron, Thomas knew, tall and stiff, with a military bearing suited to his heroes, Wellington and Nelson. Lofty too in language, apt to shoot lines of verse or prose at his comrades and confound officers not up to his level of learning. He had been the dour and balding William West, Thomas's first instructor in arithmetic, English and ancient history at Murgon's little school before Thomas moved to Brisbane. He had eulogised Thomas's father at the funeral, for which the son would be eternally grateful. At home, there was a young wife and baby, about whom Teach rarely spoke, a fact his mates put down to melancholy as much as personal privacy. Thomas would sometimes find him alone, quietly engaged with his *Complete Works of Shakespeare*, the Bible, or Homer's *Iliad*, which he called the first war story. At other times, Teach seemed to relish the role of regimental encyclopaedia who could answer every question and settle most arguments. He didn't preach or poke fun at less educated men, and was well liked for his habit of describing volunteers from the Darling Downs and Burnett districts as his 'Burnett brothers' or 'the darlings of the Downs'. Everyone admired Teach's knowledge and envied his education, though naturally they mocked him for it.

The closer they came to the Dardanelles, the more animated Teach became. At one point he announced suddenly, 'Here were once the mighty Xerxes and Alexander the Great, here Leander swam the Hellespont to his lover Hero, and Icarus flew and fell.'

'It's all Greek to me,' Kingy said.

'We'll be legends, won't we?' Thomas said.

'Or dead,' Snow suggested.

'Quite possibly both,' Teach said with a smile.

Thomas felt his heart must burst. How wonderful to be with such fellows on the eve of battle. How thrilling to aspire to be among Teach's heroes. Thomas chuckled. He was hardly a knight in shining armour, he told himself. For one thing, he had no charger. Rosie Girl was back in Egypt, left behind with the brigade's other mounts. The Light Horse – neither cavalry nor infantry – was designed to ride to war, then to dismount and fight on foot. Being horseless was the price they'd willingly paid to join the fun at Gallipoli.

Thomas took out the vest pocket Kodak that Ellen Woods had presented to him as a farewell gift. Many of the men had them and were busy capturing the distant hills in the viewfinder.

Oh, what an adventure it would be!

It rained the next morning as a thousand men packed into small boats heading for the beach, delighted by the renewed booming of Britannia's guns. Puffs of smoke and flame burst here and there on the ridges.

'No Turk can stand up to that,' a young man said with enthusiasm.

'The navy will have his head down for sure,' another said with confidence.

'He's not a patch on us.'

'One of us is worth ten of them.'

The men looked up from the boat when a sound like a factory siren screamed overhead and a few laughed at the sight of two white clouds exploding prettily in the grey sky.

'Our blokes are playing a game with us,' suggested a raw young Queenslander, believing the cloudbursts to be friendly. But the sudden squall of pellets on the water revealed their true intent, and in the boat a man grunted and slipped to the bottom boards.

Thomas wondered if any of the shrapnel would reach him, but the boat passed through the hail without further casualties.

The keel crunched on the beach and the wounded man was carried away. The rest clambered over the gunwales and raced ashore with their heavy new infantry packs.

With a shake of his head, Snow drew Thomas's attention to the shallows, where two men, stretcher-bearers to judge by their SB armbands, were scrubbing their canvas and turning the water rose.

The new chums cut across a beach of busy men and between stacks of boxes. They passed the wounded awaiting evacuation, whose bandaged bodies lay in rows on the sand, some as still as the dead, others observing the newcomers through the swish of occasional shrapnel and the insistent lap of the waves.

'Make it snappy, before one of Beachy Bill's pills catches you,' an NCO bellowed, the first time they had heard the name given to the Turkish artillery battery whose hot lead swept the beach.

Thomas wondered why the army would choose a cramped little cove surrounded by forbidding hills as its beachhead. It was such a trifle compared to the broad golden bays back home. Still, he decided, the higher-ups had their reasons.

A few dozen steps and they were across the sand into Shrapnel Gully. They passed graves with wooden crosses and brown stains in the dirt. Bloodied men swathed in bandages limped by, some with a cheerful wave as if glad to be leaving. A stream of stretcher-bearers slipped down the track with men on the canvas in various states of wretchedness. Some screamed and aimed great gaping wounds stuffed with bandage at the newcomers.

One man with a grin locked in a grey face looked straight at Thomas.

'Buck up,' Thomas told him cheerfully. 'She'll be right.'

The man clenched his teeth and looked away.

They tramped up Monash Valley. From either side, old hands – dusty, unshaven veterans of the first landing less than three weeks earlier – watched them pass with faint amusement. Thomas winced when a shell burst overhead in a puff of white smoke and sent a rain of shrapnel to snap the dirt some distance away. His action prompted a gale of laughter from a group of old hands bent around a teapot.

'Scared of a cream puff, boys,' one scoffed.

'Crikey, it's the bally Light Horse!' another smirked. 'Where's your gee-gees, boys?'

'Let's not *n-n-nag* the lads,' said a third, turning the word into a neigh.

'Ya finding them infantry packs a bit hard, eh, boys?'

'Oh, the poor dears. Best leave the toy soldiers be.'

Thomas and the others kept walking, spurred on by their NCOs. 'They think we're novices,' he told Snow.

'We are.'

'Not for long,' Kingy promised.

That first day, they dug in along the rugged slopes of the Valley, digging as they'd been trained, lying on their sides and clawing back with the entrenching tool, about 150 yards from the frontline, close enough to hear the steady crack and bang.

Kingy stopped digging to listen to a sniper's bullet – slight, like a snap of the fingers – pass overhead on its way to a silent strike further down the Valley.

'From up on Baby 700 a Turk can hit anything in the Valley,' the sergeant declared cheerfully. Sergeant Lucky Les Brett was a young brown-eyed sawmill labourer from Toowoomba. 'Best not drag the chain, lads.'

'Turks are using dumdums, sarge,' Kingy said. 'I thought they was against the law.'

'Reckon any bullet's all right if it shuts you up! Keep digging!'

Kingy turned to his comrades. 'Dumdums, I tell ya.'

'How do you know?' Snow asked.

'Those fellas we saw got holes in them big as a fist.'

'Make it snappy,' the sergeant warned.

'"Yea, though I walk through the valley of the shadow of death, I will fear no evil,"' Teach whispered to himself. '"For thou art with me, thy rod and thy staff, they comfort me."'

'Thy bayonet and thy mates, more likely,' Kingy said.

Sergeant Lucky Les lowered himself to Kingy's face. 'I said get a bloody move on, chum.'

Thomas attacked the ground, thankful that the damp yellow-brown dirt wasn't as hard to shift as the rock-hard earth back home. He remembered the handful he'd dropped into his father's grave. *You're here to find a killer*, he told himself, and hacked all the harder.

'Cut it out, cobber,' Kingy observed. 'Ya'll be in China 'fore ya know it.'

Thomas chuckled and took a break. He was in a foreign country, after all, on a mission for the King, with a task to make his country proud, and he sighed with pleasure at such good fortune. How thrilling to fight the foe all the way to the capital of their empire.

Still, it was impossible to sleep. Booms and bangs, clear and loud in the darkness, seemed to detonate on top of them. On the skyline flashes of light flicked on and off like a summer storm. Lying back on his elbows, Thomas watched pinpricks of red dance inside sweet clouds of tobacco smoke around their bivouac. The NCOs had forbidden it, but the men lit up anyway, hoping their cupped hands and the steepness of the gully made them invisible to snipers.

Thomas saw Snow had his eyes closed, but sensed that he was awake too and just as excited by what lay ahead. He felt his heart swell. Finally, they were about to go to war, to show what they could do, what Australians could achieve in a great cause. Thomas wondered if his father was watching him. Was he proud? He would make sure he was.

Next morning, Thomas's regiment received new orders – occupy Quinn's Post. On their way up the steep winding path, they tramped between clusters of spring wildflowers, purple and yellow in the thorny brush. Coming the other way were the men of the 13th and 15th Battalions who slumped by, red-eyed and exhausted.

'How's Quinn's?' Kingy asked.

The soldier looked up the hill with an expression that Thomas found hard to read. It might have been relief, horror – or both.

Someone said, 'Oh, you might get a few bombs.'

'So nuffin' to worry about, eh, sarmajor?' Kingy put to Squadron Sergeant-Major Brown who had fought the Boer.

'Bombs is obsolete, son, was last used in the Crimea,' the veteran said. 'Shoot straight, do as ya told, be right as rain. Got that, lads?'

The young men cheered.

Up ahead, Thomas looked at the ridge. The frontline. Quinn's was the most advanced Anzac position, they'd been told, and the most exposed, overlooked on three sides by the enemy. If Quinn's fell, the Turks could sweep down Monash Valley to the narrow little beachhead and take back everything.

To have a go, to be a man, to show his chums.

He couldn't wait.

Chapter 10

Rarely was a shot fired all afternoon as the bombs flowed back and forth. The Australians picked them up and returned them or pulled out the fuses before the balls exploded. Others threw half-filled sandbags, folded greatcoats or blankets over them.

'We must stick it, boys,' an officer called out. 'Catch and throw, dive or smother. There's no time to lose.'

Thomas's heart was beating hard. At some point, as the adrenalin pumped and the fear ebbed, it became the most exciting time of his life. He began to relish the hissing arc of the ball across the ribbon of sky, and the second or two between sighting it and diving to catch it. That the ball held death only heightened the thrill.

'Thank Christ for cricket,' he quipped.

'Return to keeper,' Teach exulted, as he chucked one back.

'Watch this,' Snow said as he threw. '*Boom! – erang.*'

The joke raced along the trench and lifted spirits. Thomas laughed so hard that the memory of Wag Scully, screaming at his lost toes, disappeared in a moment. Only later would he wonder at how quickly he could lose a chum and just as swiftly forget him.

Teach had a wicked grin on his face. He had taken up his rifle and was using the butt like a bat.

'Don't miss,' Kingy warned him. 'If ya get bowled, we're all out.'

Teach swung expertly. Each hit made a loud crack against the wood and – while a bomb didn't travel far – it at least cleared the parapet quickly. He had knocked three bombs back before the sergeant ordered him to stop misusing his weapon.

Muttering to himself, Teach found a damaged rifle and resumed the batting. This time the sergeant shook his head and left him to it.

Kingy nodded his approval. 'Gun's no flamin' good with nuffin' to shoot at.'

For his part, Thomas crouched back against the trench wall, waiting. As a ball sailed over the parapet near him, he would catch it and bowl it back. He never knew where the bomb exploded, but a distant blast was satisfaction enough. Soon every second man in the trench was crouching, staring up, with his offsider standing ready to smother.

'Your turn,' said Thomas, his throwing arm exhausted. Snow moved to the rear of the trench and Thomas made ready with a half-filled sandbag.

It wasn't long before the bombs arrived with shorter fuses. Now there was less time to react, a second or two, depending on how long the Turk held the grenade before lobbing it. Bombs exploded up and down the trench, sending sudden gales of dust and sand over uniforms and faces.

Thomas watched a man in the adjoining bay catch a bomb that exploded in his hand. The man collapsed in the dirt, holding the stump with his good hand, staring amazed at the sinews hanging down. 'Bastards got me good, cobber,' he said to his mate, who screamed for a stretcher-bearer.

Hour after hour they caught and chucked the bombs back, jumped away or smothered them, suffered or died. The day wore on, no longer a game.

Thomas shook from the strain of watching for the black arc of the bombs, and the instant surge of energy that followed as he decided whether to meet the bomb in midair, smother it, or fly into the bay next door. It was desperate and exhausting and, as the day wore on, more bombs exploded among them.

No one raised a head above the parapet, or attempted to step up to fire, for fear of the rattling guns in the heights. In any case, there was nothing to shoot at, for the Turk lay unseen over the rise in his own trenches.

The chaplain Sol Green passed among the men. He was much respected for his wit and kindness and for sharing their risk. Some said, 'God bless you, padre,' as they handed him envelopes. Thomas had already penned his. 'In the event of my death I give to Miss Winifred Daisy Terrier all I possess and any monies due to me,' and signed it 'T. J. Clare, May 13, 1915'.

It occurred to Thomas to run. To be anywhere but here. A picture of himself lying with his brains painted on the trench wall and his insides hanging out in the dust flashed through his mind. He found he couldn't stop shaking and the fear of fouling himself made him tighten his sphincter. His eyes met Snow's. Snow smiled, a mongrel thing of shame and joy.

Thomas knew himself in that look and felt better. Both afraid, he realised, both desperately excited beyond anything ever felt before. He grinned back. It was mad, insane, and he punched Snow lightly on the shoulder.

'C'mon, ya bushwhacking cannibals!' Kingy screamed at the Turks. 'Keep chuckin' 'em. We're game as a pissant.'

Thomas waited for the next missile. He caught it cleanly and quickly chucked it back, laughing at the dull clump it made. He tried to imagine it exploding among the men who murdered his father, and there was a satisfaction in that.

Further down the trench came a sudden explosion. Dave Browning, a lump of a farmer from west of Murgon, was bellowing like a foghorn. 'Those bastards would kill a bull,' he roared as his big face streamed with blood and bits of iron poked out of his skin and around his heavy eyebrows.

Without waiting for orders, Browning stormed down the trench, threatening to skittle anyone in his way. Thomas saw him go and wondered if he had broken, whether an officer would shoot him.

A few minutes later Browning reappeared, still mad as hell. As he passed, Thomas was unsure whether to laugh or cry at the sight of the man, a cigarette dangling from his mouth, on his way to kill Turks with a bag full of blackcurrant jam and apricot preserve – jam-tin bombs from the 'bomb factory' down by the beach, where men sat on the bare earth and forced bits of barbed wire, stones, guncotton explosive and a fuse into the empty food tins that surrounded them in piles.

Up at Quinn's, Browning hurried on to the end of the trench, blocked by a wall of sandbags over which many of the cricket-ball bombs were appearing, thrown by Turks on the other side. Clumsily at first, he lit the fuses with his cigarette and then hurled them one after the other in a trail of sparks over the bags. *Bang bang bang* went his bombs, until the cricket balls stopped coming.

As he returned to his station, he was patted along the trench.

'Good on ya, Dave, ya jammy bastard,' someone chortled.

'You showed 'em, cocky.'

'Fookin' jam tins,' Kingy grumbled. 'Why don't the brass give us proper bombs?'

No one disagreed.

Nevertheless, a hastily provided supply of jam tins did the trick. By dusk, the bombing from the Turkish side of Quinn's had died down, and the stretcher-bearers had taken away the wounded.

In the half-light at the bottom of the trench, the four shared a silent smoke, careful to cup the glow. Thomas caught the exhaustion in their hollow faces, and shared the numbness. Above all, he was utterly relieved to be alive.

'Be dark soon. The Turk won't waste a grenade in the dark,' he said hopefully.

'"A night dark as pitch, silent, forlorn and forbidding, and colder than the busiest morgue",' said Teach, borrowing Steele Rudd's description of a night in the Queensland bush.

'Black as a burnt log,' Thomas put in.

'Black as an Abo's arse,' Kingy said agreeably.

'White arses attract more bombs,' Snow said.

Thomas caught Kingy's grin. Never were such friends as these. His heart went out to them. They were the best of men. He could rely on them, hoped they would always be by his side.

'Lovely way to treat guests,' Thomas said.

'We weren't invited,' Snow observed.

'Jacko doesn't like us,' Kingy said.

'*I* don't like you,' said Snow.

Thomas was enjoying the joke when a red light rolled to a stop at his feet, hissing.

'Bomb,' said Snow.

Teach dived into the adjoining bay but Thomas grasped it. He was about to sling it over the parapet when he had second thoughts. He dropped the bomb. 'Smother!' he said.

Instantly Snow dropped a sandbag on top and Thomas added his coat to the sandbag.

With a maniacal grin on his face, Kingy placed his bottom down on both. A second later there was a dull crump, dust exploded at his feet and Kingy rose a foot in the air. 'That shook me up a bit,' he said, both hands rubbing his backside.

Thomas and Snow burst into laughter.

'Damn fools, all of you!' Teach snapped.

'I felt it, the shape of it . . . I knew what it was,' Thomas explained, as he lifted the sandbag to reveal the pieces of blasted metal.

Kingy dropped to his knees, sniffed and peered at the remains. 'Well, I'll be blowed!' he gasped.

Among the bits of smoking tin, wire, nails and old cartridges was a scrap of red paper with an image of a white bird.

Thomas read the label – COCKATOO PLUM AND APPLE.

'I saw that, trooper!' Sergeant Lucky Les was beside Kingy in a moment. 'Ya already an arsehole. Ya want another? Fancy sitting on a killjoy!'

'It was my arse or theirs, sarge. I was just lookin' out for me mates.'

'Once gets ya a mention in dispatches.'

Kingy beamed.

'But don't fookin' do it again!' said the sergeant, jabbing his finger in Kingy's chest. 'Next time ya'll be blown-to-fook. Trooper Keid of A Squadron sat on a bomb with only a coat between 'im and eternity. Stretcher-bearers carried 'im down. Gunna end up in stiffs' paddock, for sure.'

'Billy Keid, poor fella,' Thomas sighed. 'We went to the same school in Brisbane.'

'Bravest thing I ever saw,' muttered the sergeant as he passed down the trench.

With the sergeant gone, Kingy's grin turned angry. 'What the hell happened?'

'It was one of ours,' Thomas said.

'Maybe the Turks chucked it back,' Snow suggested.

'No,' Thomas said. 'Fuse was too long. We had time to choke the bastard.'

'Landed on top of ya, it did. A bloody good throw in the dark,' Kingy said.

'Well, it was more than likely an accident,' Teach said. '"Fog of war", to quote Clausewitz.'

'Clausewitz was a Hun, wasn't he? Never trust no bloody Hun.' Kingy tapped his nose with his finger. 'Better watch out from now on, lads.'

'Why do you say that?' Snow said.

'Why do ya think? Fookin' bomb coulda smudged us all . . . was no bloody accident.'

Kingy had a nose for betrayal.

As a child he was allowed to run wild by a mother busy entertaining her paying men friends, and there was no father, not one that Kingy ever met. When police discovered him living rough on Sydney's wharves, they charged him with 'sleeping in the open air'. In Egypt, as the Light Horse settled down to another night in the desert under canvas, Kingy would call out with flash larrikin pride, 'I'm sleeping rough again tonight, sarge, ya think the redcaps will pinch me?'

For all his swagger, Kingy admitted that the boyhood arrest was the making of him. 'Coppers told the magistrate they was rescuing me from evil surroundings. Magistrate said I gotta become a useful member of society,' and Kingy would laugh. 'Ya see, it was my ma who laid the charge . . . gave evidence against me. She wanted me safe, not gone off to gaol. Hated her for it, I did, but no more. Best thing she ever done me.'

He was consigned to the *Sobraon*, once the fastest clipper ship in the world, afterwards a floating reformatory school at anchor in Port Jackson. 'Worst thing about the *Sobraon* was "the dungeon", that's what we called it, deep in the hull, wet, black as night, infested with rats . . . If ya was sent there, I tell ya, ya never wanted to go back. Compared to that place, a dozen belts on the stern was a picnic.'

In the two years he was aboard, Kingy learnt to read and write. He devoured the ship's library, in between a regimen of musketry and cutlass, gymnastics and dumbbells, sailing and the endless routine of cleaning the ship. Mostly he learnt to grasp an opportunity when it appeared, particularly when the *Sobraon* cast him out aged twelve to be apprenticed as cheap labour to a squatter on the Clarence River.

'In seven years, I could ride and shoot as good as any gent,' Kingy said proudly. When war was declared, he walked to Brisbane and enlisted in the Light Horse. 'Didn't give a continental about the King or the Kaiser or Constantinople,' he said. 'I had to get away.'

Thomas first met him at a regimental boxing tournament in Egypt when he volunteered to fight the 'Prince of Kalkadoon'. Half a head shorter and full of pluck, Kingy strode up to Snow with a shambling, hunched gait, and said with a shrewd smile, 'The smaller you are, the better your chances, coz I'm closer to ya balls. Also, I never fought a dirty black bastard before.'

'Nick off, ya white bastard,' Snow laughed. 'I never fight little blokes. You fight dirty.'

'Fair enough,' Kingy acknowledged with a wide grin.

Naturally they became mates.

Snow and Thomas loved Kingy for being an antidote to the Bible-sprouting wowser in Teach and for challenging his certainties in ways that younger men could not. That Kingy excelled at tomfoolery and frequently got them into and out of trouble was a bonus. Besides which, Thomas felt a sort of kinship with this man who was abandoned by his mother and never knew his father.

'Family, ya can't trust 'em,' Kingy had said. 'Look at the King and the Kaiser – they're bloody cousins.'

'Steady on!' Teach objected. 'God save the King, I say, and down with his enemies.'

'God save us from the Hun and the heathen Turk,' Kingy replied, 'and when we've done 'em like a hot dinner, we'll start on all them empty-headed lords and ladies and dukes and dames what oppresses the working classes.'

'High treason!' Teach had cried.

'Wake up, chum, look around ya. Nuffin' will be the same after this.'

Chapter 11

MIDNIGHT, BY HIS FATHER'S WATCH, and Thomas's nerves were on fire.

Sitting, knees to chest, he stared up at the trench-long slash of darkness in which northern stars winked with no less brilliance than at home. He gave an involuntary shudder. From the cold, but was it also dread? Thomas hoped not, but in his heart he knew otherwise.

It was not supposed to be like this. After the long months of training and waiting in Egypt, he had expected to come ashore to a brass band, a parade ground and rows of tents, all spick and span. Yet, almost three weeks after the first landing, the distance to the front was barely the length of Murgon's main street. Rather than a bite out of Turkey, they'd taken a nibble. Something was awfully wrong. By now, the fighting should have progressed far into the interior, somewhere with a view down over the Dardanelles. He should be perched on a summit, looking one way into Europe and the other into Asia. They should have been potting fleeing Turks like scared rabbits.

Instead, it was a dog's breakfast. A mighty army was stopped dead in its tracks, below an unseen enemy who shot from almost every angle. At any moment a bullet might come from the flanks or from behind, or in the dead of night the Turk might creep over the parapet with bomb or stabbing bayonet.

A black mood seemed to take him. His father came to mind. Not the father alive in his memory, the flesh and blood dad, with whom he had hunted and sorrowed and shared a life. But the condemned man in his last hours.

This father knew pain, he thought, and it must have been unbearable. Thomas imagined them, the laughing thugs, the tree and the rope, the noose tightening, and the knowing how it must end. His father's untied hands, free to lift the noose, except for the muzzle at his back or against his skull. The velvet words with their underlying steel: *Do not fight it, it is inevitable, unless you tell us where. Where is the document?* No punching or kicking here, nothing obvious to mark the body and indicate foul play. He was a cop, he was a soldier, he would have understood the inevitability of what was to come.

Thomas could see it, could feel it now. The hard breathing, the thumping of his father's heart, the desperation, the struggle to stay calm, to find a way out, to speak clearly, to give truth to the lie: *What document? What are you talking about? I know of no such document. Why would I lie? If I had such a document in my possession, why would I hide it, and not reveal it as you suggest? You are mistaken, comrade, I have no such document.*

And as the noose is tightened, and his father is lifted off his feet, hands scrabbling to his throat, gagging, tongue swelling, chest bursting, the pain unbearable, until he is released, his feet touch the ground, and again the question is asked. Again he is dragged up, for a longer time, tearing the skin, sawing at his neck, choking until he is let down, hacking and gasping.

And the same question posed over and over, in frustration and then in fury: *Where is it? Your last chance, God damn you, your only hope. Make no mistake, you will die.*

I will die regardless, he gasps.

What was that? Can't hear you.

Go to hell, he croaks.

So be it, they say, and for the last time he is raised, kicking, jerking, his body fighting for life though his mind has accepted death. Dragged high until his killers on the bough lift him up to join them. There they sit him, perched between them, legs kicking air and his throat given a moment of blessed relief.

His torturers tie the rope to the bough. A push is all that stands between him and eternity.

Tell us, they say.

Fook you.

Thomas wondered what thoughts died with his father in that moment. Were they of Rose or Thomas, or of his parents in the home country?

Then comes the shove in the back and the fall until the noose snaps. And worse, far worse, before the darkness, are his eyes alive? Do those fading eyes see what happens next? Do they see the world rise and spin and come to rest in the dirt? Does his father realise?

The boy stifled a sob. His father had borne it. Strong to the end. There was a lesson in that and perhaps a gift.

Was his father's killer on Gallipoli? The boot tracks below the hanging tree had led Thomas to the Light Horse and now here was the jam-tin bomb. *One of ours.* If someone from his own side had thrown the thing, it could only mean that his father's killer was close, knew that Thomas was hunting him, and had decided to strike first.

Thomas shivered. He had never felt so vulnerable, never imagined his father's murderer waiting for him and willing to kill his mates as well. And, he lamented, he was no closer to finding the man. His promise to himself to avenge his father was turning out like the Dardanelles, like nothing he had imagined.

Kingy sat beside him in the trench, snoring soundly. Amazing how a street urchin could sleep anywhere, anytime. Thomas decided he should tell Kingy and Teach about his father's murder and what it might mean for them, that their lives were in danger not only from the Turk.

The sleepless night dragged on in bangs and flashes, screams and moans.

In the morning, during a lull in the bombing, two tall men ducked down the trench towards Thomas. One was George Bourne, their long-faced CO from Brisbane. The other was a slightly stooped man with a heavy moustache and a straight aristocratic nose, who stumbled along, saying, 'Sorry, old chap' or 'Silly me' every time he bumped into someone.

'This bloke's either cock-eyed or barmy,' Thomas suggested.

'Probably both,' Snow said.

The two officers stopped beside the boys.

'This suit you, Herbert?' said Major Bourne. 'Clare, shift over for Captain Herbert, there's a good lad.'

'Hope you don't mind, old chap?' the Englishman said in a posh voice, peering short-sightedly at Thomas.

'Not at all, sir,' said Thomas and squeezed closer to Snow.

Captain Herbert began to call out in a strange tongue. He stood up on the fire step and slowly raised his head above the parapet.

'Barmy all right,' Snow whispered, 'stark raving.'

'He'll draw the crabs onto us.' Thomas swore silently, expecting a sniper's bullet to cleave the man's skull at any moment.

The men in the trench tensed up. Thomas braced himself and stared at the sky, waiting for the black ball and spluttering fuse that the mad officer's words seemed sure to attract.

Instead, a reply came in the same language and it was neither angry nor unpleasant. A relative quiet descended on the ridge as the conversation in Turkish took the place of explosions and gunfire. Thomas closed his eyes for a few blissful moments.

When the talk ended, all held their breath.

No bombs came, nor did any Turk emerge with hands raised, but as Major Bourne escorted his guest from the trench, a voice rang out clearly in heavily accented English from across no-man's-land, 'Kangaroo-shooting bastards.'

The troopers who heard it laughed, while the Englishman and Major Bourne traded weary looks and crawled away through the exit tunnel.

Teach quizzed Sergeant Lucky Les about the exchange.

'He's General Godley's interpreter and a Pommy parliamentarian to boot,' said the sergeant. 'Tells the Turk we treats prisoners well, so they should surrender.'

'Do we?' Thomas said. 'Do we take prisoners?'

'Yes, well, now we does,' said the sergeant.

'Now?'

'I hear the boys at the start was in a bit of a rush,' the sergeant continued. 'They settled 'em right off, and the Turk was no different. Now we offers 'em smokes and bully beef – poor bastards – and Captain Herbert tells 'em we won't do 'em coz we're not the enemy. The Huns is, not us.'

Snow laughed. 'And that puss-in-boots reckons Jacko will say, "Come in, have some tea, take my land, take my wife, take everything." Would that be right, sarge?'

To Thomas, Snow said softly, 'Remind you of anything?'

Thomas nodded, recalling Tubbie's experience on Battle Mountain.

'That's enough smart yapping from you, Trooper Snow,' the sergeant said, not unkindly. 'Stay alert, you fellows, these chit-chats usually stir up more bally bombs.'

'I don't fancy being captured,' said Teach.

'Ya won't catch me staked to an anthill or some other heathen torture,' declared Kingy. 'Death or glory for me.'

Some time later, as Thomas was contemplating how he might stick a Turk with his bayonet if one suddenly appeared above the trench, the CO returned with a small man in dirty khaki and a British cap.

'Who's this, sir?' Kingy asked.

'Why, the foe, of course,' Major Bourne said.

The little figure bobbed his head as he passed, saying 'Greek, Greek', as if the Australians knew the difference.

He was Thomas's first live Turk. Bearded and stout, a farmer perhaps, grimy in a ragged uniform and torn boots, not unlike a wandering swaggie back home, and certainly not the beast Thomas had imagined.

'Permission to use the bayonet, sir?' Kingy spat.

Thomas smiled to himself, but Major Bourne wasn't amused. 'You'll do no such thing, Trooper King,' he said coolly. 'This man has surrendered. The intelligence boys will want to have a go at him.'

'He's wearin' a hat stolen off one of our poor boys, sir,' Kingy argued. 'And he's a deserter.'

'He's chucked it up, trooper, which means one less Turk aiming at you.' Major Bourne grinned at the others listening. Thomas guessed that the CO had caught on to Kingy's game.

'Plenty of our cobbers went west today, sir,' Kingy persisted.

'And brave men they were. Nevertheless, take no prisoners is not an order you will hear from me,' Major Bourne said. 'But if you box on, in the way you have today, there'll be many more like him.'

'Yes, sir,' Kingy said smugly, as the men cheered and the CO left with his prisoner intact.

'Not a bad bloke,' Kingy chuckled, adding, 'for an officer.'

Teach and Snow laughed, but Thomas felt as if he had been struck dumb. That was it, of course.

The major had said 'take no prisoners'.

TNP.

Chapter 12

LATER THAT DAY, THOMAS'S SQUADRON was relieved by veteran infantrymen and retired to the support trenches on the steep slope below the ridge. Done in, red-eyed and sleepless, shaken by a type of war they'd neither expected nor trained for, they made small fires to brew their tea and soften their bully beef.

Kingy was spreading runny apricot jam on a biscuit when the fat flies swamped it. 'Who's pinched my bread and jam?' he joked. When no one laughed, he brushed the blue-black brutes away and popped the biscuit quickly into his mouth, bit with a sour face and swallowed flies and all.

'Dead crook,' he moaned. 'Fookin' flybog.'

'I'd rather fight Turks than flies,' complained Thomas.

'"A man can fight all day if he is full fed with meat and wine,"' Teach remarked in an attempt at good cheer. 'So said Ulysses.'

'I don't give a rat's arse 'bout some bloomin' Greek,' Kingy said. 'Meat and wine is officers' tucker, not for us trench-wallahs.'

'You must be aware that the siege of Troy occurred close to this very spot?' Teach persisted.

'Blimey! No wonder we work like bloody Trojans.'

'And that the Trojan Horse was Ulysses' idea?'

'I'd eat a horse if it wasn't for the flamin' blowies,' Kingy grumbled.

'Grizzleguts, the lot of you,' said Teach, surrendering to the glum mood. They spent the rest of the meal in silence and exhaustion. No one mentioned that they had lasted less than two days at Quinn's.

After the meal they were ordered to dig, to deepen and widen, and dig again. Occasionally, a spade-full of earth tossed into the air drew a desultory slug from a sniper.

Thomas's dugout was cut into the side of the hill. Framed by sandbags, it was large enough for four and safe enough from a bullet and all but the unluckiest arc of shrapnel. There were holes scooped from the clay wall for their personal items – mess tins, shaving kit and racy postcards belonging to Kingy. Teach had placed a photograph of his wife and son next to one of the grandly moustachioed Kitchener, from the cover of the *London Opinion*, demanding 'Your Country Needs YOU'.

Inside, with his feet stretched out west and the afternoon sun warm on his face, Thomas could look down the mile of tumbling hills to the sea. The Aegean blazed in steel blue and silver, dashed here and there by little destroyers that sprinted with smoky columns and streaky wakes around the squat battle-ships and searched for a U-boat to ram.

Gallipoli was an awfully strange place, he decided, in equal measure picturesque and deadly. Thomas wondered what it would be like without the shriek of shells or whine of bullets. He wondered about the country behind the Turks and he imagined forests, bubbling creeks, and groves of orange and olive trees. Perhaps farmers tilled the soil and would allow him to hunt deer or wild boar if he shared the prize with them.

He shook his head. *Ridiculous.*

A breeze of unspoilt air blew up off the sea like a dream of home. Home, he mused, was a walk to the beach, a left turn, through the Canal, down past Egypt and Rosie Girl, then south for a few thousand miles, back the way he'd come. There was the tall slender girl in a yellow dress, on the platform waving him goodbye, tears in her eyes. For him. He let his mind drift over rolling hills, a creek below ragged trees, rough-hewn fences and animals snuffling in pasture, Winnie laid back in sunshine, warm and inviting.

'Leave her alone!' whispered Snow beside him.

Thomas grinned. 'Never knew you could read minds.'

'When it comes to my sister,' Snow scoffed, 'I can read yours like a book.'

The long-awaited post arrived to cheers. Men sat outside their dugouts, beside their little cooking fires, their spirits lifted, reading, re-reading with a desperate yearning.

Thomas held a letter from Winnie. 'My life is dull as dishwater,' he read. 'But every day I think of you and how you will make us proud. Take care, Thomas, as I would die if I never saw you again. I miss you, and in my dreams I kiss you.'

'Any message for me?' said Snow.

'Yeah. She says, "Take care of my stupid brother, mostly when he's drinking and fighting. He's good at both but never knows when to stop." And here she says, "Tell that lazybones to write, even a postcard."'

Snow snorted. 'That all?'

'She says, "The bush is lonely without you and Snow. Dad is sad too. He says he talked too much about the Kalkadoons and he says tell Snow not to be too brave."'

Snow sighed. 'No fear of that.'

Thomas opened another letter. 'This one's from Doctor Woods. She's sent a Sherlock story.' Thomas held up pages clipped from a magazine, 'The Adventure of the Dying Detective.'

'Cheery title.'

Thomas laughed. 'She says Sherlock is brave and clever like me.'

'She fancies you.'

'Nonsense. She says that if my dad were alive today, he would have volunteered. And he would have been proud of me.'

'Told you,' Snow smirked.

'Shut up and listen, will ya. "A week after you took the train to Brisbane,"' Thomas read aloud, '"a rather portly gent, a Captain Taylor, who said he was on leave from active service, arrived in Murgon in company with Sergeant Griffin. He was an Irishman to hear him speak, and claimed to be a former Boer War comrade of Jack. Griffin referred to him more than once as 'Bulala'. A strange Christian name if ever there was one. When I enquired, he said it was a Zulu title bestowed on him in Africa. This Captain Taylor offered me his condolences, though how he knew of my relationship with your father I cannot imagine. He seemed genuinely distressed at 'Jack's suicide', as he put it. Truth be told, I didn't much like the look of him. He claimed to be writing a history of their unit and wondered whether I knew of any official papers your father had in his possession relating to his military service. Naturally, I told him I knew of none."'

'What the hell?' cried Snow.

Thomas shook his head. On the document – 'Bulala'.

A moment later the wind changed and blew off the land, and the shock of unburied corruption hit them as suddenly as a shell from Beachy Bill.

*

It wasn't long before the storm of metal arrived with a roar. Occasionally a shell exploded nearby, sending bits of dirt to batter the oiled sheet that served as a door to the dugout. The ground shook around them and dirt fell from the wall. The four of them huddled closer, shoulder to shoulder.

Thomas tried to sound brave. 'Oh, for Rosie Girl and a charge against the foe. That's my idea of war, not this.'

'We're Light Horse, not cavalry,' Snow reminded him.

'Gimme cold steel and a Turk to stick it in and I'll die happy,' Kingy said.

'We are ascetics, living a life of prayer, fasting and hard labour,' Teach said cheerfully.

Thomas snorted, 'More like rabbits in a hole.'

Kingy pondered a moment. 'Nuffin' wrong with rabbit,' he said. 'Rabbit stew, rabbit on the spit, rootin' like a rabbit. Better bein' a rabbit in 'ere than a roo out there.'

'You ever seen a roo, Kingy?' Snow said doubtfully.

'I seen plenty. Don't eat none, but. Not like your mob.'

'We'd eat you too, chum, and save your bones for soup.'

Kingy chuckled. 'Black bastard.'

'White bastard.'

'Well,' Kingy concluded with a grin, 'at least you're not a Chinaman.'

Snow smiled.

Same old game, Thomas thought.

'Boys, boys, show some manners,' Teach said in his best classroom voice.

A shell exploded outside the dugout, closer than the others. Flying earth blasted their oilcloth door. They watched it snap and buckle under the impact. 'We could read Sherlock for a bit,' Snow suggested.

Thomas brightened at the idea. 'What about a story of murder and a stolen document?'

'That will do,' Snow laughed.

From his pack, Thomas pulled out Winnie's farewell present. The previous year, just before the train left the station at Murgon, she had handed him a short story torn from a magazine, 'The Adventure of the Bruce-Partington Plans'. In the nine months since, the pages had become dog-eared and tatty.

'Oh dear me, not again,' Teach said dryly. 'It's such low art.'

Thomas grinned. 'That's what Kitchener and Churchill said.'

Teach's eyes widened. 'Not the War Secretary and the First Lord of the Admiralty?'

'Ya mean them two Pommy bastards who put us in this hell-hole?' said Kingy.

'Different war,' Thomas said. 'Same bastards.'

Teach frowned at such disrespect. 'How do you know what they said?'

'My father told me. He was being treated by Conan Doyle in hospital when Kitchener and Churchill arrived and demanded that Sherlock return from the dead. For the war effort, they said, to boost morale.'

Teach appeared lost for words. Thomas chuckled. It wasn't often the student stumped the teacher.

'Ya telling me Sherlock Holmes got snottered?' Kingy said, shocked.

Thomas laughed. 'That's what I said.'

'He's not dead, not anymore,' Snow put in. 'He came back.'

'Resurrection, hope for us all,' murmured Teach.

'I wonder how the world's foremost detective would tackle our particularly sensitive case. Eh, Watson?' Thomas asked. 'Which I shall call "The Adventure of the Counterfeit Hanging".'

Snow cottoned on. 'Just so, Holmes.'

'I've not heard of that one,' Teach said.

'By golly, I like a good yarn!' Kingy said.

So they sat side by side in the cramped dugout, legs drawn up, the magazine story resting on Thomas's knees. He and Snow had read it so many times that they knew every line, but the text was there to be consulted for inspiration should memory fail them. Every so often the ground shook and Thomas would brush dirt from the pages.

'Please be so good as to outline the facts, my dear Watson,' Thomas said.

'The deceased's name was John Robert Clare,' Snow began. 'Thirty-nine years of age, widower, soldier, police constable first class, and I believe related to your good self, Holmes.'

'Listen to the toffy git!' Kingy said. 'Ya read pretty good for a darkie.'

'I got a good memory,' Snow explained, and said in a near-perfect imitation of Kingy, 'Gimme cold steel and a Turk to stick it in and I'll die happy.'

Kingy laughed loudly, but Teach wasn't amused. 'What the devil are you playing at?' he asked Thomas.

'A bit of fun is all, cobber, to take our minds off Johnny's game outside.'

'Suicide is scarcely humorous. Hardly a fit subject for . . .'

Thomas interrupted, 'It wasn't suicide.'

'Gawd love a duck!' cried Kingy. 'First Sherlock, now ya dad's snottered?'

The bluntness of it was brutal, like being whacked by a Mauser. Thomas wondered whether he could play the cool detective, while the memory of his father beneath the hanging tree lingered like one of Quinn's corpses.

'I had no idea,' Teach said.

Thomas took a deep breath. 'Gentlemen, we must not allow emotion to deter our best enquiry. A death that has engaged the greatest living detective cannot by definition be anything but extraordinary. Do go on, Watson.'

'Last seen by his son, Thomas Clare, a rather headstrong, impatient young fellow of dubious worth.'

Kingy added theatrically, 'Aha, a clue!'

'However, there was no quarrel between father and son, who may be excluded from any suspicion of foul play.'

'Of course,' Teach agreed.

'Too right,' added Kingy.

Thomas and Snow grinned. How fortunate to have such good sports as mates.

'The body was found at seven on a Friday evening by the son and his colleague, a rather impressive young chap by the name of Prince Snow of Kalkadoon.'

'Dear me, Watson,' Thomas said, 'have you not missed something? A black prince by the name of Snow. Doesn't that strike you as most odd?'

'Ya tellin' me!' Kingy agreed with a grin.

Snow ignored him. 'Hardly, Holmes. I rather like it. It is a name befitting my royal darkness.'

'That would explain it. Very good, Watson. Pray continue.'

'The son found the body lying close to the stable, beneath a tree common to those parts. The body was headless, having fallen some distance while attached to a noose.'

Thomas gulped. *Serious now.* 'Ah, yes, I believe a long drop may result in decapitation.'

At this Kingy whistled in surprise, and Snow dropped his Watson persona. 'Thomas, you don't have to . . .'

'Nonsense, Watson. The case is definite enough. The man, dead or alive, either fell or was pushed. So much is clear to me. Pray continue.'

'A local physician, a Doctor Ellen Woods, arrived soon after . . .'

'Nice bit of fluff, eh?' Kingy suggested.

'A femme fatale?' Teach offered.

'Not at all,' Snow continued. 'A friend of the deceased, with impeccable credentials.'

'Don't be too hasty in your assumptions, Watson, I have found that where there's smoke there's usually fire.'

'This is murder, my dear Holmes, not arson. There were neither witnesses nor motive. A local policeman, one Sergeant Griffin, concluded that Constable Clare had taken his own life due to grief over his wife's suicide and a large quantity of whisky.'

'Jack did enjoy a drink,' Teach said. 'He and I shared the odd tot or two.'

'Indeed,' said Thomas. 'However, the apparent lack of a motive is of curious interest. As to the absence of witnesses, on a winter's night it would not be unusual for the hardworking residents of a small country town to gather safe and warm by the homely hearth. Of far greater interest is why no one heard a noise. Almost certainly, a man being murdered must call out. Did no one hear, or was no sound uttered? One cannot simply force a head into a noose. A victim usually fights back. The deceased was no stranger to violence in war and peace, but there were no signs of a struggle, no suggestion of fisticuffs, no injury to fingers or knuckles.'

'The empty bottle might suggest the deceased was too drunk to retaliate.'

'Quite possibly, my dear Watson. Yet, as you and I have seen in this awful place, even the mortally wounded will struggle for life when it is about to be denied them.'

Snow nodded thoughtfully. 'How then do you explain the matter of the note, a most common occurrence in cases of suicide?'

'Such a note could only be written if the victim knew that death was inevitable and had a compelling reason to write it.'

'Or the bastards threatened to snotter you next, Tom,' suggested Kingy. 'That would have shaken ya pa up a bit.'

'Indeed, one must assume coercion,' said Thomas. 'Constable Clare would not want his son to be put at risk. Furthermore, we may suppose that by agreeing to compose a suicide note he may have extracted a promise not to harm the lad. In effect, a pact between victim and murderer.'

'It still don't sound right to me,' Kingy added.

'Suffice to say, the man was murdered, he went quietly and it appears his killers left empty-handed.' Thomas closed his eyes and took a deep breath.

Snow looked with concern at Thomas in the half-light of the dugout, before continuing cool as you like. 'Must I remind you, Holmes, of the horse tracks and footprints at the scene? The distinguished tracker and Boer War veteran, Mister Tubbie Terrier, identified them as army-issue riding boots. Why, Holmes! Could your father's killer be here among us?'

'I fear so.'

'The jam tin!' said Kingy.

'No, no, no,' said Teach. 'That's not possible.'

'Ya think the bomb had something to do with ya dad's murder, Tom?'

Thomas shrugged and left Kingy's question unanswered. 'Proceed, Watson.'

'You have neglected to mention the more shocking aspects of the case, Holmes. How to account for the additional violence done to the constable, the bruises on the ankles and the boot marks on his cheek?'

'There we have it at last, a most crucial piece of evidence. Torture most foul. The question to consider is why it was necessary to torture a man who, in writing a suicide note, knew he was soon to be murdered?'

'They believed he was hiding something?' Teach suggested.

'Capital, my dear Teach. There you have it, a motive. He was indeed hiding something.'

'But, hang on,' interrupted Kingy. 'Ya don't need to torture a man, do ya, when ya can threaten to kill his son?'

'Just so, Kingy. We may never know the exact degree to which threats were employed against him or his son or both. 'Tis mere supposition, after all.'

Here Thomas paused, before adding with a flourish, 'Were it not for one piece of hard evidence, central to this whole affair . . . Now, Watson, the document, if you please.'

Snow pulled the yellowing sheet of paper from his pack. 'Typewritten, dated, revealed to our good selves by the venerable Aboriginal warrior and son of a tribal chief,' Snow said with a chuckle.

'What the . . .?' Teach said, taking the document. 'This is a proclamation by Lord Roberts during the last war. How did your father come by it?'

'An excellent question, my dear sir,' Thomas said.

'Not much of a souvy,' Kingy sniffed. 'Rather have a Turk's ear or a Hun officer's pistol m'self.'

'I have perused this document for many an hour,' Thomas continued in character. 'In effect, Lord Roberts is warning that he would be tightening the screws on the Boer commandos. For our purposes, the question is what importance did this old document carry for the deceased? Why did he hide it . . . refuse to reveal it?'

'There is the matter of the note in the margin,' Snow suggested.

'Splendid, Watson. There you have the key to this entire exercise.'

Snow pointed out the handwritten note to the others.

Bulala,

TNP

K

'Curious, is it not?' Thomas said.

'What is it, Holmes?' Kingy said, playing the game.

'A mere indication, dear fellow, no more. Clearly the note is addressed to a *Bulala.*'

'Sounds like bull to me,' Kingy joked.

'Indeed, a most unusual name, Zulu in fact. I now have it on good authority that a Captain Bulala Taylor, an Irishman from Africa, served with Constable Clare during the Boer War. What's more, last year he visited Murgon. Now here is a leap in the deductive process, of which I am the world's foremost practitioner. *Bulala*, to whom the note is addressed, and this Taylor are one and the same man. The sender is K, whoever that may be.'

'Well, it ain't the King or Kaiser Bill or me,' Kingy grinned.

'And "TNP"?' Teach asked.

'Formidable, is it not? The heart of the mystery.'

'For crying out loud,' Kingy said impatiently, 'what does it mean?'

'My dear Kingy, it should be most evidently clear, particularly to you,' Thomas said smiling. 'What did Major Bourne tell you yesterday concerning our Turkish captive?'

Kingy scratched his head. 'Keep fighting.'

'And?'

Kingy jumped suddenly as if the memory had bitten him. 'Take no prisoners,' he cried.

'The major gave no such order!' objected Teach.

'Indeed, he forbade it,' Thomas said. 'Nevertheless, "TNP" is central to my father's case. You will notice the deliberate placement of the letters "TNP" to a line in Lord Roberts' message. Watson, if you will be so kind?'

Snow read, '"Field Marshal Lord Roberts will vigorously suppress guerrilla warfare by every means, which the customs of war prescribe."'

'Do you not see the connection? Find the motive and the murderer will follow. I shall be very much surprised if it does not fetch our man,' Thomas said in triumph, adding with a flourish, '"I play the game for the game's own sake."'

Snow shook his head with a half smile. '"Good heavens, Holmes, this is murder, not some parlour game!"'

'Not everything is as it seems, Watson,' Thomas chuckled, his finger tapping the pages in his lap. 'See, there it is. "I play the game for the game's own sake." I wanted to say it, that's all.'

'My God,' Teach said, 'what have you boys got yourselves mixed up in?'

Snow and Thomas shrugged.

In the awkward silence that followed, they noticed that the shelling had stopped and Sergeant Lucky Les was bellowing, 'All you timid little bunnies may leave your burrows.'

'Come, friend Watson,' Thomas said, putting the story and the document away, 'there is work to be done.'

In the reserve trenches that night, they heard a shrill whistle followed by shouts from up on the ridge where their fellow Queenslanders of C Squadron had remained at Quinn's.

As Thomas looked at the luminous dial of his father's old watch – 1.45 am – there was a sudden fusillade of rifle fire, then the rattle of machine guns from the heights and the sharp bang of bombs.

'A stunt!' Thomas said.

'Give 'em hell, Australia,' Kingy called out from his sleeping position.

'It'll be our turn next,' Snow said with enthusiasm.

In the blackness, Thomas gripped his rifle and waited for the order 'fix your bayonet', both hoping for and dreading it. Others in B Squadron were awake now, and a cheer went up. Thomas felt that they might all rush to join in, and the sergeant seemed to agree, for he shouted at them to stay the hell where they were.

The explosions and gunshots echoed through the gullies. When finally it stopped, an awful silence emerged, cut by sounds both painful and pathetic. Clear in the night came a dreadful moaning from those left behind, who cried out for rescue or water or mother.

Dark shapes hurried by – stretcher-bearers puffing up the slope to Quinn's. Thomas ached to go with them into no-man's-land. The bearers were the best and bravest of men, he thought, to coolly rescue a man under fire and not retaliate. He knew those men who were fading. They'd shared hardships and adventures. He loved them, he realised, yet he didn't move. Instead he lay back and closed his eyes, and tortured himself with shame and relief.

The morning brought word that many of their comrades were dead or wounded, and in every man's heart was a longing for revenge.

Chapter 13

AFTER THE SHERLOCK GAME AND the jam-tin explosion, Thomas wished he could talk again to Harry Chauvel. Though headquarters was a short scramble down the slope, Thomas wasn't able to visit whenever he wished. The chain of command dictated that a lowly trooper would be ridiculed by the NCOs and given additional fatigue duty should he request to speak to the commander of the Light Horse, whether or not he called him 'Uncle'.

They had last spoken when the colonel was at his ease in Egypt, had taken tea together and reminisced about his father. Chauvel had promised to look out for Thomas if he could, short of giving him special treatment in the brigade, and they had parted warmly.

Now that he was commanding the most important frontline in the entire Anzac sector, Harry Chauvel would be far too busy for a chat. His counsel would have to wait, Thomas decided. Everyone understood that if the Turks overwhelmed Quinn's Post, they could storm down Monash Valley and sweep the Anzacs back into the sea.

A week after Thomas's regiment arrived on Gallipoli, the Turks tried.

The first to notice the build-up of Turkish troops were the slow rumbling biplanes with their aerial cameras over Quinn's. After the reconnaissance photos reached the generals, everyone was put on the alert.

Thomas and his squadron sat by their dugouts and made ready. They cleaned and oiled their rifles, checked and rechecked their ammunition pouches.

Kingy sharpened his bayonet. 'Cold steel . . . puts the fear of God into the Turk.'

'Such a handy tool,' Snow said with affection. 'Opens a can and cuts firewood.'

'Trims a beard and makes a tidy hook,' Teach said.

'Saves a bullet,' Thomas added.

The blade's prime purpose was left unspoken, its true intention too breathtaking for words.

After several days, the heaviest Turkish bombardment yet experienced crashed into the valley and forced the Light Horsemen inside their dugouts.

'The Turk's a mite windy at present,' the sergeant explained.

'Let 'em come.' Kingy patted his rifle. 'We'll do 'em for what they did to our boys.'

Thomas and his mates grunted their agreement.

The deaths of so many Queenslanders, twenty-five in Major Graham's C Squadron, shot down during a charge against the Turks, was a disaster for the regiment. It devastated and horrified the 2nd Light Horse. It left them feeling vulnerable and intensely angry. They had been stung by their experience at Quinn's and embarrassed at their swift replacement by the infantry. So, anxious to prove themselves and keen to pay back the Turk, they stewed in the waterless heat of the approaching summer and vowed revenge.

Now it looked like they'd have their chance.

That night they were ordered to sleep in their full kit, but who could sleep? The shelling from the Turkish guns and the tap-tap-tapping of Maxims and rifle fire, far heavier than usual, became furious around midnight.

In the blackness, Thomas closed his eyes and strained to make out where the firing was loudest. It seemed to him that Anzac posts were being attacked both near and far, on the right at Johnston's Jolly and Lone Pine, and then on the left at Pope's Hill.

He wondered when his turn would come. He gripped his rifle and hoped it would be soon. He felt sure someone would hear his heart beating and notice his shaking hands.

'We're all a bit jumpy,' Snow said.

'I'm always nervy before a game,' Thomas said.

'Tubbie told me that before a battle his spear shook so much they reckoned he was the fiercest warrior in the tribe.'

Thomas smiled. 'My dad never talked much.'

As he sat in the dark, unable to sleep for the noise, Thomas wondered anew about his father. 'Tell me about the war?' he'd asked him once, in the hope of an heroic tale of shot and shell, bravery and pluck, of victory won against terrible odds. As in *Deeds that Won the Empire*, which Teach – when he was Mr William West of Murgon's little school – had given Thomas to read. Jack Clare had waited a while, then said quietly, 'Pray you never know, son.' For a boy dreaming of cavalry and charging lances, the answer had been a puzzle and a disappointment.

Now he knew better. Thomas clenched his eyes shut and folded his hands on his forehead. *Can you see me, Dad?* he said to himself. *I want to be brave. Is that what you want, for me to kill the bastards?*

As always, there was no answer from Jack Clare.

*

Just before dawn, the shelling stopped. They heard the urgent order for B Squadron to reinforce the infantry and the Light Horsemen burst from their dugouts and scrambled up the steep narrow path to Quinn's Post.

'Good luck, cobber,' Thomas said.

'You too,' said Snow.

'A fine day for it,' Kingy said grandly, which made them laugh.

The noise ahead was a waterfall of gunfire. Thomas felt his heart beating wildly as he climbed. He had never been this excited. But he could feel the fear too, pinching his stomach, making him want to piss. He tensed himself as he struggled upwards and hoped to hell that Snow wasn't watching. The last thing he wanted to do was make a fool of himself in front of his best mate.

Even so, he found himself being peppered with random thoughts. He had never killed a person before. It was one thing to shoot an animal, but a man . . . what would it be like? He wondered if he should fire over their heads, aim for a leg, merely wing them. They'd been trained to go for the torso, but Thomas knew he would hit wherever he aimed. He could disable a man, take him out of the war without taking his life. Kill or maim? *Which, Thomas?*

The sergeant had said more than once, '"Thou shalt not kill" is the proper commandment for home, if the Turk lets ya go back there. Remember, lads, the enemy's no Christian, 'e don't keep commandments. Except for one, which is thou shalt kill Anzacs. So if 'e ain't worried, why should you be?'

Yes, Thomas agreed, *must leave civvie street and its rules behind.*

He had to look after his cobbers, those who had made every hardship bearable. *Without them you're nothing,* Thomas thought. Wound a man, he may still shoot you or your mate. Kill him, you make sure.

He recalled other deaths: his father beneath the tree, the man without hands at Quinn's, the rows of dead on the beach, and those fellows in C Squadron who never stood a chance.

In his haste, Thomas scrambled up the slope, passing others, gritting his teeth, sweaty already. As the ridge loomed, the sound of firing became deafening. He peered over, expecting to see men huddling behind a ragged line of sandbags. Instead, the brightening sky revealed an impossible silhouette – a jumble of figures in peaked caps inside a mist of dust and smoke, acting out a pantomime familiar in training but alien to Gallipoli. It took Thomas a moment to understand.

The Australians were out of their trench. They were perched on the parapet, sitting or kneeling, raising and lowering their rifles, reloading and firing into no-man's-land. They were facing the rising sun in full view of the Turks. At Quinn's! *What madness*, Thomas thought, where to raise a hand above the sandbags was to see it shredded. Even as the idea exhilarated him, he flinched at the prospect of joining them.

Thomas and the others surged ahead and for the first time peered over the crest.

And then they saw.

A tide of shadows moving against the eastern sky. Ghostly figures flooded across no-man's-land in the hundreds. They surged from their trenches, bayonets outlined sharp against the dawn, spurred on by the martial music behind them.

The Turks trudged forward, chanting, '*Allah, Allah!*'

'*Imshi Yalla*,' replied many of the 15th Battalion men in the Cairo slang they'd invented to tell the Gyppos to go to blazes.

The infantrymen fired as fast as they could, furiously thumbing bullets into their rifle magazines. Even the officers fired their revolvers into the pack. From the flanks, Anzac machine guns made a terrific staccato, sending streams of bullets to plough the narrow earth.

The Turks were caught in a terrible crossfire. The hail of bullets punched them down one after another, or simultaneously, so that a man jerked this way and that like a ragdoll in the jaws of a beast.

Snow yelled into Thomas's ear, 'Turks got no covering fire, no artillery, no MGs.'

Thomas nodded, understanding immediately that the Turks couldn't trust their heavier weapons not to hit their own men; no wonder the Australians were out of the trench.

With their bayonets held out before them, the Turks jogged on into a wall of rifle fire. It seemed to Thomas that they were seeking death.

Such sport, he thought. He itched to shoot them, but too many Australians were ahead of him. Instead he watched with mounting excitement as the Anzacs ran their rifles hot. If only the infantrymen would tire or run out of ammo and make room for him.

Few Turks reached the Anzac trench and those who did were cut down at the last moment. Only those Turks in the front rank could fire without hitting their comrades, while others behind lobbed bombs over their comrades' heads. The Australians smothered or threw them back, and occasionally a bomb burst in a flash, spilling blue smoke among them.

As the morning light grew in intensity, Thomas watched the next wave of Turks rush forward, only to be mown down by the point-blank rifle fire and cut to ribbons by the machine guns. The Turks fell quickly, stumbling, thrown into the air and crashing against their brothers. Others would push steadily on, until they too would fall. Soon a creeping, breathing carpet of khaki lay on the strip of earth between the two sides.

Thomas remembered his friends in C Squadron, mown down similarly a few days earlier, and he itched to join the slaughter before the Turks stopped coming.

He watched a small black ball sail over the leading Turks and fall into the trench in front of him. It exploded in a swirl of dirt and dust and Thomas felt his face grow warm and wet. He turned to Snow, who was wiping white matter and blood from his tunic.

Down in the trench, a body lay crumpled and missing half a head. Another broken man was crying piteously. Two others staggered away with shattered limbs. Their comrades dropped their rifles to attend to their wounded, to scream 'Stretcher-bearers', hardly audible in the din.

Thomas saw his chance. 'C'mon, Snow,' he said and they scrambled into the trench. One man remained against the bloodied trench wall, his mouth hanging open and disbelief in his eyes, clutching his stomach, red oozing between fingers.

'I'll smother, you fire,' said Snow, collecting a wad of empty sandbags.

Thomas jumped to the fire step and hoisted himself out of the trench to join others sitting on the parapet. From there, he watched hundreds of figures fringed with dawn light lumbering ever closer. Thomas had a quick moment of fear. Unlike the earlier bombing duel, here the enemy was in sight, true and deadly and coming to kill him.

The Turks shuffled forward doggedly, zigzagging between the bodies of those before them. Light flashed from muzzles in their frontline and small black balls appeared above them, sailing towards Thomas. *Leave the bombs to Snow. Your job is to shoot.*

He steeled himself and levelled his rifle.

Here was the moment. If he saw a man close up, saw his face, read his eyes, learnt something about him, could he still fire? Should he aim high? Fire to wound?

The shuffling uniforms, running at him with bayonet and bomb, chanting their alien dirge, were hardly men, he thought, but a stampeding herd to be turned, beasts to be put down.

This lot wouldn't surrender in a fit. They were out for blood. *God help us if they reach our trenches.* His family, the men he loved above everything, all were here and some would die this morning.

Take no prisoners. Kill or be killed. Thomas knew it was true.

He found a chest, aimed for a split second and fired. The chest jerked backwards and was lost among others who passed around and then over it.

Got him fair and square. Thomas exulted. He felt his heart lurch. He was filled with an intense pleasure, a joy he had not expected. Thomas spotted a well-dressed soldier, a Turkish officer, shot and thrilled to see the man fall.

He fired and fired into the mass. He worked the bolt, aligned the sights, squeezed the trigger, saw the man fall, then repeated the process – retract, eject, close the bolt, breathe, sight and fire. Again and again. One round every four seconds. Rapid fire, by the book, as he had been trained to do. Brisk, methodical, practised, second nature.

The more he shot the more relaxed he became. Moving from one target to another, he chose who to hit and quickly fired, and did not wait to see the man fall dead or to stagger away or whether the man raised his rifle afterwards. There were too many for that.

Somewhere in his being he felt that eventually he and his comrades must be overwhelmed and that would be that. But, until the moment came, he owned an inner calm, was invincible, all fear gone in the wildness around him.

Amid the constant crack of rifle fire, sometimes a shout could be heard, and laughter too – for here the Turks were packed so tightly that a single high-velocity slug went through several at once.

'Two for one,' an infantryman crowed.

'Got three myself,' said a Light Horseman.

'Potting Turk into left pocket,' the first man said, delivering a shot through the heart.

No longer were they crouched at the bottom of a trench or sheltering in a hole. No need was there to duck under cover. The fire came from men unafraid to look over a parapet. Death was with the Turks. Here was a feast and at the table the Australians were gorging themselves.

Oh, yes, revenge was sweet. Thomas felt it. So many targets, so many hits, though he didn't keep count. Never was shooting a roo or an emu as good as this.

With lightning reflexes and years of practice, Thomas brought them down as handily as rabbits. *Dead easy.* He raised and aimed and fired in one smooth motion, shot after shot, fifteen times a minute.

Bang, and a man crumpled. *Bang*, a Turk whirled around hit in the shoulder. *Bang*, a Mauser shattered in a man's hands. *Bang*, the foe clutched his stomach, doubled up, fell backwards. *Bang*, a head exploded. Each shot was a crash and its echo in his ear lasted as long as a body took to hit the ground.

Thomas was bursting all over. In the blink of an eye he saw everything so clearly, so vividly – the surprise in faces, the red in the air, the crumbling looks. And the sounds too, the panting and grunting, bolts snapping home, blast and bugle, loud and sharp. There was such joy in being the executioner. It was godlike, this power. They were dying like flies and he was alive as never before.

Needing to reload, those nine seconds to thumb clips into the magazine were interminable, so impatient was he to resume.

Thomas fired until the oil between wood and metal seethed. The kick to his shoulder began to hurt. Sweat stung his eyes, and he wiped it away with the back of his hand. He was forgetting to breathe, and his ears rang with the hammering all around.

Thomas glanced across at Snow, who by now had taken up a rifle, and heard him shout as he fired, 'You bastards . . . you poor devils.' On his other side was Teach, wild as a prophet, chanting with each shot he fired, 'Every bullet has its billet.' Beside him, Kingy was grinning from ear to ear and screaming curses that were lost in the crash and rattle of the guns.

Thomas laughed like a schoolboy whose side was winning by a mile. As he shunted the bolt home again and squeezed the trigger, he said to himself, '"We few, we happy few, we band of brothers. For he today that sheds his blood with me shall be my brother."'

Oh, the bond he felt for them. He shared their joy and pride in giving such a lesson to the enemies of the King. *We are Australians. This is what we can do.*

The sun rising revealed a carpet seething with wounded. Over and between the fallen, the enemy staggered dazed, or blundered into each other. Others not yet hit sought a path to the Anzacs, while some turned and ran back, only to be met by Turks climbing out of their trench. Cut down in swathes by the machine guns on the flanks, they fell like dominoes back inside the trenches. A man's head exploded and he ran a few steps before crumpling. An arm flew unattached through the air. Men were spun and twisted by the rage of lead. In the early light, a red mist rose over the enemy trench.

Still the Turks came on.

Now Thomas used two rifles, his own and one bequeathed by

the dead infantryman. He fired until the oil bubbled between barrel and stock, then swapped it for the cool one.

By now, he was slowing down, taking more care with each shot, being methodical in order to keep up a steady rate. Aim, squeeze, fire, work the bolt, eject, push and fire again, all in five seconds.

Until he ran out of ammunition.

A Light Horseman behind him saw his chance, 'Give us a shot, cobber,' he pleaded.

'Not bloody likely,' Thomas snapped.

'Have a heart, matey, a shilling for your possy.'

Thomas grumbled as he took it, annoyed – not for taking the coin – but that he must give up the killing. He slipped into the trench in search of a full ammo belt. Irritated, impatient, drenched in sweat, his hands shook as he removed an ammo belt from the dead man at the bottom. He put the bandolier around his own shoulders and stood below Snow, watching for bombs but longing for him to run out of bullets.

Five waves were cut down at Quinn's Post that morning, one after the other, until the sliver of ridge was thick with slaughter. Lying, kneeling, sitting, bent over as if in prayer . . . clutching their rifles. In places, Turks had fallen on top of one another, so that piles rose here and there, mostly still.

The sun was high overhead when the attacks trickled to a halt. The Anzacs on the parapet jeered at the opposing trench, taunting their enemy to keep coming on.

'Thanks for the game,' Thomas heard one man say. 'Play ya again on Saturday,' a comment that drew laughter among the Australians.

The men looked over hundreds of corpses laid out on that little patch of scrubby earth right up to their sandbags and they congratulated themselves. Officers and NCOs warned them to be ready just in case, while the men checked their rifles and took sips of water.

They began to notice the smells, an evil brew of smoke and cordite, sweat and dust, piss and shit. A lull fell on the ridge, a sweet dearth of gunfire and explosions, shocking to those who knew Quinn's.

Gradually, as ears became accustomed to the change, other sounds emerged. '*Ahn-neh, ahn-neh*' came wretched and pathetic from no-man's-land.

Strange, Thomas thought, how alike it was, as a man would cry for his mother.

Snow sat back against the earth wall with his face in his hands. For the first time that Thomas could remember, Kingy was silent. Beside him, Teach stood with his rifle still aimed at no-man's-land, his eyes wide and wild. 'We have shown them,' he declared. 'They cannot challenge the greatest Empire the world has ever seen and her loyal subjects.'

Thomas sank into the trench, drained, parched and ravenous. Desperately tired in body and mind. There was no joy, only weariness. Already his mind was becoming blank.

Snow sighed, and Thomas noticed. 'What's wrong?'

'Nothing,' Snow said. Then, pressed by the insistent looks of his friends, he said blankly, 'They were brave, weren't they, the way they came on?'

'Indeed,' Teach agreed.

'Straight into our guns,' Snow added.

'Of course. They're fanatics,' Teach said. 'For them, to die by the sword is the key to heaven.'

Kingy, examining the seam of his tunic, stabbed a louse with his lighted fag. 'Bloody greybacks,' he declared.

'They didn't have a chance,' Snow said.

'They dunno what's good for 'em,' Kingy said. 'Oughta chuck in the towel.'

'C'mon, mate,' Thomas said lightly to Snow. 'Don't go soft on us.'

'I got plenty,' Snow said defensively.

'We all did.'

'As was our duty to God, King and country,' said Teach, 'and what we trained for.'

'Sarge says a dozen of our blokes were skittled,' Thomas said. 'Plenty more were wounded.'

'They'd have swept us away,' Teach said.

'Yes, yes, I know,' said Snow, who paused before continuing, 'and I enjoyed it.'

They all went quiet, as if an unwelcome guest had joined them.

'Nuffin' wrong with that,' Kingy said finally.

Thomas said, 'You're a warrior, Snow. Tubbie would be proud.'

'Warrior? I wasn't brave. It wasn't heroic.'

'Jesus, give ya arse a chance,' said Kingy, who had heard enough. 'They're bloody Turks, maggots, heathens, no better than boongs. Ta hell with 'em.'

Snow glared at him.

Teach said, 'Never forget why we're here, Snow. They're the foe.'

Kingy glared back at Snow. 'Ya can't *care* about 'em!'

'We're defending the Empire in a righteous and honourable cause,' Teach persisted.

'I know and I was there with you. I was cheering and laughing . . .' Snow's sentence trailed off.

Thomas wasn't sure what he wanted most – to put his arm around his friend or shake some sense into him, so he did neither.

Snow turned to him. 'Don't you see it? We knocked them for defending their land.'

'Would you rather be rotting out there with them?' Teach said sharply.

Snow ignored him. 'You remember Tubbie's story about Battle Mountain? He was *there*, Tom.'

'It's not the same,' Thomas said.

'Kalkadoons charged the guns and got massacred.'

Kingy spat with vehemence, 'Cripes, Snow, whose bloody side are ya on? We stonkered 'em dinky-di. Ya not a fookin' tinkie-tinkle, are ya?'

Thomas rounded on him. 'Have a care.'

Kingy ignored Thomas and smiled shrewdly at Snow. 'Turks are whitefellas . . . should have been easy enough to knock.'

Snow sighed. He knew Kingy too well. 'My dad ate whitefellas like you for breakfast, but he skinned 'em first.'

Kingy chuckled.

'I won't funk it,' Snow said. 'I won't let them do you or me.'

'Course you won't. We're in this together,' said Thomas, who hadn't any concerns about the Turks he'd shot. 'I've had a bellyful too. But we can't just go back, can't just leave, say sorry, we're going home now. No, we have to knock them to billy-ho or they'll overrun us and we'll never see home again.'

Sometimes Thomas didn't understand Snow. There was no joy left in killing so many, but it did no good to think of the Turk as a human being. It was Thomas's job, his duty, his reason for being there, just what he had to do. It helped his country and that was enough. Of course, the Turk was not evil, neither torturer nor mutilator, was likely fair and square and struggling to survive just as he was. Johnny was no monster, he was merely the enemy, and thinking too much about it didn't make it any better. He respected Snow and his opinions, but there was a lot about him he didn't grasp and probably never would.

'Kill or be killed, that's all it is,' Thomas concluded.

Snow looked at him sadly and said not another word.

'Christ almighty, what a mob of miseryguts,' said Kingy.

Chapter 14

THAT NIGHT, IN A QUIET gully below Pope's Hill, Thomas went to church. An altar of biscuit boxes under a scrap of canvas lay in front of an open grave. The Light Horsemen stood with heads bowed as the Anglican chaplain spoke softly in his Oxford tones. Captain George Green was a tall man in his mid-thirties, who wore a pith helmet and carried a shepherd's crook. This night, he was almost invisible in a long black surplice, except where his torchlight focused on the book in his hand and reflected a faint halo of light back on his face.

The chaplain looked up from the Bible and down at the body. 'Another thoroughbred scratched in the race of life,' he said.

The men murmured respectfully at the sporting analogy, for the chaplain's nickname was 'Sol', not 'soul' for his holiness, but in recognition of a popular Brisbane bookie of the same name.

'Here lies Dugald Maxwell Lockwood Graham, Major, 2nd Light Horse,' Sol Green said a little huskily. 'Dugald was a sugar grower from Ayr and a veteran of the war with the Boers. I was with him and C Squadron at Quinn's four nights ago. I can tell you that he and his men knew there was a good chance they would not return from their stunt that night.'

The chaplain paused. 'Probably about 6 to 4 against.'

Soft laughter rose in the men. Not bad for a funeral.

Sol Green got serious again. 'Not a chance in hell did they have. Yet, bravely silent they were, before they entered *the valley of the shadow of death*. Major Graham fell when he went to the aid of a comrade. As John, the disciple of Jesus, reminds us, "Greater love hath no man than this, that a man lay down his life for his friends."'

Again the chaplain paused. 'You may have heard that Private Simpson was knocked today.'

'So bloody what?' Kingy muttered quietly to Thomas. 'Lazy dodger, living the easy life.'

'You know him?' Thomas whispered.

'Nah, but he was no soldier, so what's he getting special treatment for? Not like he was no spit and polish officer or nuffin'.'

The chaplain went on, 'You may have seen him between Quinn's and the beach. He was an ambulance man who carried your cobbers, whose stretcher was a donkey.'

'There's your answer,' Thomas said.

Kingy grumbled but said nothing.

'A machine gun shot him through the *heart*.' Sol Green rested on the word for a moment. 'This very night, my namesake Chaplain James Green is burying Simmo down by the beach at Queensland Point. Let us consider Graham and Simpson, the major and the private, the Light Horseman and the stretcher-bearer, two quite different souls who gave their lives for their mates. Merely two of the many of you doing God's work in this place.

'Now I know that some of you were rattled by that stunt in which brave Major Graham fell, and that is only natural. But you have given a great account of yourselves. This morning there was some justice, a great defeat inflicted upon the enemy, and that is also how it should be.'

The chaplain looked down at his Bible. 'The prophet Ezekiel wrote, "Thus saith the Lord God, Smite with thine hand, and stamp with thy foot . . . and he that is near shall fall by the sword . . . Then shall ye know that I am the Lord, when their slain men shall be among their idols round about their altars, upon every high hill, in all the tops of the mountains . . ." Ezekiel was talking about the Jews worshipping false idols, but we can apply his words to the Turk.'

In the darkness, several Anzacs intoned, 'Amen.' The chaplain concluded the funeral rites and some of Major Graham's comrades shovelled the dirt of Gallipoli into his grave.

Thomas remained as the others made their way back to their dugouts. Even in the darkness, Thomas could see their faces set cold.

'Trooper Clare, Thomas, isn't it?' said Sol Green.

'Yes, sir.'

'Colonel Chauvel speaks well of you.'

Thomas was amazed the chaplain would remember him out of the hundreds in the regiment. They'd had only a brief passing conversation when he had presented himself at Uncle Harry's HQ in Egypt months before.

'Are you C of E, Thomas?' the chaplain continued.

'RC, sir.'

'No matter, we're all khaki here.' The chaplain pulled a box from the makeshift altar and sat down on it. He invited Thomas to do the same, so that they were sitting together beside the newly turned grave. The chaplain lit his pipe. 'Should you ever wish to talk about the manner of your father's passing, they tell me I am a good listener.'

Uncle Harry told him. 'Thank you, sir.'

'A shame for you to part from boyhood in such a way. Your comrades too, boys no longer.'

'Padre, there is something,' Thomas ventured. 'Major Graham

and his blokes came a gutser, sixty of them, and got nowhere. Today we knocked a lot of Turks. Well, sir, one of my mates reckons the Turks were only defending their homes. I wonder what you think of that?'

'They are certainly defending, that is true, and we are attacking. Though I suspect we are both fairly stuck at the moment. Nevertheless, it is your duty that should concern you. You are a soldier, a Light Horseman dismounted, and Turkey is the enemy of the King whom you have sworn to defend. And as my friends in the senior ranks tell me, attack is often the best form of defence.'

'Yes, thank you, sir. Can I ask you something else?'

'Of course.'

'This same fella also said he felt bad giving the knock to so many so easily, as if it wasn't brave or gallant. What do you think of that?'

'What exactly are you trying to say, Thomas?'

Thomas paused before answering. 'We do it so often, sir. Is it still wrong?'

The chaplain surprised Thomas with a smile of acknowledgement. 'Ah, well there you have it. Terrible things happen in war. Terrible things happen to men in war. The donkey man, Simpson, was a fine fellow, yet someone shot him. Shooting an unarmed man is not cricket, I agree, but I hardly consider the Turk who shot him to be a bad man.'

'Then is it acceptable to give the knock to an enemy who is not trying to kill you?'

'Some of the Lord's rules don't apply here, Thomas, I'm sad to say.'

Thomas thought of what he would do to his father's killer. 'Yes, sir.'

'Then go with God.'

*

The quiet lasted for days, except at Quinn's, where the Turks hardly stopped the bombing and rifle fire. In the support trenches, the Light Horse took a break from digging and filling sandbags. For the first time in a week, they could have a swim and a wash.

As cool as you like, the four strolled like veterans down Monash Valley, but hurried across the breaks in sandbags favoured by snipers. They picked up pace along Shrapnel Gully, drawn by the sparkle on the sea and the taste of salt in the air. It was at a point along the track where they began to hear the lapping of waves in between the usual boom and bang that Thomas was shot.

The pain was sharp and burning. 'Hey, wait a minute,' he said, putting a hand to his neck. 'I've got a bullet in me.'

'My colonial oath!' Kingy cried.

Amazed, Thomas looked at the blood on his fingers and felt faint. 'I'm shot,' he croaked.

Snow, however, burst out laughing. 'You're tickled,' he snorted.

The bullet had travelled so far it had almost expended itself, and was stuck half in, half out of Thomas's neck.

Teach giggled, 'Oh my, Eris is having sport with you.'

Thomas looked at Teach as if he were an idiot.

'Greek goddess of strife and quarrel who liked to play tricks,' Teach explained. 'Her golden apple started the Trojan war.'

'Oh will you shut up about that, Teach,' Thomas grumbled. 'I'm shot in this war, for Christ's sake.' He reached behind to stem the blood and instead bumped the bullet out.

Quick as a flash, a passing New Zealander picked it off the ground, only to find the slug so hot from its high-speed journey that he had to juggle it as he walked away.

'Ya thieving Kiwi bastard,' Kingy growled at him. 'How dare ya steal a man's souvy!' He snatched back the bullet in midair and deftly slipped the souvenir into Thomas's pocket. 'Hang on to that, cobber, ya earnt it.'

'I better get you to the doc,' Snow advised, as a fine trickle of blood ran down Thomas's neck.

'Nah, a swim'll fix it,' Thomas said, keen to show some pluck. He ran ahead, leading them towards the sea.

At the beachhead, they weaved around heaps of wooden crates, between rows of stretcher cases, and joined scores of men strolling about the narrow stretch of sand. Here, it seemed to Thomas, there was no war on at all.

They stripped at the water's edge and whooped at the gritty feel of sand between their toes and dived in with gay abandon.

Never was water so welcome. Thomas sank deep into the shock of cold, the liquid caress and escape from care. In that moment he was free of the uniform and its duties, and the sweat and gamy stink of war. And when he burst out to take a breath, the taste was clean and new.

He washed his wound and everywhere else, scraped his fingernails through his hair to take revenge on the fleas and lice, and took pleasure in the way the water turned a misty brown as a week of dirt, sweat, blood and shit dissolved away. How wonderful it felt to cast off the soldier and join the naked men splashing and hooting like schoolboys.

'This is better'n the water at Manly, though I do miss the sharks,' Kingy said with a wink. But he jumped in fright when four black poles floated by. It was a mule – on its back with legs stiff in the air – dumped at sea and now drifting back to the place where it had perished.

'Bloody periscopes . . . thought it was a U-boat.' Kingy grinned sheepishly.

When Beachy Bill sent over a cloudburst that pitched shrapnel pellets across the surface, everyone in the water rushed ashore, and while a few men fell with wounds, most laughed at their naked stampede.

In the shallows, Thomas and his mates scrubbed their clothes and waited for them to dry. They dressed as the sun set, watching steamboats and warships plough a golden sea.

'I miss the creek and our hunts,' Snow said.

'Me too.'

'Bet ya miss Winnie?'

'Ya silly old donk.' Thomas splashed him and laughed. After all, he was in grand company, in a war in which he had been shot and survived.

Laden with kero tins of water, they toiled up the track until the stench hit like a hammer in a butchery. It was sweet and sickly and seemed to stick to the skin. It caught in their throats and made them want to gag. And from up on the ridge, beneath the crash of bombs and rifle fire, came a persistent buzzing.

Sergeant Lucky Les passed on the word from HQ. 'There's thousands of 'em all along the line,' he announced. 'Five hundred in front of Quinn's, thanks to us.'

There was raucous cheering and backslapping, 'God save the King!', cries of 'Forward Australia!' and 'Onward to Constantinople!'. The men dispersed cheerfully, exchanging tales of their part in the battle. Kingy spoke of the number of Turks he had potted, while Teach said he was privileged to have played a role in an historic moment in the campaign. 'They are broken and destroyed,' he said. 'We must prevail.'

'Now's the time,' Kingy suggested, 'to winkle 'em out with the bayonet.'

Thomas said, 'We showed the higher-ups too what the Light Horse can do.'

'Even without our mounts, we're as good as the infantry,' agreed Snow.

'Better, I reckon. Wouldn't be anywhere else for quids,' Kingy said. 'What do ya say to a game of chance, Teach old son?'

'Yes, indeed.'

'Not two-up again, Teach,' sighed Thomas.

'Alas, wagering is my Achilles heel,' Teach confessed cheerfully. 'Would you rather I squander my pay on wine, women and song?'

On Gallipoli? Very funny! But Thomas bit his tongue. Most of his and Snow's six shillings each a day went to Mrs Iris Terrier, care of Murgon post office. Why Teach didn't remit his pay to his wife and child was his business.

'Dead cert, you'll do your dough,' Snow put in.

'We shall see,' said Teach as he and Kingy each fished out a brass box from their kitbags. They were identical, the size of a man's hand, with nail holes through the lids and both secured with twine. They laid them gently down and untied the strings. With the tip of his bayonet, Kingy drew a wide circle around them in the dirt and then laid sandbags over the mark to form a walled ring.

'Let the games begin,' Teach proclaimed loudly.

'It's on again,' a voice called from nearby, and a crowd gathered quickly, each Anzac with a ten-shilling note or more in his hand and his eyes focused on the boxes.

'Orright, gentlemen, arses down, ante up,' touted Kingy. 'Place ya bets.'

'Black Bill versus Our George,' cried Teach the ringmaster. 'Who shall prevail, the fiendish Prussian Kaiser or the mighty Hunter King?'

'Doubting Thomas here will hold your wagers,' Kingy added. The men bet among themselves and Thomas soon found quid notes being thrust at him. He stuffed the bills in his pocket, knowing they would remember their bets.

'Time, gentlemen,' said Kingy.

'One round, three minutes, to the death,' Teach declared. 'You know the rules, no Marquess of Queensberry here, all's fair in love and war. The Prince of Kalkadoon is our ref, and will settle arguments.'

Snow folded his arms and scowled like a sergeant major.

'And,' Kingy stressed at the top of his voice, 'in the case of a draw, ya does ya dough. Agreed?'

There were grunts of approval from around the ring as all eyes focused on the boxes.

Teach and Kingy placed a bayonet tip under each lid. In the hush, broken only by distant explosions and the occasional overhead hum of a bullet, they glanced at each other and flipped the covers.

Two black scorpions crawled out.

The men shrank back a little with horrid fascination for creatures usually crushed on sight.

Each gladiator had an armoured back and a curled tail and stinger almost as long as its body with a thin strip of blue or red ribbon looped around the base of its tail.

'Behold, the emperors of their domain,' Teach cried. 'Our George in blue, the vile Black Bill in red, fighting cousins and evenly matched. You'll recall that their last encounter was a draw.'

Inside the little stadium the creatures paused for a moment before charging and stabbing each other with lightning strikes of their stingers.

'"O full of scorpions is my mind,"' Teach intoned as dramatically as Macbeth.

'And full of poison is their tails,' said Kingy.

The animals grappled, their front crab claws trying to hold each other still while the tails whipped up and the thorns at the end slashed down.

'"Seek not a scorpion's nest, nor set no footing on this unkind shore,"' Teach said, enjoying the opportunity to wield his Shakespeare.

With Thomas's watch in hand, Snow called the time. 'Two minutes to go.'

While the scorpions struck each other continually, neither seemed wounded nor the worse for wear. Around them, the men cheered on their champion, heedless of any officer or sergeant who might arrive to spoil their fun.

'One minute,' Snow called, and still the creatures circled and stung.

The men's cheering became furious, obliging Teach to raise his voice. '"Who led thee through that great and terrible wilderness,"' he declared as if he were Moses himself, '"wherein were fiery serpents, and scorpions, and drought, where there was no water."'

But the men ignored him, so intent were they on the battle royal. When Snow called 'Time's up', they groaned.

Teach and Kingy consulted each other for a moment, after which Teach announced, 'One minute shall be added to the combat.'

The spectators cheered and Black Bill and Our George resumed their skirmish, each stinging the other until Snow again called time, eliciting another broad moan of disappointment.

'Oh dear, a draw, gentlemen,' Teach called out. 'Our warriors have survived, battered and bruised. I regret to say, the bank wins, until next time they meet.'

The men dispersed amiably enough and – like the scorpions – none the worse for the diversion.

Teach and Kingy used the tips of the bayonets to separate their champions and to flip them back into their boxes. They sprinkled a handful of smashed flies over each as a reward, carefully returned the lids to the boxes, and secured them with twine.

'We brung a little happiness to war,' Kingy chuckled with a quick grin.

'Blessed relief for our brave fighting lads,' said Teach.

'And a draw every time,' observed Thomas, as he handed over the winnings. 'How is that possible?'

Teach laughed. '"Be bloody, bold, and resolute; laugh to scorn the power of man, for none of woman born shall harm Macbeth."'

'Enough, Teach, not another word!' cried Thomas.

Teach looked around to ensure they weren't being overheard. 'They're first cousins . . . same species,' he whispered as he counted the notes.

'You mean they can't hurt each other?' Snow said.

'Immune to the venom.' Teach chuckled and handed Kingy his share. 'Never lost a fight.'

''Tis a grand show,' Kingy agreed cheerfully.

'It's a touch,' Snow said with a shake of his head. 'They'll crucify you.'

'My dear chap,' Teach said indignantly, while stuffing his takings into a pocket, 'who would tell them?'

Thomas found himself unable to speak. It was no surprise that Kingy would diddle his mates, not after the way life had cheated him.

But Teach? How could this patriot, who had risked his family and a good career to fight in a noble pursuit, be capable of such underhandedness? Was the cadger who swindled his comrades the same kind-hearted schoolteacher who had spoken of honesty and duty at his father's funeral? 'Brothers are we,' Teach had told them once. 'From every place, every occupation, every part of God's own society, we are.'

Teach the soldier seemed a different man. War had diminished him, Thomas decided. *Diminished us all, I expect.*

Chapter 15

FOR THE NEXT FEW DAYS, Thomas's squadron dug trenches and latrines, carried up rations and water from the tanks, taking care to hurry across open stretches in order to beat the sniper's bullet. Rumours were the main entertainment during meal breaks – the Turks were surrendering; a big push was coming; the British and French had broken through at Helles in the south; there would be a ceasefire tomorrow.

As the men tried to distinguish the real from gossip, the buzzing on the ridge became louder and the stink intolerable.

The last rumour proved not to be a furphy.

Ceasefire.

They were given picks, shovels and hooks. Thomas and his section would be among twenty-five from the regiment under Captain Nash who would join the Turks to bury the half-a-thousand dead in front of Quinn's Post.

Thomas hardly slept for the excitement. To walk about freely, to examine enemy positions, to look out across Turkey for the first time, to see what they were fighting for – wouldn't that be marvellous!

*

Thomas stood in no-man's-land. Such a thing! How strange to be standing in that savage place.

The day had dawned grey, wet and muggy, and now the morning sun sucked moisture from the leaves of bushes in clouds of steam. The rain had left the air rinsed and clear, laid the dust, dampened the earth and raised a fresh crop of poppies.

Here was Turkey spread out. For the first time he could marvel at the hills dark under the bright sky, the uneven line of pine trees on crests of purple-blue that lightened with every distant mile. The Ottoman capital lay unseen over more of the enemy's cliffs, along more valleys of snipers, so close and so far. Thomas breathed in deeply, filling his lungs with the high air, and turned his back on the heights.

So this was what the Turk saw. The ragged folds of Monash Valley and Shrapnel Gully that his comrades had won with their blood, less than a mile to the Aegean, a shimmering triangle streaked with darker patches of blue between the ships, and the islands Imbros and Samothrace poised majestically on the horizon. And, oh bliss, for a few precious seconds his heart sang in the absence of gunshot, bomb and barrage.

Until, as if awakening from a dream, a sound emerged supreme, beneath every other, *in* everything. It was the buzzing of a billion flies, accomplices to shrapnel and slug, the sole victors of the battlefield, seething and never silent.

With the noise was a smell so ripe that it convulsed his stomach and clutched at his throat. The stench seemed to envelop like a fog and seep into every pore and crevice. He wanted to rip it out, tear off his skin to get rid of it, wanted to run down to the clean sea.

Thomas turned to face it. No-man's-land belonged to the flies and their five hundred hosts. The insects crowded in empty eyes, in noses and ears, in stumps and entrails, in gangrene and stains of blood and faeces.

The sheer weight of corpses overloaded the senses. Wherever he walked were arms and legs thrown about randomly. The newly fallen were mounds of khaki bulging with gas, some doubled up, others with heads shattered. Here and there, lumps of flesh lay black and crawling.

The recent dead contrasted with the dried out husks of men unburied for weeks. Whitened bones poked through parchment skin, wizened and burnt. Bony claws of a detached arm grasped a rifle.

It was a sight to crush youth. Thomas felt faint, had to stop himself from falling, and braced himself by stabbing the earth with his shovel.

Where was the schoolboy glory of Wellington and Nelson or the charging stanzas of the Light Brigade? Here, where the flies droned and the hiss of gas marked an Anzac pick puncturing a corpse?

Men, with families and dreams once. Useless thought, and he thrust it away.

A flag flew on each side of the ridge, a cross and a crescent, both red. Beside each was a huge man, one an Anzac, the other a Turk, unarmed guards to enforce the conditions of the truce.

A few yards away Turkish soldiers – smaller, stockier than the Anzacs – would glance their way with a sad smile or nod as they too dug shallow graves and dragged the dead into them.

Thomas and his mates walked over to Chaplain Sol Green, a forlorn figure under his pith helmet, who was surveying a pile of cadavers. 'Poor, valiant fellows. Awful beyond imagining, isn't it, what we do to each other?'

'Everything's topsy-turvy, sir,' Thomas said. 'A graveyard upside down.'

'Sadly true of the world at present,' the chaplain said. 'There was a ceasefire in France, did you know?'

'No, sir.'

'On the Lord's birthday. They sang carols, exchanged smokes, played football together. The Tommies sent over puddings to the Huns.'

'They couldn't have been *that* friendly,' Kingy said sceptically.

'Well, while each side collected bodies they also repaired the wire,' the chaplain added.

The statement hung in the air for a few moments, until Teach filled the silence with a quotation. '"There can be no covenants between men and lions,"' he said, '"wolves and lambs can never be of one mind, but hate each other out and out and through".'

Chaplain Green shook his head. 'Homer wrote those words before Our Lord came into the world. Much has changed since.'

'Are you so sure, padre?' Teach said. 'Achilles denied Hector's request for a respectable burial, then slew him and desecrated his body.'

'And later, you'll recall, those two great armies negotiated a truce to dispose of their dead,' the chaplain said.

'A *temporary* ceasefire,' Teach said. 'The battles resumed and Troy fell.'

'Indeed,' sighed the chaplain. 'But, perhaps on this heaven-sent occasion, we might quote the prophet Isaiah, who lived around the time of Homer, and who foretold a cheerier time when, "the wolf also shall dwell with the lamb, and the leopard shall lie down with the kid, and the calf and the young lion and the fatling together, and a little child shall lead them".'

'Amen,' the Light Horsemen said automatically and were silent for a while, as they looked about the field of bodies.

'Johnny Turk is a good fighter, and fair,' Snow ventured.

'Old Paddy Bourke,' Teach said, using the rhyming slang. 'A real white man, if ever there was one.'

'Ya don't hate him,' Kingy said, 'but ya don't like him much either.'

'Yet, here we are,' the chaplain said.

Thomas gestured towards the mounds of green-khaki. 'They're mostly Turk.'

'They are, poor devils, and some decayed beyond recognition. Have a close look at footwear, lads. Many of the Turks wear leather shoes instead of boots. As to our people, you'll find it deuced difficult if they have no tags. Remember, most Tommies and Kiwis wear hobnails, the Light Horse don't.'

'Blasted boots got me into this mess,' Thomas muttered ruefully.

'What was that, corporal?' asked the chaplain.

'Nothing, sir,' replied Thomas, who had long stopped believing that he could identify a murderer by his boots.

'Yes, well, I'm afraid it will be rather a long day.' The chaplain pulled a flask from a pocket and took a nip, offering none of it to the others. 'Rum fortifies the body and the soul. I advise cotton wool for the nostrils.'

Abruptly he snapped his shepherd's crook against his boot, startling them. 'Let's get on, then. There's no time to lose and I hardly know where to start.'

Nevertheless, the chaplain ordered his party to begin by burying Anzac bodies in the communications trench, the same one from which the Turks had lobbed many of their cricket-ball bombs.

Thomas, Snow and their team worked till the sweat poured. They manhandled corpses in various stages of decomposition, some balloons of gas, others falling apart and difficult to pull, push or scoop. They rolled the Anzacs into the trench and shovelled a thin layer of dirt on top. The Turkish remains, they dragged over to the ceasefire line.

With one bloated body, Kingy lifted the boots, while Thomas thrust his hook under the shoulder and pulled. Instantly the Turk's arm parted from the torso and Thomas staggered backwards with it.

The incident prompted a stir among a group on the other side, laughter or anger, Thomas couldn't tell. A small greybeard in a ragged uniform walked across to the Anzacs. He looked down at the body of his comrade and up at Thomas's young face. He said nothing, then pulled out a pack of cigarettes, lit two at the same time and offered Thomas one.

Thomas took it and drew back. It tasted foul. He fished out a pack of Woodbines and gave them to the old Turk, who responded by handing over his pack. Together they looked at the body for a few quiet moments.

When they had finished their smokes, Thomas grasped his hand in a sudden gesture. The handshake seemed to surprise the Turk, but he didn't pull away.

'Good luck, old chap,' Thomas said.

The Turk gave a quick smile in reply.

'Waste of good fags,' Kingy said.

'He'll shoot you tomorrow,' Snow suggested.

'Not if I smudge him first,' Thomas smiled.

They tied a rope to the legs of the corpse and slipped another beneath its shoulders, carefully shifted it onto a stretcher, and added the disconnected arm. They carried the stretcher over to the Turks and tipped the contents gently at the feet of a Turkish officer, who took possession without a word.

Back on their side of the ceasefire line, leaning on a shovel to catch his breath, Thomas felt the stink envelop him like a wet cloak. The taste in his throat was bilious.

He recalled his father's body on the table in the hospital tent; he had kissed his father's forehead. Cold it was, dry and smelling of soap, he remembered. It had shocked him then. *Nothing compared to this.*

Thomas looked across the scrubby patch between trenches, where war's harvest gathered in deathly faces frozen with pain, surprise or horror. It was good, he decided, to bury these boys and men with their dreams and hopes, with the maggots and worms and flies, and let nature's alchemy welcome them back into the earth.

'Ashes to ashes, dust to dust,' he said quietly. *Rest in peace, Dad.*

'Amen,' said Snow.

'And there, but for the grace of God . . .' Teach murmured.

'Shut the fook up,' Kingy said quietly.

On their return to their burial trench, they found Chaplain Green talking to the same tall, short-sighted Englishman who had called on the Turks to surrender a fortnight earlier. Two Turkish officers stood close by with sour looks on their faces.

'Well, Herbert, you arranged this truce,' the chaplain said. 'Reason with them.'

'They are obviously, understandably, upset,' Herbert said. 'And I have to say I agree with them. You have filled a communications trench with bodies, a trench they believe they would have retaken.'

'And such a simple thing I did, without any trouble at all, for which you people lost so many lives endeavouring to capture it.'

'Quite correct,' Herbert said. 'But look around you. So many Turkish dead, so much courage. They have fought very finely. They feel your action is a major disadvantage to them and against the spirit of the ceasefire. They have promised to make a big smell about it to HQ.'

The chaplain shrugged. 'So be it.'

Captain Herbert spoke a few words to the Turks, who walked indignantly away. He returned to the chaplain. 'Their noses are out of joint, but they're up to their own tricks. They're collecting rifles. We're both setting up loopholes and sniper positions. There's spying on both sides.'

'Shame,' the chaplain sighed.

'Ghastly to the point of nightmare. This is a ceasefire, nothing more. Hostilities will resume at four-thirty and not a moment later,' Herbert said sadly.

The chaplain noticed he had an audience and he gestured for Thomas to join him. 'Herbert, this is the young man I spoke of, Colonel Chauvel's nephew, Thomas Clare. I've cleared it with the CO, trooper, you're to assist Captain Herbert.'

'Yes, sir.'

Herbert said, 'I gather you know French, Clare?'

'High school, sir.'

'Well, even that may come in handy. You and I are the umpires in this game of graves. Consider it half time and our job is to keep the players apart until the game resumes. Come along.'

As he left with Herbert, Thomas puffed out his chest for Snow. He was surprised and delighted at his new role and intensely relieved to be free of the ghastly burials.

However, it soon became clear that the short-sighted Captain Herbert didn't require much from Thomas other than to warn him before he stepped on a body, and to carry the several gifts of Turkish cigarettes he received from the enemy.

Though Thomas's role was tiny, it included an incident that would change his life.

He noticed a rotund, middle-aged officer in British uniform step over an arm lying on the ground. Nothing unusual about that, except that the officer slipped on something else beside it and stumbled into the rest of the body. Even from a distance, Thomas could see that his foot had gone into the torso. The officer cursed as he extracted his boot covered in sticky green fluid. In a fury, the officer kicked the Turk's head, which detached and rolled away.

Something burned in Thomas's guts. 'Oh, Christ,' he cried, at the image of another head rolling beneath a moonlit noose.

Thomas's cry was lost in the bellows of protest from a group of Turkish officers who, having witnessed the incident, stormed across the ceasefire line.

'That's torn it,' Herbert said and rushed to intercept them, followed closely by Thomas.

The British officer at the centre of it all regarded the approaching Turks with remarkable aplomb. He calmly scooped up a handful of dirt and threw it over the slime on his boot, then proceeded to scrape off the remainder with a stick torn from a bush. Upon seeing Herbert approach, he said with an unmistakable Irish lilt, 'Ah, just the man.'

'Taylor,' Herbert acknowledged coolly.

'Would you be so good as to explain to these *gentlemen*,' said the officer, spitting out the word with derision, 'that a British officer does not enjoy standing in a body, whether Turk or Anzac. Nevertheless, I regret my clumsiness and offer my sincere apology.'

'Is it *sincere*?'

The officer bristled. 'Perhaps I should throw myself at their feet, and say, "Oh pretty please, do not shoot me for I am a friend of Herbert Effendi." Isn't that the Turkish phrase practised by your cronies?'

'Two *clauses* joined by a conjunction,' Herbert corrected him coldly, 'which you would do well to learn.'

The two captains stared at each other with mutual loathing, until Herbert left with a curt nod to begin a conversation with the enemy officers.

While Herbert was busy calming the Turks, the other officer

looked in Thomas's direction. He had a hard face and light grey eyes. 'Head shots,' he said abruptly.

'What of them, sir?'

'Our fellows were mostly shot from above, from the heights. Enemy's wounds are in the torso. Not the first war in which I've seen what a Mauser can do. Interesting, wouldn't you agree?'

'Yes, sir.'

'Wounds to fit a fist, so large that initially my people believed the Turk was using expanding ammunition. On the contrary, they're not dumdums at all. As you can plainly see, our hits on the Turk are equally messy. Impressive, what a high velocity slug will do, wouldn't you agree?'

'Yes, sir.' Thomas didn't fancy such talk about wounds. *My people?* And why was a British officer bothering to natter to a lowly trooper? Thomas felt unsettled by this man.

'You must be Jack Clare's boy,' the captain said suddenly.

'Sir?'

'I knew your father. We served together in South Africa. My condolences, by the way.'

Thomas's stomach lurched. Herbert had called him *Taylor.* Captain Taylor. Irish. *Bulala. TNP. Oh hell.*

'Thank you, sir,' Thomas gasped through a tightening throat. 'My father never spoke much about the war. Were you two mates?'

'Comrades,' Taylor chuckled. 'We did not often see eye to eye.'

'You were there with the Breaker too?'

'Harry Morant? Oh yes. I see you know something after all.'

'Only that he wrote poems and broke horses.'

'And a host of hearts.'

A host of hearts. The phrase turned in Thomas's mind. In Murgon, Sergeant Griffin had used those same words.

At this point, Captain Herbert returned. 'See here, Taylor, we must get on. Can I suggest you refrain from kicking Turkish heads? We hardly need to start another war, at least not until the ceasefire ends this afternoon.'

'Perish the thought,' Taylor said scornfully. But he smiled at Thomas. 'I'd like to talk further about your father. Such a sad end to a fine life. Your father fought his demons and lost. Believe me, Thomas, it is so important in this business not to lose one's head.'

Thomas almost laughed at the pun. *Not to lose one's head.*

Captain Herbert gave Taylor a look of loathing.

'Yes, sir,' Thomas stammered, realising suddenly that Taylor's comment was aimed at him. Did Taylor know of his father's decapitation? It wasn't in Sergeant Griffin's police report. Then Thomas remembered that Taylor had visited Murgon. He would have heard the gossip, might have picked up the *hearts* phrase from Griffin, or vice-versa.

Taylor departed with a curt nod to Herbert.

'What did the Turkish officer say to you, sir?' Thomas asked.

'He said, "At this spectacle even the most gentle must feel savage, and the most savage must weep."'

'Yes, sir.'

'And another, pointing to the graves, said, "That's politics," and pointing to the dead, said, "That's diplomacy."'

'Oh dear, you don't believe that, do you, sir?' asked Thomas.

'I see an enemy whom I cannot dislike and a campaign that is doomed already,' Herbert said dismally.

Thomas had no answer to that. He and Captain Herbert watched in silence as the grisly work went on around them. Herbert took out his pipe, filled it carefully from a pouch and lit it. 'Ghastly man.'

'Who, sir?'

'Taylor. The kind of man to fight to the finish, who will never negotiate despite this affront to civilisation,' he said bitterly, sweeping his hand around the scene before them.

'Yes, sir.'

'You two seemed awfully chummy,' Herbert continued. 'What do you know of Captain Taylor?'

Thomas wondered whether he could trust this cock-eyed toff who seemed a little too friendly with the enemy. But there was something honest and likeable about Captain Herbert, and as an officer on General Godley's staff he might have useful information. Thomas took a chance. 'They call him Bulala, sir.'

Herbert looked Thomas in the eye. 'What else?'

'*Bulala* is an African word.'

'It is indeed. I speak eight languages, Thomas, though hardly a word of Zulu,' Herbert said matter-of-factly. 'Captain Alfred Taylor is well known in some circles. He was an intelligence agent during the second Boer War. He was arrested and charged with the murders of a number of Boer prisoners of war and some civilians, but from my memory of those events Taylor was as guilty as anyone, yet somehow he wriggled free.'

'Were you there, sir, in South Africa?'

Herbert coloured. 'No, I'm ashamed to say, missed that one.'

'My father served there, once with Colonel Chauvel, then with Captain Taylor in the BVC.'

'Yes, the Bushveldt Carbineers. Three convicted, two executed. If I recall correctly, Harry Morant's excuse was that he "came to shoot Boers . . . not to play". But they were bushwhackers who killed without rule or reason, so Arthur Conan Doyle described them.'

'He's my favourite author, sir . . . Treated my father in hospital,' Thomas said proudly.

'You don't say.'

'My father served with the Breaker, sir.'

'Well, he would have. I don't know about your father, but Morant and Handcock admitted disposing of prisoners; they

argued that Captain Taylor among others had ordered them
to do so. Doesn't exonerate them, of course. British officers
shouldn't go round killing prisoners willy-nilly, should they?'

'They were Australians, sir, Australian Britons.'

'And the firing squad was a fitting end for them,' Herbert
said firmly.

'If you say so, sir.'

'You disagree?'

'I'm hardly a lawyer, sir.'

Herbert raised an eyebrow at Thomas. 'I'd say you're barely a
man. How old are you?'

Thomas hesitated, was about to lie, decided not to. After all,
he quite liked Herbert. 'Nearly seventeen, sir.'

'Thought so,' smiled Herbert. 'I expect it helps to have a
relative as brigade commander.'

'He's not my real uncle. You didn't say what *Bulala* means, sir?'

'It is Zulu for killer . . . slayer. Best steer clear of that man.'

'Yes, sir.'

Thomas didn't need to be convinced.

Chapter 16

WHILE THE BRAVERY OF THE enemy and the burial of his bodies may have triggered a respect for the Turk, no one in Thomas's regiment was surprised that the war resumed immediately the ceasefire ended.

The very next day, any joy left over from the crushing Anzac victory sank to the bottom of the Aegean.

It was the cheering from the enemy trenches that alerted Thomas. He joined the general rush to the hillsides in time to watch the *Triumph* die. A mile away in full view of everyone, the battleship turned turtle. She showed her red keel for a time, then dived bow-first into the blue.

A groan erupted around Thomas.

'Oh, the poor devils,' sighed Teach.

In the place where the old girl met the torpedo, rescue boats were dragging sailors from the water, while destroyers scuttled about in their hunt for the submarine.

The other battleships in the fleet turned their bows westward, their belching columns of black smoke chasing them towards a grey patch on the horizon, the island of Imbros and sanctuary.

Thomas watched the retreat of the capital ships in disbelief, until all that remained were the little destroyers with their four-inch guns.

In the heights, the Turks waved rifles and flags and cried out for joy. And while the Anzacs standing in the open below made easy targets for them, no shots rang out.

Kingy shook his fist, first at the enemy and then at his allies. 'Ya nob and toff bastards,' he cursed. 'Afraid of a little U-boat.'

'They have their reasons,' Teach countered.

'Yeah, they might get hurt,' Kingy snorted.

'A prudent course of action,' Teach persisted. 'Very brave to leave us. They'd be in tears.'

'Fears, more like. The woolly dogs got the wind up. The wasters left us to rot.'

'Have a care! That is the Royal Navy you're speaking of,' Teach declared. 'They don't know the meaning of fear.'

Snow gritted his teeth. 'We'll have to spit at Abdul now.'

'Us common-ohs have the bayonet,' Kingy said. 'Cold steel is what he fears most and what makes us men.'

Thomas knew how Kingy was feeling. How could the heirs to Drake, Raleigh and Nelson flee before a little German U-boat? Where was the nobility in that? Thomas felt weak in the knees and sat down in the dirt to watch the battleships disappear over the horizon. The Anzacs were on their own. The sea was at their backs and they were clinging to a sliver of foreign shore below a determined enemy.

Not since the sudden deaths of his parents had Thomas felt so miserable.

An officer, sensing the mood, called out, 'C'mon, Australia, are we downhearted?'

'No!' came the determined reply.

Thomas cheered along with the others, and no one spoke of

the symbolism of the *Triumph*'s destruction to the prospects of victory.

It began to rain, large heavy drops, and they inclined parched mouths to the grey heavens and sucked it up.

The next day, Thomas's regiment moved to Pope's Hill, a high, sharp ridge overlooking the Turkish trenches opposite Quinn's Post. The new position was close to a cemetery holding the remains of some of their comrades in C Squadron and a few Turks from the May 19 massacre. They felt good about their new digs, because they would be able to plug any Turk foolish enough to venture into no-man's-land.

'Keep your eyes peeled, lads,' Sergeant Brett advised the men. 'Fella told me a sniper did some good business at Walker's Ridge last week, a crack shot she was.'

The comment set off a barrage of good humour among the men, as the sergeant had hoped. 'Fella told me she hid in a little pine tree, like a bird roosting,' he continued. 'Naked she was, except for a coat of leaves to fool our chaps while potting them.'

'Naked?' said one young man, unable to believe his ears. 'Turks got naked lady snipers?'

'When one of our chaps gave her the knock, he found a dozen of our blokes' discs round her neck.'

'Ooh, Sarge, I don't like that one little bit,' said another youngster, clearly disturbed by the idea.

Not Kingy. 'Come hither, darling,' he said. 'This here's me rifle. I'll show ya mine if ya show me yours.'

'It's what I was told,' the sergeant said. 'Where there's one, there's more, boys, so be careful of the ladies, treat 'em with respect.'

Kingy said, 'Gawd, how am I gunna sleep tonight?'

'What utter bosh,' scoffed Teach. 'Sheer nonsense.'

'Oh, I rather like the idea,' Thomas said and he and Snow looked at each other and laughed.

The prospect of a female sniper was soon forgotten as shells began to explode above them, and shrapnel bullets peppered the ground, prompting a cry or a grunt of pain here and there.

Thomas huddled with Snow and Teach in their funk hole, leaving Kingy – who had gone to the latrine before the barrage had started – to find his own shelter. Thomas closed his eyes as they pulled their legs in tight behind the oilskin door, not particularly concerned about the steel hail outside.

The shelling stopped soon enough and Thomas opened his eyes. A finger of light streamed through a hole in the oilskin. Thomas pushed it aside to find stretcher-bearers outside attending to a dozen wounded men. He looked back to his mates to give the all clear.

Blood streamed down the side of Teach's arm. He was white-faced and hadn't made a sound.

Thomas screamed, 'Stretcher-bearer!'

Two burly men appeared with surprising speed. 'Make way!' said one, who thrust Thomas aside to examine Teach. A moment later the bearer shook his head. 'Scratch is all, nothing to it. Off ya go, ya can bloody walk.'

'Best be off then,' Teach said cheerfully and left for the aid post.

Thomas put his little finger through the small hole in the oilskin and shook his head. He fossicked around on the dugout floor for the piece of shrapnel, and was about to give up when a sliver of lead caught his eye.

It was wedged in the trench wall. 'Ah ha,' he announced, and dug it out with the tip of his bayonet. 'Souvenir for Teach.'

In the palm of Thomas's hand was a large slug, dented on one side.

'Big bugger,' Snow observed.

Kingy returned unscathed from the latrine shortly afterwards. 'As I always say, there's nuffin' like a bog in a barrage,' he pronounced, grinning. 'Nearly fell in, I was havin' so much fun.'

Even with Teach absent, the dugout was cramped, earthy and damp during a wet and miserable night. They awoke to mud and more bad news. The chaplain Sol Green had heard that a submarine had sunk the *Majestic* down south off Cape Helles.

Another battleship, another disaster, Thomas thought.

At the regimental aid post, they found Teach resting with a bandage around his arm.

Thomas handed him the slug. 'Souvy for you.'

Teach weighed the bullet in his palm. 'That can't be right,' he said and held it up to the light. 'But it's . . .'

'It's what it's *not*,' Thomas said. 'Not shrapnel, not from a Mauser, not a Lee-Enfield. Why, it's not even Abdul.'

'Strike me,' Kingy exclaimed.

Squadron Sergeant Major Brown confirmed their fears. 'Don't look like no machine gun slug. Revolver, I'd say.'

The veteran turned the bullet carefully in his hand and held it up to the light. 'Well, well,' he said, as his grey eyes lit up in surprise. 'Flat nose, hollow point, she's a mark three Man-stopper. Fits a .455 Webley. Seen plenty of 'em before, in the last war, coup de grâce for wounded Boers or prisoners who misbehaved. Puts a decent hole in ya, she does. Where'd ya find her?'

'Fell out of a Turk,' Thomas lied.

'Best keep mum, boys,' the sergeant major said with a wink. 'One of our blokes is playing naughty buggers. That bullet was banned during the last war . . . for being unsporting, if ya get my drift.'

Thomas and Snow sat on a beam over the latrine. The smell didn't faze them, not after the festering stink at Quinn's. They were alone in the shadow of sandbags that afforded some protection from the morning's snipers.

'One of ours,' Thomas sighed.

'Officer's pistol,' Snow said. 'They all have them, Kiwis, Pommies, machine gun crews.'

'But not with illegal ammo. Jesus, *unsporting*! You know what that means?'

'Dumdums.'

'Bad enough the Turks trying to knock us . . .'

'. . . without our own side doing it,' completed Snow.

'Whoever it was shot directly into our possy. That's hardly fog of war, not twice in a week. It was deliberate, timed during the barrage when no one would notice. I should tell Uncle Harry.'

'And say what? A mate was hit during a bombardment, a jam tin exploded during a bomb attack? He'll put it down to a mistake by a trigger-happy idiot. We got plenty of them, cobber. Worse – he'll think you're windy.'

'Why's it happening, Snow?'

'Bloody hell, Sherlock, why else? It's that document of yours. Someone wants it.'

'Who . . . Bulala, or this fella K, or someone else?'

'How the hell do I know?'

'I should burn it.'

'You should,' Snow agreed.

'I can't. You know why. How else will I find who murdered my father?'

Like fighting two wars at once, Thomas thought. And it wasn't just him being targeted. *That Boer bloody War.* What else could he do but talk to Uncle Harry about it?

Chapter 17

I N THE COOL OF THE night, a huge explosion shook the earth. Thomas's squadron was quickly ordered into the trenches, from which they looked down on Quinn's Post. A mine had detonated beneath part of the Anzac line, burying many Australians, and the Turks were rushing across no-man's-land to occupy the crater.

From Pope's Hill, Thomas's squadron and the regiment's machine guns fired into the dust and smoke, while their comrades in A Squadron and soldiers from the 13th and 15th Battalions rushed up to join the battle.

The darkness was broken by the flashes of countless Turkish cricket-ball bombs as attack and counter attack consumed the night until the Anzacs retook the position. When, finally, the sun rose on a chilly spring morning, scores of new bodies lay out in the open, and the major after whom Quinn's Post was named was dead.

When the news arrived that dozens of Turks had surrendered, Thomas and Snow were among those ordered to escort them to the stockade. Keen to catch an eyeful of Abdul, they hurried down the steps from Pope's to the Valley and fell in with stretcher-bearers carrying the wounded.

The bearers grunted as they slipped and stumbled with their canvas, each bump accompanied by a piteous groan or a scream. Thomas looked away from the bloodied bandages disguising missing feet or hands and other awful wounds.

And here too were Turks, men of all ages and boys, escorted downhill in single file. Thomas was moved to pity at the sight – most of them small, ragged and wretched, and from the fearful expressions on their faces anticipating a bayonet in the guts at any moment. Not at all what he had expected. He wondered how he might appear to them – probably much the same, only taller.

The Anzacs crowded around, curious about their enemy. Thomas and Snow fell in with them as they moved past a group of officers including Colonel Chauvel and Captains Herbert and Taylor.

Chauvel nodded affably to the passing prisoners. One Turk responded with a huge grin, relieved that he would not be killed after all, and seized the colonel by the hand, pumping it furiously.

Thomas watched as another Turk tried to kiss Uncle Harry, who deftly stepped back just in time to see the enemy plant kisses on both cheeks of the next officer in line.

Thomas laughed out loud, which brought a glance from the colonel. 'Something humorous, trooper?' Chauvel said sternly, though his eyes looked kind.

'No, sir.'

'Well, I suggest you go about your duty, which is . . .?'

'Escorting these birds to the cage, sir.'

'Captains Herbert and Taylor will be interrogating the prisoners, trooper. You will join them. Wait here. Captain Taylor wants a word with you.'

Thomas had a moment of panic. 'Yes, sir,' he stammered as Chauvel walked away.

Snow marched ahead with the line of prisoners. 'Don't do anything stupid to Taylor,' he whispered in a parting warning to Thomas.

At a signal from Taylor, Thomas joined him and Captain Herbert at the tail of the column of prisoners and guards heading down the twisty path to the beach. Thomas found himself behind the last guard and prisoner, a boy about his own age. The Turk smiled cheerfully back at him, glad to be out of it, only to receive a hurry-up in the back from the butt-end of his guard's rifle.

As they dashed between barricades, Thomas heard the soft *psff* of the bullet kiss his ear. 'Sniper!' he cried.

The shot caught the rearguard in the back of his head and he fell forward without a sound. The young Turkish captive jumped back against the sandbags, wide-eyed and desperate. Several times he reached behind as if his back were on fire. Thomas grasped him by the shoulders and turned him around. The Turk's uniform was pitted with jagged white pieces, like chips of quartz dipped in blood. For a moment, Thomas wondered if the Turks were using a new cartridge loaded with stone pellets. He grasped one of the bloody chips and pulled quickly and the Turk gave a sharp cry. In Thomas's fingers was a tooth once belonging to the guard.

One by one, he tugged out the teeth, while the young enemy grunted wordlessly. When he'd finished, Thomas handed one to the boy as a souvenir and placed the rest in the dead guard's tunic pocket.

'You're quite the dentist,' Captain Taylor said coolly, and smirked as the prisoner looked with horror at the tooth in his hand. 'Poor bastard wonders who's going to finish him first, his own side or us.' Taylor pointed his revolver at the Turk and growled.

'No need for that, captain,' said Aubrey Herbert, impeccably aristocratic despite squatting in the dirt.

'We'll see,' Taylor said. 'He may make a run for it still, or invite Abdul to take another pot shot at us.'

'I hardly think Abdul needs an invitation,' scoffed Herbert, but he said a few soothing words in Turkish to the prisoner. 'Told him you wouldn't shoot him, but the sniper might if he moved an inch.'

Taylor noticed Thomas looking at his revolver. 'Lovely weapon. I've had it forever.'

'Sir?'

'Since South Africa.'

'They have new cartridges for it now, don't they, sir?'

Taylor appeared surprised. 'They do indeed.'

'Because earlier rounds were judged unsportsmanlike, isn't that so, sir?'

'Now is not the time for idle chatter,' Herbert interrupted.

Taylor ignored him and addressed Thomas. 'You are referring to Manstoppers, very efficient hollow points. Shame our right honourable politicians didn't have the ticker for them. Eh, Herbert?'

'They were hardly civilised, Taylor.'

'War is hardly civil.'

'There are rules.'

'There's only one rule in war – Rule 303. Harry Morant was quite correct on that score.' Taylor's smile hardened and grew nasty.

It turned Thomas's blood cold. 'The Turk, should we get rid of him now, sir?' Thomas asked Taylor.

'Why on earth would you ask that?' said Captain Herbert.

'Oh, it might be convenient.' Thomas looked at Taylor. 'TNP and all that?'

Taylor smiled. 'What on earth are you blathering on about, trooper?'

'Take no prisoners, Captain Bulala, sir. Isn't that what you used to do?'

Taylor laughed without mirth. 'Now that is downright impertinent.'

'Have a care, Thomas,' Captain Herbert said evenly. 'This Turk is my captive and I intend to interrogate him. Furthermore, he is entitled to proper treatment . . .'

'Do shut up, Herbert,' Taylor snapped, then addressed himself to Thomas. 'You're the one with the rifle.'

'We don't shoot prisoners, do we, sir?' Thomas said. He stared for a long moment at Captain Taylor. Could this be the man who killed his father? Did he throw the jam tin at Quinn's Post and fire the bullet that wounded Teach?

Thomas jerked his head towards the sniper in the heights. 'Better to scupper the body-snatcher, wouldn't you agree, captain?'

'Well, get on with it.'

Thomas checked the magazine and palmed a round into the breech. He would show Taylor he was not to be trifled with.

Beside the sandbags was one of the new periscopes. The sniper would be hidden in the scrub, Thomas thought, with his Mauser trained on the next gap they would have to pass. He carefully raised the periscope, an inch every few seconds, so slowly he hoped it would not draw the Turk's attention. When it was above the sandbags, he looked into its lower lens, and swivelled it to scan the terrain. As he did so, he caught sight of a muzzle flash, and the periscope flew out of his hands.

It was enough.

Thomas took up his rifle and calmly adjusted the sights. In a smooth movement, he brought the gun to his shoulder, felt it nestle comfortably against his cheek, as familiar as home, and his father's words came back to him. 'It's the rifle and not the drill that makes the soldier, Conan Doyle once told me. Give an Australian a rifle, son, and he's the best in the world.'

'Captain, if you please?' Thomas gave quick instructions to Taylor, who gathered up the guard's rifle and peaked cap. At a signal from Thomas, Taylor balanced the hat on the end of the rifle and proceeded to walk down the line of sandbags away from Thomas. At the end of the sandbags Taylor stopped, but moved the rifle and hat as if its wearer was about to jump the next gap in the barricade.

Thomas rose quickly and sighted as the Turk fired and the hat went flying. Two hundred yards away, he caught a speck of flashing light in an otherwise featureless terrain. He fired once and ducked down.

'Now,' he said, 'to test my marksmanship.'

Thomas took his rifle, put his own hat on the end of the barrel, and tried the same trick at the other end of the sandbags. This time there was no shot from the sniper. 'Either I got him,' Thomas said proudly, 'or Johnny's trickier than I thought.'

'Only one way to find out,' said Taylor with a malicious grin. He waved his revolver at the prisoner, a clear order for him to walk across the gap in the sandbags.

Herbert was about to object, but Taylor forestalled him. 'By all means lead, captain, if you are so sure that young Thomas has silenced our sniper friend.'

Herbert snapped, 'Go to hell, Taylor, and stay there!' In the next moment, the half-blind captain had jumped to his feet and plunged across the gap in the prisoner's place.

No shot rang out.

Taylor pointed his revolver at the prisoner. '*Imshi*,' he ordered in Anzac slang with a knowing wink at Thomas. The Turk got the message and followed Herbert safely across.

'Did you want to speak to me about something, sir?'

'No, I have my answer.' And Taylor smirked as if it were all a joke.

Not long afterwards, Thomas was ordered to present himself at the brigade commander's dugout. It was a room carved into the hillside, sheathed in sandbags, while inside heavy wooden beams supported the ceiling.

As he entered, he found Chauvel seated on an upturned ammo box. The colonel was dressed impeccably in a tailored jacket with polished Sam Browne leather and brass belt, diagonal shoulder strap and knee-length boots. By comparison, Thomas felt ragged in his stained tunic and torn trousers, but Chauvel didn't seem to notice. He invited the boy to sit and served tea, biscuits and proper jam with the manners of an English gentleman.

'I've not seen you since Egypt, Thomas. You've shot up fast,' he said. 'Our hardtack must agree with you.'

'Hardly, sir, though I am partial to apricot flybog. You look fighting fit.'

Uncle Harry chuckled. 'These hills and gullies keep an old man trim. My belt's back to its old hole. I'm told the Turkish newspapers call us the "white cannibals". Have you been feasting on the odd Turk or two, my boy?'

'Can't tell what's under the flies, sir.'

They laughed together easily and stopped only when half a dozen bullets smacked into the sandbags protecting the opening.

'My God, the Turk can shoot,' Chauvel sighed. 'He's made

rabbits of us. Our writerly friend Charles Bean says we live in a cross between a cave and a grave.'

Thomas was surprised that Chauvel appeared downhearted. 'They can't beat us, sir.'

The colonel changed the subject. 'Aubrey speaks well of you.'

'Aubrey?'

'Captain Herbert, General Godley's interpreter. He tells me you traded shots with a sniper, saved his life and Captain Taylor's.'

'Got the bastard, sir.'

'Excellent. Just like your father.'

Thomas puffed out his chest. 'How did he do that, sir, save your life I mean?'

'Jack didn't tell you? No, of course he didn't. Your father was not one to boast. We were in the Queensland Mounted in the Transvaal. I was a company commander, and Jack was a young fellow not much older than you. We'd dusted Johnny Boer up a bit at Nooitgedacht, a poisonous place if ever there was one, and the *bittereinders* dearly wanted to get back at us. Although there was this pretty little Dutch girl . . .'

Chauvel stopped for a moment and smiled vacantly at a memory.

'Sir?' asked Thomas.

'Yes, well, as I was saying, one night in camp, awful jumpy we were. Everyone had turned in, and I was in my easy chair as it happened, playing the harmonium. I was fired on, missed me by a whisker. Jack shot them, one, two, three, nice as you like before they could blink. Had it been anyone else but him on sentry duty, I wouldn't be here today . . .'

Chauvel hesitated. '. . . Wouldn't be on Gallipoli,' he added with a quiet smile. 'Did you know, Thomas, that the first Australian troopers to fall overseas were Queenslanders shot by snipers.

Vic Jones and Dave McLeod on New Year's Day, 1900, at Sunny-side, poor fellows. I was their commander and I'll never forget it. Later we trapped the Boers and they fired a few shots after they put up the white flag. I had the devil of a time preventing our fellows from bayoneting them.'

Thomas jumped in. 'So, you wouldn't execute prisoners, sir?'

'Of course not. That's murder, plain and simple.'

'Glad to hear it, sir.'

'Mind you, the Kaiser might.'

'Might what, sir?'

'Execute prisoners. While we were wrestling the Boer, Kaiser Wilhelm sent troops against the Boxers in China by invoking the spirit of Attila the Hun. Told his men, "No quarter will be given, no prisoners will be taken."'

'Goodness!' Thomas cried, taken aback. There it was again, *TNP*.

'Indeed, though I imagine he regrets it now, particularly since we make free use of it in our public pronouncements.'

'Sir?'

'The "*diabolical Hun*". Our propaganda against German barbarism . . . Huns raping women, bayoneting babies, murdering prisoners, that sort of thing.'

'What happened, sir, in China?'

'The Germans did as the Kaiser ordered, of course. Mind you, so did the Russians and the French.' Chauvel coughed. 'Now, enough of that. To matters at hand. Snipers – they're killing the best of us here, stretcher-bearers, water-carriers, generals like Bridges. Even Birdwood was hit.'

The colonel paused, his natural reserve surfacing, cautious about revealing too much. General Birdwood, the Anzac commander, had been looking through a periscope at Quinn's when a sniper's bullet had shattered the device and sent metal fragments into his skull. Rather than damaging morale among the men, Birdwood's standing had increased.

'The general recovered, of course, and was quite complimentary of the Turk,' chuckled Chauvel. 'Birdie fancies himself a good shot, claims he did some real sniping for grouse in India with K and the Maharaja of Bikanir back in o-six.'

Thomas gasped. K. Who the devil was he?

Before he could ask, the colonel ploughed on, 'Must stop these troublesome Turks if we're to control our supply routes. Which is why I have approved the formation of a squad of marksmen. I want you to be one of them. Fight fire with fire, so to speak.'

'Me a sniper!' Thomas was horrified. 'Sir, I should be with my cobbers, not sneaking around and hiding in some hole.'

'A hole is the best place when all hell breaks loose.'

'Yes, sir, in it with my mates.'

'You will be protecting your mates, son.'

'But, sir . . .?'

Chauvel put up his hand. 'Sniping's a dangerous job, but you have shown you are a crack shot. You have a talent for the job. Like father like son, eh?'

Thomas's shoulders slumped in defeat.

'Now, none of that, lad. You may choose a spotter from among your comrades. What about that young fellow you mentioned, the son of the tracker? Snow, yes, that was it. I imagine he will be most useful.'

Thomas knew an order when he heard one. 'Yes, sir.'

The colonel got up and walked over to his desk. 'Was there something else, Thomas?'

'Sir, you were with my father in South Africa, as was Captain Taylor, who goes by the nickname Bulala. I've since discovered that the word means killer. Who did he kill?'

'Who on earth told you that?'

'Captain Herbert, sir.'

'Yes, well, Aubrey was quite correct. The Zulus had some experience of Taylor. I imagine the name described his exploits in Rhodesia before the Boer hostilities. Later, he was court-martialled along with some officers in the BVC, the Bushveldt Carbineers. That said, I have no misgivings as to his loyalty to King and country.'

Thomas hesitated. The document was inside his tunic. Should he show it to Uncle Harry? Some instinct caused him to keep it to himself. 'Why were they prosecuted, sir?'

'They shot a number of Boer prisoners and civilians. Morant and Handcock were executed, Witton was gaoled, Taylor was acquitted.'

'Was my father involved, sir?'

Chauvel took a deep breath. 'Your father was a good man, too good for that bunch of scallywags. Jack was among those who informed on his officers. Why do you ask?'

Thomas gasped. Had his father betrayed his comrades? It didn't seem possible. He blurted out, 'Could there have been a connection to my father's death, sir?'

'What are you suggesting?'

Murder! Thomas wanted to shout. But again, a niggling doubt kept him from speaking his mind. 'Just trying to understand it.'

Chauvel sighed. 'Jack testified that Morant ordered the death of the missionary Hesse and a number of Boers. But there were other incidents, including one in which Jack and his comrades fired on a wagonload of Boers coming in to surrender. They stopped when they heard the screams of women and children and the pleas of the men. Your father admitted to me much later that he disobeyed orders to finish them off.'

'Sir, wouldn't he have been arrested for not following orders?'

'He fired to miss. That was his way of dealing with such atrocious orders.'

'From Morant and Bulala?'

'It was said Taylor was the true commander of the BVC. At the time, he was Lord K's intelligence officer . . . all most unfortunate.'

K.

Thomas jerked as if he had been shot. *Of course.* How stupid of him. It was so obvious, why hadn't he realised?

Kitchener's initial in the margin. The general's personal order to *Bulala*, his man. Captain Taylor. *TNP* – take no prisoners.

'What's on your mind, Thomas?'

'Sir, would a general ever write to a captain?'

'What do you mean?'

'A handwritten note?'

'Most unlikely.'

'And what about a personal order to a captain?'

'Again, unlikely. As you know, there's a chain of command. A general has an aide to take care of such things.'

Thomas decided that Uncle Harry didn't know about the document. But why hadn't his father told Chauvel, his old comrade?

The colonel sighed. Clearly he wanted to bring the discussion to an end. 'Anything else, Thomas?'

'Sir, what part did Lord K play in the Morant case?'

Chauvel furrowed his brow as he looked carefully at Thomas. 'Nothing, as far as I know,' he said evenly. 'Morant and the others claimed they'd received direct orders from HQ, but nothing was ever proved. As commander-in-chief, Lord K could have commuted their sentences of death, but he didn't. Some claimed he was anti-Australian, which was not true. I accompanied the field marshal on his visit to Australia some years back, and I found him a good soldier, though a tough bastard.'

Evidently, Uncle Harry admired Kitchener. Even 'Birdie', the Anzac commander, went hunting with K. And now his intelligence agent Taylor was here. Thomas was surrounded by K's men. He felt his throat constrict, but managed to ask, 'Did my father testify against Captain Taylor, sir?'

'I believe he did, yes.'

Thomas found himself taking sharp little breaths.

'Are you well, lad?' Chauvel said.

Thomas shook himself. 'Did my mother know?'

'Like most of us, Jack kept the war close to his chest. Nor did he wish to burden Rose.'

'Yes, sir.'

'With a comrade, he might talk over a drink or two. Your father was bitter and regretful – about his own testimony against friends, about Lord K's refusal to show mercy to Morant and Handcock, about Taylor's acquittal. It played on his mind. I suspect it contributed . . . at the end.'

It certainly did, Thomas wanted to shout, *but not in the way you think*. He might have pulled the document out of his pocket there and then, had it not been for Chauvel's admiration of Kitchener.

In any case, the colonel clearly had other matters on his mind. 'It was a tragedy for you, and my loss of a particular friend and comrade. But that is in the past, Thomas. You have a life to live and death is all about. We must defeat the Turk and save as many Anzacs as we can. That's where you come in, my boy. Are you able to do what's best for your King, your country and for your comrades?'

Thomas stood up. 'Yes, sir. I shall become the best sniper in the Light Horse.'

'You will indeed,' smiled Chauvel. He selected a note from among several on his desk and handed it to Thomas. 'Take this to Lieutenant Grace of the Wellingtons. Good luck, lance corporal.'

'Sir?'

'A promotion, Thomas. Congratulations. I remember how marvellous it felt twenty-five years ago when I got my first stripe.'

'Thank you, sir.' Thomas beamed and saluted and went off to find the Kiwi officer, Grace.

As he left Chauvel's dugout, Thomas recalled the colonel's words, *You have a life to live and death is all about.*

Of course, it could have been wise counsel from an affectionate uncle or a call to arms from his commander. Or something else entirely.

The end of May saw another welcome delivery of mail to the trenches. Among the letters for Thomas (most were from Winnie) was a plain package, postmarked Brisbane. Inside was a dull cloth-covered book, entitled *Scapegoats of the Empire* by a Lieutenant George R. Witton, accompanied by a letter from Ellen Woods.

'Doctor Woods has gone,' Thomas announced aloud. 'They wouldn't let her join the army, so she's sailed for England. She's going to treat the wounded in France!'

'War is no place for a woman,' Teach said.

'Oh, to be sliced, diced and stitched by the fair Ellen,' grinned Kingy.

Thomas ignored him. 'She says, "I shall be like Harry Houdini and escape the straitjacket of my gender."'

'What does that mean?' said Snow.

'How should I know? But we need more good doctors if we're to defeat Fritz and Abdul.'

It was a long letter and he read the rest silently:

Thomas, I too have been playing at Sherlock. Upon consulting back copies of newspapers in the Brisbane library I chanced upon the name of George Witton, a lieutenant in the Bushveldt Carbineers when your father was in South Africa. Like Morant and Handcock, Witton was sentenced to death, but unlike them was reprieved by Lord Kitchener. He spent several years in gaol in England but was released after protests from Australia.

By a stroke of luck, I discovered that he owned a farm in the Burnett. Recently I visited him and found him and his wife Mary a most charming couple and quite popular in the district. Despite his military experience, Witton is bitter about this war and has refused to put his hand up. He was good enough to give me a copy of his book. Take particular care of it, Thomas, for Witton told me that the government tried to suppress its publication and that most copies were destroyed in a quite suspicious fire at his publisher's warehouse. He was shocked to hear of Captain Taylor's visit to Murgon.

Upon reading the book, I have learnt that it was Taylor who ordered him, Morant and Handcock to take no prisoners, yet somehow managed to be acquitted himself. Witton's account reflects poorly on Lord Kitchener, as you shall see. Nevertheless, for all his fine words and softly spoken ways, Witton was hardly an innocent. If I were you, Thomas, I should take what he says with a grain of salt.

What all of this has to do with your father's murder I cannot imagine, except to say: be careful. You are very young to be playing at the detective and there are others far shrewder and more dangerous in the game. You may have enemies more treacherous than the Hun and Turk.

Thomas opened the book and began to read hungrily.

WOLVES

Monash Valley, June 1915

'We must fall back upon the old axiom that when all other
contingencies fail, whatever remains, however improbable,
must be the truth.'

– 'The Adventure of the Bruce-Partington Plans',
Arthur Conan Doyle, 1912

Chapter 18

FOR THE FIRST TIME, THOMAS felt the morning's hint of warmth. Faint touches of sun caressed the line of his back, buttocks and legs, a delicious feeling that promised to banish the night's chill. It wouldn't last, of course, for June was turning hotter than a Queensland January. By noon the sun would sear the skin and dull the senses, and his mouth would be as dry as dust. The greybacks would bite and the big black blowies would tempt him to swat when any such move might give the game away. Thomas consoled himself with the certainty that Johnny Turk would suffer too.

He and Snow were settled into a snug spot above Monash Valley. In the darkness they had crept among the gorse and thyme and worked for several hours with spade and stone to build a hide, one that was close enough to a sap should they require a rapid exit.

No Anzacs were allowed anywhere near the boys, on orders from the sergeant. Their comrades had moved away without complaint, lest they draw unwanted attention to the boys who would otherwise eliminate the feared and loathed enemy sniper.

'Ya just wave, lads,' Sergeant Lucky Les had said. 'We'll make a right fuss, have Abdul waste a shot and show 'imself so ya can pot 'im.'

Thomas lay on his stomach with his eyes closed, forehead resting on his arm, hands on the rifle. Beside him, Snow peered through the brass telescope trained on a patch of scrub at the head of the Valley.

Until a Turk revealed himself, Thomas would stay motionless for several more hours. The gathering warmth was making him sleepy. He was also exhausted – they all were – after weeks of hard slog and constant tension, awful grub and interrupted sleep.

'Hey, slacker,' Snow hissed him gently awake, 'Abdul.'

Thomas gritted his teeth and strained his muscles to wake himself without moving. He peered along the barrel, saw nothing.

Like them, the Turk had been in his foxhole for hours, hungry for a target. Abdul had the advantage of dawn when a wash of light at his back crept above the hills to paint the invaders. Some mornings, twenty or thirty Anzacs were lit up in their little patch of Turkey and cut down.

Thomas's job was to wipe out Abdul first. It was not an easy thing to shoot into the sun, when the Turk could see him better, at least until noon when the sun evened the odds. In the afternoon, the advantage switched as the rays slanted eastwards over the Aegean into the eyes of the Turk.

So damned hot, he thought. He wondered how Uncle Harry was faring. Thomas had heard that the colonel had been evacuated, probably to a hospital on one of the Greek islands or, if he was lucky, to Alexandria or Cairo. Pleurisy, they'd said.

Thomas had written to Winnie, 'I swear the flies follow me around. You wouldn't come within a bull's roar of me, I can tell you!' He'd added, 'Snipers have hit some of our officers and a dozen or so of the men.' Then he had scrubbed the line out, before the censor did it for him.

By mid-June the Light Horse been five weeks on Gallipoli.

He had written to Ellen, 'Our regiment is in a gully between one hill and another, not far from Quinn's which is the hottest of all. We're a bit stuck now, but it won't be long before we advance again.' He had scrubbed that out too.

Neither moved. Nor spoke. Be quiet, hear more, Lieutenant Grace had said. Not that they needed to be told. The Turk was as attentive to noise as they were. The rifles were loaded, each round wiped clean as a whistle. Once Snow found him a target, Thomas could fire.

'Abdul,' Snow whispered again.

'Get rid of that,' the Kiwi subaltern had said a week earlier, pointing to Thomas's wrist. 'The glint in the sun will give you away quick smart.'

Reluctantly, Thomas unbuckled his father's watch and put it in his pocket.

'Place your cartridges beneath you, hide your ugly moosh, cover your arms,' continued Hami Grace, addressing the group of sharpshooters. 'Pick a good pot-hole, make yourself invisible. Use the land. Disappear into the earth – or Jacko will do it for you.'

Second Lieutenant Grace had heavy eyebrows, prominent ears and a squashed rugby nose in an open brown face. They called him 'the sniping king'. Thomas and Snow were among the thirty riflemen he had selected, all of whom were sitting around a fire over which a large billy of tea was brewing in a rest gully off Monash Valley.

Grace nodded at Snow. 'Whoever has Snow beside him is lucky indeed. Unlike you lily-whites, he's harder to spot. I imagine he has the eyes of a hawk, the ears of a cat and the patience of a tiger. Would that be correct, trooper?'

'No tigers where I come from, sir,' Snow beamed. He was in awe of Hami Grace, who was a Maori and reputed to be the son of a warrior chief. They all knew that the Wellington Battalion had awarded him a field commission on account of his pluck and skill at potting Turks.

'Make no mistake – Abdul can shoot,' the young lieutenant said. 'The Turk doesn't care that you can put down a charging boar in Kaweka or a roo on the hop in Goondiwindi. He doesn't care that you can shoot the eye off a blowfly at a mile. Your quarry shoots back and he will hit you if he *sees* you.'

Grace let that sink in. He peered into the billy and checked the contents. He put a few small pieces of wood into the fire and slowly stoked the blaze. No one said a word.

The officer turned back to them. 'You take your time. You watch, listen, be silent. You make no sudden moves. You become invisible. Do that and you might live to kill more Turks.'

Hami Grace began to allocate teams of snipers, one man to observe, the other to shoot, and to swap roles every so often. When he came to Thomas and Snow he said, 'You two together?'

'Yes, sir,' both said.

Thomas and Snow were the youngest in a hard bunch serious about their shooting, no mucking about, single-minded about killing Turks for reasons none spoke of. Among them were the Kiwi quartermaster sergeant Charlie Swinard, who stalked deer in the South Island; the soft-voiced traveller, rabbit poisoner and miner Jack Idriess from Sydney; and a half-Chinese horse driver with a jet-black moustache, Billy Sing from Queensland.

Sing looked the two boys up and down with amusement. 'Bit young for the sniping game, ain't you? Where from, lads?'

'Murgon,' Thomas said. 'Used to pot wallabies there, scrub turkeys, plenty of rabbits.'

'Me too, in Clermont,' Sing said agreeably enough, then narrowed his eyes. 'But this ain't like home, boy. These bunnies shoot back.'

Thomas felt everyone's eyes upon him. He remembered something Uncle Harry had told him. 'First Aussie killed by a sniper was from Clermont,' Thomas said. 'He was with Colonel Chauvel in South Africa when he got knocked.'

Brown eyes flashed hawklike in Sing's quick grin. 'Yeah, Vic Jones, at Sunnyside. Time to get even, eh?'

'Knocking off Johnny Turk to pay back Johnny Boer? Can't see the connection myself,' Thomas said.

Sing gave Thomas a friendly slap on the back. 'It's simple, you put the poor cuss out of his misery. You shoot, you kill the bastard, you take the money.'

Thomas repressed a shiver. Something about Billy Sing reminded him of Bulala Taylor. He exchanged a look with Snow, who replied with a raised eyebrow.

The next day, Billy Sing brought his commanding officer over to meet the new group of snipers. This was Stephen Midgley, 'the Old Bird'. Major Midgley was something of a legend in the Light Horse. He had won a DSO against the Boers, and in subsequent campaigns he had been wounded by a Zulu spear in the buttocks and bitten by a black mamba. Both incidents sparked equal amounts of amusement and awe among his men.

But it was Midgley's service with the Bushveldt Carbineers that interested Thomas. He tried hard to hide his surprise when the Old Bird was introduced to the group. For Midgley was indeed birdlike – a skinny Queenslander in his forties, narrow across the shoulders, small compared to most Anzacs. He was dressed in a knockabout, mismatched combination of tunic and trousers, his sleeves rolled up past the elbow, his hat inclined at a rakish angle, and – most impressive of all – a revolver hung on an ammo belt around his waist like some Wild West shootist. Major Midgley was like no officer Thomas had ever encountered, but his casual bearing, without an ounce of stuffiness, told Thomas that he was every inch a natural born leader.

The reason for the major's visit soon became clear. Like a coach encouraging his fighter before a bout, Midgley fired up the group. 'Your job is to knock out snipers, not once, not twice, but every day until they are no longer a threat,' he said. 'Rid the Valley of them, lads, for everyone's sake.'

The men didn't need much convincing. All knew someone hit by a shot from the heights and they gave Midgley a lively three cheers.

When Lieutenant Grace brought the Old Bird over to speak to each of the snipers in turn, Billy Sing piped up, 'Tom's father was in South Africa with you, sir.'

Midgley merely grunted.

'My father was Jack Clare, sir.'

'Was he now?' said Major Midgley with sudden interest. 'And how is Jack?'

'Gone last August, sir.'

Midgley narrowed his eyes.

'Tortured, hanged and decapitated, sir, and made to look like a suicide.'

'Well, tiddly om pom,' Midgley said quietly through clenched teeth.

An odd expression, Thomas thought. 'Did you hear what I said, sir?'

'I did, corporal. Jack was a good man. You have my sincere condolences.'

'You don't sound surprised, sir.' The words came out almost like an accusation and Thomas instantly regretted it.

Midgley looked hard at him. 'Jack had enemies, as do we all.'

Thomas decided to go a step further, since Midgley appeared to be the sort to appreciate frankness. 'I believe he was murdered because he testified against members of the BVC in South Africa, sir.'

'Ah, yes, the courts-martial resulting in the execution of Morant and Handcock.' Midgley nodded sagely, before turning to Billy Sing and Snow who had listened to the conversation so far in surprised silence. 'Carry on, you two. I'm sure there is a great deal more that Lieutenant Grace can teach you about potting Turks.'

'Yes, sir,' Billy and Snow said together and left to join the others.

Midgley said quietly, 'Sit, son,' and squatted down in the dirt beside Thomas. 'All right, proceed!'

Thomas took a deep breath. He had a good feeling about Midgley, who was neither distinguished like Herbert nor sly like Taylor. He was a Queenslander: direct, solid and, Thomas felt, trustworthy. The words came out fast and desperate. He told Midgley about the tracks left behind by the killers in Murgon and the tree markings and Taylor's visit, but he left out the part about the document with the TNP note to Bulala. Kitchener was Midgley's commander-in-chief, whom he was sworn to obey.

'Do you know who might have wanted to harm him, sir? I've spoken to Colonel Chauvel, to Captain Herbert, to Captain Taylor.'

'Quite the detective, I see.'

'Thank you, sir.'

'You're aware that Colonel Chauvel wasn't with us in the Bushveldt Carbineers?'

'Yes, sir. My father served with him before joining the BVC.'

'And Aubrey Herbert, what of his view?'

'He said British officers shouldn't go round killing prisoners willy-nilly, and that the firing squad was a fitting end for them.'

Midgley smiled. 'That's a tad harsh, wouldn't you say?'

'I wasn't there, sir. Colonel Chauvel said some of my father's comrades viewed his testimony as a betrayal.'

'Are you suggesting *they* murdered Jack?'

'I don't know, sir.'

'Testimony given twelve years earlier . . . a rather long time to wait for revenge, wouldn't you agree?'

'Yes, sir, but why else would Captain Taylor turn up in Murgon?'

'I have no idea. Why don't you ask him? Bulala is the War Secretary's eyes and ears, no doubt here to check up on us.' Midgley tapped the side of his nose. 'Military Intelligence.'

'I potted a sniper who'd nearly got him.'

'Shame,' Midgley said under his breath.

'What, sir?'

Midgley ignored Thomas's question. 'What was the good Captain Taylor's opinion of your suspicions regarding Jack's death?'

'Only that they were comrades in arms. That they didn't always see eye to eye. That my dad was a fine soldier, but had his demons, and that it's important not to lose one's head.'

'Taylor said that – "It's important not to lose one's head"?'

'Yes, sir.'

The major was silent for a few moments. Thomas wondered whether he had misjudged him. Maybe he wouldn't help at all.

But Midgley resumed, 'Let me just say that when the BVC murders occurred I was away on detached duty elsewhere in South Africa. By the time I returned, Lieutenants Morant and

Handcock, Captain Taylor and the others were already under close arrest. In point of fact, HQ made me responsible for Morant as he awaited the court's verdict. Certain officers, I won't say which, asked me to tell Morant that they had a horse standing by so he could escape to Portuguese East Africa. I didn't much like Morant, not one iota – he was a scoundrel – but to his credit he refused the offer, said the British would not dare shoot him.'

'He was wrong about that,' Thomas pointed out.

'About a lot of things,' Midgley agreed. 'And you wonder what this had to do with your father, correct?'

'Yes, sir.'

The major paused to extract a small piece of black felt in the shape of a cat from inside his tunic. 'Silly thing, this,' he said, stroking it. 'Middle of the night some years ago, a black cat jumped on my chest, gave me one hell of a fright, woke me just in time. The Zulus had the place surrounded, you see, and we were able to fight them off.'

'So it's a lucky charm, sir?'

'Indeed, so far,' Midgley chuckled. 'Your father was lucky to escape South Africa alive. I knew him, not well mind you, but enough to know why he testified against his officers.' He hesitated, as if contemplating how to explain a complex situation. 'Would you say he was a good cop?'

'Of course, sir. Never heard anyone say otherwise.'

'If I remember correctly, Jack joined the BVC about the same time as Morant and Percy Hunt. Before that, the Carbineers were notorious for being a band of drunks, thieves and scally-wags. They stole from the army and the Boer farms. They looted alcohol, horses and cattle, and outraged the womenfolk, and Taylor was among the worst for cattle duffing. The BVC was verging on mutiny when Captain Hunt and Morant cracked down hard, with the support of men like Jack. They packed

many of the scoundrels off to Pietersburg. Not Taylor, of course –
he was too shrewd, too well connected.'

'My dad helped the Breaker?'

'Yes.'

'So, why did he turn against him?'

'Well, you must understand that everything changed when
Percy Hunt – Morant's great chum – was shot by the Boers.'

'But that's war,' interrupted Thomas.

'What upset Morant was that Captain Hunt had been
mutilated.'

'How, sir?'

'Hunt's neck was broken and there were boot marks on his
face.'

Thomas flinched as if struck. *My father, neck broken, decapitated, those cuts to his cheek.*

'Gruesome indeed,' said Midgley. 'Most likely the handiwork
of a Boer commando wearing boots stolen from some poor
Tommy.'

'But – but –' stammered Thomas, his thoughts whirling.
Tortured and killed like Percy Hunt, Morant's best mate.

Midgley continued, 'Morant simply fell to pieces, ordered
the deaths of Boer prisoners and unarmed civilians, particularly
those caught in stolen British khaki . . . went on a killing spree.
And Jack Clare, being a copper before the war, refused to turn
a blind eye. He and a number of comrades from Fort Edward
wrote a letter to HQ with details of what they had witnessed,
twenty or more shootings by Morant and the others. But your
father went further.'

Thomas took a deep breath. 'How, sir?'

'In the courts-martial that followed he turned King's evidence.
He blew the whistle on just about everyone, on officers, on
NCOs and lower ranks who'd behaved badly, even some of

those who'd co-signed the letter with him, accusing them of seeking revenge on Morant.'

'He made enemies on both sides,' Thomas muttered.

'Both tried to kill him.'

Thomas opened his eyes wide in surprise.

Midgley continued with a chuckle, 'Didn't tell you, eh?'

'Not a thing.'

The major patted the revolver on his hip. 'Oh, it was the wild west then. They murdered the Dutchman Van Buuren, one of the Boers who joined the BVC. Handcock put three bullets in his back. Your father witnessed it and described it for the courts-martial, and for that they shot at him later. Missed.'

'And Taylor?'

Midgley took a deep breath. 'Bulala had a reputation going back many years for bribery, theft, intimidation and murder. They said he liked to shoot at the blacks just to see them jump. Jack testified that Taylor effectively commanded the BVC, that he ordered troopers to kill unarmed Boers, to give no quarter, all the while claiming such orders came from Lord K.'

'And did they come from Lord K?'

'Ah, well, there you have it.'

'Lieutenant Witton thought so,' Thomas said. 'I have his *Scapegoats* book. He said HQ told officers, "No quarter, no prisoners".'

'Of course George Witton would say that, wouldn't he? He was gaoled for murder, after all.' Midgley shrugged his small shoulders. 'Lord K was pitiless. He implemented the scorched earth policy, burnt the farms and threw hundreds of thousands of Boer and black women and children into his terrible camps. He ordered Boers found in British khaki to be court-martialled. Anything to defeat the *bittereinders*. But did he sanction indiscriminate murder? His military secretary, Colonel Hamilton, denied it. Taylor denied it, but he was K's agent, and who could believe him?' Midgley exhaled loudly. 'Personally, I don't believe K ordered anything of the sort. It would be contrary to the rules of civilised warfare and plain barmy to boot.'

'Sir, what if my father had a document from HQ, with a note addressed to Bulala with the letters TNP and signed K?'

Midgley raised an eyebrow. 'TNP?'

'I believe it's Lord K's personal order to Captain Taylor. I think Taylor knows I have it now, but I have no intention of giving it to him. Not until I find out whether the document is the key to my father's murder and whether Taylor had a hand in it.'

'Ah, revenge, is it?' Midgley regarded Thomas closely. 'Morant sought to avenge his friend Captain Hunt and was executed for doing so. I hope you're not planning something similar, because if you do I will put you up against a wall and shoot you myself.'

'Not revenge, sir. Justice.'

Midgley sighed. 'And where is this document of yours?'

'With my kit,' Thomas said.

'Then I should very much like to see it,' said the Old Bird.

Chapter 19

THEY RETURNED TO FIND KINGY sharpening his bayonet. 'Ya cagey idlers! Leaving us to dig shitholes, breaking our backs, and the flamin' sergeant breathing down our necks.'

'*Protecting* you good-for-nothings,' Snow said. 'While you sissies stay warm and cosy in your holes, we'll be in no-man's-land looking for Abdul to snotter him good.'

'Pig's arse!' said Kingy. 'Doing bugger-all more likely, one hand swatting flies, the other on ya old fella.'

'We'll give Johnny a right bloody nose,' Thomas promised seriously.

'Better to jab him in the guts with cold steel,' Kingy said.

'I'll have you know that one of our greatest kings, Richard the Lionheart, died at the hands of a sniper,' Teach said.

''Ere we go again, another sermon,' Kingy groaned.

Teach ignored him. 'A boy fired a crossbow bolt from a castle wall in France, claimed Richard had killed his father and brothers, changed the course of history.'

Thomas asked, 'What happened to the boy?'

'He was captured, but, as the King lay dying, he pardoned the lad, sent him off with a hundred shillings in his kick, or so the story goes. Mind you, Richard died soon after and one of his officers had the young fellow flayed alive and hanged.'

'There ya go, boys, see what happens to the sniper who gets caught,' commented Kingy. 'Hardly seems fair.'

'There's a moral in it for us,' Thomas said cheerfully. 'After we skittle the Sultan, we'd better . . .'

'. . . scarper the hell away,' said Snow, and they laughed together.

'Indeed,' Teach said. 'All hail our gallant heroes who sally forth bravely onto the field of combat!'

'Sword for sword, my Lee-Enfield against his Mauser,' Thomas said.

'You're a better man than I am, Gunga Din,' Kingy said, picking his teeth with a shell splinter.

Teach shook his head in admiration. 'You do surprise me, trooper King.'

'Ya ain't the only sod what can read,' Kingy said.

From his kitbag, Thomas pulled out the document and passed it to Teach. 'Hang on to this while I'm away, will you?'

Surprised, Teach said, 'Are you sure you want me to look after it?'

'Taylor may find some excuse to search my kit. He won't look in yours.'

Then the boys whooped at their good fortune and set off down the gully to meet the Sniper King. In the small hours of the next morning Lieutenant Grace would place his group of marksmen in various hidden positions at the top of Monash Valley.

Through the telescope, Snow scanned the opposing scrub where snipers were sure to be, while Thomas and his rifle lay on a strip of canvas, the muzzle hidden among the undergrowth.

At a quarter past eight as arranged, trooper Dave Browning walked along the forward trench on Pope's Hill holding up his bayonet with his slouch hat balancing at its point. As he passed a dip in the sandbags, he tensed for the shot from the heights. When none came, he waited a few minutes and then repeated the motion. Again there was no response. On his third pass, a shot rang out and his hat flew through the air.

'Damned shame,' Browning muttered, as he picked up his hat and pressed a finger through the neat hole.

In his telescope, Snow spotted a wisp of smoke and whispered, 'From their trenches, not a sniper.'

The boys waited, motionless, mouths closed against the flies.

An hour later a second shot came, the one they'd been waiting for. It buzzed like a bee well above their heads, and half a mile away an Anzac carting water threw up his arms, spilling the precious fluid into the hungry earth.

'Hundred yards, below the rise, left of tree stump,' Snow whispered and passed over the telescope.

Thomas focused on the spot. It was dark, in shadow. He could make out a round shape, part of a face perhaps. Maybe it wasn't. What was it that Hami Grace had said? 'Fire along the flash. If you don't hit the barrel, you'll hit the head. But shoot only when you are sure.'

'Well?' Snow whispered.

Thomas knew that, if the Turk fired again, someone else would probably die. Yet to fire and miss would be to reveal himself. The next to die might be him. Resist the temptation, he thought. The Turk might take fright and move away. *Must get him first shot.* Thomas said nothing, refused even to shake his head.

Snow took back the telescope while ever so slowly Thomas brought his sights to bear on the mark. They both waited. Time passed like a headache. If their mark was a sniper, he was damn good. He hadn't moved, hadn't wasted a bullet. Thomas was beginning to wonder if their man wasn't a patch of sunlight caught in the undergrowth.

A soft crack.

Somewhere down in the Valley, a young man spun in a macabre dance.

'Shoot,' Snow said.

Thomas saw the flash too, held a breath, squeezed the trigger. *Crack!*

This was the moment. Thomas had revealed his position. He clamped his mouth shut, tensed, waited for the return bullet. In the telescope, Snow watched the mark shiver and throw up a hand, legs kicking the bushes.

Snow kept the telescope on the spot for a while longer. Then he laid his head down face to face with Thomas and smiled grimly.

The boys left in darkness and returned at dusk. Each night they fashioned a new possy and settled in for the dawn. Every few hours they swapped roles and, while Snow was the better spotter and Thomas the superior shooter, by the end of a fortnight each had confirmed a score or more of kills. Their tally, while not the highest, was considered respectable by those who kept score as if it were a game. When added together, the total bag was enough for Hami Grace to declare they had all but cleaned Abdul up. Food and ammo were passing up the Valley with rarely an interruption, he said, and the stretcher-bearers had an easier time of it carrying down the wounded.

So it was that in late June Thomas and Snow returned to their unit and to the gratitude of their mates. They were ordered to keep sniping and were allowed a degree of independence, free of the endless digging and carting that their comrades despised.

B Squadron now held the frontline at the head of the Valley, with A and C in reserve. It was a critical position, wedged between Pope's Hill and Russell's Top, with the Top itself overlooked in the north-west by the giant yellow crag they called the Sphinx for its likeness to the beast beside the pyramids at Giza.

Johnny Turk waited for the morning. With the sun behind them, the Turks had a fine view of any movement above the parapet in the Anzac trenches – the best time to kill the invaders.

During the night, Thomas and Snow had fashioned a discreet nest of camouflaged sandbags at the end of their trench. As Thomas carefully loaded his rifle, Snow stood on the fire step behind a piece of naval plate wedged between the bags. This iron shield contained a loophole with a hinged flap. Snow slid the flap aside slowly, revealing an opening the width of his eyes and the length of his nose. Gingerly, he put his telescope to the hole.

'Anything?' Thomas asked.

'Not yet.'

Thomas dozed, even as he marvelled at Snow's patience: swivelling the lens back and forth, Snow could sweep the land for hours and still inform him with enthusiasm of a minute change just observed.

This morning they were seeking a particular Turk who had wounded two Light Horsemen and killed another with precise marksmanship at the same spot. Ordered to clean him out, Thomas and Snow had examined the place where the men had been hit and had found a pattern. Each bullet had neatly passed through the loophole in another iron plate nearby and hit a passing man in the head.

Snow stabbed his bayonet into the centre of brown bloodstains on the trench wall. He pulled a roll of twine from his pocket and tied one end to the bayonet. Next he stretched the string tight and fixed it to the closed loophole.

'Open,' Snow said.

Thomas slid the flap aside. With his head against the blood-stains, Snow closed one eye and put the other to the twine, following the path of the bullets back through the loophole. He caught a quick glimpse of a shadowed rise 100 yards away. 'Close!' he said quickly. Thomas slid the flap back as a slug rang against it like a smithy's hammer. Now with a rough idea where the sniper was, they waited.

Half an hour later, a Mauser bullet smacked into a man a little way down the trench. They heard the sickening thud and the shouts of his comrades. There was no cry of pain or scream for a bearer, just a mate's lament.

Watching the spot in the scrub, Snow had caught the opening of the enemy loophole, marked the flash, noted the rifle's quick retreat.

He nodded.

Thomas stood up with his rifle.

A slight breeze blew off the Aegean and over the Anzac positions. No stink from dead-man's-land. The best wind, Thomas thought. No crosswind, no need to correct his aim. Slowly he slipped the flap on the loophole, poked out his rifle barrel with infinite care and sighted.

It was in shadow, a socket of steel around a closed eye. When it slid open, he would be ready. He would have his mark. But when the eye did open, it winked continually, as quick darting shapes flashed across the hole – passing Turks, nothing to indicate a marksman.

Thomas withdrew his rifle. 'Smart bugger,' he said.

Snow stuck to his telescope, eye fixed on the target.

No sniper.

They waited.

Thomas was dozing, knees to chest, hat low on his face, watching Snow, when the bullet rang loudly on the steel plate an inch from Snow's lens. He flinched. Without taking his eye from the telescope or looking at Thomas, he flicked his fingers: their signal.

Thomas was there already, looking along the sights through his own loophole. On the other side of no-man's-land, the hole in the metal blinked. A tiny dark circle and behind it a lighter colour: flesh and the snout of a rifle.

Peering through his telescope, Snow reported, 'Eyebrows.'

Thomas squeezed and fired. He didn't bother to pull back. Such was his opinion of his rifle that he knew with a certainty that his bullet had gone where he wanted it.

Opposite, the muzzle jumped and the loophole went from dark to sudden light.

'Farewell, my friend,' Snow confirmed.

A moment later, the Turks closed the hole.

Thomas smiled to himself. There was no elation, not anymore. How many was it now? He wondered when he had stopped keeping count.

Chapter 20

THE NEXT NIGHT, AS SNOW and Thomas were preparing to set up a new sniping position, a summer storm came in from the sea. The wind blew dust and lifted rubbish from the Anzacs' sector onto the Turkish trenches. It gave Kingy an idea.

As they huddled in their dugout, eyes closed against the dust, Kingy grabbed newspapers, toilet paper, filthy cans of food and handfuls of dirt, and threw them up in the air, so that the westerly whooshed them over to the Turks. From the cigarette hanging from his mouth, he lit a jam-tin bomb and threw it, laughing at its distant explosion.

'Oh 'tis a lovely night to put the wind up Jacko,' Kingy grinned.

The others joined him in throwing bombs until Sergeant Lucky Les screamed above the howling wind not to waste them, as others in the frontline were firing star shells and flares.

The Turks, blinded by dust and wind, and seeing the coloured lights swirling in the storm, responded in a panic of rifles, cannon fire and a barrage of artillery, none of which came close to Thomas.

'Abdul is a wee skittish,' Teach observed cheerfully.

The rain began falling in sheets and by midnight the moon had disappeared. Lightning lit up the sky and thunder roared over the ridges as if God was firing His big guns.

'Blimey, He's opened the gates of hell,' exclaimed Kingy from under his greatcoat.

'Brought down damnation on us all,' Teach pronounced, touching the pocket that held his Bible.

'Johnny will think we're going to attack,' Thomas said.

'No moon and black as ink, not a bad night for it,' Snow agreed.

As if the Turk had read their minds, a distant sound emerged in between the claps of thunder. A barrage of artillery fire, with shells landing over the ridge, moved onto the trenches at Quinn's Post, followed by an eruption of rifle and machine gun fire.

In the distance they heard the steady, rhythmic *Allah, Allah* of the enemy advancing down Monash Valley towards them. In the darkness, the chant was unnerving. Thomas heard his heart thumping and wondered if Snow could hear it too. Their rifles lay cocked on the parapet aimed at the blackness ahead. Dimly at first, the Turks emerged from the gloom.

Thomas heard the order to fire. A crash erupted from their rifles with a thunder to get the blood up. Each man fired rapidly into the shadowy figures. The first line of Turks seemed to fall, but in the darkness it was not possible to be sure.

'They will not stand the bayonet,' Lieutenant Chisholm declared, with one foot on the firing step.

Thomas and Snow made to move, but Sergeant Lucky Les ordered them to remain. 'You boys is more use to us here. Snotter as many as ya can, lads. Don't 'it us, but.'

Kingy looked from Snow to Thomas. A smile crept over his face. Almost angelic, Thomas thought. Many times Kingy had spoken of his desire 'to tickle up the Turk' in a grand bayonet

charge. For the first time in their ten months together, from
Enoggera to Gallipoli, Kingy was lost for words.

'Good luck, cobber,' Snow told him.

'Greater love hath no man than this, that a man lay down his
life for his country,' Teach intoned.

'I thought it was for his friends,' Thomas said.

'Well, yes, strictly speaking,' Teach conceded.

'It don't matter neither way,' Kingy said finally. 'C'mon, let's
have a cut at 'em.'

Teach was a pale contrast to Kingy's bravado. He looked hard
at Thomas. 'In my kit there's a package. Make sure it goes to my
wife, in case I'm kicked out, there's a good lad.'

Thomas said, 'Never fear, mate.'

Teach took a deep breath, then pronounced portentously as
if summoning up courage, '"Stranger! To Sparta say, her faithful
band, here lie in death, remembering her command."' He
paused before adding, 'Simonides concerning Thermopylae.'

Thomas, wondering if Teach had the wind up him, whether
he would falter, looked hard at his old teacher. 'And "England
expects that every man will do his duty" . . . Nelson at Trafalgar.'

'Always a fine student.' Teach smiled sadly as he patted
Thomas on his shoulder.

'Come on, Australia!' cried Lieutenant Chisholm, pistol in
hand.

The whistle blew and Teach was up onto the fire step and
over the parapet as B Squadron went out with a cheer like a roar.

Thomas and Snow leant their rifles over the sandbags and
began firing over their comrades' heads at the shadows lumbering down the hill. As fast as they could reload, they fired until
the two groups came together in the gloom.

Thomas stared. 'What are we supposed to do now?'

'Dunno.' Snow shook his head. 'Wait, I s'pose.'

'Fook that.'

'Time to become a warrior.'

'C'mon, then.'

Together, they sprang wild over the parapet, yelling. They stamped up the wet slope together, rifles out, bayonets outmost, breathing hard, chasing their comrades.

With the storm's wind at their backs, speeding them forward, it seemed to Thomas that Divine Providence was on his side. Here at last was the ultimate test. To charge like a knight, to join with the foe hand to hand, dreamt of, feared and yearned for, where bayonet was sword, where heroes were made and deeds lived for evermore, where Australians showed their steel. On this night, he would prove himself.

A mass of men loomed in the rainy dark. All were in sodden khaki, stabbing and plunging, thrusting and slipping in mud, and occasionally firing. Thomas soon recognised his target: the Turk was shorter and more ragged in his cloth hat than the taller Australians.

The boys ran screaming past their comrades. Thomas plunged his bayonet into the side of a Turk, and with his own momentum pushed the man down onto the ground. With his foot in the man's back, Thomas withdrew his rifle and left the man curled up, moaning.

Around him others were fighting shoulder to shoulder with a steady routine: stamp, parry, lunge and engage, pull back and stab again. He heard the dull thud of rifle butt on skull and the sharp crack of bones, cries of pain and screams. He stepped around men on the ground twitching, friend or foe he didn't stop to see.

Thomas's breath came in gasps. He lost sight of Snow. A Turk came at him suddenly from the blackness, thrusting his bayonet. With a teenager's reflexes, Thomas stepped aside and

swept the butt of his rifle around crashing into the man's ear. As
the Turk staggered, Thomas plunged the bayonet into his side,
felt it scrape over ribs. He tried to extract it but the blade would
not come out. Thomas fired, blasting the man away. A mixture
of relief and elation rushed through him and he felt the joy
again in his opponent's defeat and in handing out death.

I am touched by God, he thought, his heart bursting as he
gasped for breath.

All around, shadows in khaki stabbed and slashed. The
ground trembled to their stamping, while the air was a confusion of grunts and cries, sour sweat and sweet diarrhoea.

Figures rushed past, difficult to distinguish. A man was
suddenly there. Thomas noticed the eyes first, wide and wild. In
a split second, he had registered the streaks of blood on his face,
the wide nose, the beard below a snarl of teeth. Even in the dark,
Thomas could see the Turk's bayonet was dripping crimson.

He parried the man's thrust, sensed the Turkish bayonet
slipping into his tunic, as he drove in his own and saw it disappear into the chest. Swiftly he pulled it out, stabbed again
mechanically, short and sharp, not too deep, saw the blood
spurt, watched the horror in the man's eyes fade. He put his
left hand to his tunic where the Turk's bayonet had gone and,
examining his fingers, grinned at the absence of blood.

Killing was a delight, Thomas decided. *He tried to do me,
but I got him first.* Sniping was a boy's game compared to this.
True combat was hand to hand, man to man. Words he'd long
imagined flooded his mind – valour, mettle, dash and pluck –
and were just as quickly forgotten as he looked for someone else
to kill.

Everywhere, bayonets flashed and butts swung in wide arcs.
Thomas saw a Light Horseman push his blade into a groin and
the enemy's legs kick and buckle. He recognised Sergeant Lucky

Les knock a man off a comrade and then impale the Turk, the
bayonet slipping through the neck like an arrow.

The Light Horsemen were moving further up the slope. The
Turks had broken off the fight. Both sides were leaving behind
men who lay twisted and convulsing in the dirt.

'Give a good account of yourselves, lads,' he heard an officer
shout. 'Forward the Light Horse. Advance Australia.'

Thomas cheered and ran with them in the chase. A Turk
loomed ahead, a big lumbering man, slower than the rest. He
glanced backwards and saw Thomas. As his expression changed
from desperate to despairing, Thomas lunged. The bayonet
pushed into the Turk's shoulder and spun him around, whipping
Thomas's rifle from his hands. Side on, the Turk tripped in his
rush and began to fall, fear written on his face. The man crashed
heavily to the ground and slid a little way in the mud. With
Thomas's bayonet locked in his shoulder, he screamed as the
long blade moved in him.

Thomas was on the man in a scramble to retrieve his rifle,
just as the Turk brought up his own. In that second, Thomas
saw the man's finger on the trigger and the muzzle at his chest.
He knew how it must end. The certainty of his death slowed the
moment. Thomas had time to be surprised and to wonder how
agonising the bullet would be.

He stood frozen, looking down on the man who would kill
him. In that moment, he noticed the rain falling on his enemy's
face, the mouth open revealing uneven teeth, the brown eyes
lose focus, the man grow still and the finger die on the trigger.

A flood of relief swept through Thomas. His legs went weak
and he dropped to his knees. He brushed the Turk's rifle aside
and looked about him. Light Horsemen were wandering past,
heading back down the Valley. Lieutenants Burge and Chisholm
were calling out orders to withdraw.

Where was Snow? Nor could he see Kingy or Teach. In vain Thomas searched among the returning men. Their faces were blank, drained, empty of energy and passion. If there was pleasure in their victory, Thomas couldn't see it. Some carried comrades, others hobbled or shuffled in their own agonies. The more seriously damaged staggered on the shoulder of a companion, or rode in pain or oblivion on the stretcher-bearers' canvas.

Thomas passed silently among Turks on the ground. He watched a man bayonet any of the enemy who moved. The officers, as weary and spent as everyone else, hardly seemed to notice.

Thomas was grateful beyond words when Teach emerged suddenly from the gloom. 'Nash is gone,' he announced sadly. 'A chance shot at Pope's, of all the rotten luck.'

Even in the darkness, Thomas could see Teach shaking. Major Nash was an old pal; they'd enlisted together, shared classes at the school where Nash had been head teacher.

'Good bloody officer, he was,' croaked a familiar voice.

For the first time they saw him. Kingy, with his eyes closed, sitting on the sodden ground. A dark stain pooled between his legs and trickled away with the rain.

Snow was with him, kneeling, fixing field dressings over the gash in his belly. With utmost gentleness, he laid Kingy's hands on the bandages. 'Hold those, will you?'

Kingy gasped, 'For a black bastard, ya been a good mate.'

'Shut up, ya mug.' Snow's reply was almost a sob. 'The doc will fix you up.'

'Bit late for the butch,' Kingy said with an effort, as blood seeped between his fingers.

Teach screamed, 'Stretcher-bearer!'

Beside Kingy, an older man in a ragged uniform lay curled up and groaning piteously with a bayonet impaled deep in his stomach. His hands were bloodied where they slid up and down the blade as he struggled to pull it out, an impossible task with the heavy rifle attached.

'I skittled the bugger, dinky-di,' Kingy said.

Thomas wanted to weep. 'Yes, you did,' he said, wishing for something better to say.

'Then he plugged me, fair and square.'

'Oh dear, oh dear,' Teach said. 'Oh my goodness.'

'Nuffin' good 'bout it,' Kingy said. 'Don't ya worry 'bout me. There's others worst off.'

'Worse,' Teach corrected automatically.

Kingy grinned. 'We had a bit of fun, didn't we?'

Even in the dark, Thomas could see the grin. It shone, lighting up Kingy's face like the cat in the Alice story his mother used to read to him. Thomas had forgotten that until now. The memory prompted a rush of tears, but he blinked them away. *Not now.* Thomas's legs went to water. He sat down heavily beside Kingy, whose wound gave off an awful smell, where the bullet had ripped across his belly, where he was holding his guts in.

Sergeant Lucky Les passed by in a rush. 'I thought I told you to stay behind, corporal.' Upon seeing Kingy, the sergeant said, 'Quick now, carry 'im down before Johnny starts up again.'

'What about him?' Thomas asked, indicating the wounded Turk.

The sergeant looked meaningfully at Thomas and shook his head, before moving on, joining the tide of dark shapes stamping past.

'We can't just leave the bastard,' Thomas said.

'Can't take him, either,' Teach said and aimed his rifle. 'They'll patch him up and he'll come back at us.'

The Turk saw the action and squirmed and moaned. His bloody hands slipped along the bayonet like some pitiful self-abuse.

'Don't!' Kingy's shout startled them. 'Ya leave him. Let some Turk butch have a go, might fix him. Poor bastard deserves a chance.'

'It'd be a mercy . . . to put a man out of his misery,' Teach said.

'Don't ya fookin' touch him,' Kingy insisted, with an effort that brought new pain to his face.

Seeing it tugged at Thomas's heart. Dying yet respecting his executioner, fair-minded and generous, that was Kingy. A good man who would die as painfully as Thomas's parents. Sudden images flashed through Thomas's mind – the Turk grasping the bayonet stuck in him, Kingy holding down the bloody bandages on his belly, a boot on his father's face and men hanging him from the tree, and his mother grasping her throat as the poison burnt through her.

Hadn't they done enough? Hadn't he suffered too much already? And there was the Turk trying to pull out Kingy's blade. A shabby, dishevelled man wearing – Thomas's gaze fell to the man's feet – brown leather Anzac boots. *Thieving bastard!* A red rage exploded inside him.

Kingy cried, 'Jesus, no!'

Thomas plunged his bayonet into the Turk's chest. For a second he felt a guilty thrill, the momentary pleasure of dispensing justice to a murderous creature who had all but killed his mate.

'Oh, what did ya do that for?' Kingy wailed.

'Mongrel got you, didn't he?' Thomas hissed. He put his boot on the Turk's chest and pulled at his rifle and the bayonet emerged with an obscene sucking sound. In that moment, Thomas saw clearly the man he'd killed – stout, past middle age, grey beard, someone's grandfather. Suddenly the killing fever left him and, in its place, exhaustion. Thomas crumpled to his knees beside the corpse, overcome with a desire to weep. *Not now.* But his body refused to obey, and he sobbed quietly.

After a while, blinking back tears, he got to his feet.

By then, Teach had taken Kingy under the arms and Snow had grasped his legs and they were carrying him crab-like down the Valley. Thomas followed with the rifles as they sat Kingy down behind a wall of sandbags.

A pair of men with SB armbands arrived puffing. 'Make way,' said one, shouldering them aside. The bearers moved Kingy onto the soiled canvas quickly, if none too gently. 'Mother of Christ,' Kingy cursed, with a moan that sent a knife through Thomas's heart.

'For pity's sake, have a care,' Thomas told the bearers.

They ignored him and took up their handles, grunting as they lifted their load. Thomas, Snow and Teach followed them down the track towards the regimental aid post. 'Make way,' the bearers repeated, obliging men to move aside for them and their passenger, until they were forced to stop at a narrow point on the edge of a ravine where the track was clogged with exhausted men going down and reinforcements struggling up.

The SBs conferred and then placed the stretcher on the edge, where it teetered above the slope. The first bearer, a burly six-footer, sat behind Kingy on the high end of the stretcher and drew him back in a hug. The other straddled the lower end of the stretcher, faced forward and held Kingy's legs between his arms.

'Right,' one bearer said.

'Righto,' answered his partner.

Without further word they pushed forward together. The stretcher sped down the wet slope with Kingy between them. Thomas watched open-mouthed as the front bearer dug in his heels to slow down the sled, until at the bottom they regained the track and carried Kingy away.

The three of them watched him disappear, until Teach filled the silence. 'I imagine he enjoyed that.'

They trudged back to their dugout, lost in their own thoughts. Teach lit his pipe and a faint red light marked his face in the darkness. Others were lighting up and the NCOs were turning a blind eye. The pleasant smell of tobacco filled the air.

Kingy was gone. Like a dozen others whom Thomas had known, men from Murgon to Brisbane and plenty of places in between, old mates and new. He would never see them again. Not in this life. He wondered how his time would end. Shot, shell or bayonet? Who knew? Who cared? When you were dead, it no longer mattered how you died or what killed you. Or who.

There was icy blackness there, at the edge of his mind, creeping across his consciousness like the storm in the distance. Thomas felt it coming full of thunder and tears, there beneath his eyelids, and feared it. He struggled to put the thought away. Whatever fate awaited him, he hoped he could face it as well as Kingy.

He grabbed at his water bottle, took a sharp swig and passed it to Snow. 'We showed them what Australia can do, eh?'

'Cold steel.' Snow nodded and took a drink.

'What Kingy wanted,' Thomas said.

'Face to face,' Snow continued. 'There was one my age, didn't have a clue about the bayonet.'

'Nearly bought it myself,' Teach admitted.

'It was . . .' Snow paused, as if searching for the right word, but leaving the sentence unfinished.

Neither Thomas nor Teach spoke.

Snow said, 'You know, in a fight, you're in the ring and everyone's screaming for blood, and you go at him, and you never stop, even when you've hurt him bad.'

'It doesn't help to dwell on these things,' Teach offered.

But there was no stopping Snow. He spoke with a bitterness Thomas had not heard before.

'You know you've hurt a bloke by the set of his body and face, and he goes at you harder like a trapped animal. And you step back, you hear the cheers and everyone yelling, rip into him, get him in the guts, tear his head off, spike the bastard.' Snow paused, took a deep breath. 'I never felt that. In the ring he was the enemy, but I didn't hate him. When the match was over, we would hug each other.'

Thomas said, 'It's not boxing.'

'Johnny Turk – I don't hate him, Tom.' Snow had tears in his eyes.

'None of us do. Not anymore.'

'I understand him.'

'Now steady on, old boy,' Teach objected.

'It's his country. It's only fair he's trying to stop us,' Snow said.

'It's dangerous talk . . . treasonous,' protested Teach.

'Teach, you know history. Don't you see?' Snow was pleading now.

'Oh, for Christ's sake, we didn't start this, the Huns did. Turkey joined them, now they're trying to kill us. End of history lesson.' Teach stood up to leave. 'You swore an oath to defeat the Empire's enemies. They killed a lot of good men today, probably Kingy too. How dare you sympathise with them?'

'Fair go, Teach,' Thomas said, coming to Snow's aid. 'I'm not proud of myself, either. You saw what I did to that Johnny.'

'He deserved it for what he did to Kingy,' Teach answered simply.

'He was just lying there,' Thomas said miserably.

'Enough! Kingy wouldn't stand for it and neither will I,' Teach growled, suddenly fed up, and walked away.

Snow called after him, 'You know I'll kill anyone who threatens you.'

'I know it,' Thomas sighed. 'You're a fighter like your dad. We'll be all right, chum, you'll see.'

But Snow didn't answer, and both of them stared silently into the darkness where Teach had gone and where Kingy had been taken.

Chapter 21

THERE WAS NO SLEEP FOR the rest of the night. The officers had ordered 'Stand-to-Arms' and Thomas's squadron was on tenterhooks. Lieutenant Chisholm said, 'An attack is unlikely after the beating we gave them. Still, best to be prudent.'

Thomas and Snow set up a new camouflaged possy where they awaited the dawn and new targets. But their hearts weren't in it.

Thomas sat with his eyes closed, craving sleep that wouldn't come. Snow sagged. He swivelled his telescope back and forth slowly across their field of fire, staring into the darkness.

'Anything?' Thomas said finally.

'Like the grave,' Snow said.

'Licking their wounds,' Thomas said quietly.

They didn't speak for an hour.

Snow whispered finally, 'You know what you said last night, about me being a warrior like my dad?'

'Uncle Tubbie wouldn't want you worrying about it.'

'Snow's a funny name for a blackfella, isn't it?'

'Not especially. First day at school, the kids took one look at my red hair and I was *Bluey* ever after. Here, I'm just plain Tom.'

Snow sighed. 'Never told you this. My old man's a whitefella. From that Macdonald station up north where Tubbie and my mum lived for a while.'

'Oh,' Thomas said.

'Tubbie told me one day. He said did I ever wonder why I wasn't shiny black? If you was mine, he said, you'd be dark as night. I wasn't surprised. Well, not much anyway. I must of always known.'

'So Winnie . . .' Thomas said and stopped.

'Same as me. Never knew our real father. Tubbie looked after Mum and us.'

'That makes him a top bloke, I reckon, better than a real dad.'

'Yeah, but all that stuff about me being a prince, Kalkadoons and all . . .'

'Wishful thinking?' Thomas suggested.

'Something like that.'

Thomas waited.

Snow took a deep breath and continued, 'This is hard to say, coz you're my best mate and all. But being here makes a fella think about things.'

'Yes.'

'Don't matter how hard I fight, I reckon I won't ever be like you, even with a white father.' Snow shook his head sadly. 'I'll always be some sooty native.'

'Not to me.'

'Funny thing is . . . I dunno whether I wanna be one of you.' Snow frowned at his own words.

'What do you mean?'

'There's no black and white in the army, right?'

'Only khaki.'

'Khaki is the colour of hate, Tom. Johnny wears it too.'

'You don't have to hate them. You just have to stop them.'

'It's hard to kill without hate.'

'Listen, I don't care what you say, you're a warrior – you're my brother.'

Snow nodded gratefully. He took a deep breath and his face softened. 'A bloke gets a bit low, Tom,' he said and went back to the telescope.

These days, Thomas realised, Snow was doing most of the observing. Those few times when Snow took the sniper role, when the target was an eye in the enemy loophole, he fired and missed. The bullet invariably hit the edge of the Turkish plate. If the target was a flicker of passing khaki, Snow fired and winged the man. The result was there in the telescope for Thomas to see as plain as day. At first he'd thought it was mere chance or a puff of wind or a faulty rifle sight or that Snow wasn't quite the marksman Thomas was. Soon enough, he realised that Snow was a very good shot indeed. Thomas might ask him straight out, but he might not like the answer and he feared what he would have to do as a result. It became one of the things they didn't talk about. Instead, Thomas spent longer as sniper and Snow as spotter. If their target were a sniper, and not some ordinary Abdul, Thomas would suggest he have a go and Snow would agree. It was an arrangement that seemed to suit them both.

Thomas watched his friend carefully as the pink rays of dawn crept over the hilltops. He remembered Snow's pluck in the bayonet charge and his unflinching eye at the telescope when a Turkish sniper's bullet might funnel down the lens at any moment. He recalled the savagery of the Kalkadoon song, *Kill the white man,* and how Tubbie had cared for a white man's bastards, and how Snow and his family had helped him endure the bleak aftermath of his father's murder. It struck Thomas that the old Aborigine had been a better father than his own.

Jack Clare had grieved terribly for his darling Rose, but was that reason to ignore his son? He'd not confided in Thomas, never spoke of her suicide, or why he hid the document. *Did he think I wouldn't understand? Did he not trust me? Oh, what we might have said to each other . . .*

His mind wandered back to the murders of the Boers. In his book, George Witton claimed that Harry Morant had murdered out of anger and pain only after his best friend Captain Hunt had been mutilated. *Is that me?* The idea shocked him. Wasn't that what he had done to the old Turk who'd shot Kingy? How far would he be prepared to go to avenge his father? Whatever the intrigues of Kitchener and Bulala Taylor, Morant had gone too far. One of Witton's lines came to mind – 'War is calculated to make men's natures both callous and vengeful.' That was certainly true on Gallipoli, Thomas thought. It was one thing to finish off a dying Turk, but could he line up Taylor and shoot him in cold blood as easily as he would Abdul?

As the morning light grew in intensity, and at a signal from Snow, Thomas stared down the sights of his Lee-Enfield.

'Dead ahead,' Snow had whispered from behind his telescope. 'Hundred and fifty yards, left of the rise, beside the bush with yellow flowers. See him?'

'Got him.'

Teach returned from Anzac Cove the next evening just before another thunderstorm came out of the west to sweep over them. His eyes downcast, Teach said in a faint, hoarse voice, 'On the beach, Kingy. Gone, I'm afraid.'

Snow and Thomas groaned, though neither was surprised. They had seen the intestines flowing hopelessly from Kingy's belly and knew his only chance was a speedy evacuation. They knew men lay for hours on the beach waiting for a barge to ferry them to a hospital ship and that the medical officers gave priority to men with lesser wounds and better chances.

Teach continued, 'Your document too, while I was away. Someone's been at my kit.'

Thomas gasped. He sat down in the dirt, speechless. He was more surprised about the theft than about Kingy's death. For a moment, he was ashamed of himself, but only for a moment. They would have Kingy's burial, and after that – well, better to keep his mind on the job at hand. The document, his father's murder, there was no forgetting that.

'Taylor,' Thomas hissed. Bulala would either destroy it or take it straight to Lord K.

Though he was stopped from time to time by nosy officers and NCOs, Thomas's status as a sniper gave him free rein to roam at will over the Anzac sector. Yet recovering the document was easier said than done. Finding out Taylor's whereabouts was almost as difficult. With Uncle Harry evacuated, Thomas's best source of information would be Aubrey Herbert.

The morning after Kingy's death, Thomas walked down to HQ, where he found the stooped figure of Captain Herbert conversing in English to a prisoner almost as tall. The short-sighted Englishman broke off when Thomas arrived, leaving the prisoner under the watchful eye of a burly guard.

'Ah, Trooper Clare, just the man,' Herbert said.

'Corporal now, sir.'

'Gracious! At this rate, you'll outrank me by Christmas. For your information, I hear your Uncle Harry will be Brigadier General Chauvel when he returns from sick leave.'

'He's not my real uncle, sir, but that is good news.'

'Quite,' Herbert said. 'Now see here, Thomas, I need your help, your rifle actually, for a spot of prisoner-gathering. There are wounded crying on Walker's Ridge.'

'Sir, I was hoping . . .'

'I need you to discourage any of your ilk who might care to snipe me.'

'Yes, sir.'

'Lead on, I shall follow. Your sight is sharper than mine.'

As they walked up the steep track to the ridge, Herbert asked, 'How fares the sniping, Thomas?'

'We're cleaning them up, sir.'

'Capital. And your tally?'

'I stopped counting, sir.'

'I'm very glad to hear it. Did you know, my dugouts have been demolished five times by shellfire. Dashed good fortune that I'm never in them. My batman, Johnny, was hit by shrapnel in the calf and evacuated, poor devil.'

'Lucky devil, I'd say, sir,' Thomas quipped, then quickly added, 'I mean if it's a Blighty, sir.'

'Quite,' Herbert smiled knowingly. 'Speaking of sudden departures, the Admiralty has removed Churchill as First Lord of the Admiralty.'

'Sacked? Not Mister Churchill, sir?'

'My dear wife has written to say he's quite broken about it,' Herbert said cheerfully. 'As for Winston, I would like him to die in some of the torments I've seen so many die in here.'

Thomas was taken aback. Usually, officers didn't speak so openly and certainly not to the lower ranks. 'But sir, wasn't the whole Gallipoli campaign Mister Churchill's idea?'

'Indeed it was. London is not pleased with our progress or lack thereof. Yet it seems Winston's only regret is that he will miss being PM.'

Thomas had no idea what Captain Herbert meant, but – as gossip in the trenches – such information was as valuable as gold. To keep the conversation going, he said, 'My father met Churchill during the last war, while he was being treated by Doctor Conan Doyle.'

'Your favourite author, if I'm not mistaken, which I'll warrant explains your fondness for playing the detective.'

Thomas laughed, pleased and a little surprised that Herbert recollected anything of their previous conversation.

'Abdul the Damned also had a passion for Sherlock Holmes,' Herbert announced.

'Who, sir?'

'The old Sultan, brother to the current Emperor. He had Conan Doyle's works translated into Turkish.'

Thomas had no answer to that, so he said, 'You do seem to like Turks, sir?'

'Why, of course! I like the Turks themselves immensely. They're genial and polished, unlike their rulers who've been cruel and unjust.'

'They're the enemy, of course, sir,' Thomas reminded him.

Herbert laughed. 'And here I am fighting an enemy I like in a campaign that I find ill-conceived and abhorrent.'

Again, Thomas was astonished and confused by the man's candid nature. His comments seemed at least disloyal and at worst unpatriotic.

'Sir, remember the incident with the Turkish sniper? Why did you risk jumping the gap before the prisoner?'

'You mean, apart from my intention to shame Bulala?'

Which failed, Thomas thought. 'Yes, sir.'

'I was captured last year in France.'

'Sir, I had no idea!'

'I was in a bad way, lying wounded, when a German came up like an angel of death and prodded me with his bayonet,'

Herbert said. 'But he turned out to be extraordinarily kind and polite, offered me wine and water and cigarettes. Another German told me he would like to put his bayonet in my throat and turn it round and round. Still another covered me up from the overnight cold. Then they took me to hospital and cut out the bits of bullet from my side. I spent many days recovering and, until the advancing French liberated us, was well treated, if occasionally insulted.'

'What has that to do with the Turk and Captain Taylor, sir?'

'Nothing really, I expect,' Herbert admitted. 'Except that one German shot me while others saved my bacon. Make of that what you will.'

They climbed the rest of the way in silence, and were dripping in sweat by the time they reached the trenches on Russell's Top.

A tall, well-built officer in a pith helmet greeted Herbert warmly. He was in his mid-thirties, with a noble face, a strong nose and full lips. 'Game has been plentiful hereabouts,' the officer said. 'We bagged a few hundred of the blighters last night. Others are awaiting your tender ministrations, Herbert.'

'Major Reynell, this is Thomas Clare, one of our snipers. I've brought him along to keep their heads down. Hope you don't mind, old chap?'

'My fellows should be more than adequate to your needs, Herbert,' Reynell said, with an easy assurance.

'Clare's uncle is the brigade commander,' Herbert said matter-of-factly.

'With respect, sir, Colonel Chauvel is not my *real* uncle, more of a family friend,' Thomas said, tired of explaining it. 'My father shot three Boers who were trying to kill him in the last war.'

'Ah, I missed that one,' the major sighed. 'I was about your age, but sadly my father vetoed my enlistment.'

'It was my dear mother who prevented me from going,' Herbert chimed in, 'that and my dashed abysmal eyesight.'

'Yet, here we all are, at the service of Empire in its time of need.' Major Reynell smiled, then turned to Thomas. 'War forges splendid friendships. A hundred years ago my grand-uncle Thomas was with Wellington inside a British square at Waterloo when Napoleon's cavalry charged. He won a knighthood after that.'

'Yes, sir,' Thomas said cheerfully. He guessed the major was the sort who played polo. Herbert had told him that Reynell made wine in South Australia, which impressed Thomas, though he had never tasted any.

'Your corporal might well be useful after all, Herbert,' Major Reynell said with sudden decisiveness. 'Come along, then.'

Captain Herbert winked at Thomas and gestured for him to follow.

The major led them along what he called 'the secret sap', a deep gutter in the undergrowth invisible from the Turkish trenches. Not a pleasant experience, as they had to crawl over numerous flyblown bodies, Turks whose heads had been blasted away by bomb or machine gun. They stopped some thirty yards from the Turkish trenches, and Thomas set up his rifle to cover the officers and watch for any threatening movement. Before them, scores of bodies lay unmoving among patches of prickly scrub in no-man's-land, but when Herbert called out in Turkish, inviting any wounded enemy to surrender, he was rewarded at once with a reply.

Thomas watched in horror as Herbert and Reynell stood up.

'Wouldn't do that if I were you, sir,' Thomas suggested.

Herbert laughed. 'Don't you know that I'm mad, Thomas?'

Reynell scoffed, 'That's hardly sporting, old chap. The boy will believe you're actually serious.'

Thomas marvelled at their nerve as both men stepped out in plain view of the enemy positions at The Nek. The pair located the wounded Turk and between them carried him back to the sap, occasionally stumbling over bodies as they did so.

Not a shot was fired. Perhaps the Turks were still licking their wounds, Thomas thought, because any other day would have brought instant death.

Herbert and Reynell conveyed the man down the trenches, a tight fit where the walls narrowed, and passed him over to an Australian doctor.

By the time they returned, Reynell's men were watching with a curious fascination. The slight, stooped figure of Herbert always seemed to draw a crowd.

'You go out again, sir,' one Light Horseman suggested to him. 'It's as good as a show.'

Herbert grinned at Thomas. 'Mustn't disappoint our fans.'

When he called out again in Turkish, the response came in a frightened whisper.

'What did he say, sir?' said Thomas.

'I asked if he wanted water. He said, yes, by God. But he's shamming, and terrified his people will kill him.'

'Shamming, sir?'

'Lying doggo, pretending to be wounded.'

This time Major Reynell threw out a rope. When they felt a tug at the other end, Herbert and Reynell dragged the Turk in, receiving not a single gunshot but some energetic applause from the Light Horse.

The soldier who tumbled into the sap was a thin young man in his twenties, dressed in bits and pieces of various Turkish uniforms. He was shivering from fear, but Thomas thought the expression on his face also spoke of intense relief.

'The doctor will see to the prisoner,' Herbert said. 'When he's finished, Thomas, be so good as to escort him back to HQ.'

'Yes, sir.'

Some time after Herbert and Reynell departed, the doctor led the blindfolded Turk through the web of frontline trenches, with Thomas bringing up the rear. But at the entrance to a particular sap, where the Anzacs had piled the bodies of Turks slain in the previous night's fighting, the young man staggered as if shot, slipped his blindfold and gave a terrible yell at the sight of his comrades.

Thomas understood immediately. The man believed he was at the place where the Australians killed prisoners. In a panic, the Turk grabbed the doctor around the neck, and they fell together on the bodies and rolled about in the blood, dirt and gore.

Instantly, Thomas aimed his rifle at the prisoner. There was a small risk he might hit the doctor, but far worse would be to disappoint Captain Herbert. He put up his rifle, and with one hand grabbed the prisoner by the scruff of the neck and dragged him off the doctor.

'Now, don't carry on so,' said Thomas, shaking his head vigorously and trying to make the Turk understand. 'No one is going to shoot you.'

The doctor got to his feet and looked at the sticky mess that covered him from head to toe. Shocked at his appearance, he seemed unable to speak and, without a word, walked down the track towards the sea, leaving the prisoner with Thomas.

When they reached headquarters, Captain Herbert was sitting bootless on a bench between ammo boxes, with his back against a wall of sandbags, and dabbing iodine over numerous cuts to his bare feet. He ordered a guard to take charge of the prisoner, then returned to his injuries.

'Blasted barbed wire,' he explained. 'Talking of prickly characters, are you still exchanging pleasantries with our beloved Bulala?'

'That's what I came to see you about, sir.'

'Fortunately, I've not encountered Taylor recently, but I will look out for him at Helles when I'm next down south,' Herbert offered.

'Someone dropped a jam tin on us, then took a pot shot at us with a Webley.'

'There are scores of such pistols here, Thomas. I have one myself,' Herbert said patting his holster. 'Yet you suspect Captain Taylor?'

'You know his history, sir.'

'And why should that concern you?'

'He killed my father.'

'I see,' Herbert said evenly and invited Thomas to join him on the bench. 'To accuse a British officer of such a crime is a serious matter.'

'I'm aware of that, sir.' Thomas told Herbert about Kitchener's note to Bulala, how his father had hidden it, and his suspicion that Taylor had stolen the document from Teach's kit.

Herbert said nothing. He leant towards Thomas until their faces were close and peered into the boy's eyes, studying them intently. Finally, he said, 'A most extraordinary conspiracy! Who else have you told?'

'Only Major Midgley and my mates, sir.'

'Not Chauvel?'

'No, sir.'

'Why in heaven not?'

'I dunno, sir. Worried he wouldn't believe me, I suppose.'

'And Midgley said what, exactly?'

'He wanted to see the document, sir.'

'I'll bet he did,' Herbert sighed. 'I grant you that Taylor is of questionable character, but without solid evidence and possession of the document as motive, your suspicion hardly constitutes proof of murder.'

'Yes, sir,' Thomas said blankly.

Herbert sat back. 'I lost my father at the age of ten . . . a terrible blow. But, Thomas, do not allow it to make you vengeful. You must not become another Harry Morant and shoot Taylor down like a dog.'

When Thomas refused to respond, Herbert said, 'For God's sake, you're a sniper in wartime. Don't confuse that with a licence to murder. As I told you once before, steer clear of that man. He is dangerous.'

'No more so than Johnny Turk, sir.' Thomas wondered if he could ever make the Englishman understand why he must kill Taylor. *Not murder, but justice.* 'As I said, sir, the man killed my father.'

'That is by no means proven and you are no vigilante.'

Thomas remained silent.

'Oh, don't be a damned fool. Or have you become so familiar with killing that you forget it is wrong?' Herbert said and turned back to his injured feet. 'Now, if you'll excuse me, corporal, I have important matters to attend to.'

As Thomas stood up to leave, Aubrey Herbert pointed to the Turkish prisoner. 'That feeble stick is my enemy, Thomas, but killing the fellow serves no purpose. Apart from everything else, he has information that may save a life, perhaps even yours.'

Chapter 22

JULY WAS A TORTURE OF heat and dust. As dry as chips, two stale-mated armies lay inert under a blanket of flies. On both sides of no-man's-land their rabbit holes fell away in the roasted earth.

The invaders' trenches sagged with listless half-naked men. By noon every dugout was an oven. The Australians baked slowly, barely able to summon the energy to swat at the legions of flies that flew from the wounds in no-man's-land to the shit in the latrines to the melting mush that passed for rations. When an Anzac ate, he swallowed as many flies as food. With precious little water to wash with, disease collected in mess tins and faeces and on men's bodies. Everybody was thirsty and exhausted, stripped down and stinking of sweat, vomit and diarrhoea. Dysentery was the very devil.

Gas would soon be fired at them from the enemy trenches, they were warned, contrary to common sense and the whims of the wind. The Anzacs were issued with gas helmets and prac-tised working in them. The officers deprived the men of sleep by forcing them to Stand-to-Arms from an hour after the moon set to an hour before dawn during the Muslim holy month. The Turks were starving themselves for Ramadan, the officers claimed, and likely to attack because of it, which brought a grim satisfaction to the Australians sick of bully beef, hardtack and runny jam.

Small groups of troopers crept over no-man's-land to raid and harass during the cool of the night. 'Must keep Abdul nervy,' Major Bourne explained.

Thomas and Snow were too valuable to waste on such missions. They remained apart from the others in the prized role of snipers, never returning to the same position twice.

Snow was ill. He would shuffle silently away from their possy with a rushed excuse. 'I'm bloody sick as a blackfella's dog,' he would say, 'gotta trot,' leaving Thomas with both telescope and his rifle. Sometimes he would be away for hours, only to hobble back with humiliation in his face. As the days passed, he seemed to diminish, grow weaker.

Thomas would say, 'See the doc, he'll give you something.'

Snow would shake his head and smile, 'Can't leave you alone with Abdul. You wouldn't last two shakes.'

His sudden departures became frequent. In the early hours one morning, Thomas awoke to find Snow had not returned, and he went off in search of him.

Along the track, patches of brown liquid showed up clearly in the moonlight where men had failed to reach the pit in time. Thomas could smell the sweet, noxious odour before he reached the latrine. He took the stink in his stride. He was as filthy as anyone, and in any case there'd been worse, particularly during the ceasefire.

As he rounded the corner, he expected to see a few figures with vacant eyes, perched like crows on a fence, side by side, their shorts on their boots, their sad white buttocks bright as lamps, straining with soft groans and louder grunts.

Instead, the pole was bare, with only the hum of flies filling the dark recess, and no other sound except for the occasional bang over the hill.

'Snow, where are you, mate?'

Thomas wondered if he had passed him on the track. He turned to retrace his steps when he heard a soft reply, 'Tom.'

He turned back and hurried to the pit. There was Snow, his arm hooked around the pole, his head resting on his wrist, and his body lost in the pit. Somehow he had become wedged between the seat and the side of the latrine. In the half-light he looked all done in, as if he couldn't hold on much longer.

Snow raised his eyes. 'I'm in the shit, brother.'

Thomas grasped Snow's wrists, put his back into it and pulled slowly. Snow came up with a sickening, sucking sound. 'Thank Christ,' he whispered.

Thomas laid him on the ground. His lower body was covered in a dark slime of excreta and black flies. 'C'mon, chum, it's down to the beach with you.'

Snow lifted a hand weakly to the side of his head, where a long black mark appeared to be bubbling. His hand pushed the flies aside for a moment to reveal a runnel in the flesh, and when he took his hand away the flies returned.

'Sitting duck,' Snow laughed weakly. 'A bloke can't shit without being shot.'

Thomas trembled. It occurred to him that Snow might die. He wanted to scream, *Not you*, but a voice inside steadied him, told him to think carefully, examine the wound. He saw it wasn't bleeding. That was good. The bullet had cut along the side, scored the skull.

'Lucky it was my head,' Snow said weakly, the old joke.

'Best place for it, all right.'

'Nearly drowned,' Snow said.

'Better get you cleaned up, mate.' Thomas pulled up Snow's shorts and hoisted him onto his back. For a big bugger, Snow wasn't heavy, Thomas realised, stripped of fat and muscle. They were all skinny, the sick ones most of all.

In the moonlight, Thomas walked fast down the track towards the beach. No shots rang out. *Thank God we cleaned up most of Jacko's snipers, but my cobber is going to die from Anzac shit.*

A sentry challenged them and quickly let them pass.

Thomas was blowing hard when they reached the beach. He struggled across the sand, careless of anything that got in his way. An officer objected when shouldered aside, then shrank back at the steel in Thomas's face and the stink of his load.

He ran pell-mell into the sea and tripped, tumbling Snow into the cool water. The shock seemed to revive him, for Snow grunted and Thomas was happy to hear it.

Thomas lifted his friend and sat back with him in water up to their chests. With one arm around Snow's chest, Thomas splashed water over his bloodied head. 'Deep breath,' he said. 'This will hurt like blazes.'

Snow gulped and Thomas pulled Snow backwards on top of him. With Snow's weight on him, keeping him underwater, Thomas began to rub his fingers back and forth, and up and down, along the path of the bullet, scouring out the filth.

Snow kicked his legs furiously. He grasped Thomas's knees so hard he thought they must break.

Beneath the water, Thomas heard the pain. He knew it was torture, but he kept at it, cleaning the wound. Then, using all his strength, he pushed Snow up until they both broke the surface.

In his arms, Snow was deathly still. Thomas grasped his chin and turned his face around. He put his ear to Snow's mouth and, even against the lap of waves on the shore, heard a faint breathing, felt a breath.

He dragged Snow to a new, cleaner patch of water. There he rubbed the wound again, glad that this time he was unconscious. Finally he dragged Snow out of the water and laid him down gently. His friend looked deathly pale. The gash along his head was weeping red, a clean flow down his ear onto the sand. Thomas walked a few yards to the medical tent and roused a sleeping orderly, who applied a bandage to the gash without saying a word. Together they laid Snow on a stretcher and placed him with the lines of sick and wounded lying on the beach. Thomas walked away as the moon fell in the final hours before dawn and left an inky blackness in its wake.

He trudged back along the gully and up the Valley, a trip made a hundred times. He took his time, balancing two tins of water from a strap over his shoulder and another in his hand, careful not to spill a drop.

He felt the tears welling. His best mate might die on the sand like Kingy, or on the hospital ship like Billy Keid. They'd sat on cricket balls, Billy and Kingy, he remembered fondly. Gone forever. It wasn't supposed to turn out like this. It was supposed to be an adventure, with hardships shared fair and square. In such a place, stuck as they were in alien dirt between the sea and death, fear and horror were tolerable only with Snow to share it. Together.

Thomas arrived to find Sergeant Lucky Les rousing the men into the daily routine. He dropped off the water and told him about Snow.

The sergeant shook his head. 'A damn shame that is. Two bloody good boxers out for the count.'

The other was Thomas Reynolds, the Queensland miner from the 5th Light Horse, shot through the heart. He was famous for winning the army lightweight title in Egypt. He and Snow had fought a 'friendly' in the Wazza and though Snow was heavier and younger, he'd taken a punishing at the hands of the wily Reynolds before the redcaps put an end to it.

'I was looking forward to a rematch,' the sergeant said wistfully, before telling Thomas that he was required down at headquarters. 'Captain Taylor wants a word.'

Bulala. Killer. Thief. Slippery as a snake, sarcastic and shady, a beastly fellow who chilled him to the bone. Who had stolen the document from Teach. What more could Taylor want? Thomas collected his rifle. He walked back down the Valley, each step a drumbeat to the anger in his heart.

He thought of the others. His father, a good man tortured in mind and body, and murdered. His mother, left lonely and abandoned, in despair and dead by her own hand. Kingy, the nuggety larrikin with a whore for a mother, whose cheery grins had made their trials bearable. And Snow, the warrior who hated to kill, now shot and humiliated and probably dead. Thomas should have looked after him better, stayed with him. He might have potted the Turk sniper before he fired.

He was almost running now, the rifle strapped on his back, swinging with each furious step. He had to see Snow again, tell him he understood, apologise for not protecting him. Only then, when it was light, would he see to Taylor.

The sun was peeking over the eastern ridges when Thomas got to the beach. But on the sand where he had left Snow the wounded had gone. Out past scores of men skylarking in the water, a crowded barge was heading towards a little ship with three red crosses along her white hull.

Thomas sank to his knees. *It shouldn't be like this.* It should be as it was at home. There, a rabbit was finished with a swift chop to the neck. A goanna was swung by the tail to bash its head on a tree. An animal would quiver and blood would flow, and life would end quickly, properly. Killing came with a joy there, never regret, never revulsion. Life and death were valued and honoured. And the prey did not shoot back.

Thomas pitched forward and sobbed into the sand.

Shapes and shadows poured through his head – the smells and sounds, the pain in its screaming viciousness, the savagery of bullets and shrapnel, the brutality of holes torn through stomach and chest, and blood and bone shattered and sprayed about, all waste and purposelessness. The blasts with their hammering waves of concussion, the dirt in everything, the dust in eyes and ears and hair, and always the fear, the belly-gripping fear, burning then freezing like snake venom.

What's happening to me? Thomas held his head in his hands and shook with the nightmare of old pals and new mates, comrades half-remembered or purposely forgotten in the need to go on, to be quick, to duck – weave – jump – throw – fire – hide – again and again, whatever was needed to stay alive and sane.

And in that mishmash of terrors, a tide of chanting spectres flooded his mind and then receded, leaving one behind – an old man twisting with Thomas's bayonet in his guts.

A shriek like a train whistle roused him. In the next instant the beach shook and men flew in an eruption of sand. A blast knocked him over, stung his ears, ran up his nose and down his throat. He struggled for breath, hacking and spluttering. Sand and pebbles fell like rain about him.

Not twenty yards away, a knot of smashed bodies lay on the edge of a steaming crater, some crawling, others still. As men hurried to help, Thomas got unsteadily to his feet and began to run along Shrapnel Gully towards Brigade HQ.

You can't duck it, he thought. No possy is safe, no trench is deep enough. Whether from one of Beachy Bill's pills or a bullet from a Mauser. When it's your turn, you're gone. Once he had hidden deep, thinking it made a difference. Others had determined his fate, whether his country, his friends, or his enemies – Abdul or Taylor.

No longer, he decided. He would not wait for the jam tin in the night or the Manstopper in the back. He would hunt Taylor as he hunted Johnny Turk. Find him and settle things once and for all.

Chapter 23

B RIGADE HEADQUARTERS WAS A CAVE in the side of the hill with a corrugated-iron roof topped with a heavy layer of sandbags. The curtain across the entrance was drawn, suggesting that any officers inside were not yet awake.

Taylor was.

He sat outside on a wooden bench against a sandbag wall, smacking his swagger stick impatiently against his boots. When he saw Thomas, he said with typical sarcasm, 'Glad you could finally make the effort.'

Taylor led the way, setting a brisk pace for a stout middle-aged man. He turned off into a ravine and Thomas followed, his fury growing with every step. Rifle fire and the occasional rat-tat-tat of a machine gun came from just over the ridge. They walked wordlessly along the narrow track, passing no one, until they came to the end of the gully. There, cut into the slope, was a dugout, a smaller version of headquarters, framed by sandbags and with an oilcloth covering the entrance.

Taylor held the cloth aside.

Thomas paused. It was dark in there and God knows what else was waiting for him. One of Bulala's accomplices? Or would

Taylor simply shoot him? He began to tremble. Where would the bullet hit? Would the Manstopper break the spine, shatter his head, destroy a leg? Thomas took a deep breath. *If he shoots, I'm gone, nothing I can do about it.*

Curiosity drove him in. The cave was empty, but for two chairs, a folding table, and a hurricane lamp hanging from an overhead beam.

Taylor lit the lamp and took one of the chairs for himself. 'Cool and comfy, is it not? And quite conducive to the flow of information. Herbert and I interrogate the odd Turk in here, where a man may betray his comrades in confidence.'

Thomas hesitated.

'Sit, Thomas. Put your rifle down. This is a friendly chat.'

Thomas found the talk of prisoners not at all reassuring, but – confident of his ability to get the better of Taylor – he leant the rifle against the cave wall, within easy reach, and sat on the other chair with the table between them. 'Will Captain Herbert be along, then?'

'Oh, haven't you heard? While you and I risk our very lives, the chap is having a holiday, swanning around the islands, chatting to his Greek and Turkish friends. We can expect no interruption from that quarter.'

In a flash, Taylor brought out the Webley from under the table. He rested his elbow on the table so the revolver was pointed at Thomas. A faint smile touched Taylor's lips as he held out his left hand. 'The document, if you please.'

So this was it, Thomas thought, the confrontation, when he would learn the truth. He would die, of course, for the pistol would brook no other choice. But why was Taylor asking for a thing already in his possession? Thomas had assumed that Bulala had stolen it from Teach's kit. If not him, who? Thomas's mind whirled. Who knew of its significance? Aside from his cobbers, he had spoken about it only to Major Midgley and Captain Herbert. Not them, Thomas shook his head. *Ridiculous.*

Taylor took the shake for refusal. 'Give it to me or I shall fire!'

Thomas was surprised at his calm. He reached inside his tunic as if the document was there, and then pulled back. 'First, a few questions.'

Taylor looked smug, in no hurry. 'Well?'

'TNP – you passed on Kitchener's orders to murder prisoners?'

Taylor sniffed as if the matter was unimportant. 'I gather you are quite the sniper, Thomas. How many, ten, a score?'

'That's different.'

'Is it? War is brutal and ugly. It requires speedy termination. South Africa differed not a jot from this one. We were ordered to clear out the Boers, not fill up the burgher camps with them. That meant exercising a certain discretion when dealing with the white flag.'

'You murdered prisoners.'

'Dear boy, it's a practice as old as Methuselah.'

'So you admit it?'

'Let's just say a captive didn't last long.'

'You denied it at the court-martial.'

'I denied everything.'

'On orders from Lord K?'

'Of course. You've seen the document.'

'But in court . . .'

'Oh, don't be naive,' interrupted Taylor.

'You could have told the truth.'

'Yet here I am, a jolly fellow of middle years with a farm, a lovely wife, children and a fortune awaiting me at home. Whereas, Morant and his pals confessed all, implicated the boss, and . . . well, you know what became of them.'

'Why did Lord K write to you personally?'

Taylor chuckled. 'Ah, there you have it, the nub of the issue. Usually K put nothing down on paper, made sure his secretary Hammy Hamilton passed on such orders verbally to his officers.'

'What changed?'

'Why, the Boers killed Percy Hunt, of course. Before that, Captain Hunt's officers and men had been bringing them in alive. Morant had even refused Hunt's and my direct orders to give no quarter.'

'But that all changed after Hunt died?'

'Indeed it did. K was as furious as Morant. Ironic, isn't it, that Morant followed the orders only after his chum Hunt was killed. Oh, our dear Breaker was quite the horseman and had a marvellous way with words, but he was hot-headed. Vengeance has its place on the battlefield, I admit, but the best killing is cold. You of all people know that, Thomas. Sniping is murder by telescope, after all.'

'Nonsense!' Thomas said. 'It's a fair fight. We each have our rifles. I'd never do an unarmed man.' But as the words came out of his mouth, he remembered. *I stuck the old Turk.*

'What a splendid fellow you are,' Taylor went on. 'But believe me, if you want to murder someone you do it immediately upon his surrender. Or if you must shoot him when he's in your custody, make damn sure there are no witnesses. That was Morant's failure. Incidentally, we are very much alone here.'

Thomas forced a smile. He wondered whether Taylor had tortured or murdered Turks in this very cave.

'Morant and company shot civilians in front of witnesses, and prisoners well after they had surrendered. I could see that it would go badly, so I approached K, and insisted on receiving written orders. At first, he refused, said he never committed such things to paper, but on a whim grabbed the first thing to hand, which happened to be the Lord Roberts document, and scribbled a few cryptic lines in the margin. I remember his exact words. "There! Are you satisfied?" He laughed, thinking himself clever, and he threw the dashed paper at me. Of course, he bungled. He admits it now, regrets it still. Mind you, even those measly letters were enough.'

'For what?'

'To prove the orders came from the top.' Taylor flashed the sly smile of the cardsharp with an ace up his sleeve. 'And to ensure my acquittal.'

Straight away, Thomas saw the implications. 'You blackmailed him! Your commander-in-chief.'

'Steady on, that's a bit harsh. Put it this way, I followed K's orders to the letter.' Taylor chuckled at his pun. 'I denied his involvement, perjured myself. But yes, the note was a form of insurance that the evidence presented against me in court would be insufficient to convict. Dear Lord K, a thorough gentleman, dashed decent of him, wouldn't you agree?'

'And my father?'

'An idealist and a fool, and no friend of Morant or Peter Handcock. Jack testified against all of us, pronounced us guilty of murder.'

'But you were all comrades. He wouldn't have wanted them shot, not even you.'

'You're right there. Jack believed Kitchener had given verbal orders to forces across South Africa to take no prisoners. He was as surprised as the rest of us at the guilty verdicts and the severity of the sentences. Odd, don't you think, that Jack would testify against Morant and then try to save his skin?'

'No, not at all. Even bastards like Morant deserved a fair shake. A death sentence was far too harsh,' Thomas said. 'How did my father come by the document?'

'Once a copper, always a snoop,' sniffed Taylor. 'While we were rotting away behind bars, awaiting the verdicts, he ransacked my office in the Spelonken, found it and stole it. Your father was a thief, boy.'

'He was a good cop searching for evidence,' Thomas said evenly, 'in the pursuit of justice and to save lives.'

'Oh, dear boy, not you too!' Taylor shook his head. 'I imagine you're a Holmes enthusiast like your father?'

'Of course I am.'

Taylor sniggered. 'Jack fancied himself a proper Sherlock, and he failed. By the time he returned to Pretoria with my document, Morant and Handcock were cold in the ground.'

'Why didn't he expose you and Lord K?'

'Why should he? Morant and Handcock were already dead, and had your father attempted to make the document public, Kitchener would have destroyed him. *I* would have shot him.'

'Did Lord K order you to kill him?'

'Kitchener is ruthless, but even he wouldn't stoop so low.'

Taylor raised his Webley and smiled down its barrel at Thomas. Perhaps Thomas should have been afraid, but he found that he wasn't. 'But you have no such scruples, am I right?'

'If you refuse to hand over the document.'

'On K's orders?'

Taylor's voice fell to a whisper. 'Lord K doesn't know you exist. You are merely a louse to be popped. I shall kill you if I must.'

'Colonel Chauvel wouldn't appreciate it.'

'We both know your precious Uncle Harry is in Cairo, sick as a dog.'

'So it was you who tried to kill me with the jam tin and pistol?'

'Of course,' Taylor said with mock surprise. 'It's far easier to appropriate a document from a dead man's kit than to convince a live one to hand it over. You are proof of that, dear boy.'

'You'd have killed four of us for a scrap of paper, you heart-
less bastard.'

'Steady on. That is a most improper manner in which to
address an officer. I should shoot you for mutiny or, at the very
least, insubordination. Or I shall shoot you for being an insuf-
ferable brat and I shall enjoy it all the more.'

'Better shoot then, captain. The document's gone.'

Taylor sneered in disbelief.

'Stolen,' Thomas added.

'Not again.' Taylor seemed almost amused, even as he cocked
the pistol and brought the barrel closer to Thomas's face. 'You
must do better than that.'

Thomas sensed that this was his last chance. Numerous
thoughts crossed his mind. *Make Taylor stand up somehow. Tackle
him, grab the revolver, call for help.* The choices flashed through
his mind, only to bounce back dismally. Taylor wouldn't
hesitate. They were alone in a cave. Outside was alive with
gunfire and no one would think twice about a single shot. *It
would be suicide.*

Thomas sighed. 'You tortured my dad, then hanged him.
What makes you think I'd lift a finger to help you?'

'What are you talking about?'

'You stomped on his face and then murdered him.'

'That's not what happened, old boy.'

'You decapitated him.'

'So I heard.'

'Bastard.' Thomas was set to explode. The seedy little man
was going to kill him and yet still he refused to tell Thomas the
truth. 'I don't care two hoots about the document. You can have
it, for all I care,' Thomas said. 'Just admit you killed him.'

'You are mistaken,' Taylor said. 'Jack betrayed us. He testified
against me, as did several others. Yes, perhaps I should have
killed him. However, I did not.'

Thomas bent forward and screamed into his face, 'Liar!'

Startled, Taylor leant back and his pistol shifted. The boy seized his chance and leapt. He seized Taylor's wrist in his left hand and pushed the gun away, even as it fired. A bang deafened him, reverberated off the cave walls. A Manstopper cut through Thomas's left ear. The iron tang of blood filled his nostrils and a warm liquid flowed down his neck.

Thomas punched Taylor with his right fist, again and again in the face and head, with a young man's vigour. The table collapsed on top of Taylor, with Thomas on top of it. All the time, Thomas was punching, until he felt the older man weaken, and he wrenched the Webley away and turned it on him.

Thomas stood up and kicked the broken table to one side. He took a handkerchief from his tunic pocket and held it to his bleeding ear, while Taylor righted his chair and sat unhappily. With his left hand on the handkerchief and his right holding the pistol, Thomas kicked his chair over to Taylor and sat so that their knees touched. 'You are pathetic,' the boy said through gritted teeth. 'You can't even admit you killed him.'

Taylor coughed, spitting blood from his damaged mouth. 'I didn't . . .'

'Liar!' Thomas repeated. 'Bulala, killer and liar.'

'Of course I lie,' Taylor sighed. 'Many times and wholly by necessity, I assure you. It is what we do, after all. My God, boy, if the public realised the slaughter taking place now in France . . .'

'Murderer.' Thomas cut him short. Of all the men he had shot on Gallipoli, this man most deserved it. He put a little extra pressure on the trigger. Every instinct told Thomas to finish him, to squeeze harder. A sniper fires or is himself killed. *Don't hesitate.* A hunter shoots or his prey escapes. *Shoot the bastard.*

Taylor read the look in the boy's eyes.

Thomas saw Taylor hold his breath, and enjoyed the power

he had over the man. *Yes, you'll die*, he thought. *You will feel the pain. Like my father.*

Taylor exhaled finally. 'Oh, go ahead if you must, but believe one thing – I didn't touch him. He was well and truly dead and buried when I arrived.'

'Liar.'

'Not this time.'

'Show me your boots.'

'What, are you mad?'

'Your boots. Now!'

Thomas shifted backwards to allow Taylor room to lift his leg.

There was a U-shaped plate in the heel and heavy hobnails on the sole. Taylor was wearing British infantry boots, not the rider's sort that had left its stamp below the hanging tree and on Jack Clare's face. A memory niggled at the back of Thomas's mind. Doctor Woods had written that Taylor and the police sergeant arrived in Murgon after Thomas left. *For once, was Bulala sincere?*

'What a lovely little pantomime,' Taylor sneered as he dropped his leg.

'There were tracks beside my father's body and boot marks on his face, like Percy Hunt.'

'So you think a Boer commando killed your father? Or was it a Bushveldt Carbineer or a Bantu witch doctor?' Taylor sniggered as he spoke. 'Daniel Heese of the Berlin Missionary Society was one of Morant's victims, so perhaps it was a German seeking revenge. Or maybe it was me in my wellies.'

'This is no game, captain.' Thomas pressed the pistol back against Taylor's forehead and hissed, 'I will enjoy this.'

The smirk died on Taylor's face. 'How the hell do I know why the Huns were wearing those boots?'

'Huns? Pig's arse!'

'Germans.'

Thomas shook his head. 'I gave you a chance.'

Taylor took a deep breath. He was surprisingly calm for someone with a gun at his head. 'Germany wants that document intact as much as K wants it destroyed. Why else would I be here?'

Thomas drew the revolver back an inch.

'Old Kaiser Bill has taken a personal interest. One of our agents in Berlin confirmed the involvement of German military intelligence. I don't know who it was killed your father, but I know which side he was on.'

Thomas shook his head. 'Why the devil would Huns kill him?'

'Because the propaganda value of that document is incalculable. Berlin would make a colossal song and dance of it, portray the revered hero Lord Kitchener of Khartoum as ordering the deaths of innocent civilians and prisoners.'

'Which he did,' Thomas pointed out.

'And has frequently denied. The document would prove otherwise. Imagine K's disgrace! To be condemned by friend and foe, judged dishonourable, unprincipled, and worse – unfit to command. It would force his resignation as Secretary for War and quite possibly bring down the British government. Not to mention, alienate one of the Dominions. Public outrage in Australia would erupt at the worst possible time.'

Taylor paused and looked hard at Thomas. 'You don't give a damn about the killing of prisoners. What you Australians cannot abide is that your precious Breaker was scapegoated while his superiors got off scot-free.'

Thomas stayed silent.

'So much so that it might induce your government to withdraw troops,' continued Taylor, 'leave the Empire to fight her own fight.'

'Never,' Thomas cried. 'Australia is loyal.'

'London could not take the risk.'

'The German, who is he?'

'I don't know. Wish to hell I did. But it's the only plausible explanation.'

Thomas sat back in the chair. '"Whatever remains, however improbable, must be the truth",' he muttered.

'What was that?' said Taylor.

'Nothing . . . a line from Sherlock Holmes.'

'If my people learnt I had passed this information to you, they would shoot me.'

'One can hope.'

'I say, that's a tad harsh. We are on the same side, after all,' Taylor said, confident now that Thomas would not be shooting him. 'I wouldn't want to overstate it, dear boy, but I would regard myself in some small sense a friend.'

'Not that, never that.'

'The document is most likely still here. We must work together to find it.'

Thomas laughed at the man's gall. 'You and I may be allies, captain, but we are definitely not mates,' he said, standing up. He tucked Taylor's Webley into his pocket. 'And I'll keep this.'

Thomas left the cave elated and relieved.

Not only had he bested Bulala man to man, but if Taylor was to be believed, one or more Germans had murdered his father. He would much rather kill the enemy than someone from his own side. To kill the Hun was neither illegal nor wrong and he would be doing his country a service. Thomas could scarcely credit it. Never had revenge seemed so simple, appropriate and right. If there was one good thing to come out of his father's death, he realised, it was that Jack Clare had died bravely at the hands of their common enemy.

Thomas recalled Uncle Harry's story about the Kaiser giving orders to German troops: 'No quarter will be given, no prisoners will be taken.' Already, London was using the Kaiser's own words against him. Of course, Berlin would want Kitchener's TNP document. With it, Kaiser Wilhelm could turn the tables.

Sweet revenge, he thought. *It all makes sense.*

What did Thomas know of spies?

Conan Doyle was no help. In 'The Adventure of the Bruce-Partington Plans', the spy was 'Oberstein'. The name sounded German all right, but there was no useful description of the man. Thomas had always suspected that Sherlock's brother, the corpulent Mycroft, was shady enough to fit the bill, with his steel-grey, deep-set eyes, but he turned out to be on the right side after all.

No, the spy would be devious and sinister and have a foreign accent. Thomas chuckled to himself. No such Germans would dare be on our side of the line. What sensible spy would infiltrate an enemy army only to run the risk of death by shot or shell at the hands of his allies? A very brave one, that was for sure, but hardly likely. His Hun was not on Gallipoli, Thomas decided.

Then, why had the document gone missing so late in the day?

Who stole it? Where was it now? Thomas had carried it for a year. Any one of hundreds of soldiers with time on their hands and access to his kit could have nicked it. He had judged it secure simply because so few knew of its significance. What's more, none knew of its value to the Germans, he'd supposed, and none had a reason to steal it.

Might the Hun have an accomplice? A traitor? Such an agent would blend in, be able to move easily about the sector and not be subject to the predatory whims of an NCO. All of which suggested an officer of substantial rank. Again, he considered Aubrey Herbert - the man who liked Turks - short-sighted, eccentric, and a member of parliament, but hardly the sort to betray his country, for God's sake. An Australian officer or one of the senior sergeants? *Absurd*. Simply didn't bear thinking about.

If and when Thomas recovered the document, what should he do with it? His father had hidden it for more than a decade. Would he wish it destroyed or handed back to Taylor, a man he'd wanted punished for murder? It was one thing to keep an incriminating paper secret, Thomas thought, but quite another to allow Taylor to benefit from it. Jack Clare would never have wanted that. He would have expected his son to do his duty.

Somehow, he would recover the document. That much seemed clear enough. If Bulala got in his way again, he would kill him. If the thief turned out to be a German spy - snotter the bastard! If he had to go all the way to France or Flanders to find him, so be it.

Strange, though, that business of the stamp on his father's cheek, particularly when a Boer had stomped on Captain Hunt's face years earlier. Jack Clare's killer could hardly be a Boer. Was there a connection, or was it mere coincidence? *Not important*, he decided.

Revenge was still Thomas's mission. The murderer would get his just deserts, the kind the Breaker had once dispensed - Rule 303.

LAMBS

Lone Pine, August 1915

'Come, friend Watson, the curtain rings up for the last act.
You will be relieved to hear that there will be no war, that the
Right Honourable Trelawney Hope will suffer no set-back in
his brilliant career, that the indiscreet Sovereign will receive no
punishment for his indiscretion, that the Prime Minister will
have no European complication to deal with, and that with
a little tact and management upon our part nobody will be a
penny the worse for what might have been a very ugly incident.'
My mind filled with admiration for this extraordinary man.
'You have solved it!' I cried.
'Hardly that, Watson. There are some points which are as dark
as ever. But we have so much that it will be our own fault if we
cannot get the rest. We will go straight to Whitehall Terrace and
bring the matter to a head.'

– 'Adventure of the Second Stain',
Arthur Conan Doyle, 1904

Chapter 24

THOMAS PUSHED ASIDE THE OILCLOTH. In the dugout, Teach held his rifle upside down. His eyes were closed, he was breathing heavily and the muzzle was pressed against his left boot.

'Don't!' Thomas shouted.

Startled, Teach looked up as he pulled the trigger.

The shot was thunderous in the small space and dirt filled the air. When it cleared, both men were staring at Teach's boot. The bullet had gone clean through the sole, missing the foot.

'What the blue blazes did you want to do that for?' Thomas sighed, though he knew the answer already.

Teach examined the hole. 'Going to report me, corp?'

'Don't be daft.'

Sergeant Lucky Les tore the oilcloth aside and poked his head in, his face a picture of fury. 'What the fook?'

'Rifle malfunction, sarge,' Thomas lied. 'Ruined a perfectly good boot.'

The sergeant's expression did not change. 'Ya better fookin' not be scrimshankin',' he grumbled, 'or ya'll be on a charge, both of ya.'

With the sergeant gone, Teach grinned sheepishly at Thomas. 'Given a choice, a teacher may cripple a foot but will leave his blackboard hand intact.'

Filthy fingernails, chewed ragged, were at Teach's mouth, in a face that was gaunt and burned red. He showed neither anger nor resentment at being found out. It was a shell of the man who once had stood tall in the classroom and inspired Thomas with *Deeds that Won the Empire*.

'I'm no good anymore, Thomas.'

Like the rest, Teach was sick, shitting his trousers and spending much of the day on the pole. No one on Gallipoli was healthy, not even the brass, not anymore. The heat, sickness and rotten food had made skeletons of them all. They were sleepless and exhausted, having had no break from the constant racket and the endless repair of trenches, dugouts, saps and tunnels. Some were wondering aloud whether they would beat the Turk.

'You have to stick it, Teach.'

Strange to be reproaching his old teacher, Thomas thought, and not a little hypocritical. Teach wasn't the only one who had contemplated a self-inflicted ticket home. Thomas had wondered if a slug through the hand might not save him worse damage, though he had almost instantly rejected the idea.

'Do they even know what they're doing?' Teach said.

'They're our superiors and we must follow orders,' Thomas said without enthusiasm, for he had seen his officers order night raid upon raid across no-man's-land that had resulted in heavy casualties for no appreciable gain. Still, it was a shock to hear Teach – the most dutiful, patriotic, and deferential of all – express such doubts. 'It's our duty.'

'It's murder,' Teach said under his breath.

'We have no choice.'

'Kingy's dead and Snow has probably . . .'

Thomas wanted to strike him. 'Don't say that! He'll be back.'

'Has this place taught you nothing?'

'It's taught me that we mustn't let each other down.'

Teach shook his head and muttered, '"But their heart turned cold and they dropt their wings."'

'Jesus, Teach, give it a rest.'

'"Thou shalt wander obscure even in the house of Hades, flitting among the shadowy dead."'

'Cut it out.'

'It's Sappho, Thomas.'

'It's ancient bloody history.'

'It's here, staring us in the face.'

'If you must quote, why not "Fight on, brave knights! Man dies, but glory lives! Fight on! Death is better than defeat! Fight on, brave knights! for bright eyes behold your deeds!" Walter Scott, remember? You taught me that, at Murgon, in your classroom. I believed you.'

Teach lay back against the dugout wall, closed his eyes and shut Thomas out.

What had happened to him? Thomas wondered. Once, Teach had embodied the cultivated Australian, well regarded for volunteering, for leaving his wife and child to risk his life. Once, his stirring quotations had reminded them all of their duty to defend the Imperial race against the threat of barbarism.

But months of association with English, Welsh and Scottish allies had shown the Australians how different they were from those of the home country, how the small and acquiescent Tommies treated their officers like kings and how impossibly stuffy British officers could be.

Men who were strangers to fine prose and poetry had seen the noble sentiments Teach espoused crumble in gullies and dissolve in blood-soaked trenches. His ready quips and self-important lines of memorised text came to sound like nothing an Anzac would utter. Teach had become quaint and eccentric.

'Put a sock in it, Socrates,' they would say.

'Stop bunging it on.'

'You're no better than us.'

Thomas saw the weariness in every face. They were no longer fighting for something fine and civilising and Teach knew it as much as anyone. Now, Gallipoli was all about survival.

Snow had been little more than skin and bones when Thomas had left him on the beach. Now, here he was heavier and healthy and wearing a grin that would have done Kingy proud. He inclined his head so they could see the angry pink scar that marked the path of the bullet.

'Lucky it got your noggin,' Thomas joked, 'where you're tough as a mulga root.'

Snow beamed, until Thomas enveloped him in a hug. 'Jeez, cut it out, cobber,' he protested.

'Thought you'd be on the boat home,' Thomas stammered.

'What, and let you get to Constantinople without me?' Snow chuckled, until he noticed the cleft in Thomas's ear lobe. 'Cut yourself shaving?'

'A Manstopper – bled like the dickens,' boasted Thomas. 'One of Bulala's.'

'Bastard. Hope you beat the shit out of him?'

'Not quite, not yet.'

Teach pumped Snow's hand. '"Be glad, for this thy brother was dead, and is alive again; and was lost, and is found."'

'Crikey, can't a bloke say g'day without you two fussing like old chooks?' Snow said, before spending the next hour regaling them with tales of hot food, clean water and willing nurses, some of which they believed.

Chapter 25

FROM RUSSELL'S TOP, A SHELL from the Kiwi howitzers rushed overhead with a witch's shriek and fell with a thump somewhere along the line.

Thomas stared into the darkness. By his father's watch, it was four o'clock. The bombardment of the Turkish trenches had been going on for days. At night the red and green star shells lit up the night three-quarters of a mile away at Lone Pine.

But against the trenches opposite, there had been precious little in the way of a proper shelling, merely a few shrapnel bursts, not enough to cut the wire.

He was back at Quinn's. A few days earlier the 2nd Light Horse had replaced the Auckland Battalion, grateful that the Kiwis had put in a new fire trench and strung up some chicken wire as protection from the cricket balls.

The 'game' was drawn after fifteen weeks of play, as Thomas had overheard an officer say. Both sides had failed to move the other; the ugly reality was stalemate. Now, the Anzacs would try a new push and the excitement in the air was palpable. It would be a blessed relief from the demoralising cycle of thirst and sickness, from the heat and stink and more flies than in a thousand Queensland summers. The whole squadron was done in, almost to a man, and as bored as it was exhausted. Here at last, at least, was liberation from tedium; after all, deliverance unto fate was not a bad thing when most were convinced that whether you lived or died was a matter of luck.

Sergeant Lucky Les moved along the fire trench with a hearty word here, a jaunty laugh there, keeping spirits up, reminding the troopers of the essentials, which boiled down to run, get through the fookin' wire, 'op over the bags and skewer the so-and-sos.

Thomas shared the enthusiasm even as he trembled. Beyond everything else, the men were still keen to win.

In half an hour they would tear across the narrow patch of no-man's-land swept by machine guns. It would be glorious, Thomas knew, and it would be suicide.

The signal to charge would come in the pre-dawn at the moment a mine blew an almighty hole under the Turkish trenches. Four waves of men would sprint, B Squadron to the left and A on the right, with Thomas, Snow and Teach in the first wave of fifty.

Thomas thought that Major Bourne looked a worried man as he conferred with his officers, Major Logan and Lieutenants Burge and Norris, who would be first to go over the top.

'This is it, mate,' Thomas said. There was a gleam in Snow's eyes but he didn't reply, only grasped his hand and nodded.

It was heartening to have Snow back, but how he wished Kingy were with them to grin and joke. Not Teach. Teach was no help, slumped in his shrunken world of prayers and psalms, muttering old hymns of Empire, jumbled up with texts he'd recited for the innocent boys they had once been.

'". . . men and lions, wolves and lambs can never be of one mind, but hate each other out and out and through",' intoned Teach.

'Which are you, Teach?' interrupted Thomas.

Teach didn't respond, so Thomas kicked his leg. 'Which, Teach?'

'Oh God, Thomas, what a question! Not a lion, not today.'

'Me either.' It didn't bother him that Teach was scared, but that he was letting it show. 'Growl just the same, Teach, that's the thing you must do.'

Teach looked vacantly at Thomas and went back to mumbling, '". . . till one or other shall fall and glut grim Mars with his life's blood".'

Why couldn't the man shut up? Thomas tried not to listen. He felt the weariness return. He hadn't slept for ages. His nerves were strung like barbed wire, he strained to keep his sphincter tight, and he was terrified that tears – or worse – might burst free at any moment. He ground his teeth to keep the fear hidden.

Kingy had said, 'If you're not fookin' scared, you're a fookin' fool.' Brave and no fool was Kingy and sharp as a bayonet. But it had made no difference. He had died with his guts hanging out.

As the shrapnel shells exploded in sharp, close bangs over Turkish Quinn's, Thomas put his free hand over his eyes and held tight to his rifle with the other. Breathing deeply, he struggled to hold back the memories of men with faces shot away, legs and arms blasted asunder, black death in yellow sand, abandoned to flies and maggots.

Hell is no worse than here, he thought. *What a fool I am!*

When the regiment had been selected to make the assault from Quinn's, Thomas might have suggested he and Snow could be more useful sniping Turks instead of running at them with a bayonet. Yet, in a burst of enthusiasm, he'd insisted that they be in it. Now he yearned for home, to ride Rosie Girl with Winnie bareback behind him over a dawn track, or sit beneath a wide spreading tree with Ellen. He wanted his mother's lullaby and his father's arm around his shoulder. He was too young for this. My God, he'd hardly started.

Teach was still mumbling, '". . . valiant though you be, shall slay you at the Scaean gates".'

Thomas knew they would be for it. Bravery mattered little. The machine guns would see them out. If they were lucky, perhaps a few would reach the Turks. *Yes, that was it.* He would be one. Of course, he would. He would get there. It was only a short way. He was younger, stronger, faster. He had done it before, would do so again. It would be him to get there, to show Johnny a thing or two about Australians.

Teach's voice was rising, louder now, '". . . Moloch, horrid king besmeared with blood, of human sacrifice, and parents' tears, though for the noise of drums and timbrels loud their children's cries unheard, that passed through fire".'

Thomas knew it – Milton's *Paradise Lost* – had studied the poem at school. But to be reminded at such a time was infuriating. To hear it before an attack was bad for morale. He was a corporal, a cool veteran and cold sniper. Men looked to him. *Mustn't let them down, must hold fast to King and country, and trust to the Lord.*

He had to act. Thomas glanced up and down the trench. Most of the Light Horsemen were scribbling last notes or leaning back with eyes closed, others reading a Bible, one or two tearful, all of them waiting.

With a sudden lurch, Thomas burst across the gap and put his hand over Teach's mouth. His friend's eyes opened and widened.

Thomas spat words like bullets, 'Will you shut up! And that's an order.' He waited for the nod before releasing his hand and left Teach staring at his former pupil with surprise, sorrow and regret.

Thomas saw that one of the reinforcements had witnessed the exchange, a fresh-faced six-footer barely older than himself. Hamp was his name, Thomas recalled, and he wore a clean and neat uniform unlike the torn clobber of the old hands. He had arrived only the day before, full of enthusiasm as if expecting a picnic. Now he was shivering, though it was a warm August morning.

Bloody shame to come and go in a day. Thomas said, 'By jingo, it's chilly, eh, Hamp?'

'Yes.'

'Be over in a tick, you'll see,' Thomas said. 'We'll stonker the beggars, send Abdul trotting back home, eh?'

'I'll give it a go,' Hamp said, with downcast eyes.

'Maybe you don't know this, being new and all – but everybody feels a bit dicky.'

Hamp's eyes flicked up to Thomas.

'You heard of Lonesome Pine, Hamp? It's along the ridge south of here. Abdul holds it. It had a pine tree, though I don't expect it's there now, what with the artillery and all. Lone Pine, eh? On our lonesome. We all feel a bit like that from time to time. A chap would have to be stupid in the head not to.'

In the distance, the sounds of gunfire and bombs were plainly audible. Thomas cocked his ear. 'Listen,' he commanded. 'That's the lads taking Lone Pine and German Officers' Trench. By now the Enzeds will have chucked Abdul off Chunuk Bair. See, you're not alone, we're all in this together, and we don't go over till the artillery skittles his wire, all right?'

Hamp said nothing, so Thomas continued, 'You must aim for something in Abdul's trench and you had better bloody well run your hardest. Wanna bet I'll be there before you?'

The new man gave the faintest nod, closed his eyes and returned to his own little hell.

Thomas sighed. He'd done his best. The rest was up to Hamp, Johnny Turk and Lady Luck.

Already, the sergeant had outlined how their action fitted neatly into the jigsaw. At the same time, at half past four, other elements of the Light Horse would assault Baby 700, the Chessboard and The Nek. To their right, Australian infantrymen were storming the Turks at Lone Pine; the Poms were attacking from Suvla in the north; the Kiwis at Chunuk Bair, while the British, French and the rest would go at it from Helles in the south. The big guns firing from land and sea had been softening up the Turks and everything would go like clockwork in one combined breakout. Together they would overrun Johnny Turk and take the peninsula.

Thomas looked at his wristwatch, glad to be taking along a piece of his father. Not long now.

A lieutenant called a final roll. A sergeant went over their instructions again. The men checked their rifles and ammo clips, took a swallow from their canteens, and said their goodbyes. Some were still bent over, scribbling on scraps of paper on their ragged shorts, waiting for the chaplain to come by.

Thomas unfolded the magazine article, 'The Adventure of the Dying Detective' and began to write over its black-and-white illustration of Holmes and Watson.

'They're not a bit like us,' Snow laughed and then added, 'but we're just as good.'

'One of life's great moments is upon us, Winnie,' Thomas wrote on the picture. 'We welcome it. If we fall, remember us well.'

By the time the chaplain Sol Green had arrived, dispensing an encouraging word in each ear, Thomas had finished the letter and persuaded Snow to add a line at the end.

Teach handed the padre a piece of paper, explaining, 'For

the dispersal of my goods and chattels.' Captain Green merely nodded and took Thomas's letter also.

'August the seventh today, sir,' Thomas announced. 'My birthday.'

'Many happy . . .' The chaplain stopped before the next word, and looked quite uncomfortable.

Many happy returns. Thomas chuckled. 'And many more, eh, sir?'

Sol Green smiled. 'How old are you, corporal?'

'Seventeen, sir.'

'I'm afraid I have neither cake nor candle for you, and the sergeant will not allow us to sing.' He grasped Thomas's hand. 'All the same, I wish you good fortune and I'll say a prayer for you.'

'That will do nicely, sir.'

When Captain Green had passed on, Teach said, 'I didn't realise, Thomas. Congratulations.'

Thomas nodded his thanks. 'I buried my father on this day a year ago.'

'Yes, I was there. Terrible shame you never solved the puzzle about who killed him.'

Thomas shrugged. 'Too fricking late for that, I reckon.'

'I wanted to say, well, whatever happens, I'm sorry it's worked out this way.' Teach hesitated. 'And that I've been a disappointment to you.'

'No need.' Thomas shook his head. 'I've no regrets.'

The sergeant passed down the trench to check that each man was set. 'Ready to make the missus a rich widow?' he quipped, raising a few laughs.

'What's your wife's address, sarge?' Thomas replied. 'So's I can tell her what a hero you were and comfort her when you're gone.'

'Thank you, son, I'd appreciate that,' the sergeant chuckled and moved down the trench.

'Send my things on to Anna, there's a good lad,' Teach said. 'That's foolish talk.'

'If you say so, old sport.' Teach grinned awkwardly. 'Then it's "Once more unto the breach, dear friends".'

'That's more like it.' Thomas reached out and shook his hand. 'You've been a marvellous teacher and cobber. So long.'

'Good luck.' Teach closed his eyes again.

'Three minutes to go,' called out one of the lieutenants.

'"For England, home and beauty – eh, Watson?"' Thomas said to Snow, as one of Sherlock's lines sprung to mind.

'"Martyrs on the altar of our country",' Snow quoted back at him. 'Tom, remember what Tubbie told us about Battle Mountain and how the Kalkadoons ran into the guns?'

Thomas gulped. 'He said, "Be brave, be bloody careful, be clever."'

'"And don't jump in front of no bullets."'

They smiled grimly at each other.

'Two minutes,' said the lieutenant.

'You tell him his son was a Kalkadoon,' Snow said.

Thomas grasped Snow's hand. 'Mate . . .' was all he could say. He felt tears in his eyes and saw them in Snow's.

'All right, lads, stand-to,' a sergeant whispered from somewhere along the trench.

'One minute.'

Thomas looked at Hamp, the newcomer pale as a ghost. 'It'll be over soon,' he reminded him. Thomas looked at his watch. The hands glowed 4.30. Zero hour.

'Quiet now. Save your breath for the Turk,' the sergeant said.

'Steady,' said the lieutenant.

Thomas and many others stood with one foot on the step, while the rest crouched on the floor of the trench. Everyone listened hard for the blast of the mine under Turkish Quinn's.

Off to the left, they heard the sound of battle – their comrades had begun the attacks on Dead Man's Ridge and at The Nek. A minute passed, and then two. Nothing from the mine.

'What the hell?' Snow grumbled.

'Another bloody bungle,' someone scoffed.

As the minutes ticked by, an engineer brushed past Thomas with an urgent whisper. 'She's gone, boys, she's blown, mine's exploded,' and passed quickly down the trench with the same message.

Beside Thomas, Hamp shook his head with a barely suppressed panic. 'Are they sure, corp? It made no noise at all.'

Poor bugger, Thomas thought, poor us.

'Prepare to jump out,' said the CO, Major Bourne.

Suddenly he gave the order, whistles blew. 'Up and at 'em!' someone yelled.

'Come on, boys!' Thomas cried as, heart hammering, he scrambled over the parapet and ran as fast as he could into the darkness.

He flew at the little red flashes that danced ahead. A mighty crescendo enveloped him – the thunderous rattle of Anzac machine guns behind, combining with those of the Turks echoing from the heights. The ground seemed to tremble as if in a hailstorm. With blinding sharpness a flare converted night into day, revealing a blistering pantomime of khaki figures running and falling. Zephyrs of lead sliced his clothes and singed his skin. Something sticky and vile drenched one side of his face and he spat it out. His rifle, with a mind of its own, sprang from his hands. A moment later a burning pain shot through his thigh and a sledgehammer smashed his head. He crumpled, and felt himself tumbling until a gouge in the scarred earth stopped him dead.

His last image was of a man who seemed to shudder and come to pieces beside him. *Was it Hamp, or Teach, or Snow?* Thomas wondered, before the darkness took him.

Chapter 26

IT HURT LIKE HELL. His thigh burned and his head hammered. Dirt filled his mouth and tasted foul. His cheek scraped along the earth. Something was pulling him, something iron-hard around his ankle, a grappling hook, he guessed, feet first through a narrow space. Hands grasped his ankles and dragged him down. He slid over sandbags, face crashing until, once more, blackness.

He pitched and rocked. His right arm trailed down over the edge of something hard. A gunwale of a small boat, he imagined, in a rough sea. Until a sudden bump sent a shiver of agony through him, he opened his eyes and understood – a stretcher. There were muffled voices he couldn't understand and even the neighing of horses amid an endless background thunder. Rosie Girl. Above was blue sky and a sun so piercing he closed his eyes and slept.

The light was dazzling, right into his eyes. He decided to keep them closed. Must be facing the dawn, he thought. No, that couldn't be right. Not from Anzac, not without getting shot.

A drumming ache filled his head. He tried to move his hands up there, but found them roped to a pole pressed against his back. He half-opened an eye, long enough to see a grey strip of cloth wrapped around his left thigh, oozing blood.

Something hit his foot with a sudden violence that sent an almighty pain through him. He screamed. A long blade confronted him and behind it the angry unkempt face of Abdul. Other soldiers stood behind him and Thomas was shocked by the fury in all their faces.

The Turk pulled back his bayonet to plunge it forward into Thomas's eye, when a voice rang out.

'Halt!'

Distracted for a moment, the Turk turned towards whoever had given the order. He hawked and spat, and then quick as a snake snapped back to stab with the bayonet. A loud crack rang out and the Turk crumpled, falling onto Thomas and sending another tremor of pain up his side.

Thomas awoke to find the Turk's head laid across his knees. Blood trickled from the small hole in the man's skull.

'German officer did for him,' said a familiar voice. Teach was sitting on the bare earth, tied to another of the bunker's heavy wooden supports.

'Oh, am I glad to see you!' Thomas cried.

Teach responded with a sad smile.

Thomas tried to move his legs, to kick the head away, but only succeeded in generating another burst of pain.

'You'll start the bleeding,' Teach advised. 'You got a crack on the head and a bullet in the thigh.'

'You?'

'Not so good.' Teach twisted slightly away and grunted. A wide strip of greyish cloth circled his torso, with a dark black line spread horizontally across his back. 'Took one in the back, can't feel my legs.'

'Shit, mate.'

'We're a pair, aren't we?'

'Did Snow fall?'

'I couldn't say.'

'What about the others – the three waves after us?'

Teach shook his head. 'I don't think so. The major would have seen us cop it, and called a halt.'

'Thank Christ,' sighed Thomas. *It would have been murder.* He looked around. The bunker opened above a deep gully, through which snaked a long line of Turks. 'Where in hell's name are we?'

'They took us south. Somewhere near Lone Pine.'

'I could have sworn I heard horses.'

'Yes, must be a stables nearby.'

Thomas tried again to move his legs, gently this time. Though every inch was a dagger in his thigh, he shifted enough for the Turk's head to slip to the ground. He breathed deeply until the pain receded. 'Odd, don't you think, Hun shooting Turk?'

'Saved your hide. He's German intelligence, wants to know what's going on, left Abdul there as a warning to other Johnnies to leave us alone.'

'Well, he'll get bugger-all from me,' said Thomas with a show of pluck for Teach, though he felt completely drained and utterly helpless.

From close to hand came a rat-a-tat-tat and the occasional shriek of a shell. When one exploded nearby, the ground shuddered and dust fell from between the ceiling timbers. Thomas noticed that his watch was still on his wrist but that his feet were bare. 'Bastards took my boots.'

'And your pistol,' Teach said.

'It was Bulala's.'

'Officer's weapon, dashed lucky you had it. They'll want to interrogate you.'

Thomas faded in and out of consciousness. The next thing he knew a young soldier was shaking him awake and his leg was throbbing again.

On a chair opposite, an older man in a grey, well-tailored double-breasted jacket sat smoking a cigarette. Beside him, the body of the Turkish soldier was propped up against another pole. Thomas wondered what kind of officer would shoot an ally in cold blood. Then he remembered Bulala.

The German officer caught him gazing at the corpse. 'Regrettable, but necessary,' he said in heavily accented English. 'The Turk is a simple soldier. Your comrades attack. He sees you, he wants to kill. That is war, no? *Pfft*, simple.'

The officer dragged deeply on his cigarette. 'So, you are alive, but for how long? That is why you will answer my questions, no?'

'Thomas Robert Clare,' Thomas said. 'Corporal.'

'Ah, not an officer. *So jung*. How old?'

Thomas saw no harm in the question. It might be to his advantage. 'Seventeen.'

'*Ja.*' The officer nodded. 'Pity.'

Teach interrupted, 'We are Australians, sir, simple soldiers ourselves,' and then continued to speak in rapid German.

Thomas wasn't worried. Teach had taught the subject at school. He wouldn't let anything slip. 'Stick to your guns, mate. Don't tell the bastard anything,' he said softly. Teach was smart, smarter by a long shot than any Hun.

As they spoke, Thomas thought hard. The enemy had destroyed a squadron of Light Horse. The Turks and their German officer allies would want to know the extent of the offensive and where the Anzacs would strike next. So it was not to be TNP, not yet. On the other hand, Abdul would need every available man for the fight and would not wish to waste time with POWs. No wonder Teach was talking.

Thomas felt ashamed. He had not expected this. Shot, maimed or crippled, yes, even blown to bits. But not the indignity of years spent behind enemy wire. There was nothing about being a prisoner that was gallant or brave and no way to do his duty.

And what if Snow got back, what would he think? That his friend was in no-man's-land, wounded and unreachable? Or food for grubs and best forgotten? Or that Thomas got windy, chucked it up without a fight, a coward who went over to the foe? *God no, not that.*

Thomas wrestled with his fears. If the Turks discovered he was a sniper, would they castrate him? Would they gouge out his right eye or sever his trigger finger? He'd heard they did that to a sniper. Or would they simply bayonet him and move on? The Anzacs had taken hardly any prisoners in the first days after the landing, the sergeant had said, neither had the Turks. In the face of another Anzac offensive, would they again TNP? He shivered as he remembered the wounded old greybeard he'd stuck. Or would they put him in front of a firing squad like the Breaker? Would they force him to betray his mates first and then kill him? Was he strong enough to resist torture?

Thomas screwed his eyes tight. His war was over. Oh, he was such a failure. As a soldier he'd been captured and as a son he had not avenged his father. The thoughts stormed through his head and filled him with shame.

Thomas awoke to loud and strident voices speaking in German. He looked across at Teach, who was sobbing.

The enemy officer was waving his Luger in a threatening manner. Teach cried out something in German, prompting the officer to strike. The pistol barrel whipped across Teach's face, opening a long red slash in his cheek.

'Thomas,' Teach pleaded, his face a picture of blood and pain. 'Tell him! The document, Kitchener's signature.'

Thomas shook his head, confusion welling up inside him. 'What the blazes?'

'He knows, Thomas.'

'You told him?'

'Just now, but he doesn't believe me. Make him believe, Thomas. I told him it's in my kitbag. Please, it's our only chance.'

The officer turned his pistol on Thomas. 'Your comrade says he works for Berlin, and that there is a document that will help Germany. He is lying, yes?'

Thomas struggled to make sense of things. He looked across at Teach, who whimpered as blood flowed down his cheek. What did he mean, 'It's in my kitbag', when he'd told Thomas it had been stolen? Had Teach kept it and what could he possibly want with it?

'I'm sorry, Thomas,' he said in a voice filled with despair, 'but you must see, I had no choice.'

'I don't understand.' Thomas shook his head, dumbfounded.

'They gave me no choice,' Teach repeated.

Did he know something about his father's death? No, such an idea was ridiculous. Teach had known his father for years; he had given the eulogy at Jack Clare's funeral. Teach would never betray him; not this gentle, educated man, who had been Thomas's teacher, father figure and mate. Working for Berlin? Never! Not this patriot who had fostered his love of Empire and its heroes.

'What are you talking about?'

'When Jack died . . . I was there.'

At the murder. 'Oh, Teach,' Thomas sighed, as a deep pain cut through him, worse than the agony in his leg.

'Thomas, I can explain. But please, tell him, or we're both dead.'

'Where is this document?' snapped the scowling German.

A cold hard resolve filled Thomas. His father had refused to give it to a Hun and neither would he.

Thomas took a deep breath. 'There is no document.'

The German swung his pistol and fired. The shot rang loudly in the bunker. 'It will take time, *mein freund*,' the officer said as he stood up to leave. 'As much of my time as you have wasted.'

Chapter 27

Not even the noise of battle in the distance could drown out the wretchedness of Teach's groaning. At one stage, he moaned, 'Why could you not have told him?'

Silent, Thomas stared at him. The neat hole in his tunic told him what he needed to know. Bullet in the stomach, nearly always fatal.

'Oh, it's probably for the best,' Teach said. 'Not much of a life left for me anyway.'

Filled with anger, sorrow and confusion, Thomas said nothing.

A little later, Teach whimpered, 'Oh God, grant me a quick end.'

'You don't deserve it,' Thomas snapped, 'not after betraying your country and my father. You were *there*, that night, when he died?'

'I never meant him to die. Please believe me. He said Jack would be released when they found the document.'

'Who's *he*?' Thomas croaked.

'I never knew his name.'

'Tell me.'

'They referred to him as the Boche.'

'Traitor!'

'We weren't at war. Not then. It hadn't been declared.'

'But my father . . . your friend.'

'They swore they wanted the document, nothing more. But you know Jack, he was stubborn, wouldn't co-operate. It was only when they threatened to harm you that he wrote the note.'

Thomas knew it by heart. *My son . . . grievously sorry to leave you . . . would rather die this way than live without my dearest Rose . . . regret having been such a poor father . . . do not blame yourself . . . your loving father.*

'By then he knew he was for it,' continued Teach. 'When they used the same threat – to kill you – unless he produced the document, he just laughed in their faces, told them they were bluffing, said you hadn't a clue about it, killing you wouldn't help them in the slightest.'

That's why he kept it secret. Thomas gritted his teeth to strangle the tears before they could begin. *To protect me.* 'This Boche, what did he look like?'

'It was too dark, he kept his distance.'

'Tall, short, young, old – which, Teach?'

'I couldn't tell, never spoke to him. He was on his horse in the trees the whole time.'

'Did my father know him?'

'I don't know. It all happened so quickly. They strung him up and tortured him.' Teach groaned with the effort of telling the story.

'And you did nothing to stop it?'

'How could I? There were too many of them, and they'd threatened my Anna and little Felix. "Of evils, choose the least," Cicero said, and I chose my family.'

Thomas wanted to reach out and throttle the life out of him, stop his stupid quotations, shut him up for good. *No need*, he decided. The man wouldn't last much longer.'

'There were three of them with the rope,' Teach continued with a moan. 'They tied one end to the bough and two of them hauled him up by the neck, while the other was on the ground and pulling on Jack's ankles, demanding answers. Your father refused to speak, so they lifted him up and sat him on the branch. His hands weren't tied so he fought them, and they couldn't hold him. He fell, Thomas, too far for a big man like your father. It was ghastly. You know the rest. They made it look like suicide. They had it all worked out, except for the decapitation.'

'And what were you doing when your friend was being butchered?'

'I never meant it to end that way,' Teach gasped and started a trickle of new blood down his blackened khaki.

'Oh, how you twist everything!' Thomas cried. 'You were in the company of murderers. That makes you equally criminal. How do you explain that? What's your next quotation going to be, Teach, more parroting of the masters? Some fancy line, maybe a stanza or two? What poetic excuse for betrayal of friendship, your country and King? What about the stab in the back, the unkindest cut of all, "*Et tu, Brute?*"'

Teach's bloodied face bent into a pained grimace. 'I've taught you well.'

'Taught me enough of treason to last a lifetime. You gave me hope after my father's death and when I learnt of my mother's suicide. But you've made a sham of it.' Thomas stopped, exhausted, feeling that his anger might dissolve into tears.

Teach's breathing had grown laboured, but he whispered, 'There's more you need to know. Griffin approached me when I was appointed to teach in Murgon.'

'The copper?'

'From Wondai.'

Thomas drew a surprised breath. Sergeant Griffin had investigated the hanging and pronounced it suicide. The policeman had taken Thomas to the hospital to view his father's body and informed him of his mother's suicide. *Blunt but honest.*

Teach went on, 'Griffin claimed to be working for the British government and said Jack possessed information to damage Lord Kitchener in the event of war with Germany. He wanted me to observe your father. I believed it my duty to co-operate, so I sought Jack out.'

'Why didn't you simply ask him?'

'I did and he laughed at me. I told him that London knew the document was in his possession, but Jack said he would never lift a finger to help Kitchener, said the document was the "smoking pistol in his hand", whatever that meant.'

'Proof of murder.' Thomas sighed as the memory filled him with affection for his father. 'From a story he and I once read together – Sherlock's first case.'

'Ah, the world's greatest *boy* detective.'

'You bastard!' Thomas's anger flared. 'How much did they pay you?'

'Thomas, you know me,' Teach groaned. 'I'd blown my dough.'

'How much?' Thomas repeated. 'Thirty silver pieces?'

'I was dead motherless broke . . . desperate!' Teach pleaded. 'I thought they would merely search your house, find the damned paper and leave. You were away, the place was empty with Jack at the pub until late. But he came home early and found us.'

'Us?'

'The Boche, his thugs and Griffin.'

'You said Griffin was working for the British.'

'*And* Berlin. Both wanted the document.'

Thomas shook his head. 'He was Dad's comrade in the war.'

'Griffin had a lot of bottled-up anger towards Jack. He forced him down at gunpoint, stepped on his face, said something like "That's for Percy Hunt and the Breaker, for testifying against us, what the Boer does to bastards like you."'

'Oh, the swine!'

'Griffin was the one who held the rope. After your father died, they were going to kill me because I was a witness, but Griffin said I should watch you, that it was their best chance to find the document. That's when I enlisted with you.'

'Were you ever my friend, my comrade?'

'Always, Thomas, and no one despises the Kaiser more than I. But I had to think of my family. For God's sake, it's a scrap of old paper, that's all it is.'

Now Thomas understood why Teach had tried to shoot himself. A Blighty would have seen him evacuated to Egypt, where he could easily have passed the document on.

'It's stashed with my kit,' Teach said. 'Post it to my wife. She'll see to it.'

'Not much chance of that. Abdul will pack me off before long.'

'Please, Thomas, I'm done for. You must give it to them.'

'Are you blind?' Thomas said. 'I'm shot and liable to be gutted any moment.'

Teach groaned – a rasping, deathly thing. 'Remember the one you took in the neck? You have the luck.'

'I'm no use to anyone.'

'If anyone can get back, it's you.'

Despite his anger, Thomas couldn't help but smile. *High expectations*. Teach always had them, from the very first time in Murgon's little schoolhouse when – as his teacher Mr West – he'd demanded Thomas give of his best. Teach had challenged and inspired him with stories of Britannia's victories against overwhelming odds. It was William West's encouragement that had driven Thomas to aspire to higher education in Brisbane, when he might just as easily have opted for a job as a farmhand or at the butter factory. Teach had been passionate about his books and Thomas had loved him for it.

Now, he was near death and Thomas was likely to join him soon enough. *He's not got long.* Thomas met the man's pleading eyes. 'All right,' he said.

Teach sighed, whether from gratitude or exhaustion, or with relief at finally making a clean breast of it, Thomas couldn't tell. In a weak voice, he said, 'It's eaten me, Thomas, this secret, my role in Jack's death. I am so sorry for it.'

Thomas was silent, his anger diminished, but he was not about to forgive.

'And there's something else you must know.'

Thomas's ears pricked up. *What could be worse?*

'Years before the Germans got wind of the document, Bulala Taylor hired Griffin, whom he'd known from the Boer War, to work for British intelligence. Taylor had Griffin search your home while Jack was out bush and you were in Brisbane.'

Thomas shivered, as if a cold hand had plucked at his heart.

'Your mother was there, of course,' Teach continued. 'Griffin tried to convince her that he was on police business, but she didn't believe him, said she'd report him if he didn't leave. He threatened her and she ran. He caught her in the stable and poured Lysol down her throat, watched her die.'

So unexpected was the story that Thomas jerked back against the pole and sent a knife through his wounded leg. But it was nothing compared to the agony in his heart. *Not suicide.* She had fought for life. A moment later, he felt as if a terrible weight had lifted. *She didn't mean to leave me.*

'Griffin told me to my face,' said Teach. 'Said he'd do the same to my Anna if I refused to help him.'

The country copper, his father's comrade, had murdered them. Mother and father, Thomas realised. *Both.*

'Griffin played both sides' – Bulala and the Boche,' Teach added. 'I imagine he did well out of it.'

It took Teach hours to die. Thomas looked away. He had seen enough of it, more than most boys his age, had learnt to harden himself to the last agonies.

Teach did not pray, at least not aloud. Instead he spoke for Thomas to hear, '"If I must die, I will encounter darkness as a bride, and hug it in my arms."'

Thomas knew how Teach wanted him to respond – *There spake my brother; there my father's grave, did utter forth a voice. Yes, thou must die.* He could recite the line from memory, learnt well in Teach's classroom: *Measure for Measure*, Act III, Scene 1, 'A room in the prison'. But he remained silent. When, finally, he glanced back, his old teacher was slumped, hanging from the pole, his face grey, chin on his chest, mouth yawning.

Thomas began to sob. Not for Teach, he told himself, but for what they had shared. For Teach who had been the man his father never was – educated, eloquent, whose every word sang of romance, history and adventure, as if British values and the duty to uphold them were bound up in one man. Teach had been England and Empire.

'You lived too long in the past,' he shouted at the corpse. 'You believed in a fantasy. There's nothing noble left in the world. Nothing. Look at us, Teach, look at us.'

Thomas knew also that he was weeping for himself. The teacher had betrayed his students, his mates, his country and

Thomas's father. Most of all he had betrayed Thomas, and at the end Thomas had betrayed Teach.

Now Thomas knew his father's killers, but it was no job well done, no Holmesian moment to crow. There was no description of the Boche. He'd gained little of substance from Teach's death. He could have told the German interrogator the truth about the document. His failure to do so had killed his friend as surely as the Hun's bullet, as surely as his bayonet had finished the old Turk, as surely as Kitchener had failed to stop the firing squad that disposed of Morant and Handcock. *I'm no better than any of them,* he thought.

In his mind, his mother appeared, her face hazy with the years. No longer dead by her own hand, she was screaming as the poison seared her insides. He saw the desperate struggle, her questioning what she had done to deserve this, the fear and surprise as death took her.

And his father's pain at finding her. *As I found him.* For the first time, Thomas understood the demons that drove his father. How he must have agonised over losing her and tortured himself with guilt by believing Sergeant Griffin's story that she had taken her own life.

Griffin had murdered her while working for Taylor. Griffin had murdered his father while working for the Boche. Later, as Ellen had written in her letter, the copper had joined Taylor in Murgon to search again for the document. Griffin had taken the King's pound and the Kaiser's deutschemark.

All this time, in war and peace, Griffin had been both comrade and colleague of Thomas's father. The man had waited twelve years to settle accounts with Jack Clare for testifying at the courts-martial. It staggered Thomas to think how cold and patient, how vicious and deceitful, Griffin was.

It seemed everything began and ended with a lie. Began, he realised, with the lies that sent Morant and Handcock to their graves and entangled his father with the document. Griffin's lie about the manner of Rose's death had sentenced Jack Clare to years of shame and regret. Griffin's claim that his mother had once tried to kill Thomas as a baby had caused a son to doubt his mother's love. Even his father had lied by pronouncing Rose's death to be an accident when he believed it to be suicide. Then Griffin had lied to Thomas by claiming Jack Clare had taken his own life. Taylor's lie had led Thomas to think finally of him as an ally, when he was an accomplice to his mother's murder. Teach's lies had betrayed his father and, yes, by God, Thomas's own lie to the Hun officer had sealed Teach's fate.

So many lies.

Thomas felt crushed under their weight.

Was everything he knew a lie? He could hardly breathe, he was shaking, his thigh burned like the devil.

At some point in the afternoon someone called his name, but when he looked around the bunker, he found it empty.

The voice was in his head, he realised, soft and enticing like a cool stream on a summer's day and as close as a kiss. *Say goodbye to the lies*, she whispered. *You did your best. Let them go.*

Winnie, he thought.

And another voice broke in, stern like a father's and far away. *Never surrender! There is more to do. Get up, get out.*

And Winnie – or was it his mother? – purred, *Do you want to go on like this? You can leave the pain behind so easily . . . sleep, sleep.*

Thomas smiled, dropped his head on his chest and slept.

On the shore his mother is calling. He struggles through the water to reach her, dragging a leg that pains terribly. He looks down, expecting clear water over golden sand, but sees instead a floor of crushed skulls and green slime squeezed from the bones with each step he takes. The skulls are laughing at him. One with Snow's face says, *I'm dead.* Another with Kingy's argues, *No you're not, I am, I'm dead,* while Bulala's face laughs with slitted cat's eyes, *Off with his head.* The skulls become giant scorpions and he runs from the water onto a beach below exploding clouds. He ducks and weaves but a heavy black cricket ball smashes into his leg. He falls and, upon examining the wound, finds the enormous mouth of his father's severed head eating him.

Thomas struggled violently. The leg was agony, people were pushing and pulling, doing painful things to it. He decided it must be a nightmare and fell back into darkness.

Chapter 28

WHEN HE NEXT WOKE UP, his thigh was newly bandaged and Teach's body was gone. There was a heavenly taste in his mouth and a delightful coolness spilling down his neck. When his eyes focused, he found a Turk drawing back a canteen from his mouth.

The soldier muttered darkly as he stood up, but not before hawking a gob of spittle that caught Thomas on the cheek. Another voice rang out sharply in Turkish and the soldier departed, grumbling.

'He says you are an infidel who would steal his land and dishonour his wife.' The voice came from the same chair occupied earlier by the German. 'He says you deserve to be treated as you treat his comrades.'

'And how is that?' Thomas asked.

'To be rolled over the cliff.'

Thomas shivered.

The newcomer was a thin-faced young man with a slight moustache. He was neatly dressed in a khaki uniform, polished boots and leggings and a pistol in his belt. 'I am Mehmet *Effendi*, Captain Mehmet in your language,' he said quietly in fluent

English. 'You have recovered. That is good. Your wound and the fever – we believed you would die.'

Thomas looked down at his bare feet. 'Is that why your men robbed me?'

The young officer smiled. 'It is the custom in the Ottoman army to address an officer with "sir". Is that not the case in yours?'

Thomas paused. 'Yes, sir.'

'Then, I must apologise for the loss of your boots. Sadly, there is a shortage and at present our need is greater than yours.'

Thomas nodded. *Fair enough, I'm not going anywhere.*

'With or without proper footwear, we will prevail over you English.'

'I'm Australian, sir.'

The Turk snorted. 'You are hardly our allies.'

'Allies?' Thomas was confused. Was this a trick to make him talk? Then he realised. 'Not Austrians, sir. Australians.'

The captain narrowed his heavy eyebrows. 'Not English? What is the difference?'

'We are bigger, smarter, braver.'

'Bullets do not discriminate,' said Captain Mehmet. 'What regiment?'

Now it's down to business, Thomas thought. He gave his name and rank. Then, seeing no harm in stating the obvious, he added on a whim, 'Light Horse, sir.'

'I see no horses. Perhaps you ate them, instead of your awful bully beef.'

Thomas wondered if his interrogator was serious or playing with him. 'We left them behind.'

'You are weak without them.'

'We do well enough.'

'What is your main objective?'

'I'm just a trooper, sir.'

'Is your objective here, or in the north? I suspect it is in the north, yes?'

'Officers know that kind of stuff, not me,' Thomas said.

'Your comrade said you would advance along the entire front.'

'Of course, until we take Constantinople,' Thomas agreed. *That'll put the wind up him.* But, privately, he wondered what else Teach had told the German interrogator. 'That Hun murdered him.'

'Much to my regret. We are not all barbarians. One may choose a friend, but sadly not one's ally.' Captain Mehmet paused before continuing, 'Of course, you are lucky to be alive. It is difficult – is it not? – for a soldier to take prisoners.'

Thomas laughed a little nervously.

The Turk raised one eyebrow. 'What is humorous?'

'It's a long story,' Thomas said. 'I have escorted many Turks safely to the stockade, and I've seen Captain Herbert question them.'

'Ah, the honourable Herbert Effendi, a fine English gentleman.'

'I was with him during the ceasefire when we buried our dead.'

'A sad day,' nodded the Turkish officer. 'But a moment of sanity.'

Thomas recalled Captain Herbert's speech to the Turks at Quinn's Post and decided it wouldn't hurt his prospects to repeat it. 'We have no fight against the Turks, sir. The Germans are our enemy, not you.'

The Turk sighed. 'Such pretty words from one who arrives without an invitation and shoots at us!'

He's right there, Thomas thought. The man was no mug. 'My uncle is Brigadier General Chauvel.'

'In that case, we will *not* shoot you.' Captain Mehmet chuckled. He opened a silver case and placed a cigarette between Thomas's lips. 'After we defeat this attack of yours, *inshallah,* we will escort you to a comfortable hotel where you will be well treated, according to the usual conventions.'

Captain Mehmet flicked the flame on a silver lighter and lit Thomas's fag. He stood up to leave. 'Do not concern yourself. For you the war is over. The doctor will return to see to your leg. Good luck.'

Is that all? Thomas wondered as the chivalrous young officer departed. He'd scarcely asked any military questions, had not employed threats, and seemed more interested in practising his English. Aubrey Herbert had described ordinary Turks as genial and polished and Herbert had been right about so many things. On the other hand, perhaps the not-unpleasant captain, or his German ally, would return with the thumbscrews.

If I last that long. He looked down at the black stain on the bandage. *Doesn't smell. No gangrene, thank Christ. Not yet.* But the leg might soon fester. He might wake up in the fine hotel that the Turk had promised, only to find the bloody thing sawn off. No, Thomas didn't fancy that. He would have to see a proper doctor.

A gammy leg wouldn't get him far. The Turks would shoot him leaving and the Anzacs would shoot him coming. Either way, he was buggered.

Escape seemed impossible. Certainly the Turks believed so. Confident that Thomas was crippled, they had left him unguarded and untied his hands so he could feed himself from the food left in a bowl – olives, wheat kernels and bread. After the monotonous Anzac diet of slimy meat and hard biscuits, it tasted like heaven. Thomas wolfed it down as if it was his last meal. *True enough*, he thought grimly.

From inside the bunker, he could see a large part of the eastern sky. A reconnaissance aircraft grated through the pink and mauve twilight, whether Turkish or British it was impossible to tell. Every so often a shell would explode in a burst of flame on the far ridge, as the Royal Navy sought out enemy reinforcements, and around him the sounds of battle continued in shrieks and thuds and an almost ceaseless rat-a-tat-tat, near and far.

The bunker stank with the familiar mix of sweat, urine, shit and ash, no different from the other holes he had lived in. But Thomas no longer felt beaten down.

In his waking hours since Teach's death, with little to do but reconsider his life up to that point, Thomas had drawn some surprising conclusions from the information Teach had bequeathed him. His mother had bravely fought an attacker twice her size, which meant that she had not willingly abandoned him to the care of an absent father and distant relatives. 'Say goodbye to the lies,' the voice had whispered in his dream. *She did love me.*

Teach's description of his father's last hours had filled Thomas with as much pride as anger. His father had endured terrible torture to keep the document secret and Thomas thought he knew why: the man had no intention of using it against Kitchener or of returning it to Bulala or of allowing the Germans to use it against the Empire. The tough bastard simply refused to give it up. It was Jack Clare's stubbornness, pure and simple. He had lost his wife and would lose his life, but he would not give in to threats.

My father was a hero. His was the angry voice in Thomas's head, refusing to let the son yield to death or captivity.

If his father and his mother would not submit, then neither would he. He had been captured, yes, but he had never surrendered. He would not now. Better to die than to eat crow at the hands of the enemy. He would make a break for it. He would scarper or, far more likely, die trying. In either case, escape was his solemn duty and the only way to bring the sorry saga to an end.

He would retrieve the document from Teach's belongings. What he would do about the Boche and Griffin, he had no idea.

First things first. He must make a break now, while close to the Anzac trenches, for even if he survived his wounds, a faraway Turkish gaol would end his chances, along with his soldiering and career as the boy detective.

'More like the *dead* detective,' he muttered.

Thomas remembered the story Ellen Woods had sent him, 'The Adventure of the Dying Detective'. He'd read it so many times that he knew it by heart.

Holmes had appeared to be dying from a rare disease. He had neither eaten nor drunk for several days and, with the help of a little vaseline, belladonna, rouge and beeswax, had contrived to make himself appear to be at death's door. The world's greatest detective had declared, 'The best way of successfully acting a part is to be it.'

A *disguise*. Sherlock might be a proper git, a stuck-up Pommy from an old-fashioned world far away, but that did not make him entirely useless on Gallipoli.

For rouge, Thomas could apply blood from his wounds. Instead of beeswax, belladonna and vaseline, he could substitute the one thing he had plenty of: Turkish dirt. Yes, that was the ticket. Blood and earth for a mask. Dirt would disguise a white boy from Queensland. There were bound to be sick and wounded aplenty in the Turkish trenches, and one more filthy, bloodied soldier might go unnoticed. He would use the sniper's skills of camouflage and concealment, and *imshi* the fook out.

As for the rest, well, he would make it up as he went along. *Just when you think Holmes is done for, up he pops,* Thomas chuckled. *If I'm to die, might as well have some fun first.*

Chapter 29

WHEN DARKNESS HAD WELL AND truly settled around the bunker, Thomas hoisted himself up the support pole. The move sent such agony through his leg that he had to grit his teeth against screaming. Standing unsteadily with his back braced against the rough wood, he pushed down his trousers and sent a stream of urine three feet to splash into the soup bowl. He slipped down the pole and sat waiting for waves of nausea to subside. He dipped his hands in the bowl and then smeared the blood from around his thigh onto his face and neck. Next, he pulled the souvenir Mauser bullet from his pocket and scored the hard ground with it, then poured the last of the piss onto the scratched earth and with his hands transferred newly-made mud to as much of his skin, tunic and regimental patches as he could reach.

'Earth to earth, dust to dust,' he murmured, and wished he had a mirror. Darker, grubbier, less like an Anzac, he hoped.

On the path outside, shadows hurried past too busy with war to look in. Once, a group of soldiers carrying cardboard boxes of cartridges entered and stacked them in the space formerly occupied by Teach. Half an hour later, another group came to collect them. They afforded Thomas barely a glance. He felt invisible and it strengthened his resolve. Perhaps they'd forgotten about him.

He looked at his watch, still amazed it had not been stolen. Abdul might take your boots if he had none himself, but he was not a thief.

It was nearly midnight. Gingerly, he stretched his legs and slivers of agony flew up his wounded limb. That wouldn't do; both legs had to carry him. Thomas raised and lowered each slowly, gently, testing himself against the pain.

He rested and tried to imagine his father's last day on earth. What was Jack Clare thinking as the noose tightened around his neck? He would have known his chances of escape were zero, that he would die. His father had borne the pain, struggled to the very end, and would have expected nothing less of the son.

Thomas would escape, would survive the war, would find this Boche and settle things with Griffin. He owed it to them, father and mother.

Night would be his friend. But he would wait for the right moment, whenever that was.

The answer came in a roar and a flash of light as shells exploded around the bunker. The ground trembled and the roof shook a load of dirt over him, plastering his hair. He began to brush it out, until he realised, *I'm a bloody redhead.* He looked up at the roof. *Thank you, God.* He mixed mud and urine on his hands and rubbed them over his scalp.

Go now, he thought, while Abdul has his head down.

Thomas pulled himself up the pole until he stood hugging it. He took a step towards the opening. Bullets of pain shot through him, threatening to topple him in a sickening wave of dizziness, until he grasped the next pole and hung on. The shells were falling further away, like distant thunder, so he stumbled out and began to limp along the track beside the bunker. He was grateful that the dust raised by the explosions would hide him, though it meant he might blunder into an unseen Turk at any moment.

After fifty yards, he leant against an earth embankment and breathed a sigh of relief. So far he had met no one. It was wonderful to be free, but he had no idea where he should be going, other than uphill towards what he expected to be no-man's-land. When a side track leading upwards presented itself, he took it, dragging his wounded leg and sliding his hands along the embankment for guidance and support. In this way, he travelled another thirty yards, where he came to a sap and was startled by the sight of bodies choking the opening, stacked like freshly hewn logs. The latest to die were thrown hurriedly against the pile, their shadowed eyes full of searing malevolence as if Thomas were an intruder in hell.

Hearing voices approaching from up ahead, Thomas sat down beside the nearest body, a boy about his own age. The corpse was black with blood and flies whose buzzing drowned out the stamp of the oncoming footsteps. Thomas lay doggo even as the insects invaded his own wound. Droning like bees, they entered his ears and nose, and pushed at the edges of his eyes and the wet corners of his mouth. He clenched his eyes tighter and prayed that the rising bile in his throat would not make him vomit. It seemed to take forever until the shadows passed by and the tramp of feet receded.

Thomas stripped the dead boy of his cap, khaki jacket, leather shoes and puttees. As he put on the enemy uniform, every move was agony. Just deserts, he supposed, for robbing a grave and stealing from the poor unfortunate. As an afterthought, he ripped away the flyblown bandage around the boy's wound and wrapped it around his own neck. Exhausted by the effort, he lay back, until the thunder of shells exploding a hundred yards away prompted him to struggle to his feet.

In his disguise, Thomas felt a renewed confidence. A soldier returning to the fray would go unnoticed. On the other hand, he knew little of the Turk. Perhaps a wounded soldier stupid enough to return to battle was rare and immediately suspect. And of course if discovered in Turkish uniform he would be shot. Thomas recalled Lord K's orders to shoot all khaki-clad Boer prisoners pretending to be British and smiled grimly to himself.

He limped along, always uphill, towards no-man's-land, where the ridge was black against a sky lit by flares. Turning a corner, he found a wide trench and smelt tobacco. Shadowy figures, a dozen or so, were sitting, cradling rifles, smoking. Not daring to hesitate, Thomas limped on, between them. The soldiers ignored him. They had their heads down, apparently exhausted, not speaking to each other.

He had gone barely ten yards when a cry rang from behind, clearly directed at him. *Dur, dur.* Evidently, the Turk wanted him to stop. Thomas froze, then turned to face his fate.

An officer, judging by the cut of his uniform and the holster on his belt, was gesturing at him with a sword.

Thomas pointed to the bandage around his throat and then opened and closed his mouth wordlessly while shaking his head slowly.

The officer nodded that he understood and issued another order.

Thomas grunted louder and shook his head harder. He held his arms up as if he was aiming a rifle, and growled as if nothing would stop him from returning to the frontline to kill the enemy.

The officer barked at the other soldiers while gesturing at Thomas with the point of his sword. The soldiers hardly moved, and in disgust the officer wrenched a rifle from one of them. In what sounded to Thomas like barely contained fury, the officer ordered the soldier to take off his belt and bayonet, canteen and cartridge case, and a few moments later he handed them to Thomas.

Thomas took the articles quickly, with a nod and a grunt. He threw the belt over his shoulder and planted the rifle butt in the ground. With the Mauser for a crutch, he limped away towards what he hoped was the front, his body tensed for a sudden bullet in the back.

None came.

Disguise and bluff, Watson, that's the ticket.

So far, so good.

It was relatively easy, if exhausting, to follow the zigzag path up to the ridgeline and the din of battle.

At one point he heard the heavy rat-a-tat-tat of a machine gun nearby. He stopped and waited until another flare exploded over no-man's-land and threw the gun emplacement into stark silhouette. A hundred yards away the crew was pouring fire in an ear-splitting stream. The gun was almost side-on to Thomas, clearly enfilading a Turkish trench that the attacking Australians had taken. He imagined a torrent of bullets slicing down the trench.

Thomas leant back against the dirt wall, taking his weight off his wounded leg. He felt the heft of the Mauser in his hands and he pulled back the bolt. The magazine was full – five rounds. He pushed the bolt home. Piece of cake, he thought. He could wipe them out before they knew what had hit them. One less machine gun to kill our lads. He aimed first at the seated gunner.

As his finger squeezed gently, something unexpected came

to mind. *The Trojan Horse*. Wasn't Thomas the enemy in sly disguise, the stab in the back?

Like Teach.

Thomas thought of his father. What would he do? Jack Clare had fired in the air rather than shoot surrendered Boers and innocent civilians. But the enemy machine gun was killing Anzacs, probably many of them. Australian lives were at stake, whether or not Thomas was acting within the rules of war.

His finger tightened on the trigger.

The crash of each shot spitting from the mouth of the gun reverberated inside his head. As he steadied his aim, he began to calculate. With a Lee-Enfield, he could fire every four seconds. But wounded and using the unfamiliar Mauser, he might manage one round every six seconds. It could take him twenty-five seconds to shoot the four-man crew, during which time one of them might well spot him, swivel the gun and rake him to pieces. It would be touch and go, probably suicide.

A shiver went through him. Thomas took his finger from the trigger and a voice screamed inside his head, *Coward!*

No, cried a second voice, *plain good sense. There's another way*, he thought, and lowered his aim. He would try a single shot, go for the breechblock. Better to kill the gun.

A shell burst over no-man's-land and a white star below a parachute sank slowly to earth. Thomas sighted and squeezed. The shot seemed to explode in his ear. Without looking at where his bullet had gone, he ducked below the lip of the trench. In the shadow he waited, heart in mouth, still as a statue, gritting his teeth against the sudden pain in his leg.

Silently, he counted to a full minute. When the gun had not restarted, he resumed his journey with a sigh of relief and some pride.

To kill as a Turk was wrong, Thomas told himself. Too much

like murder. Too much like an assassin, like the Boche killing his father. Later, he decided, when he was properly attired, he would make up for it. But even these arguments couldn't dispel entirely the notion that he hadn't been brave enough.

He came to a trench in which the dead were stacked four deep on either side. Passing through, he felt as if the very walls were swarming and he did not look at them but moved along as fast as his limp would allow. He emerged into a communications trench crowded with slow-moving reserves and was able to join them and hobble along at their pace. In the flow of these silent, nervous men, Thomas went unnoticed. No one questioned why a wounded man would return to the front. So unthinkable was it that an enemy would come from the rear to be among them that even the Turkish officers, pistols in hand, did not look twice at him.

Thomas had an awful thought. If he turned back, an officer might shoot him for desertion. If he stayed with these reinforcements, he would be expected to shoot Australians or be shot by them.

The traffic in the trench was heavy. Every so often the line paused to allow men carrying ammunition to overtake, or stretcher-bearers with wounded to squeeze past the other way.

At one such halt, Thomas pretended to drop, falling sideways towards a connecting sap. But before he could reach it, the Turk behind grasped him under the arm and pulled him up. Thomas grunted his thanks and resumed his shuffle forward. At the next opening he fell again, and this time the helpful Turk passed him by.

As Thomas struggled to get to his feet, as painfully slowly and theatrically as possible and hardly difficult under the circumstances, he checked to see if he was being watched. The line of Turks streamed by with scarcely a glance in his direction.

He made his way up this new route in the hope that he was heading towards the front, allowing the increasing sound of battle to draw him along.

Turning a corner, Thomas was confronted by men in a frenzy of firing. There were dozens of Turks with their rifles spitting flashes of red fire through gaps in sandbags. Every so often, one of them would pitch backwards in a spray of sand and blood.

He started along the trench, through the dusty air stinking of cordite and excrement that caught in his throat and made him want to gag. He passed behind combatants on the fire step and between men lying wounded where they fell or sitting slumped against the far wall. Many were full of holes, victims of the nails, stones and bits of wire packed into jam-tin bombs. Some of these wretches grabbed at Thomas, mouthing desperate pleas for help unheard over the fury of battle. Their hands brushed his thigh with a scalding pain, but he hobbled doggedly on, knowing that to stop meant death and grateful that those fighting the Australians remained oblivious to his identity.

Further along, a group of Turks huddled behind a wall of sandbags blocking the trench. One after another, they lit cricket-ball bombs and waited a few seconds before throwing them over the bags. As the bombs burst, he heard the swish of shrapnel pellets overhead and the crack and crash of rifles and machine guns, as loud as anything from those first days at Quinn's Post.

He was back in a bombing war, he realised with a shiver. His comrades were close by on the other side of the blockage. *And me on the wrong side.*

No sooner had Thomas formed the thought than a wave of explosions blasted the air, sending gusts of smoke and dirt, coughing and cries, racing towards him. He dived sideways into a possy in the wall moments before a shower of small cylinders exploded around him.

His ears howled from the hammering of the jam tins. Red flashes lit up a scene of flying bodies in a whirlwind of shrapnel and smoke, both the dying and the already dead being torn to bits.

A heavy weight fell against him, thrusting him deeper into the hole. His leg erupted in pain and he screamed his throat dry, even as he closed his eyes and knew his life was over.

He couldn't move. He was pinned beneath a body that struggled and gurgled and shook in time to the blasts beating at them. Thomas felt a warm liquid soak his lower regions, but whether it was him or the Turk on top of him, in the dark he had no means of knowing.

The detonations moved away, leaving in their absence the sounds of men grunting as they lunged and others screaming as they were spiked. Voices emerged with familiar accents. The man who had Thomas pinned beneath him suddenly convulsed as if shuddering under the impact of repeated blows. Thomas felt a sharp pain in his forearm and another in his shoulder, each a stabbing, burning sensation.

'Oh, you bastard shitting mongrel of a thing,' he shouted.

All at once the blows stopped and he felt the weight lift as the body of the Turk was pulled off him.

'Hullo, Australia,' said a pair of wide wild eyes in a big open face streaked with dirt. 'Ya been havin' fun under that Turk, cobber?'

It was a comforting voice, even though its owner kept his bloodied bayonet poised over Thomas's stomach. The soldier turned to his partner. 'Ernie, 'ere's a bloke dressed like Abdul, 'cept 'e talks like us. Wot ya think, should I belly the bugger?'

'Lemme 'ave a look-see, Billy,' said Ernie.

Another grimy face peered at Thomas. 'Jeez, what sorta game you playing at, mate?'

'It's a bloody disguise, you fool,' Thomas said. 'I'm Corporal Clare, 2nd Light Horse.'

'Can't see no horse, corp.'

'Fook you,' Thomas growled. 'I was captured. I'm escaping.'

'Are ya now, chum? Well, today's ya lucky day,' Ernie said as his mate swiftly applied field dressings to the small wounds he'd given Thomas.

The Australians didn't apologise or linger. 'Off ya go,' Billy told Thomas, pointing back the way they had come, before he and Ernie and others behind them departed in the opposite direction.

Now that he was among comrades, Thomas peeled off his hat, jacket and neck bandage. Each move was agony, but he counted himself lucky. There was enough light to see that as many Australians as Turks lay along the floor of the trench. Some were missing arms or legs or parts of faces. One with bulging eyes held up his hand close to his face to examine the absence of fingers. Several squirmed and twitched, others groaned or spat out blood in great racking coughs.

One poor wretch had half his head missing. Thomas mumbled an apology to the corpse and pulled off the Anzac tunic and bandolier and put them on, adding another man's peaked cap. *At least I'll die properly dressed.* Thomas set his face hard and picked up a discarded Lee-Enfield to use as a crutch.

As more Australians dashed past with hardly a glance, Thomas was completely surprised when a hand grasped his arm and voices whispered in Turkish. He felt his insides squeeze into a ball. He knew what to expect. In the next moment, a bayonet would carve through his belly or a bullet would explode in his chest.

The hand pulled him towards the trench wall and Thomas stared at three faces buried within the gloom of a dugout.

'Holy Christ,' Thomas swore as he brought the rifle and bayonet around. The Turks shrank back. *Three shots, one-two-three*, he thought, *easy*. 'Out. *Imshi*,' he ordered.

Three boys barely older than himself tumbled from the hole. In the uneven glare of the flares lighting up the sky, Thomas could see their bodies trembling and eyes wild with fear in hairless faces. They stretched out their hands to show they held no weapons.

'Now POQ,' he growled. 'Piss off quick.'

The boys replied in a flood of Turkish.

'Don't care,' Thomas said, with a shake of his head, wishing they'd go away and let him get on with his escape. '*Imshi*,' he repeated, gesturing with his thumb for them to leave.

One of the boys grabbed his arm, while another grasped his good leg. They hung on tightly, pressed against him, constricting his movements so that he could not use the rifle to push them away.

Thomas felt the panic rising. 'Jesus, let go, you bastards. *Imshi, imshi*.'

Clearly, they wanted a shield against what they believed would be certain death at the hands of the Australians. They seemed harmless enough, Thomas thought, and even reminded him of the smooth-faced sons of farmers at home, too young to shave. What were such boys doing fighting us? And what was he supposed to do with them? How could one wounded bloke take command of three Turks? He could hardly get himself home, let alone shackled to prisoners. They would slow him down, attract attention, draw Turkish or Anzac fire, probably both. Either way, they would be sure to get him killed. An image of the stooped, half-blind Aubrey Herbert came to mind. What would Herbert do?

Thomas palmed the bolt, putting a bullet into the breech. He gestured to the largest of the boys. 'Come,' he barked, pointing to himself. The youth shrank back in fear, until Thomas grabbed his arm and placed it around his own shoulders. 'You help me,' Thomas explained, and together they staggered up the trench with the other two close behind.

By the time they came to a junction, Thomas's strength was failing. He called 'Halt', as he had heard the German officer do, then struggled ahead to the corner, and listened. Nothing. No sound. Still, something told him to go no further.

Thomas took a hat from one of the youngsters and put it on his bayonet, then moved it an inch past the corner. A shot rang out and the hat went flying.

'Don't shoot, you stupid bastards,' Thomas cried. 'I'm wounded. I have prisoners.'

'Well, move ya flamin' arse an' show y'self.'

With his heart beating hard, Thomas stepped forward to find a bayonet in his face. Another man, gaunt and dirty, was poised with a jam-tin bomb in each hand and a lit cigarette in his mouth, while a third, a great gob of an Anzac, stood haggard and wild, poised to behead him with a spade.

'Thomas Clare, corporal,' he said quickly.

'Seen any flippin' Turks?'

'Only these three.' Thomas gestured at his prisoners to show themselves, which they did with hands held high and terror on their faces. 'They'll be a mine of information for the intelligence fellows,' he said carefully, placing himself between them and the Australians, who were rigid with hostility. Thomas could read the desperation in their gaunt faces, the determination to kill and the despair that comes with expecting to be next to die. He knew battle lust when he saw it and half-expected the man with the bayonet to run the boys through. But the soldiers pressed on without another word.

The boy and his captives resumed their slow progress. They came to a trench partially covered by heavy logs. Now Thomas knew where he was. The Turkish frontline, or at least it had been before the Australians had taken it, at a terrible cost.

The timbers overhead had been wrenched apart. Rays of red and green from flares and star shells slipped through the breaks and danced along the trench to reveal a glimpse of hell. The floor was carpeted with broken bodies, friend and enemy, the dying and the dead, still in the grip of close combat.

As Thomas hobbled, his boots squelched. *Mud, impossible in summer*, he thought, until he realised with a miserable certainty what the liquid was. The horror of it pushed him through the roofed trench as quickly as he could, between the piled dead and the hopeless left to die.

'I can't stand it no more,' one man sobbed.

'Finish me, cobber,' another said.

His heart went out to them, but Thomas could never do that again.

Every so often, one or other of the boys would pat Thomas on the back with encouraging gibberish or babble with fawning gratitude. Twice he slipped in a mass of stickiness and fell among bodies already trampled into the ground. One of his Turks dragged him up, gagging. At times they trod on a springy floor that brought a groan from some unfortunate underfoot. Turkish and Australian, Thomas struggled not to step on their faces.

They passed scores of soldiers and officers simply too drunk with exhaustion or too busy preparing for a counter attack to impede their progress.

Until, finally, they came to an open sap and the heavens alive with flares. Here, bodies lined the parapet, twisted limbs silhouetted against a multicoloured night sky, and men with a red cross on their arms loaded the living onto canvas.

He called, 'Thomas Clare, Light Horse, and I have prisoners.'

'Bully for you, mate,' said a weary bearer. 'If you can walk, keep going.'

Chapter 30

H<small>E AWOKE TO FIND HIMSELF</small> in a tent, with a dog-tired face examining him. 'Missed the femur, old chap,' the face said kindly. 'You'll be back in no time at all.'

'My prisoners, sir, what happened to them?'

'The usual, I expect,' the doctor said, and jabbed him with a needle.

As he was carried from the tent Thomas wondered where he was going. And before he lost consciousness, there was a moment when he asked himself another question. Once, he was merely the boy and son. Somehow he had become his father's avenging angel, the sniper, and the cold, callous killer of Teach. Was there still room in his life for Thomas the friend of Snow, the lover of Winnie, and the bringer of truth to K?

He woke several times with the sun burning his face, sand beneath him, waves lapping nearby. He lay in a neat row of men, some crying for water, others simply crying, and one giving voice to his horror, 'Murder . . . we are being murdered.'

When next Thomas was conscious, he was squeezed among various bodies on a hot steel deck that rumbled as it heeled. He hardly knew what was wakefulness and what was sleep, what was real and what was nightmare. Both held an impossible mess of horror and pain, with heads separating from necks, scarecrows tumbling in a hailstorm of gunfire, red foam bubbling from the mouths of Kingy and Teach, and Snow drowning with Thomas crushing him beneath the waves. He imagined the troubled face of Uncle Harry and the heavenly form of Winnie wiping a cool cloth over his face, until the darkness returned.

One day, the sunlight streaming through the door of the tent brought a vision of loveliness in a white cap and pinafore. 'Well, it's high time you were awake,' she chided him.

'Winnie?'

'She your sweetheart?'

Thomas nodded.

'What a lucky girl to have such a fine fellow for a beau,' smiled the nurse.

Was there ever such a smile? Thomas blushed. To see the feminine form, to hear such a voice, and homegrown too – he'd thought never to have that pleasure again.

'You're on Imbros,' she said cheerfully. 'You've got a nasty gash in your thigh, nothing that can't be fixed.'

The nurse told Thomas that it had been touch and go for a week, but that he would recover from the loss of blood and the fever. She would, she added with a heavenly grin, pop back shortly with breakfast.

Once, Imbros had been a Greek island seen often from his dugout, a fierce craggy lump in the distant west, a haven wondered about, dreamt of, yearned for, when the bullets were flying.

Now, here he was hobbling about it, forcing strength back into his leg. From the shore, he observed British warships skirting the windy cape and aeroplanes overhead returning to base. He watched prisoners from the stockade chop firewood for the Australian bakery, while another gave a haircut to an officer. Each time he limped past the wire, he looked in vain for the three boys he'd brought out. A Turkish woman passed him on a donkey and one of her children laughed as he struggled with his crutches and he laughed back and made a mental note to describe the scene to Winnie.

For once, there was plenty of paper. 'It's heaven,' he wrote. 'I have a bed in a tent with other blokes and most nights I sleep. Oh, the quiet is magical, not a shot, and you can eat the food. The nurses are wonderful, but not near so pretty as you.'

To Mrs Anna West, he wrote, 'Teach fell while doing his duty. I was with him at the last and he left this world bravely, his final thoughts being of you and Felix. He was shot by a German officer who demanded information of great value to the foe but went away empty-handed. Ever the teacher, he reminded us constantly of the link between past and present. It may be of comfort to know that Teach was laid to rest not far from his beloved Troy.' That much was true, at least.

To his Aunt Mercia, Thomas described how his mother had been poisoned by the man who had murdered his father, and that on no account must she involve the police.

To Ellen Woods, he wrote that Snow was gone, that Teach was a Judas, and that so many had fallen – Kingy, the officers Logan, Burge and Hinton, and others he liked such as Hami Grace, Doctor Luther and a poor chap named Hamp who'd lasted one day. 'Once I dreamt of being a knight in a noble cause,' he wrote. 'No longer. They murder us and we return the favour. Only a boy or a fool believes in war.'

All the while, Gallipoli lay on the horizon – distant as if he were back on the *Devanha*, seeing that place afresh, as if his three months there were to begin again.

Walking with barely a limp, Thomas returned to the peninsula in mid-September to find his regiment held in reserve at the old No. 3 outpost, close to the beach, their frontline work over.

He stopped in Shrapnel Gully first, found Kingy and Major Nash in the cemetery there and said a prayer. Next, he recovered the TNP document. It had lain in Teach's kit, beside his own, in a holding area for the belongings of those missing, presumed killed.

He reported to Chauvel with the document in his pocket. 'Congratulations on your promotion, sir.'

'And I'm jolly glad to see you in one piece, Thomas,' the brigadier welcomed him. 'As for myself, pleurisy is such a dashed inconvenience, too much bed and idleness, enforced by lovely nurses who, regrettably, I am too long in the tooth to charm.'

Thomas smiled politely.

Chauvel went on cheerfully, 'I ate better than a butcher's dog, my boy, none of your dreadful bully beef and biscuits, and I could walk about without chancing a bullet in the head like Birdie or one of Beachy Bill's whizz-bangs up my nether regions.'

Thomas laughed. It was good to have his uncle back.

As they swapped yarns, Thomas toyed with the idea of telling Chauvel the other story. Let the document become the commander's problem, he thought. Let him decide whether to burn it, pass it on to Australian authorities or hand it over to Bulala.

But Thomas kept his hand away from his pocket. To palm the document off would be an insult to the memory of his mother and father who, in one way or another, had died for it. He had no idea what he would do next, other than to ensure the document would not find its way into the hands of the Boche.

The brigadier listened in silence as Thomas recounted how a German intelligence officer had shot Teach for 'refusing to co-operate' during their interrogation. While a less than complete telling of Teach's action in captivity, it was the least he could do for an old friend and for the memory that a young Felix would hold forever of his father.

Chauvel surprised him with a sudden question. 'At Lone Pine, you brought out three Johnnies. Why?'

'They surrendered to me, sir.'

'You might have left them.'

'They seemed pleased to be out of it, sir.'

'You were wounded, you had every reason to pass them on to your comrades.'

Thomas paused. 'I wasn't confident they would survive, sir.'

'I see.' Chauvel sighed and leant back in his chair. 'And did they?'

'As far as I am aware, sir.'

'Like father like son,' Chauvel grinned. 'Your father told me once how he'd personally captured a *bittereinder*, a young Boer about your age who happened to surrender while wearing khaki looted from some poor Tommy.'

'What happened to him, sir?'

'He was shot.'

'Under Rule 303, I suppose, sir.'

Chauvel smiled ruefully. 'Morant commanded your father to finish him, but Jack refused. Morant ordered your father away at gunpoint, and Handcock did the deed. Jack was furious.'

'I never knew, sir.'

'It was the final straw for your father, why he testified. Jack couldn't abide murder.'

'Even if he was following orders, sir?'

Chauvel looked at Thomas keenly. 'Ah, you mean Kitchener's orders?'

Thomas jumped as if he'd been shot. *He knows.*

'You seem surprised? Many were under the clear impression that the general wanted no quarter given but, unlike those in irregular units such as the BVC, few acted on it. Jack claimed to have proof, so he said, a document that would nail Lord K's hide to the wall. I never believed it and told him so. I refused to accept that the general would be sufficiently stupid or callous to give such a direct order. I think your father rather suspected I was in K's camp.'

'Did you ever see such an order, sir?'

'Of course not.' Chauvel looked hard at Thomas. 'I believe that you may suspect that Lord Kitchener somehow conspired to have a hand in it. Let me say to you now, as one who has observed the field marshal closely: he is as hard-hearted as needs be, but he would not have been party to murder.' Chauvel narrowed his eyes and added, 'Whether of surrendered prisoners or anyone else. Put bluntly, Thomas, it would not have been in Lord K's interest to do so. I would urge you to dispense with any such notion.'

Was this the moment to bring it out? Thomas wondered.

'Strange, murky business we're in, eh, Thomas?' Chauvel continued. 'Deciding when and when not to kill? It's what separates man from wolf.'

'I wish I'd known him better, sir,' Thomas said quietly.

Chauvel knew whom Thomas meant. 'He'd have been proud of you, as I am.'

Thomas's heart swelled, but he said, 'I did my duty, sir, no more than many others.'

'And far too many have fallen. I have precious few of your calibre left, Thomas, and I mean to make the most of them. Which is why I've recommended you for promotion.'

'But, sir . . .' *Not again.* Thomas didn't want another bloody stripe. He wanted to be with his mates. What was left of them.

Chauvel seemed to read his thoughts. 'They will follow the man in you, Thomas. I need leaders who won't flinch from risk but neither will they waste men's lives. Death creates vacancies, which I must fill. I have no choice in the matter.'

'Yes, sir.'

'The paperwork will come through in due course. Was there anything else?'

Thomas sighed. 'No, sir. Thank you, sir.'

The brigadier nodded and dismissed him with a wave.

Thomas walked up the gully to his regiment. He had no idea what he would do next, other than to ensure the document would not find its way into the hands of the Boche.

When he arrived, Snow was waiting.

At autumn's end, the boys went swimming off North Beach below the huge spur of the Sphinx. The water was cold there now and busy with flat-bottomed transports heavy with stores for the coming winter's siege. Mid-November found the two sides still locked in their trenches, Abdul with all of Turkey at his back, and the Anzacs clinging to their sliver by the sea.

As always, the sea – no matter how icy – was a welcome distraction from the cold art of sniping, to which the boys had returned. They found they could come and go pretty much where and when they pleased and were needed. But there was a difference now that neither acknowledged to the other nor to their comrades.

Since their joyous reunion, Snow seemed quieter and more serious. Thomas wondered what had brought about the change, whether his dance with death or his distaste for killing. Whichever it was, or indeed whether it was something else entirely, Thomas did not ask and Snow did not tell.

Thomas bore his own regrets, his secret guilt at finishing the Turk who'd shot Kingy and at provoking the Hun to murder Teach. And as he looked down the sights of his rifle and watched the forms of men pass quickly across the Turkish loophole, the old justifications for squeezing the trigger appeared hollow and he knew that he was heartily sick of it.

Where once it was Snow who had fired only to wound, now Thomas joined him in shunning the head shot.

'Missed,' he said, having sent a neat bullet through the eye of a steel plate in Abdul's trench, 'but smacked him good.'

To which Snow replied, 'Keep practising, cobber, you'll do better tomorrow.'

Or after Snow took the shot, he shook his head. 'Nicked him in the shoulder. Put the blighter out of action, but.'

And Thomas smirked, 'Tsk, tsk, losing your touch.'

It was a soldier's duty to kill and both knew better than to acknowledge openly what they were doing.

Thomas found comfort in his father's refusal to shoot into the wagonload of women and children in the previous war. It felt as if he were paying his respects to the father he wished he'd known better.

Not being privy to how or where the bullets struck, everyone else seemed more than happy for the boys to keep Abdul's head down. Equally impressed, the CO insisted that – while the rest of the regiment sailed to Mudros for a spot of leave, undisturbed sleep and better food – Thomas and Snow should keep up the good work and remain behind.

So it was that they were scrubbing themselves in the shallows
when a little steamer chugged past, packed with top brass from
headquarters. Never before had Thomas seen so many stiff-
necked red-tabs.

The boat tied up to the pier, and the staff officers disem-
barked and walked the boards to shore, all of them deferring to
a tall man with a most familiar face.

Instantly recognisable from the poster.

Your country needs YOU.

Thomas gave a wild yell and raced from the water, with Snow
hard on his heels, through a mountain of stores to where their
clothes lay. Hastily donning trousers, tunics and boots, they
burst into a crowd of curious Anzacs who had swarmed down
from their hillside dugouts to surround the generals on the
sand, craning their necks to see.

Thomas forced his way through.

'The King has asked me to tell you how splendidly he thinks
you have done,' said the tallest red-tab, his chinstrap framing the
ruddy face and famous handlebar moustache. 'You have done
splendidly, better, even, than I thought you would.'

The men cheered and Lord Kitchener strode purposefully
on, up the steep track to Walker's Ridge.

'Come on,' Thomas said to Snow.

Uncle Harry saw Thomas coming even as he arrived at HQ.
'The field marshal is spending a couple of hours at Anzac, seeing
the lay of the land for himself,' the brigadier explained. 'He'll be
visiting our positions inland of the Sphinx and at Lone Pine.'

Thomas looked at him keenly.

'Would you care to meet him?' Chauvel said, with a mischievous glint in his eye.

Thomas nodded gladly as the brigadier hurried away to join
the official party.

'Settle down,' Snow smiled a warning. 'Look. Don't touch.'

Thomas caught up with the field marshal's entourage at Rest Gully, close to North Beach. The War Secretary was quickly surrounded by scores of men in drab khaki, many with hands in pockets against the chill. Thomas brought out his vest camera. He wasn't the only one. Several Anzacs took photographs as Kitchener stopped to chat to some of the men queuing at the YMCA's canteen tent.

'Hello, YMCA!' Lord Kitchener declared before turning to a grizzled old hand. 'What can you get in there?'

'Nuts.'

'Oh yes, but I mean, generally, what have they got in there?'

'Nothing,' said the soldier.

As Kitchener looked disappointed, the soldier said, 'Nuts is OK, 'cept I've no teeth to crack 'em.'

Lord K laughed. 'Well, we shall ensure that softer items, such as vegetables, are sent over immediately.' He said to an aide, 'Make a note of that.'

Kitchener turned to see that Chauvel had joined the group of senior officers. The brigadier spoke to the field marshal and then gestured for the boy to join them.

Thomas was making his way over when Captain Taylor blocked his path. 'So, Abdul caught you, then threw you back. Too small a fish, I expect,' Bulala grinned. 'Have you recovered the document?'

'I have. A mate took it. He's dead. A Hun intelligence officer, one of your ilk, shot him in cold blood.'

'Oh dear,' Taylor said without emotion.

'Teach told me everything, how you and the Boche both hired Griffin, how Griffin murdered my father, how he poisoned my mother while working for you.'

'I regret that, Thomas. I don't kill women,' Taylor said, with genuine concern. But in the next moment he hissed, 'Tell K none of this, or you will regret it. Hand it over.'

Thomas laughed in Bulala's face, loud enough for Kitchener and his officers to notice.

'Still want to blackmail the boss, eh?' Thomas said. 'You're a scoundrel, captain, with the scruples of a slaughterman. But nothing much scares me anymore.' He walked over to his Uncle Harry.

'Sir,' Chauvel said, 'may I present my nephew, Sergeant Thomas Clare, of the 2nd Light Horse, a sniper, captured and escaped, wounded a number of times. Seventeen years old, sir.'

'My word, what wonderfully good work, old chap,' Lord K said. 'You have fully done your part in upholding the British flag and British honour here, where you have fought so well.'

Thomas suspected the speech was as much for everyone within earshot as for him. Up close, Lord K appeared older than expected, middle-aged, stout and square-jawed, impressive in his sharply tailored uniform, red patches and gleaming belt. Thomas was roughly the same height, but face to face the field marshal's cold blue-eyed stare and the odd squint in his left eye were unnerving.

Behind K, Bulala was looking daggers.

Kitchener continued, 'It is not easy to appreciate at their full value the enormous difficulties which attended the operations in the Dardanelles or the fine temper with which our troops met them.'

'Sir,' Thomas began, 'I have something you will be interested in.'

Bulala pushed forward, almost injecting himself between the pair. 'Sir, we are exposed here to enemy artillery in the Olive Grove. Might I suggest you move on?'

'Arrant nonsense, captain, we're quite unobserved,' Chauvel snapped.

'What's got into you, Taylor?' Lord K hissed his annoyance. 'Let the boy speak.'

'My apologies, sir,' Bulala muttered and withdrew a few paces.

'Well, lad?' Kitchener said.

'I have something you want, sir.' Thomas pulled the document from inside his tunic and handed it to Lord K.

The field marshal scanned the old paper. 'What the devil!'

'Yours, I believe, sir.'

Kitchener looked Thomas hard in the eye. 'How did you obtain this?'

Thomas took a deep breath. 'My father, Constable First Class John Robert Clare, late of the Bushveldt Carbineers, died keeping this from the Boche, sir.'

Lord K calmly folded the document and tucked it into a pocket. At no stage did he take his eyes off Thomas. 'Are you aware of its significance?'

Thomas returned his stare. 'I am, sir. What it means to you and what its value is to others.'

'Yes, well, we shall say no more, eh? There's a good chap.'

'Just so you're aware, sir, I think the sentiments expressed in that note are *despicable*.'

Kitchener took a sharp breath. His eyes narrowed dangerously and his mouth opened to fire a barrage that would be withering.

In that instant, Thomas wondered what foolishness made him speak so. He thought of his father's last moments, recalled Tubbie's description of his tribe's last stand, remembered Teach's dying request for his family, and he faced Lord K unafraid.

The field marshal's cheeks burned with a ruddy glow, but his restraint was impressive. 'All of us err from time to time,' he said quietly. 'I sincerely regret your father's passing, lad.'

'And Morant and Handcock, sir . . . Any regrets?'

Kitchener glanced coolly at the wondering red-tabs and the curious other ranks around him. 'Not at all. That war is finished. We have a new one to fight, eh what?'

'Yes, sir,' Thomas said automatically. 'But why did you do it, sir?'

Lord K answered with blistering emotion but so softly that Thomas alone would hear, 'You would do well to keep your personal views to yourself, sergeant. It is most certainly not for you to question your commander-in-chief.'

The words hit Thomas like a battering ram. The field marshal saw him flinch and spoke up loudly, for the benefit of the crowd, 'As I have said repeatedly here, the methods of warfare pursued by the Turks are vastly superior to those which have disgraced their German masters.'

'Sir?' Thomas said uncertainly.

'Which means,' Lord K explained, 'that we must treat our enemies who surrender with every consideration.'

'Yes, sir.'

Kitchener shot a cold glance at Bulala, then settled on Chauvel. 'You knew about this?'

'Only in the most general of terms, sir,' Chauvel said.

'Humph,' Kitchener grunted. 'Let's ensure it stays that way. Splendid nephew you have there, Chauvel, a credit to you.'

With a curt nod of dismissal, K took a step forward to leave, when – almost as an afterthought – he turned sharply back to Thomas.

'Can we win this, lad?'

Thomas didn't hesitate. 'Not in a week of Sundays, sir. We're snookered.'

Several of the senior officers gasped, but Kitchener gave a faint smile and spoke softly in Thomas's ear. Then he turned on his heel and, with his red-tabbed subordinates in tow and to the cheers of the Anzacs, walked down to the beach towards the picket boat that would ferry him to the destroyer and his voyage back to London.

When they were alone outside their dugout, Snow turned angrily to Thomas. 'Bloody hell, after all we've been through, you just handed the thing to him.'

'He's my commander-in-chief.'

'He's a mongrel.'

'He's *our* mongrel,' Thomas smiled. He had kept his promise to Teach. *Just never said to whom I'd return it.*

Snow said, 'If you'd given it to the newspapers or to the Huns, you'd have exposed Kitchener for a lying bastard.'

'That would be the act of a traitor,' Thomas said.

'The man executed Australians for following his orders. TNP. That's what the document shows, doesn't it? Taylor said Australia would be so bloody furious it'd pull out of this stinking war. We could all go home.'

'Taylor is a liar. Anyway, it'll all be over by Christmas . . . not this one, though.'

Thomas had never believed Bulala. *He'd just as soon peddle the document to the Huns for a higher price.* On the other hand, if Thomas had held on to it, Bulala might have killed him or he might have had to kill Bulala. *Either way, I'd be in trouble.* 'Better K has it than the Boche,' he said, 'and better K than Bulala.'

Snow, unconvinced, shook his head. 'Your dad died for that bit of paper, and your ma too.'

'To keep it from the Huns. They had it for twelve years and it brought them only pain and made me an orphan.'

'You could have given it to Chauvel.'

'Uncle Harry's got his hands full fighting Turks without getting into a scrap with his boss.'

Snow sighed. 'At least you know who murdered your parents.'

Thomas nodded. Kitchener was not his enemy. Neither was Bulala, who'd never expected Griffin to murder his mother. His target was clear – Sergeant Griffin and the Boche. 'One's at home and the other's probably back in Berlin by now.'

Snow shook his head sadly. '"Our scent runs cold, Holmes."'

'"We advance, Watson, but the goal is afar."'

'"The cunning dog has covered his tracks."'

'"You can write me down an ass this time,"' Thomas said cheerfully. '"I'm afraid that all the king's horses and all the king's men cannot avail in this matter. Come, Watson, we have done all we can here . . . we must leave that question to the future."'

Snow dropped his imitation. 'Dunno what you're so cheery about.'

Coz it's a relief to be rid of the damned thing. 'It's not every day a sergeant tells off a field marshal,' Thomas laughed.

It was early evening and a winter chill was in the air. Small groups of Anzacs huddled beside their fires brewing tea. Thomas looked casually about to make sure they were not overheard. He leant close to Snow and took out his vest camera. 'Oh, and by the way . . .'

Snow understood immediately. 'You crafty devil, you photographed it.'

'Might come in handy one day.'

Snow grinned. 'And what did Lord Bloody Muck say to you?'

'That he should have me shot.'

'That all?'

'And it's time we left this godforsaken place.'

Acknowledgements

T HE MOST IMPORTANT PEOPLE TO acknowledge are the six old men, veterans of Gallipoli – the late Harry Benson, Ernie Boston, John Cargill, Bill Greer, Maurice Jessop and Jack Nicholson – who in 1980 invited me into their homes for a cup of tea, a biscuit and a long spell at the end of an ABC microphone. A decade later, when covering the 75th anniversary of the first Gallipoli landing for national radio, I was privileged to walk the battlefields with the likes of Bill Bevis, Jack Ryan and Sam Thompson, among dozens of World War I veterans.

None was more mischievous than 94-year-old Bill Bevis, who dined with us later at an Istanbul night club and then cavorted on stage with a belly dancer. He brought the house down. When I observed that he'd been a perfect gentleman with the lady, Bill replied with a laugh, 'Well, before a couple of thousand people, what else could you be?'

More recently, Professor Kenan Çelik OAM guided me with wisdom and sensitivity between Shrapnel Valley and Quinn's Post and to the burial site of some 3,000 of his fellow Turks; and Eric Goossens was invaluable navigating the short cuts between Anzac and his Gallipoli Houses hotel.

A number of others were particularly helpful with advice and encouragement: Ken Dray, Tim Bowden and Anna Fienberg; James Unkles for his lawyerly insights into the case for and against Harry Morant; Aboriginal elder and Vietnam veteran Eric Law in Murgon; Gary Oakley, indigenous liaison officer at the Australian War Memorial, also a Vietnam veteran; the AWM and the Australian Light Horse Studies Centre for their extensive online archives; and Bianca Anderson, archivist at St Joseph's College, Gregory Terrace, Brisbane, and Kristen Thornton at Deakin University library in Geelong, Victoria, for their help with rare material.

You wouldn't be reading this book if it weren't for my agent Gaby Naher and fiction publisher Beverley Cousins and her editors at Random House Australia who showed an enthusiasm for the story that was a delight and a reassurance to the first time novelist.

Most of all, thanks to my wife and daughters, who weeded out early errors and were supportive in all things, and to the young Felix, whose dogged presence kept me company in the writer's chair.

Steve Sailah
Sydney, 2014

Author's Note

A *FATAL TIDE* IS A work of fiction with roots in actual events and characters both real and imagined.

The towns of Murgon and Barambah (now Cherbourg) in Queensland are real, but Thomas Clare and his father Jack are not. A first constable John Thomas Clare became Murgon's first policeman in 1910, but he neither fought in the Boer War nor died a grisly death at the hands of the Boche.

Doctor Ellen Woods was the first woman to be appointed government medical officer in Murgon in 1914, described as a reliable, competent doctor on a 'big and spirited black horse'. There is no evidence to suggest she had an affair with Murgon's first copper or ventured to Europe to assist the war effort.

Tubbie Terrier was the son of a Kalkadoon chief and a rare survivor of the 1884 massacre of his tribe at Battle Mountain in north-west Queensland. He would have known the 'kill the white man' war song, taken from Sir Hudson Fysh's *Taming the North*, quoted with the kind permission of his son John Hudson Fysh.

Tubbie Terrier was not one of the black trackers invited by Lord Kitchener to chase Boer commandos in South Africa and marooned there after the Australian colonies became a nation.

It appears that Tubbie lived at Barambah for a time before he died in 1930 in Cloncurry, not far from where his people were massacred. The characters of his wife Iris and stepchildren Snow and Winnie are fictional.

Hundreds of Aborigines served their country in the First World War, mainly in the Middle East or France, while a few served at Gallipoli. It's likely that under the *Defence Act 1909* the Light Horse would have knocked Snow back for not being of 'substantially European descent'. However, I preferred to see him slip through the recruiting process by claiming to be Maori, as some did.

Doctor Arthur Conan Doyle treated enteric fever (typhoid) patients among the Boer War wounded at Bloemfontein hospital in 1900. I have no record of him being visited there by the likes of Kitchener or Churchill, who were not far away in Pretoria, or that those two august gentlemen ever sought to convince the author to resurrect Sherlock Holmes killed off years before. But for my purposes, I found it impossible to ignore the fact that Lord K, Winston and the creator of Holmes were in the same theatre of war at the same time.

Lord Kitchener of Khartoum must have been too cunning a campaigner to openly order that no quarter be shown to the enemy, let alone to scribble *TNP* to *Bulala*, his intelligence officer in the Spelonken region. If K ever gave such orders, he would have delivered them orally and via subordinates, as the deeply flawed Harry 'Breaker' Morant testified and as reported in George Witton's 1907 *Scapegoats of the Empire*. The case for such orders lies at the heart of attempts to secure a posthumous pardon for the Breaker, being championed by the lawyer James Unkles among others.

By all accounts, Captain Alfred 'Bulala' Taylor was a villain of the first order and shrewd enough to avoid conviction on charges of murdering prisoners. There are reports that Bulala served on the Western Front, but no suggestion that he visited Australia or Gallipoli. It appears that Taylor died in 1941 at a ripe old age at his farm near Plumtree in modern-day Zimbabwe.

While Teach and Kingy are not real, the exploits of B Squadron of the 2nd Light Horse regiment on Gallipoli – the bombing duels at Quinn's, the massed Turkish attack, the ceasefire and the unit's offensives – are as close to their descriptions in the regimental history and war diary as I could make them. Unlike the appalling August attack at The Nek made famous in the film *Gallipoli*, in which successive waves of Light Horsemen were cut down, follow-up charges by the 2nd Light Horse at Quinn's were cancelled by Major George Bourne in consultation with Harry Chauvel after the first wave was all but wiped out.

Real life characters Chauvel, Bourne, Sol Green, Aubrey Herbert, Carew Reynell, Billy Sing and Stephen Midgley had experiences similar to those described, some of which can be found in their diaries, memoirs, unit histories or biographies, although their dialogue with Thomas is clearly invented.

To suit the flow of the narrative I made minor changes to some dates. For example, Chauvel arrived at the War Office in London and took command of the 1st Light Horse Brigade in mid-August 1914, some days after the funeral of Thomas's father; the official record has Major Graham's 1915 burial on the day of the 19 May massacre, although Chaplain Sol Green's diary records it taking place four days earlier; and Chauvel narrowly missed being kissed by a Turkish prisoner a few days later than portrayed.

'Scorpions are maniacal fighters,' wrote sniper and Light Horseman Ion 'Jack' Idriess about scorpion duels in Palestine. So it was a small stretch to imagine a similar contest on Gallipoli. Kingy's seat on an exploding jam-tin bomb mirrors that of William Keid, of the 2nd Light Horse regiment, a former student at St Joseph's Gregory Terrace. Billy Keid was mentioned in dispatches for just such an act, died of his wounds and was buried at sea. His memorial stone lies at Lone Pine, the first of four Keid brothers to die in the Great War.

Thomas's capture at Quinn's and escape from Lone Pine was fortunate indeed; more than 2000 Australians and perhaps three times as many Turks were killed or wounded in that vicious four-day battle in August 1915.

When Lord K visited Anzac three months later, his conversations were recorded pretty much as portrayed in the novel, though of course he did not encounter Thomas or Bulala, and as far as I'm aware Harry Chauvel had no nephew with him on Gallipoli.

Further Reading

FOR MUCH OF THE DETAIL in the novel, I owe a debt to the following titles, whose authors can rest assured that any errors of fact in this book are all mine:

A Dumping Ground: Barambah Aboriginal Settlement 1900–40, by Thom W. Blake,

Birds Without Wings, by Louis de Bernières,

Breaker Morant and the Bushveldt Carbineers, by Arthur Davey,

Chauvel of the Light Horse, by Alec Hill,

Crack Hardy: From Gallipoli to Flanders to the Somme, by Stephen Dando-Collins,

Gallipoli, by Les Carlyon,

Gallipoli Correspondent, the Frontline Diary of C. E .W. Bean, by Kevin Fewster,

Gallipoli Sniper, by John Hamilton,

Gallipoli, the Frontline Experience, by Tolga Örnek and Feza Toker,

Gentlemen of Terrace, by T. P. Boland,

In the Kalkadoon Country, the Habitat and Habits of a Queensland Aboriginal Tribe, by S. E. Pearson,

In Their Own Words, Writings from the First World War, by Norma
     Hempenstall,
Is that you, Ruthie? and *Jack's Story*, both by Ruth Hegarty,
Killing: Misadventures in Violence, by Jeff Sparrow,
Kitchener, the Man Behind the Legend, by Philip Warner,
Landscapes of Change: A History of the South Burnett, by Tony
     Matthews,
Mons, Anzac and Kut, by Aubrey Herbert,
Quinn's Post: Anzac, Gallipoli, by Peter Stanley,
Scapegoats of the Empire, by George R. Witton,
Shoot Straight, You Bastards, by Nick Bleszynski,
*Six Australian Battlefields: the black resistance to invasion and the
     white struggle against colonial oppression*, by Al Grasby & Marji
     Hill,
Stories from Gallipoli, by Steve Sailah, Australian Broadcasting
     Corporation,
Taming the North, by Sir Hudson Fysh,
The Australian Guerrilla: Sniping; and *The Desert Column*, both by
     Ion L. Idriess,
The Australian Light Horse, by Roland Perry,
The Australian People and the Great War, by Michael McKernan,
The Battle for Lone Pine, by David W. Cameron,
The Black Trackers of Bloemfontein, by David Huggonson,
The Boys who Came Home, by Harvey Broadbent,
The Broken Years, by Bill Gammage,
The Brothers Keid, by Cedric Hampson,
The Great Boer War; and *The Complete Sherlock Holmes*, by
     A. C. Doyle,
The History of the 2nd Light Horse Regiment AIF, by G. H. Bourne,
The Hunting of Man, by Andy Dougan,
*The Kalkadoons, A Study of an Aboriginal Tribe on the Queensland
     Frontier*, by Robert E. M. Armstrong,

The Legend of Breaker Morant is Dead and Buried, by Charles Leach,
The Man who was Greenmantle, a Biography of Aubrey Herbert, by
    Margaret FitzHerbert,
*Too Dark for the Light Horse: Aboriginal & Torres Strait Islander
    People in the Defence Forces,* by the Australian War Memorial.

GALLIPOLI

©Peter Morris

Peter FitzSimons

On 25 April 1915, Allied forces landed on the Gallipoli Peninsula in present-day Turkey to secure the sea route between Britain and France in the west and Russia in the east. After eight months of terrible fighting, they would fail.

Turkey regards the victory to this day as a defining moment in its history, a heroic last stand in the defence of the nation's Ottoman Empire. But, counter-intuitively, it would signify something perhaps even greater for the defeated Australians and New Zealanders involved: the birth of their countries' sense of nationhood.

Now approaching its centenary, the Gallipoli campaign, commemorated each year on Anzac Day, reverberates with importance as the origin and symbol of Australian and New Zealand identity. As such, the facts of the battle – which was minor against the scale of the First World War and cost less than a sixth of the Australian deaths on the Western Front – are often forgotten or obscured.

Peter FitzSimons, with his trademark vibrancy and expert melding of writing and research, recreates the disaster as experienced by those who endured it or perished in the attempt.

Coming in November 2014

THE DAUGHTERS OF MARS

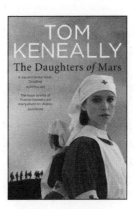

Tom Keneally

In the tradition of *Atonement* and *Birdsong*, the Durance sisters leave Australia to nurse on the front during WWI and discover a world beyond their imaginings.

Naomi and Sally Durance are daughters of a dairy farmer from the Macleay Valley. Bound together in complicity by what they consider a crime, when the Great War begins in 1914 they hope to submerge their guilt by leaving for Europe to nurse the tides of young wounded.

They head for the Dardanelles on the hospital ship *Archimedes*. Their education in medicine, valour and human degradation continues on the Greek island of Lemnos, then on the Western Front. Here, new outrages – gas, shell-shock – present themselves. Naomi encounters the wonderful, eccentric Lady Tarlton, who is founding a voluntary hospital near Boulogne; Sally serves in a casualty clearing station close to the front. They meet the men with whom they would wish to spend the rest of their lives.

Inspired by the journals of Australian nurses who gave their all to the Great War effort and the men they nursed. *The Daughters of Mars* is vast in scope yet extraordinarily intimate. A stunning tour de force to join the best First World War literature, and one that casts a penetrating light on the lives of obscure but strong women caught in the great mill of history.

Available now

Loved the book?

Join thousands of other
readers online at

AUSTRALIAN READERS:

randomhouse.com.au/talk

NEW ZEALAND READERS:

randomhouse.co.nz/talk